SOULDRIFTER

THE
DREAMWIELDER
CHRONICLES
—
BOOK TWO

GARRETT CALCATERRA

DIVERSIONBOOKS

Also by Garrett Calcaterra

The Dreamwielder Chronicles
Dreamwielder

Diversion Books
A Division of Diversion Publishing Corp.
443 Park Avenue South, Suite 1008
New York, New York 10016
www.DiversionBooks.com

This is a work of fiction. Names, characters, places and incidents either are the product of the author's imagination or are used fictitiously. Any resemblance to actual persons, living or dead, events or locales is entirely coincidental.

For more information, email info@diversionbooks.com

First Diversion Books edition September 2015.
Print ISBN: 978-1-62681-707-4
eBook ISBN: 978-1-62681-706-7

For Mandy, who taught me true love is nothing like what you read in fairy tales, that, indeed, it is a bond infinitely more profound and rewarding than anyone could ever describe in a book.

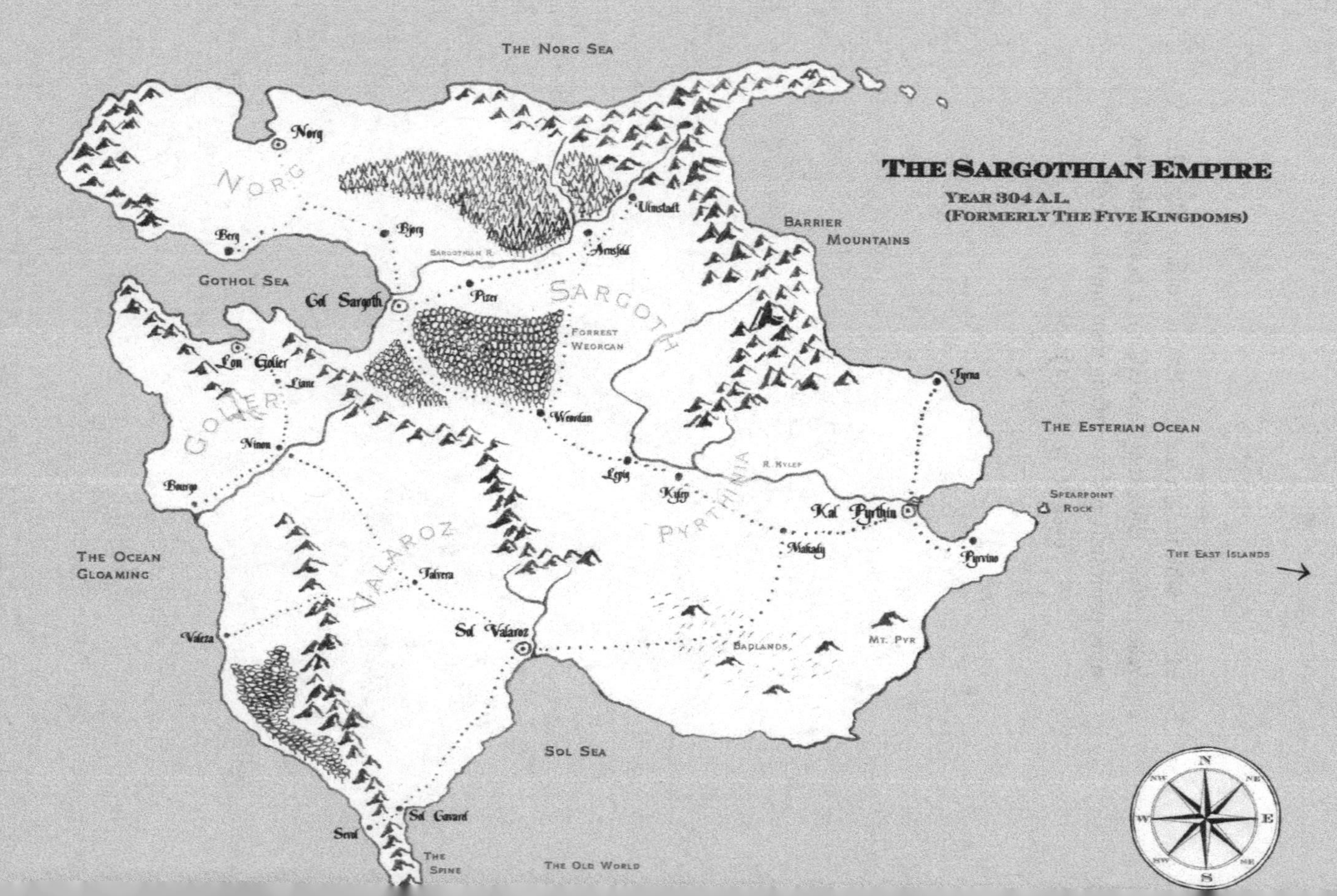

The Sargothian Empire
Year 304 A.L.
(Formerly The Five Kingdoms)
The Norg Sea
Norg
Berg
Bjorg
Sargothian R.
Uinstadt
Arnsfeld
Barrier
Mountains
Gothol Sea
Gol Sargoth
Pizer
Sargoth
Forrest
Weorcan
Lon Golier
Liane
Golier
Ninon
Bourgo
Weordan
Lepig
Kylep
R. Kylep
Pyrthinia
Kal Pyrthin
Tyrna
The Esterian Ocean
Spearpoint
Rock
Pyrvino
Makady
The East Islands
The Ocean
Gloaming
Valaroz
Talvera
Valeta
Sol Valaroz
Badlands
Mt. Pyr
Sol Sea
Sol Gavard
Serol
The
Spine
The Old World

1
Enter Darkness

Khal-Aband, the underground prison, was four hundred miles south of Sol Valaróz, shrouded in the broad-leafed rainforest that clung to the jagged, mountainous terrain of the Spine. There was no path, no gate marking the entrance, only a spire of rock known as the Finger to find one's way, and even then it was only visible in the waning hours of the evening, when the setting sun over the Ocean Gloaming backlit the angular, straight lines of the Finger in stark contrast to the undulating silhouette of the forest. It was no wonder it had taken Makarria so long to discover it.

It was nearly a year since Makarria's coronation, and Emperor Guderian's fallen empire still cast a shadow over her every action as Queen of Valaróz. Don Bricio, the usurper Guderian had placed on the Valarion throne, had turned Valarion politics into a knot of corruption, and even with Don Bricio and Guderian both dead and gone, their reign of terror had scarred Makarria's people. More than anything, they were apprehensive about sorcery. Guderian had all but exterminated sorcerers in the Five Kingdoms, so what were people to think of Makarria, a dreamwielder, when the only sorcerer they had ever known was Guderian's shape-changing monster Wulfram? At best, they were grateful to Makarria for having liberated them from tyranny, but distrustful of the changes she tried to bring about. At worst, they openly questioned her ability, saying sorcerers couldn't be trusted and that a fourteen-year-old girl didn't have the strength to rule.

That's why this trip to Khal-Aband was so important.

Inside—locked away in the secret prison where Emperor Guderian and Don Bricio had sent the enemies they hated too much to kill—was a man who could make the people of Valaróz trust the throne again. Assuming he was still alive.

Makarria tore her gaze away from the Finger and glanced to the far side of her encampment where four scouts emerged from the forest, having returned at last. "Well?" she asked, striding forward to meet them in the middle of the encampment. "Is the perimeter clear?" Patience was something she was working on, but not today, not when she was so close to her goal. Not when Caile was off searching the prison without her.

"Yes, Your Majesty, the perimeter is clear," the lead scout said. "My team searched the forest a mile to the north and south, across the entirety of the Spine. There is no evidence anyone has been here in months. All we found was an abandoned skiff in a cove along the western shoreline."

"Abandoned?"

"Yes, Your Majesty. It appears someone tried to sink it. The hull was shattered and someone filled it with rocks. If the tide hadn't been out, we wouldn't have noticed it at all. By my estimation, it's been there a year or more. There's not much left of it."

Makarria frowned, not liking the sound of someone purposefully sinking a boat. "Don't be so sure it's been there as long as that. The sea is harsh to sunken vessels, particularly on rocky shores. What do you think, Lorentz?"

Captain Lorentz—her advisor, friend, and personal bodyguard at Prince Caile's insistence—stood up from where he had been sitting on a rock, gazing up at the Finger. His face still bore the scars of the torture he had endured as Emperor Guderian's prisoner: part of one ear gone and three of his front teeth missing, in addition to the crosshatch of thin pink scars on his forehead from knife wounds. "A year sounds about right," he said, his words tinged with a slight lisp due to his missing teeth. "That would have been the last time Don Bricio could have sent anyone here."

"But why on the western shore?" Makarria asked. It didn't

make any sense. "If he were sending word from Sol Valaróz, the vessel would have landed on the eastern shore, the same as us."

Lorentz shrugged. "Perhaps he sent word from one of the western cities. Or perhaps Guderian sent someone from Col Sargoth."

It was possible, but Makarria didn't buy it. A skiff was too small for transporting prisoners, and even if Don Bricio or Guderian had merely sent a messenger, they wouldn't have risked sending a message in such a small vessel. Makarria knew all too well how dangerous it was sailing the open sea in a skiff. She and her grandfather had nearly died in one fleeing from Guderian when a storm came upon them. It seemed so long ago now, but Makarria still recalled how small she had felt in the skiff, a toy against the fury of the sea.

Makarria had new and more pressing concerns now, though. She shook the memory away and eyed the sun, looming ever closer to the treeline to the west. "We only have an hour or so of daylight left. Still no word from Caile?"

"Nothing," Lorentz said, stealing a glance up the hillside toward the Finger and the prison entrance. "I can't imagine what can be taking him so long."

It was clear Lorentz was as worried about Caile as Makarria was. She couldn't blame him. Lorentz had, after all, been Caile's protector and mentor, his father practically, for over ten years, and here he was, stuck waiting outside with Makarria while Caile searched the interior of the prison with only a small contingent of troops. He had been gone the entire day now. It was time to go after him. Makarria had been a fool not to go with him in the first place.

"We're going in," she decided. "Gather our two best men and follow me."

Lorentz's eyes widened in alarm. "I don't think that's a good idea. It's not safe."

"That's why I'm bringing you along."

"Pyrthin's arse, you're as pigheaded as Caile is," Lorentz swore. "It's no wonder the two of you get along so well."

Makarria grinned despite herself. Apart from her parents and

Caile, Lorentz was the only one who spoke to her like a real person, not a queen. That wasn't to say he was all jokes and quips. He, out of all of Makarria's advisors, had been the most outspoken about her remaining in Sol Valaróz and leaving this expedition to soldiers. She had overruled him, but that didn't mean she took his counsel lightly.

"Hurry along now, Captain," she told him. "Meet me up top, or I'll go in alone."

Lorentz frowned at her, but said nothing before jogging off to gather two guards and leave orders for the others to stand watch. Makarria turned to regard the Finger one last time, then began the climb up the loose shale embankment on her own. The footing was treacherous. She had no idea how a forest was able to thrive in the barren, rocky soil. *Anything that manages to live here must be more pigheaded than me,* she mused, testing each foothold before shifting her weight and continuing her ascent. The roots of the trees and ferns were woven into the cracks of the rock itself, creating a crumbling matrix of jagged footholds. She was glad, not for the first time on this trip, that she had set aside the burden of her cumbersome royal gown for leather boots, breeches, and a vest.

By the time she reached the plateau at the base of the Finger, she was nearly out of breath. She didn't have the leisure to bemoan the climb, though. In front of her lurked the entrance to Khal-Aband, a dark fissure in the rock face no more than four feet tall, shored up with two diagonal beams of rotting timber. Makarria shuddered. Although the Spine couldn't have been more different than the snow-covered Barrier Mountains two thousand miles to the north, the entrance to Khal-Aband looked eerily similar to the entrance to the Caverns of Issborg. Makarria had been a prisoner herself there in Issborg, along with Taera, Caile's sister, trapped in the ice, under the control of the sorcerer Kadar. Kadar's black teeth still haunted Makarria's memories, as did his horrible fate at her hands. She had used her power as a dreamwielder to trap him in the rock of Issborg, and his body was as much a part of the mountain now as was the glacier that carved the cavern centuries before.

Makarria closed her eyes and forced herself to push the

memory away. *No more reminiscing. No more daydreaming.* If she needed to use her power, she would need to control her dream visions, not be caught up in past memories.

"Well?" Lorentz asked, huffing to a halt beside Makarria along with two soldiers. "Now what?"

"Like I said, we go in," Makarria replied, retying the leather strap that held her brown hair back in a ponytail. "One of you in front of me, two behind. If we run into trouble, stay close, protect me for just a moment, and I'll do the rest."

Lorentz grabbed the hilt of the short sword at his waist, thought better of it, and instead pulled out a dagger. "I'll go first."

The others fell into place behind Makarria and they entered the tunnel leading to Khal-Aband. No more than ten steps inside, the passageway made a sharp turn to the right and they were plunged into utter darkness and silence. The hair at the nape of Makarria's neck stood on end and she felt a brief surge of panic.

"This is madness," Lorentz whispered, shuffling to a halt. "Caile has all of our equipment. We have no torches. Nothing."

Makarria closed her eyes and let out a long, slow breath to drive away her fear. A year before she wouldn't have been able to control her thoughts like this, but she had been practicing, and now she was able to slip into a dreamstate almost effortlessly. She pictured a floating light in her mind—a lifeless, formless lightning bug—and made it so, drawing upon the energy within her to push the object from her dream vision into reality. Lorentz gasped in surprise when the glowing blue sphere appeared in front of him from nothingness, and almost simultaneously a gust of wind blew past them from the entrance of the cave. The light was undeterred, but Makarria shivered. She should have planned better. It was foolish wasting her strength to dream up a light when unknown danger lay before them. There was nothing for it now, though, but to move on.

"Let's keep moving, Lorentz," Makarria said.

Lorentz nodded and led the way, following the curves of the passageway, ever to the right and downward, inexorably spiraling deeper into the mountain beneath the Finger. The air grew stagnant. Then repugnant. By the time the passageway leveled out and they reached a rusted gate baring their passage, the stench was unbearable, a palpable haze of rot and death. Makarria had to cover her nose and mouth with one arm to keep from retching, and even then saliva filled her mouth and she had to choke back her gagging reflex.

"It's locked," Lorentz whispered through gritted teeth as he examined the padlock on the gate. "One of ours, but we don't have the key. Caile does. Of course."

Makarria took it all in with a glance: the original rusted padlock Caile had split apart with a hammer and chisel only to toss aside on the passage floor, and then the new one in its place to protect his back and make sure no one snuck in behind him. It was a simple matter for Makarria to separate the new padlock from the hasp mechanism, just like her first test as a dreamwielder back in the Caverns of Issborg. She slipped into her dreamstate, then imagined the two rings melding together into one solid piece, and then individual again, this time apart from each other. When she pushed through the resistance of rearranging matter and opened her eyes, the padlock fell to the ground alongside the other one.

"We won't be needing that anymore," she whispered. "The outside is secure, or as secure as it's going to be, at least. Let's keep going. Quietly."

Lorentz opened the gate and led the way on, Makarria's airborne lantern still illuminating the way before them, but he stopped again after only a dozen steps. He motioned toward the wall on their left, outlining something with the tip of his dagger—a door, Makarria realized. It was a solid iron door, rusted to the point it was nearly indistinguishable from the rock wall itself. The charnel house stench was so overpowering here Makarria knew the source of the smell had to be coming from inside whatever chamber was on the other side. Lorentz, likely suspecting the same, knelt and peered through the keyhole, but stood up a moment later shaking his head. *Too dark*, he mouthed silently.

Makarria knelt and peered inside, pressing her face close to the door so her left eye was almost touching the keyhole. A thin beam of sunlight shone high up against the far wall, but too high and too dim to illuminate the room itself. All she could see was a swarm of insects darting across the shaft of light. Everything else was veiled in shadow. She held her breath, closed her eyes, and dreamed into existence another floating lantern inside the room. She could feel the blue glow of her efforts shining on her closed eyelid, but couldn't bring herself to look. Whatever was in the room was an abomination, she knew. She could sense it. Her hands were trembling and she wanted nothing more than to turn around and run right out the way she'd come. *No. You have to know. You're a queen, not a child.*

She opened her eyes.

The scene before her, lit up in her own eerie blue light, was worse than she could have ever imagined. She shoved herself away from the door with a gasp and fell into the soldier behind her. Her lanterns winked out like candles in the wind. And then her stomach upturned and she vomited on the boots of the soldier trying to hold her up. When she was done retching, she was left gasping for air, shaking.

"Makarria!" Lorentz hissed, fumbling in the darkness to grab her by the shoulders. "Are you all right? What happened?"

The muscles beneath her lungs were convulsing, making her breaths come in quick, staccato procession. She couldn't even apologize to the poor man whose boots she had retched on. She forced herself to exhale slowly, and then breathed in and out three more times to calm herself. "I'm fine. It was…worse than I expected. There are dead bodies piled in there, dozens of them, turned to liquid and rot. Bones and maggots, melting away into the floor. There's a chimney vent in the ceiling—otherwise the smell would be worse."

She forced the image out of her mind and refocused on forming a new lantern. Her men sighed in relief when the light reappeared, even Lorentz, whom Makarria had never seen exhibit fear of any sort. There was some comfort in knowing she wasn't alone in being afraid, but not much.

Lorentz helped her to her feet, and she dusted off her breeches. "I fear we've come too late," she said, thinking out loud. "There are so many bodies in there. Can the man they called Conzo still be alive? Can any of the prisoners still be alive?"

"Someone must still be alive down here," Lorentz assured her. "Otherwise Caile would have returned by now."

Makarria hoped he was right. "Let's hurry then. We have to find out what's going on."

They proceeded warily, deeper into the prison. The path was level, but it curved again to the right and they found themselves at another gate baring their passage. Makarria examined the lock and saw it was another of Caile's replacements. They were on the right track, at least, and Caile had made it this far. Makarria removed the lock with her power and stepped aside for Lorentz to lead the way again. When they rounded the next corner, they began to hear voices. The words were muffled but clear enough to make out that a shouting match was going on. They hurried onward, around another bend, this one to the left, and then quite abruptly came upon the rear guard of their own troops.

"Who's there?" one of the soldiers cried out in surprise as he leveled his short sword at them.

"Easy, it's me," Lorentz assured the man, holding his hands up in peace.

The orange glow of torchlight flickered deeper on in the passageway where the shouting was coming from, but the men in the rear had been standing in darkness. Once the soldiers saw Lorentz and Makarria lit up in the blue glow of the floating lamplight, they too sighed in relief and lowered their weapons.

"Where's Prince Caile?" Lorentz demanded.

"Up front," one of the soldiers replied. "Negotiating with the prison guards."

"And this shouting you call negotiating has been going on all day?" Makarria demanded.

The man cast his eyes downward. "Yes. Negotiating and

fighting, Your Majesty."

"Pass word to Prince Caile to come speak to me. If he objects, tell him it's a royal command."

The soldier did as he was told and passed word to the man in front of him. The chain message made its way through the ranks, and a minute later the yelling ceased and Caile pushed his way back through the soldiers. He was not happy to see Makarria, as was evident by his deep scowl.

"Why are you down here? It's not safe."

Makarria met his glare with her own steely gaze. "Clearly. Otherwise you would have returned hours ago. What's happening?"

"A standoff is what's happening! A very dangerous one that's already cost us two men. You need to go back outside and wait. I promised your mother I wouldn't let you come to harm."

"You and Lorentz and my mother can all lecture me later," Makarria retorted. "We're here to rescue people, not to see more die, and I'm not about to stand idly by when my power can help."

Makarria watched as the anger went out of Caile. He couldn't stay angry with her any more than she could with him. They had gone through too much together over the last year in trying to remake Valaróz the realm it deserved to be. In every hearing, every council meeting, and every court appearance, Caile had been there at Makarria's side, coaching her along, supporting her decisions, even when they were wrong. And when the official work was over, he was the first to crack a joke to lighten her spirits, or to sneak her out of the palace to explore Sol Valaróz in plain clothes. She realized that the anxiety she had felt waiting outside the prison had less to do with freeing Conzo and the other prisoners of Khal-Aband, and more to do with worrying about Caile's safety.

"Can we go save some people now," she asked him, "or are you going to lecture me some more?"

With an exasperated sigh, Caile brushed his neck-length blond hair back from his face. In the blue light of Makarria's lantern, his stubbly beginnings of a beard shone almost silver. "Fine," he relented. "But please stay behind me and do as I say if more fighting breaks out."

"We'll see. Now tell me what's going on."

"The passage turns to the right up ahead and there are a half dozen side passages with at least a dozen guards holing themselves in. We caught them unaware at first. Half of them surrendered, but then their leader riled the others up again. We had to retreat. They have a ballista of some sorts—a giant crossbow on wheels. It punched a bolt right through Brunco's shield and chainmail. Rocio got it in the back. Both of them are gone. If we try to go around the corner, we'll get it too."

The news of the fallen soldiers left Makarria heavy inside, but she focused on the task at hand. If she had learned anything as a new queen, it was that ruling was rife with sacrifice and remorse. If she let it weigh her down, she'd not be fit as a queen.

"You've spoken with the leader?" she asked Caile. "Tried to treat with him?"

Caile nodded. "The man is unreasonable. I've explained the situation. He believes well enough that Emperor Guderian and Don Bricio are dead, I think. I mean, he has to know something has changed—it's been a year since they've received any new prisoners, and probably provisions."

"That might explain the bodies in the chamber above," Makarria said.

"You saw inside? We weren't able to see anything, but I had my suspicions."

"It's horrible, Caile. I'm afraid we've come too late to rescue Conzo, or anyone, for that matter."

"Don't give up hope yet. The leader told me he'd kill the rest of the prisoners if we don't retreat. I suppose he might be lying about there still being prisoners, but why would the guards have all stayed here if there was no one to guard anymore?"

"I hope you're right," Makarria said. "Go on, take me to the front then. Let's see if this leader of theirs will trust me more than he trusts you."

Caile nodded and led the way with Makarria and Lorentz right on his heels, the three of them worming their way single file past their soldiers in the cramped corridor. When they reached the front of the line, Caile held up a hand for them to halt and Makarria extinguished her blue light. The corridor curved to the right at a sharp angle. Beyond that was only sputtering torchlight and shadows. The air reeked now not of decay and rot, but of dust and the metallic sourness of spilled blood. Makarria could glimpse the shadowy forms of her fallen soldiers lying on the passage floor a short distance away.

"Who here is in charge of Khal-Aband?" Makarria shouted, still angry she hadn't insisted on coming with Caile from the outset. She could have saved those men.

Harsh whispers emanated from around the corner, and then a clear voice. "I'm in charge here. Warden Aymil. Who speaks? Is that a woman?"

"Don't say your name…" Caile started to say, but Makarria ignored him.

"I am Makarria Pallma, Queen of Valaróz, Dreamwielder. Don Bricio is slain and along with him Emperor Thedric Guderian and the sorcerer Wulfram. The Sargothian Empire is no more and the Five Kingdoms once again thrive as independent nations. I am here to relieve you of your duty, Warden Aymil, or reassign you if you wish to continue your service as a loyal servant of Valaróz. Either way, you must come with me. Khal-Aband will be no more. The prisoners will be released and retried for their crimes, if indeed they committed any. The prison will be sealed and collapsed."

"A dreamwielder, said you?" the man asked, forcing a laugh. "Such evil was eradicated from our land a long time ago."

Makarria closed her eyes and through his voice she could envision him, hunkered down thirty paces away behind the massive crossbow mounted on wheels. Warden Aymil's once dark complexion had turned sallow and the skin hung from his limbs loosely, nearly indistinguishable from the tattered remnants of his uniform. Makarria could see it all through his voice—a dream vision of the flesh and blood man hiding in the shadows. His hair and beard hung in long, feculent strands down past his shoulders.

"You heard correctly—I am a dreamwielder," Makarria said, dreaming his whiskers and hair into a bouquet of sweet violets to prove her point. "And I'm not evil. I come in peace."

Warden Aymil shouted out in surprise and Makarria could hear the men around him muttering to one another as they took in the sight of their leader suddenly cloaked in flowers.

"You have my word, all of you," Makarria said. "We mean you no harm. Too many have suffered and died already. Disarm your crossbow, drop your weapons and we'll take you back to the sun of Sol Valaróz unharmed. You have my word, as granddaughter of Parmenios Pallma, as the true heir to the throne of Vala."

More muttering, only to be silenced by Warden Aymil.

Caile leaned in closer to Makarria. "They've been down here so long I think they're afraid of the sun."

"You swear in Vala's name you won't hurt us?" one of the prison guards hollered.

"Silence!" Warden Aymil yelled, clubbing the man with the blunt end of a spear. Makarria could feel the feral anger in him.

"If we could only convince their leader, the others would fall into line," Makarria whispered to Caile.

Caile shook his head. "Trust me, it's not going to happen. I tried. We're going to have to take them by force."

"Can you disable that ballista?" Lorentz asked. "You know, close your eyes and dream it into something else? With the ballista out of the way, we can make short work of them."

"I can disarm it, yes, but we're not attacking," Makarria said. She'd already lost two men. She wouldn't watch more die, not if she could help it. "I swear in Vala's name I will hurt no man who lays down his arms and swears fealty to Valaróz!" she shouted into the passageway. "If I wanted to hurt you I could do so now without bothering to waste my breath." She closed her eyes and visualized the wooden stock frame of the ballista. She pushed the energy in and around her into the timber and ignited it, bypassing open flames altogether and triggering instead an instantaneous combustion of wood into ash, which crumbled away before the prison guards' eyes. Makarria gathered the heat released from the combustion and held it at the ready to draw upon if need be. "You see my power, now trust me. I mean you no harm."

There was a long moment of silence. Makarria held her breath, hoping to hear the sound of swords and pikes dropping to the ground. Instead, it was Warden Aymil's voice that shattered the silence.

"She'll kill us all! Execute the prisoners!"

"No!" Makarria shouted, nearly unloosing the ball of pure energy into the man but catching herself at the last moment.

No more killing!

Instead she re-imagined Warden Aymil; immediately, his arms flopped to his sides, his legs went stiff, and he fell to the floor. Makarria dreamed the impediment of his clothing away and the skin of his torso expanding to encase his limbs—binding his arms to his sides and his legs to one another with his own flesh. She'd seen the skeleton of a sea creature once, a small whale of some sort, and had been fascinated to find its tailbones were comprised of legs that could never walk. Makarria imagined it in her mind, a Warden Aymil with arms and legs still, but now a part of his body, buried beneath a layer of skin.

She released the energy and made it so.

Warden Aymil screamed out in terror, so Makarria enclosed the skin of his lips over his mouth.

The sounds of guards scrambling around, swords clacking—a key ring jingling—echoed down the chamber. Even with her eyes closed in a dreamstate, she could hear it all.

"STOP!" she shouted, her voice sounding far away to her, disembodied almost. "ALL OF YOU, STOP!"

Not a single soldier or guard so much as whispered.

Makarria opened her eyes only to find herself sitting on the ground, propped up in Caile's arms. Her head swam with dizziness.

She had collapsed, she realized.

"Guards of Khal-Aband!" Caile shouted above her, "Lay down

your weapons and place your hands on your heads! Our men will bind you, but only until we return to the safety of Sol Valaróz. You heard the promise of the dreamwielder. Even Warden Aymil she has spared."

The clanking of swords and spears dropping to the floor echoed down the passageway.

"Go," Caile ordered his men, urging them forward to take the guards prisoner.

The soldiers rushed past Makarria with manacles and chains in hand, and Caile looked down at her, brushing her hair back to see her face. "Are you all right? What happened?"

"I'll be fine," she said, not wanting to admit to herself even that she had almost pushed herself too far. "It just took a bit out of me to transform the warden, I guess. Here, help me up."

Lorentz was there, too, and the two of them helped Makarria to her feet.

"That was foolish, but well done," Lorentz said, placing a hand on her shoulder.

Makarria smiled. "It will be worth it if we've managed to rescue Conzo, or anyone else even. Any enemy of Emperor Guderian and Don Bricio who earned imprisonment here is probably a friend of ours."

"We can hope," Caile said, turning to Lorentz. "If you've got Makarria, Lorentz, I'll go make sure we have all the prison guards secure."

"Yes, go," Makarria told him, eager to search the cells for survivors.

Caile trotted off to oversee the binding of the prison guards, and a few minutes later the first of them was ushered past Makarria and Lorentz, the guard's hands manacled in front of him. Makarria smiled for him and said thank you, and also to the next guard, and the next, showing them that her words were not empty, trying to put them at ease as much as she could, although her own thoughts kept turning now to whether the man known as Conzo was still alive back there somewhere. According to legend, Conzo had been a simple beggar when Emperor Guderian and Don Bricio stormed Sol Valaróz thirty-five years before to kill the royal Pallma family, but that atrocity had transformed Conzo into something much more. A patriot until his capture two decades later, Conzo was a constant thorn in Don Bricio's side, stealing from imperial tax collectors, sneaking prisoners out of the dungeons, painting the words "Usurper!" and "Murderer!" on all of Don Bricio's coaches in the shroud of night, and perfoming all sorts of other vigilante acts that turned him into a folk hero among the people of Sol Valaróz. Even now, fifteen years after his capture, people still spoke of Conzo, the man who stood up against tyranny and fought for the common people. If he was still alive, Makarria meant to make him one of her counselors, a public official that her people knew and trusted. It might just be what she needed to finally gain their confidence.

The last of the prison guards were being ushered past Makarria, and she smiled at them absently, still caught up in her own thoughts. She didn't even notice one of the shackled guards pull a dagger from the front of his trousers and lunge toward her. Luckily, Lorentz did.

Lorentz jumped forward and the two men tumbled to the floor, grunting, Lorentz's hands locked around the guard's manacled wrists to hold the dagger at bay.

"Caile!" Makarria screamed, but before Caile was halfway there it was all over.

The guard inexplicably went limp in Lorentz's grasp and stared in horror up at him. "No," he whispered as Lorentz tore the dagger from his grip and plunged it into his chest.

"Wait!" Makarria yelled, but it was too late.

Lorentz stabbed him twice more in quick succession, and the man was dead, bleeding out onto the dust and gravel of the tunnel floor.

"No! Lorentz, why?"

Lorentz stood slowly and turned to regard her. "My apologies, Your Highness. It won't happen again."

A chill ran down Makarria's spine. It was Lorentz's voice she heard, but something was wrong. He rarely addressed her formally except in court. Had he been shaken? More afraid, perhaps, than Makarria realized?

"What happened?" Caile demanded, rushing to her side.

"This scum tried attacking the queen," Lorentz replied.

Caile looked from the slain prison guard to Makarria and saw the horrified look on her face. "You did well, Lorentz. Go with the others and make sure we don't have any more problems with the prison guards. I'll stay with Makarria now." He put an arm around her to keep her steady, and she gratefully leaned into his shoulder, shocked by the sudden violence, even after everything else she had seen.

The last of the guards was ushered past them, or at least the last of the mobile guards. One of Makarria's soldiers had to pick up Warden Aymil like a sack of potatoes and throw him over his shoulder to carry him out. The warden's eyes bulged at Makarria as he was lugged by, but Makarria hardly noticed him. Even in Caile's arms, she felt disoriented. Dizzy. Everything had happened so fast, and using her powers had drained her.

"Go on, all of you," Caile said. "Wait for us at the camp. Makarria and I will see to freeing the prisoners. Send a few men back down once the guards are secure to grab our fallen men."

Lorentz nodded wordlessly and followed the soldiers back out the way they had come. Makarria watched him go, still unnerved by the death she had witnessed, but Caile was tugging at her hand for her to follow him deeper into the cavern. "Are you up for this?" he asked, jingling the key ring to the prison cells.

"Yes."

Her dizziness and all thoughts of Lorentz were washed away by the prospect of finally releasing the prisoners they had come to save. Especially Conzo.

Seeing her look of determination, Caile grabbed a torch from a wall sconce and led the way. They walked past the pile of ashes that minutes before had been the ballista, and then through another barred gate. The cells were embedded into the wall to their right. Caile unlocked the first one, peered in and shook his head. He started to close the door again, but Makarria stopped him.

"I need to see," she told him.

"But, Makarria…"

"It's all right. I saw the room with the corpses. I can handle this."

Caile closed his eyes and let her pass. She peered through the doorway and saw the prisoner lying on the floor, half decapitated, his atrophied, mangled neck still tenuously holding head and body together.

"The guards panicked in the moment before you stopped them," Caile said. "Followed the orders of their warden until the end. There was nothing we could have done to save him."

"Is it him? Is it Conzo?"

"Who can say?"

Makarria could only nod. Whoever he was, she had failed him.

Caile grabbed Makarria's hand and the two of them moved on to the next cell. Inside was another dead prisoner, but this man had died of starvation, not execution.

"For the love of Vala, please tell me some of them survived," Makarria whispered.

They moved on and she had a moment of hope in the next cell, but when they called out to the man lying on the floor he did not respond. Caile went to him and checked his breathing. "Gone," he said, shaking his head in disappointment. "And recently. He's still warm. He must have heard the yelling and known that his rescuers were here, but it was just too much for his weak body. All of them are starved. Even the guards. They've been cut off for nearly a year now, ever since Don Bricio's death. No supply ships, nothing. I don't know how they managed to survive this long. Perhaps those corpses you saw…"

Makarria motioned for him to stop, not wanting to even entertain what he was suggesting. They continued on wordlessly, past a series of empty cells, and then a larger cell—a torture chamber furnished with the most barbaric tools of the trade. Makarria shivered at the sight of the rack, the shelves of pliers and pincers, and, in the far corner, the drowning table. Bloodstains covered the stone floor like inky shadows beneath the flickering light of Caile's torch. *How many of those people in the burial chamber were murdered here?* Makarria wondered. *And how many more were murdered before them during Don Bricio's and Emperor Guderian's long reign? How many young, hidden-away sorcerers like myself were given up under the pains of torture?*

Caile grabbed Makarria by the hand again and pulled her away from the gruesome scene. Beyond the torture chamber were a dozen more cells. Makarria's heart sank as she passed by each one only to find it empty. Each and every one until only one remained.

"The last cell," Makarria said.

"Do you even want to look?"

"Yes."

They walked together and peered inside. Makarria started to cry at seeing the two prisoners slumped on the floor at opposite sides of the cell. *After all we've gone through to get here. No survivors. Two of my soldiers dead. All for what?*

"We came too late, Caile."

"No look," Caile said, going to the nearest prisoner. "He breathes. We're not too late at all."

"Too late for what?" the other prisoner wheezed, stirring. It was a woman's voice.

Makarria gasped. "You're a woman." She rushed to the prisoner's side and helped her sit up.

The woman was emaciated, but strong enough to raise her head. "What else would I be but a woman?"

Makarria couldn't help but smile. "I don't know. I'm just glad we found you and that you're still alive."

"Of course," the woman replied, smiling in return, the dried skin of her lips cracking over the top of her front teeth. "I would never give Don Bricio the satisfaction of dying here."

Tears poured down Makarria's cheeks she was so happy to have found this woman, and the man too. *Could it be Conzo?*

"What's your name?" Makarria asked the woman.

"Fina."

"And your partner there. His name?"

"Thon," the woman replied.

"Not Conzo?"

"No, not Conzo. Conzo was here once, but he died a long time ago."

Disappointment filled Makarria, but only for a moment. The light in this woman's eyes—the joy of being rescued—made Makarria realize she had done the right thing. No one deserved this sort of incarceration and torture. She and Caile had found only two survivors out of perhaps dozens of prisoners, but still two, and that made her forget everything else: the fatigue in her, the chamber they had found full of decayed bodies, her fallen soldiers, and even the peculiar behavior of Lorentz.

2
Ravens Descend

Any ordinary man in his position would have turned tail and run as far from Col Sargoth as possible. Indeed, that was what the High Houndkeeper had done—disappeared from Lightbringer's Keep with dozens of Emperor Guderian's innermost confidants and advisors the day the dreamwielder had killed the Emperor. Natarios Rhodas was too clever by far to be ordinary, though. Where there was turmoil there was opportunity. With the demise of Guderian, the Sargothian Empire would be no more, and for the first time in decades, each of the Five Kingdoms would be truly sovereign. There would be a new order of power, and Natarios meant to be part of it.

When everyone else in his position was off running, he had marched right back into Col Sargoth, took charge of the Houndkeeper's tower, and nominated himself as a member of the high council in charge of electing a new Sargothian king. His boldness had been rewarded; he received everything he demanded, and now here he was—a virtually unknown Houndkeeper from Pyrthinia—brokering deals that would shape the Kingdom of Sargoth. If all went to plan, it would make him more rich and powerful than he dared to hope.

A squawk emanated from the perch at one of the four windows in the tower chamber and Natarios hooted in delight. Just in time, his raven from the Kingdom of Golier had arrived! He grabbed a jar from a storage cabinet, lifted away the stopper and dumped the grisly contents into a wooden bowl. No matter how many times he had smelled it before, the stench still made him gag: chicken livers fermented in their own blood. Not what he thought of as a delicacy, but the other ravens in their cages were clamoring for it, crescendoing in a cacophony of yawping. Natarios ignored their racket and placed the bowl down for his new arrival to eat, its reward for dutifully returning to Col Sargoth from Lon Golier. The bird quivered in delight as it choked down the rotten meat, oblivious to Natarios, who removed the folded parchment from the leather sleeve attached to its right leg.

Natarios broke the wax seal away, opened the letter and smiled as he read. The bribes had been made. They would have enough votes when the council met today. He refolded the letter and slipped it into a pocket on the inner breast of his black robe. Already, the messenger raven was finished and crying for more fermented livers.

"Sorry, you'll get more when you return to Lon Golier next."

Natarios nimbly snatched up the bird, pinning its wings against its sides and avoiding its sharp beak, and tossed it into the cage with the three other Golier messenger ravens. It would be back to a vegetarian diet for all of them for the time being. In the three other cages, the ravens from Norgland, Pyrthinia, and Valaróz squawked their protest.

"Leave me be, you rotten creatures," Natarios hollered, covering his ears. He grabbed a bag of nuts and seeds and threw a handful into each of the cages. "There now. Be quiet."

With that, Natarios stepped out of the chamber into the spiral stairwell and ascended the steps to the uppermost chamber in the tower, the scent-hound chamber. The creature within—half-woman, half-dog, splayed out and melded onto a giant compass—did not stir when he entered. Talitha, the sorceress from Issborg, had ensorcelled it into perpetual slumber almost a year before. It was a good stroke of luck she didn't have the courage to kill it when Guderian died. In recent weeks, the steam-engineer's guild had been pushing for the re-awakening of the hound to help enforce the sanctions they were demanding on sorcery. They were out to inhibit the manufacture of any vehicles powered by magic that might threaten their booming steam-wagon industry—that was the sort of quibbling the Sargothian council had devolved into, when its entire purpose had been to elect a new ruler. It was all the better for Natarios.

In reality, the scent-hound would do the steam engineers no good. It detected and pinpointed the usage of magic, yes, but even with only the meager emergence of sorcerers and magical doings since Emperor Guderian's death, the poor creature would be overwhelmed and go mad, howling and spinning itself in circles on the axle through its navel every time a stormbringer summoned a breeze to push ships out with the tide or a beastcharmer coaxed a plowhorse to pull harder. No, the scent-hound was obsolescent now, but Natarios didn't tell anyone, of course. If the steam-engineer's guild thought he could help them, all the better.

In the meantime, he had to keep the idiot creature alive. That meant pouring a meat broth down its gullet with a funnel twice a day. Unsavory, but not any worse than tending to the ravens. He tried not to think about it too much, but still he couldn't help but feel a bit of pity for the hound. He had tended to the scent-hound in Kal Pyrthin for almost ten years before King Casstian's sympathizers killed it and chased him out of the city. Casstian was dead now, but as far as Natarios was concerned, his daughter, the bitch Queen Taera, was one and the same: closed-minded and meddlesome.

She and the dreamwielder both will be in for a surprise soon enough, Natarios consoled himself.

When he was done feeding the hound, he bounded down the steps, all one hundred and sixty-seven of them, and into the main pentagonal hallway of Lightbringer's Keep. With its basalt floors and dark-stained walls, the cavernous hallway was dim and dreary, even with the full light of day shining in the bay windows. Natarios was well accustomed to it now, though, and hardly thought of the clear, warm days in Kal Pyrthin anymore.

From the main hallway, it was a short jaunt into the inner council chambers of the keep where a half-dozen council members were trickling in for their afternoon meeting. Natarios found Ambassador

Rives already seated at one side of the massive, oblong table that dominated the room, and wordlessly handed him the raven's note. The Golierian ambassador glanced over the letter and gave Natarios an almost imperceptible nod.

It happens today then! Natarios could hardly keep himself from openly grinning as he took his own seat.

Over the course of the next quarter hour, a procession of council members entered the chambers to take their seats at the table. In addition to Rives, there were the ambassadors from the other three kingdoms, and then there were the guildmasters, a baker's dozen of them representing everyone from the steam-engineers and sorcerers, to craftsmen, farmers, and sailors. These were the voices that had bogged down the search for a new ruler with endless proceedings and proposed laws. Aiding them, though perhaps not willingly, were the scholars and scribes who were slavishly dogmatic about the ancient laws and texts of Sargoth Lightbringer, the original founder of the Five Kingdoms. And then there were the power players: the noblemen who had made claim to the throne. There were seven claimants in all, and also Lady Hildreth, who, while not eligible to rule under Sargothian law because of her gender, had insisted on her right to vote in the proceedings.

Last to enter the chambers was Talitha of Issborg, mightiest of sorcerers in the Five Kingdoms, and lord of the proceedings, as decreed by the conqueror, the dreamwielder Queen Makarria of Valaróz. Talitha wore a simple brown dress and had her walnut hair pulled back in a ponytail, and while she carried her head high and shoulders back, Natarios could see the weariness in her. The subtle wrinkles on her face had deepened over the course of the last year, and dark circles had formed beneath her eyes. Natarios had no sympathy for her. *Politics doesn't suit everyone. You shouldn't be here if you don't like it.*

Talitha took her place at the head of the table and rapped her ebony gavel three times to silence everyone. "I bring this meeting to order," she began, and the scribe sitting beside her began scribbling every word she uttered. "The couriers have delivered you each the day's agenda. Are there any new orders of business to add before we proceed?"

Ambassador Rives stood. "Yes, I motion that before we proceed, the council shall vote on the matter of new leadership."

Talitha shot up one eyebrow in surprise, but Rives continued on before she could object.

"The council has become mired in bickering over orders of procedure for too long now. We have before us seven worthy candidates to the throne, and instead of weighing their merits and electing one, we argue over voting procedures that delay matters, which leads to arguing over intermediary laws to keep the realm at peace, which only further delays voting. It is not only Sargoth that suffers, but also the other four kingdoms. Golier cannot be expected to guard the Gothol Sea all alone indefinitely."

"These are the very things I have been saying for weeks," Talitha replied, rubbing her brow in clear annoyance. "If we could set aside our brinkmanship for a day even, and hear the candidates out rather than playing these backdoor dealings to win candidates to our causes, I believe our choice will become clear. We can vote and let the new king be the arbiter of law and order."

Rives shook his head. "It's too late for that. As leader, you are responsible for our path and this path is one that leads nowhere. Again, I motion that we vote for new leadership."

"I second the motion," said the leader of the steam-engineer's guild.

"Of course you would," Talitha remarked. "We all know here that the two of you are only out to protect the steam-wagon industry."

Natarios wrung his hands beneath the table in excitement. It was plain by the look on Talitha's face that she had been caught off guard. No one had ever challenged her in this capacity before and now it would all be over before she had a chance to even fight back.

"The motion is seconded," Rives said, ignoring Talitha's accusation. "All in favor of voting on new leadership?"

All but five hands raised up in the air, and of those five, one of them was Natarios's. It was all part of the plan, to abstain from voting so as to appear neutral.

"The motion is passed," Rives said. "The council is now open to discuss and vote on the removal of Talitha of Issborg as lord of proceedings. I herby motion that she be removed from her station and the counsel entirely, and that a new lord of proceedings be elected, one who is neutral and has done all in his power to assist these proceedings in moving forward in a fair and equitable manner."

And here it comes…

"I nominate Natarios Rhodas."

"I second the motion," said the steam-engineer's guildmaster.

Natarios tried his damndest to look surprised.

One of the scholars stood. "A vote on this matter needs a third confirmation of the motion before proceeding to voting."

"I third the motion," the leader of the sorcerer's guild said without pause.

That was unexpected, the motion coming so willingly from the sorcerers, but Natarios didn't mind. It simply meant they were looking for a favor from him.

Rives nodded. "Very well then, we move to vote."

"Wait," Talitha said, rapping her gavel and rising to her feet. "The floor is still open for discussion. You will hear my piece before you proceed with this ridiculous vote."

Rives did not sit but waved at her with a flippant motion, indicating she was allowed to speak. This time, Natarios couldn't help but crack a smile. It had been so easy for Natarios to steal her power away, without saying so much as a word.

"Listen to me, all of you," Talitha said, letting her gaze sweep across the table. "You are only here at Queen Makarria's bidding. She was in her right to claim Sargoth as her own if she wished, or to choose her own despot to rule the kingdom, in the same way Thedric Guderian chose Don Bricio to rule Valaróz. She could have kept Guderian's empire intact if she had so desired, and ruled it with an iron fist as he did. She chose otherwise, though. She instead put the power into your hands, the hands of the people who were for so long under the rule of a tyrant. She returned to her own kingdom and gave you the opportunity to make Sargoth whole again, to raise your kingdom back to a height it hasn't seen since the Hundred-Years' Peace. And you've squandered it, fighting for scraps of the realm like carrion birds. Choose whom you will to oversee your proceedings. I have no ties to Sargoth and am happy to return to my people in Issborg, but know this: I have fought at every moment to ensure these proceedings have moved on justly, so that the people of Sargoth may have a ruler worthy of them. If you send me away and remake this kingdom into what it was when Guderian ruled; if war and chaos breaks out to spill over the border into the other four kingdoms; I can promise you that the dreamwielder and I will return."

"Thank you for your lecture," Rives said. "The child-queen had her chance to create a new order and she chose instead to flee. She can barely rule her own kingdom if the rumors are to be believed. Our fate is in our hands now and we take it gladly."

Natarios shot a glance at the ambassador of Valaróz, sitting at the opposite side of the table from Rives, to see if he would object to the insult of his queen, but the man was either too much a coward or too prudent to speak up. It was all but done now.

"All those in favor of removing Talitha of Issborg from this council and electing Natarios Rhodas as lord of proceedings, raise your hand."

The hands shot up around the room, all of them but Talitha's and the ambassadors' from Valaróz and Pyrthinia.

"It is done," Rives said.

Talitha glared openly at Ambassador Rives and then turned to Natarios. For one terrifying moment, Natarios thought she might turn him to flames, but she simply set the gavel down on the table and walked out of the council room, defeated.

Natarios smiled and stood when the door closed behind her. Now it was time to really put things into motion.

"Thank you all for your trust in my loyalty and abilities. I have to admit, I am much surprised, but I do not take this charge lightly. As my first order of business, I move that we proceed to the candidate voting process immediately. Each candidate will have up to two days to present his claim, and we'll allow for an additional two days of recess for the council to debate matters in between. That is little more than two weeks total, lords and ladies. Sixteen days until we elect the next King of Sargoth. Do I have a second motion?"

Rives had a surprised look on his face, but Natarios paid him no heed. Did the man think that Natarios was his servant and not the other way around?

"I second the motion," the steam-engineer's guildmaster said.

"All in favor?" Natarios demanded.

Again, a near unanimous vote in his favor.

"It is done then," Natarios said. "Lord Penter shall be first, making his case before us on the morrow and the next. I call this meeting adjourned."

And like that it was all over. Ambassadors and candidates alike crowded around him to shake his hand and congratulate him, to thank him for moving forward so expeditiously. He took it all in, knowing that the next two weeks were going to be very busy for him. The backroom negotiating he had been doing thus far would pale in comparison to what faced him now. It was all in his hands, just the way he wanted it.

The only surprise waiting for him as the counsel members poured out of the chambers was Talitha re-entering the room to approach him. Natarios tried to ignore her, pretending to be immersed in conversation with someone else as he made his way toward the door, but she barred his passage.

"Congratulations," Talitha said. "I hope you fare better than I have, houndkeeper."

Natarios merely nodded, not trusting himself to speak. It was one thing to undermine her power behind her back and through bureaucratic proceedings, quite another to insult her to her face.

"I have a favor to ask," Talitha went on. "I assume you'll be notifying the other monarchs of the impending vote. Would you mind sending along a note from me with your raven to Sol Valaróz?"

Natarios wet his lips as a new thought came to mind. Talitha had an airship at her disposal—the only one of its kind, in fact—and if he refused her, she would be sure to jump aboard and go running to the dreamwielder in Valaróz along with the beast of a northman who was her man servant. Natarios wouldn't have to worry about her meddling around here in Col Sargoth anymore. It was so perfect, he couldn't believe he hadn't thought of it before.

"I'm sorry, but I cannot," he said. "There will be no ravens, no outside influence on this election."

"You can't be serious."

"I am very serious," Natarios told her. "As houndkeeper, and now the lord of proceedings, it is very much my prerogative when and where to send ravens. I'm sorry. Good day."

And with that, Natarios turned and walked away from the sorceress as quickly as his legs would carry him without looking ridiculous.

3
Blood in the Water

Perched upon its plateau overlooking the city and bay below, the white-marble palace of Sol Valaróz glinted in the late morning sun. It was already hot in the practice yard, but Caile hardly noticed. He guffawed—half-laugh, half-grunt—as he parried Thon's overhand sword stroke, then countered with a backhanded swing. Thon parried in turn, their blunted sparring swords clanging dully. If he hadn't know better, Caile never would have guessed the man had been near death in a Khal-Aband prison cell three weeks prior. Though still wiry thin, Thon was strong and graceful in his movements. His visage was no longer gaunt and obscured with a mangy beard. Cleaned up and well fed, he looked to be no older than twenty years at the most, not the forty or fifty years Caile had initially surmised. Most surprisingly, the man was a damned good swordsman. Caile was holding back, but just barely.

"I yield!" Thon finally grunted, lowering his sword.

Caile pulled off his practice helmet and handed his sparring sword to a nearby squire. "Good thing," he said between heaving breaths. "If we'd gone much longer, you or I or both would have passed out."

Thon threw his own helmet onto the ground and brushed back his newly trimmed black hair. His smile was broad, reminding Caile of someone, but he couldn't put his finger on whom. The déjà vu feeling nettled at him, but he brushed it aside.

"You're taking it easy on me," Thon said. "It's a bit obvious. But I am feeling stronger. Give me another week and a flail and I'll give you a proper challenge."

"Luckily for me, we don't have any flails in the armory. No one in Valaróz uses them." That was the truth of it. As far as Caile knew, no one but the Sargothian cavalry used flails. Caile still couldn't comprehend why Thon, a Sargothian cavalryman himself, had been sent to Khal-Aband. Thon claimed to not know why either, and while Makarria had yet to hold his official retrial, Caile took the man at his word. Emperor Guderian had been a madman. He could have simply not liked the way Thon looked and sent him away for fun.

"Is it my turn now?" someone asked from the observation bench next to the sparring stock.

Caile turned to see Fina, the other newly released prisoner from Khal-Aband, sitting there. She had snuck up on them without either of them noticing. She too had recovered well. Her ebony hair had been neatly cropped, shorter even than Caile's, but there was no mistaking her for a man. She had filled out in the three weeks since her release, leaving her with full cheeks and lips, and a bosom her loose-fitting, sleeveless tunic did little to hide. Only the faintest hint of crow's feet at the corners of her eyes suggested she was older than a maiden.

As with Thon, Caile felt like he'd seen Fina somewhere before. But again, he couldn't place her.

"Well?" she asked.

"I'm sorry," Caile said. "Your turn for what, my lady?"

"For sparring," she replied, hopping over the waist-high fence toward them. "And you can call me Fina. I'm no lady."

"Lady or not, you're still a woman," Thon said. "You'd be better suited to spinning wool, I think."

Caile regarded them, unsure whether Thon was joking or not. The two of them had shared a prison cell for some time at least, but neither had spoken much of what they experienced there or how much they had spoken to one another. Had they become comrades in the darkness and isolation? Enemies? Or had they simply remained anonymous strangers?

"If spinning isn't your thing, perhaps milking cows would be more to your liking," Thon suggested, grinning.

The kick came so fast, Caile hardly realized what he was seeing before Thon hit the ground with a thud. He had never seen someone move so quickly and with so little effort. Fina had kicked Thon square in the chest and was standing back in her original stance before he landed in the dirt.

Caile instinctively reached for his sword hilt only to find it wasn't there. Of course not. He'd set it aside to take up the sparring sword, which was now in the hands of the squire who stood staring slack-jawed at Fina. Caile eyed Fina warily, trying to decipher her intention.

Luckily Thon began laughing. "Sargoth's hairy arse, woman. You kick like a mule."

Fina smiled and offered a hand to help him up. "All the times I saved you from beatings and you still doubted it?"

"I didn't doubt your ability, just your temperament," Thon replied, dusting himself off. "I thought maybe it was only the ill environment of the prison that made you so violent. It seems I was mistaken."

"You were," Fina said, grabbing up Thon's discarded helmet and sparring sword. "Well, how about it, Prince? Is it my turn now or are you too tired?"

Her name suddenly fell into place in Caile's mind. How had he not realized it before? "I am a bit winded, now that you mention it," he said. "But our young squire here is always eager to spar."

"Uhm, what?" the doltish lad asked.

"Into the ring, son," Caile told him. "Helmet on and sword up, that way she doesn't hurt you too badly."

Though skeptical at the prospect of sparring with a woman, the squire did as he was told. He made the first tentative pass with his sparring sword in the direction of Fina and she nearly swiped it out of his hands with her own sword. He took the sparring more seriously after that. Despite being only fourteen, and a numbskull at that, the boy knew his way with a sword and he was oafishly strong. Caile had observed him enough times in the sparring yard to know he was no slouch.

Fina disarmed him and knocked him to the ground in less than three seconds.

When he got up and engaged her again, she disarmed him with a flip of her sword and kicked his feet out from beneath him. The second time he got up she knocked him senseless with a sword blow to the head that left him gasping on the ground. Her movements were fast, purposeful, restrained—each one meant to position her body within close proximity of her opponent so he overreached with his weapon, each movement positioning her own weapon to finish its tightly arced trajectory and strike her opponent in a vulnerable spot.

"Enough," Caile said, grinning. "I figured it out. I know who you are."

"Of course you do," Fina replied, tossing her helmet aside with a dissatisfied frown. "I told you my name, didn't I?"

"Not your full name, no. You are Mistress Alafina Infierno, protector of Don Bricio's harem. I remember you now. You should have told us when we released you."

Fina let the tip of her sword dip to the ground. "Yes, that was my station in life once. The old ways come back quickly, it seems. I was going to say nothing until my retrial with the queen, but when I saw the two of you sparring…well, I guess I've grown restless sitting around in the infirmary."

Caile smiled, excited at the prospect of telling Makarria who it was they had rescued. "I was here as ward of Don Bricio during the same time you were here. Some of it, at least. You and I probably only ever met in passing, but Don Bricio spoke of you often and how you protected his women from drunk guards and jealous merchants who thought themselves stealthy enough to slip into the harem. What happened? You were still here when I left for Pyrthinia, yet when I returned with Makarria, you were nowhere to be found."

"Parmenios Pallma made his claim to the throne is what happened. Don Bricio was livid and came to the women in a drunken rage, not to bed them, but to take out his anger on someone weaker than him. I did not stand for it, and he in turn did not take kindly to my defiance. He sent me away before he set sail to make war on Pyrthinia."

That was all she said, and Caile respected her enough not to push the matter. "Well, they are all free now, all the women of the harem," he said instead. "If I'd known who you were, I would have urged Makarria to hold your retrial sooner, so you could be officially appointed to a position suited to your skills. Your fighting prowess is practically legendary. You should have said something."

"I suppose I like to let my weapons do the talking."

Caile opened his mouth to ask her more about the prison, to ask Fina and Thon both, but thought better of it. They had suffered much and were just now starting to feel like themselves again. There would be time enough later to question them about Khal-Aband when Makarria was ready. He was anxious to know, but he could bear to wait, he decided. That's what Lorentz was always preaching to him and Makarria both: to work on their patience.

"Well, let's get ourselves dusted off and out of this armor," Caile suggested.

"Indeed," Thon said. "I'm thoroughly thrashed, and didn't you say that you had a hearing to attend to?"

Caile cringed. Usually, he had Lorentz around to keep him on task, but since returning from Khal-Aband, Lorentz had maintained his role as Makarria's bodyguard, following her around like a lost puppy and leaving Caile to his own devices. Caile checked the sun to gauge the time and cursed inwardly. "Looks like I'm running late," he told Thon and Fina, and with a wave goodbye, he dashed off toward the palace.

• • •

Makarria looked up from the sheaf of documents in her lap and gave Caile a dissatisfied glare when he finally arrived in the private sitting room adjoining the throne room. He was bathed and dressed now in his formal doublet bearing the red and gold stripes of

Pyrthinia with the Valarion seal at his breast, pronouncing him not only a Pyrthin Prince, but also an official advisor to the Valarion throne. He glanced sheepishly from Makarria to Lorentz, who stood guarding the doorway to the throne room.

"It's about time," Makarria said. She too was dressed in her royal garb, in her case a blue gown. She had refused from the beginning of her reign to wear anything with a corset, no matter what her handmaiden and tailor said about tradition, but the royal gown they had tailored for her was still tightly fitted from the waist up and had more pleats and folds in the skirt than she knew what to do with. The damned thing took her an hour to get into and revealed more of her developing figure than she was comfortable with. She was already self-conscious enough as it was wearing it in front of Caile, and seeing him stroll in late only made her more aggravated.

"What took you so long?"

"Sorry, I was in the practice yard sparring with our new friends and had to get myself cleaned up."

"Friends?"

"Yes, Thon and Fina. There's more to them than we have guessed."

"Of course. They wouldn't have survived in Khal-Aband if they were unremarkable people. You'll have to tell me about it later, though. We have more pressing issues. A ship arrived this morning with official ambassadors from Khail Sanctu—the Old World has come calling."

She stood up from where she had been sitting in the ring of padded chairs and handed Caile the official writ from the Khail Sanctu delegation, trying not to let her nervousness show in her shaking hands.

"What do you suppose they want, Caile? It says they are only here to make an official state visit, but I don't believe it."

"Who can say? We had no interaction with the Old World during Don Bricio's rule."

"But I thought Don Bricio was *from* the Old World."

Caile shrugged. "Sure once, but he was an outcast, living at the far north end of their empire, just south of the Spine. Guderian and Wulfram recruited him and his underlings when they made their way north to reclaim the Sargothian throne. With the stifling power Guderian wielded, I don't think the Old World wanted anything to do with the Five Kingdoms. Unfortunately, I've had as few dealings with them as you have."

"That's it then," Makarria said. "That's why they're here, because they know Guderian is gone and it's just a girl sitting on the Valarion throne, barely old enough to be considered a woman."

"Not just a girl," Caile said, handing the documents back to her. "A girl with Vala's blood running through her veins, descendant of the Pallma line, true heir to the Valarion throne, and the dreamwielder who killed Emperor Guderian."

"Right. I keep forgetting that part." She straightened the folds of her gown and made her way to where Lorentz stood. He had been strangely quiet lately, but she didn't have time to worry about him right now on top of everything else. Going to Khal-Aband herself had perhaps been a mistake. Her mother had ruled in her stead while she was gone, but the Valarion people trusted her no more than they trusted Makarria, and now there were all sorts of new political problems to sort through, chief among them this visit from the Old World.

"Well," she asked Caile with a sigh, "are we ready?"

"Yes, just remember that this is Sol Valaróz, not Khail Sanctu. This is your throne room—you're in charge. Feel free to remind them if need be."

"Right," Makarria said with a nod, and Lorentz pushed his way through the double doors that opened upon the white marble dais of the throne room.

The vast, rectangular throne room was not even filled to half capacity, but even so, there were dozens of onlookers standing on the main floor beneath the glass-domed ceiling overhead. Makarria recognized many of the attendees: mostly merchants, traders, guildmasters and a variety of others who were always around to try to bend Makarria to their will, and profit. Even worse, the spokesman for the Brotherhood of Five was in attendance, she saw. *Master Rubino.* He was her most outspoken critic, and cared not to make money, but rather to get her married so she could hand off the throne to a man and focus on having babies. The only friendly faces in the crowd were those of her mother, Prisca, and her mother's bodyguard, Captain Haviero.

Makarria steeled her countenance, then strode toward the throne with Caile trailing behind her. The two of them took their seats, Makarria in her throne and Caile in the advisor's seat to her side, and then Makarria nodded for the herald to begin.

"Her Majesty, Queen Makarria Pallma!"

Everyone in the audience kneeled.

"Please rise," the herald continued. "By decree of the Queen, all hearings scheduled for the day have been postponed in order to welcome a special delegation. Your Majesty, lords and ladies, I present to you Ambassador Mahalath and Senator Emil of the Old World Republic."

A surprised murmuring echoed through the throne room from the audience as the delegation entered from the far side of the room. The two Old World officials strode forward, both garbed in white togas. Behind them came six attendants, also wearing togas, and four legionnaires, clad in maroon cuirasses and bearing long pikes. Makarria felt an urge to glance behind her to make sure her own guards were at the ready, but didn't dare do so at risk of offending them. *I might be an inexperienced farm girl still, but I've learned that much, at least.*

When the delegation came to a stop before the dais, Makarria inclined her head in recognition. "Welcome to the realm of Valaróz, good sirs. It is our pleasure to receive you. To what do we owe this honor of your visit?"

"Thank you, Your Majesty," replied Ambassador Mahalath, a tall, slender man who wore a turban on his head and sported a giant, black mustache. "We visit here from the Old World Republic to officially recognize your rule as the new Queen of Valaróz. Your predecessor was hesitant to interact with us, your southern neighbors, but we come here in peace, hoping to forge a new relationship between realms. If you will have me, the Republic has sent me as ambassador to work with you in opening new avenues of trade and commerce, and ensure peaceful interactions."

"Of course," Makarria told him, hoping that was indeed all the Old World was after. "We would be honored if you would stay with us in our embassy wing, along with the ambassadors from the Five Kingdoms and the East Islands. I think you will find the Kingdoms are much friendlier now with the dissolution of the Sargothian Empire. In due course, I would even like to send my own ambassador to Khail Sanctu."

Ambassador Mahalath bowed his head. "It would be my great honor to facilitate the very thing."

Makarria smiled at him. She found the gesture surprised most petitioners and dignitaries, in a positive way. Mix strength with kindness, her mother always told her.

"It is settled then, Ambassador. We will make arrangements for your permanent residence immediately. In the meantime, I'm sure you all must be weary from your journey. Unless there is something pressing we need discuss, it would be my pleasure to have the palace staff see you all to your temporary quarters where you can rest. We can meet again tomorrow in less formal circumstances."

"I beg your pardon," the other delegate said, "but I'm afraid we do have pressing matters to discuss." It was the senator. He was a nondescript man, of average height and coloring, clean-shaven, and with a crisply cut head of graying blond hair, but there was something about him that put Makarria on edge. It had to be his facial expression, she decided, the way his mouth curled up at one side and how the outer corners of his eyes were raised in disdainful amusement. He exuded arrogance.

"Please proceed then, Senator Emil," Makarria told him.

"Word has reached us that the Kingdom of Sargoth is in turmoil. We have learned that a king is still not in place, and in fact, your own lord of proceedings, Talitha of Issborg, has been impeached. As you can well imagine, we in the Republic are concerned the turmoil might spread. If widespread revolt were to occur, it could easily spill over into our lands."

"Did you say Talitha of Issborg has been impeached?" Makarria asked, stunned by the very thought.

"Yes, Your Majesty."

"That cannot be. We have heard nothing and we are in regular communication with both Talitha and our ambassador in Col Sargoth."

Senator Emil shrugged apologetically. "We have means of communication that travel more quickly than ravens. I do not mean to challenge your assertion, Your Majesty, but I promise you, we have it on the highest authority that Talitha of Issborg is no longer in charge of the proceedings. If you have not received word yet, it is simply a matter of time. Time that can be well spent in preparation. The Republic requires assurance that Valaróz will stymie any civil unrest in the northern kingdoms."

Nervous whispers passed through the audience.

"I find it interesting that the Republic is suddenly so interested in turmoil and unrest in the Five Kingdoms," Caile said, an edge in his voice. "Where was the Old World's concern when Parmenios Pallma reclaimed the Valarion throne and joined my father in war against Emperor Guderian?"

"We were standing at the ready, prince," Senator Emil said. "All King Casstian needed to do was ask for our aid and we would have been there. Neither Guderian, Don Bricio, nor Wulfram were any allies to the Republic. We would have come to your aid gladly."

"He speaks the truth of the matter," Ambassador Mahalath said. "And we do not entreat you today with an unreasonable demand. Rather, we come offering aid. The Republic has many resources: armies, sorcerers, ships, supplies, money. Together we can ensure a new epoch of peace."

"That's right," Emil added. "For better or worse, Emperor Guderian did provide stability during his reign. If a new leader were to step in to control the Five Kingdoms and maintain that stability, and then openly trade with neighboring realms, we could lead both of our realms to unprecedented prosperity."

"Are you suggesting Queen Makarria re-form Guderian's empire?" Caile asked.

"Empire, Five Kingdoms—call it whatever you like. If strong leadership does not rise to the occasion and keep the realm under control, the Republic Senate will vote to take action."

Caile rose to his feet and glared down at the senator. "How dare you threaten us? You think we are weak because we are young? I'll have you know it was Makarria who killed Guderian. I who killed Don Bricio and Wulfram. My sister who led the Pyrthin army to force the Sargothian and Golierian armies to surrender. We did what none of your senators or sorcerers ever dared to attempt."

"Children can win a war," Emil replied with a sneer, "but it takes men to rule a realm."

This time the crowd did more than whisper. It was their surprised gasps and muttered insults toward Senator Emil that prompted Makarria to stand.

"That is quite enough," she said, staring down at Senator Emil.

Ambassador Mahalath pushed his way in front of the senator. "Your Majesty, our apologies. Senator Emil is accustomed to debating in the Republic Senate where discussions are more…lively. I'm certain he meant no disrespect. Isn't that right, senator?"

"Of course," Emil responded.

"You see? Again our apologies. We simply mean to impress upon you the importance of taking timely action on this matter."

Makarria motioned for Caile to sit, then took her own seat, trying to appear as dignified as possible. "Whether disrespect was intended or not, Senator, I do not take demands upon me or my station lightly. I have heard your concerns. I will consult with the Sargothian ambassador on the proceedings in Col Sargoth. I will meet with my advisors to devise a course of action if necessary, and I will meet with you again on the morrow. I too wish for nothing but peace and prosperity, and let me remind you—no fighting or 'civil unrest' has yet broken out in Sargoth. We will not resort to preemptive violence to prevent violence. That is all, gentlemen. My staff will see you to your quarters. This hearing is over."

4
Unknown Soldiers

"What was all that?" Makarria demanded of Caile back in the small sitting room.

Caile pulled his doublet off over his head and plopped himself down into one of the cushioned chairs. "That was a good show of strength. Well done!"

"Is that what you call it?" She turned to find Lorentz for his support, but he was gone, having stayed back in the throne room apparently. With a frustrated growl she began pacing the room. "Did you see yourself in there? You were standing up, yelling at an official delegation, in front of an audience!"

"What? You didn't really think I was as angry as I made out to be, did you?"

Makarria narrowed her eyes at him. "You faked it?"

"Well, not entirely, but yes, I overreacted on purpose. If they were really out to enact some sort of treaty or agreement, they would have met with us in private to hammer out the details, but no, the senator insisted on confronting us in the throne room in front of everyone."

"To undermine us in front of our own people," Makarria said, annoyed with herself for not having silenced Senator Emil sooner.

"Right, or to plant the idea of revolt and civil unrest in their heads. Either way, we had to respond with conviction. That was why I raised my voice. Plus, it allowed us to get a better sense of what they were after, which I think is clear now—they're after exactly what you feared, a foothold, if not absolute control of the Five

Kingdoms now that Emperor Guderian is gone. My little act made it clear we're not afraid to fight, and, more importantly, it gave you the opportunity to show you are in charge. Which you did a nice job of, by the way."

Makarria stared at him. He never ceased to surprise her, and as much as she wanted to still be angry with him, she couldn't help but return his stupid grin. He was so proud of himself. "You are too much for me to handle sometimes."

"Oh, you do all right," he assured her. "The only thing I might have done differently in there was take what you did a step further and send the entire Old World delegation packing back to their ship. I'm not sure it's a good idea having them here so close at hand."

This time it was Makarria's turn to surprise him. She might be relatively new to politics, but it didn't mean that she hadn't been taking the time to learn as much as she could. Her tutor, the scholar Natale, had already taught her much in the last year.

"It did cross my mind to send them away," she said, "but as Sargoth Lightbringer once wrote, 'It is always best to keep enemies close at hand so you can keep an eye on them.'"

"See what I mean?" Caile said, holding his hands up. "You're better at this than you think."

Makarria rolled her eyes. "It's just something my Natale taught me."

"Well, he is a smart one. Now to the important questions. Did Talitha really lose control of the proceedings in Col Sargoth? And if so, how in Sargoth's hairy arse did those bastards from the Old World find out before us?"

Before Makarria could respond, the side door opened and three people entered the chamber.

"I think I can answer those questions for you."

It was Talitha, along with Siegbjorn and Makarria's mother, Prisca.

"They arrived just now in their airship," Prisca informed Makarria. "They said they had urgent news so I brought them immediately."

"Thank you, Mother," Makarria told her, and she went to embrace the two friends she hadn't seen in months, giving the enormous, hairy Siegbjorn an extra hard squeeze. She missed his quiet strength and the simple pleasure he found in sailing his airship. If it hadn't been for him, she doubted she would have survived the fear and solitude of being trapped in the Caverns of Issborg. And though Makarria had spent less time with Talitha than Siegbjorn, Talitha too had been a mentor and friend that Makarria suddenly realized she missed more than she could put into words. She wished she were meeting them both in better circumstances, but she was queen now and had responsibilities. They all did.

"Please sit, all of you," Makarria said. "What's happened? As glad as I am to see you, you aren't supposed to be here."

"It's the houndkeeper," Talitha said. "He's been plotting with the ambassador from Golier and who knows who else. I knew the steam-engineer's guild and Golier were in backdoor talks, but then the sorcerer's guild voted right along with them. The two have been at opposite extremes during the whole process. I never expected to see them join forces. I'm sorry, Makarria. I didn't even realize what was happening until it was too late. They voted me out and now Natarios Rhodas is in charge of the proceedings. We only have fourteen days left until they elect a ruler, and I'm afraid whomever they choose will not be to our liking. I don't know what's happening, but this goes beyond a meddlesome houndkeeper."

Makarria and Caile exchanged a look.

"The Old World Republic perhaps?" Caile suggested.

"The Old World?" Talitha asked, leaning in closer.

Makarria nodded. "They arrived this morning, an ambassador and a senator. They knew what happened to you already and are 'offering us help' to restore order. How could they have found out about what happened before we did?"

"That's a good question," Talitha replied. "The houndkeeper refused to send a raven, but even so, Siegbjorn and I left within a day and we flew faster than any raven could be expected to. We would have been here yesterday, but I had to make sure Guderian's war machine factory was secure. Let the Sargothian council think they control the kingdom for now. The only danger in Col Sargoth is those war-wagons, and whoever controls them controls their power. We have that in our hands, at least."

"Good," Caile said, nodding in approval. "I've seen firsthand what those machines can do. My father's cavalry was mowed down like wheat beneath the scythe against those things. How many are left?"

"More than you want to know."

Caile frowned. "You're sure you trust whoever you left guarding the factories?"

"The Sargothian cavalry itself guards the war machines. They are sworn to me until such time a new king is coronated. I trust them completely. For the next fourteen days, at least. After that, whoever is elected king will take control of everything."

"But how did the Old World know before we did?" Makarria repeated.

"Sorcery," Talitha replied. "What else? Their knowledge of magic far surpasses what we have here in the Five Kingdoms. They have some relic of antiquity, no doubt, that allows their informants to communicate directly with Khail Sanctu. I spent years there during my own training as a sorceress and I've seen such relics, studied them even."

"Khail Sanctu is nine-hundred miles from here, and yet their ship arrived this morning," Caile pointed out. "It doesn't add up, not if the message went from Col Sargoth to Khail Sanctu. There's no way they could have dispatched a ship to arrive here so quickly."

"They communicated directly to their ship then," Makarria said. "They brought a relic onboard their ship because they were expecting a message. This was all planned. Coordinated."

Talitha frowned. "Or maybe it's all just a coincidence. But you're probably right. It seems a little too convenient for all this to be entirely random. The sorcerer's guild has long been supported by the Old World. And I'm convinced the houndkeeper could not do this on his own. There has to be a unifying force behind them, and the Old World Republic definitely fits the mark."

"What do we do then?" Caile asked.

"Simple," Prisca chimed in. "Make sure the right man becomes King of Sargoth."

Makarria smiled. Her mother rarely spoke up in meetings of this sort. She was content to let Makarria and her advisors rule the kingdom, and instead focused on running the palace staff. Still, when she did speak up, she spoke with a wisdom that belied her demeanor.

"Exactly," Makarria said. "We put the right person on the throne and there's no longer a void of power in the region. The Old World will have no excuse to meddle in our business. No fighting. No warring."

"Sure, that's simple in theory," Caile agreed. "But who's the right man, and how do we make sure he gets elected?"

"Not so simple," Talitha said. "There is no clear, best choice for the Sargothian throne. There are many bad choices, including the man Golier's ambassador and the steam-engineers support, but no perfect candidate. And then there's the matter of how to influence the council's vote. I have no more authority to sway their minds. Caile could go, perhaps. He has had some dealings there in the city. This houndkeeper—Natarios Rhodas—he is originally from Pyrthinia. Perhaps you would hold some sway with him, Caile?"

"Not likely. We've never met, and he and my father were at constant odds. The bastard even put himself upon the Pyrthin throne when my father was imprisoned."

Siegbjorn spoke then, his *Snjaer Firan* accent thick and musical. "It was you who killed Guderian, Makarria. It is your right to choose a new king if you do not take the land as your own. Return to Col Sargoth and make it so. I will take you."

"Thank you, Siegbjorn, but I wouldn't even if I could. That is the way Guderian did things. We will not crown a king by force or trickery. We will respect the laws and traditions as Sargoth Lightbringer, Vala, Pyrthin, Norg, and Golier decreed them. Otherwise we're no better than Guderian."

Talitha sighed. "Don't be so certain. The Old World, the so-called Republic, follows its laws to the letter and I can tell you from experience that they are no less corrupt, their leaders no less power-hungry, than Guderian, Don Bricio, or Natarios Rhodas."

"I won't do it," Makarria insisted. "The Five Kingdoms have survived for over three hundred years, marred only by Guderian's reign. I won't perpetuate his tyranny."

"There were many more dark times in our history," Talitha said. "You forget the Dreamwielder War, the betrayal of Golier, the Norgmen uprising, and the wars with the Old World in the first century. But still, you have the right spirit. If you are going to make right the ill deeds of Emperor Guderian, you must do right by the people of the Five Kingdoms. I would not have it otherwise."

"That brings us no closer to a plan of action," Caile pointed out. "Are we to sit idly by while the council elects a new Sargothian king? Can we appease this Senator Emil that long? I'm doubtful."

"Lord Kobel is the candidate the houndkeeper and the ambassador from Golier are pushing," Talitha said. "If he is elected, he will be a puppet for the steam-engineer's guild and the Kingdom of Golier. I don't know what they envision, but you can be certain it involves those war wagons, or the technology to make new ones at least. Combine their steam technology with sorcery, and we'll be elbow deep in infernal devices we haven't seen the likes of since the Dreamwielder War. No, we can't allow Kobel to take the throne. He is arrogant and cruel. The others are cut from the same cloth, but less severe. I have a complete report that your ambassador in Col Sargoth prepared for you. Perhaps you will see something in one of the candidates I do not."

"I will read it," Makarria began to say, but a low rumble reverberated through the sitting room, like a distant explosion or an earthquake. It grew in intensity, a tension that Makarria sensed more in her stomach than with her ears. "What's happening?"

"Sorcery," Talitha answered. "And close."

"Lorentz!" Caile shouted.

Captain Lorentz burst through the main doors into the council chamber almost immediately, along with Captain Haviero of the

Royal Guard and six soldiers in his wake.

"There's smoke, coming from the fishery borough," Lorentz reported. "The city watch has already sounded the alarm. Shall I go and investigate?"

Caile glanced at Talitha, who sat pursing her lips in worry. "No, you stay here and watch the Queen," he commanded Lorentz. "This is something Talitha and I need to investigate."

"I'm not going to just sit around again waiting for you," Makarria objected.

"That's exactly what you're going to do," Talitha said. "Too much has gone awry for this to all be coincidence. It could be a trap, using sorcery to draw out the dreamwielder. Few, if any, know I am here. Caile and I can handle whatever we may encounter. We've faced worse together before."

"Right," Caile agreed. "Lorentz, stay here and protect Makarria. You too, Siegbjorn. Summon the rest of the Royal Guard to hold the throne room and this chamber. There are no other ways in or out. You'll be safe here."

"Lady Prisca," Captain Haviero interrupted, bowing his head. "I'd best escort you to your private quarters. I'm sure everything will be fine, but we need to follow the contingency plan, just in case something…" He couldn't bring himself to say it.

In case something happens to me, Makarria finished in her own mind. *Until I take a husband and have children, Mother is the heir to the throne.* Captain Haviero had been there when Makarria's grandfather, Parmo, had been assassinated. He never spoke of it, but it was obvious to Makarria that it drove him to be even more vigilant when it came to keeping Makarria and Prisca safe.

"Go on, Mother. I'll be safe here."

"Of course," Prisca agreed. She kissed Makarria on the head and then hurried out of the chamber, followed by Captain Haviero and two of the soldiers.

"Good, let's go then," Caile said to Talitha.

Makarria wanted to protest, but she saw the reason in their plan. It was pure selfishness to insist on going herself. She had a duty to her people. "Be safe," she told her friends.

Caile shot her a quick smile, as if to suggest he would do anything but the sort, and then he swept out the door with Talitha close on his heels.

• • •

"What's happening?" Thon hollered as Caile and Talitha ran past him on their way to the stables.

"Trouble," Caile said. "Come along if you're feeling up for a real fight."

Wordlessly, Thon joined in behind them.

"Who's this?" Talitha asked beneath her breath.

"A friend," Caile replied, leaving it at that, and not questioning the wisdom of bringing someone he knew barely three weeks. Caile couldn't explain why, but he trusted Thon.

At the stables, the squires were standing by with weapons and saddled horses at the ready, and within moments the three companions were mounted and charging through the courtyard and out the southern gate of the royal palace. The people in the main boulevard cleared a wide path for them as they rushed by to descend from one terraced borough to the next, passing first by opulent marble mansions, and then smaller shops and homes with stucco walls and terra cotta roofs as they neared the harbor.

The smoke billowing up from the fishery borough grew closer and darker as they approached. By the time they pulled their horses to a halt in front of a dilapidated warehouse, the smoke was an impenetrable dark column that blotted out the sun in the western sky. The air reeked of dead fish and a pungent tang like rotten eggs that burned their noses and eyes. The city watch was there already, clearing people away and evacuating the nearby warehouses. The fire brigade had arrived too, and was crowding tentatively around the entrance of the smoking warehouse. There were no flames to be seen, but smoke meant fire in their profession, and they were preparing to enter with axes and hoses connected to the horse-drawn water tenders they had brought.

"Stay back, all of you," Talitha shouted. "This is no ordinary fire. There are no flames you can put out with water."

The men stared up at this strange woman on horseback whom they had never seen before.

"Do as she says," Caile commanded as he dismounted. "Fall back, all of you. Stay at the ready in case the fire spreads to the nearby buildings, but do not enter this building. We'll handle it."

Talitha waved for Caile and Thon to come to her. "Listen carefully, both of you," she said. "This is very likely a trap. I'll go through the front, because that is where they're expecting Makarria to enter. I'm no dreamwielder, though. While not as powerful, I can act faster—I don't have to enter a dreamstate—so the advantage is mine. Each of you: take a half-dozen soldiers from the city watch and go in opposite directions around the perimeter of the building. Leave guards at any exits you find with orders to detain any who come out, then make your way in through the rear. Remember, when dealing with sorcery, quickness is your greatest weapon. Surprise our assailants from behind and strike before they can gather their thauma to attack. Otherwise, you'll be dead."

• • •

Makarria paced the circular space between the ring of chairs in the sitting room, hating that she was stuck there while her friends were off investigating. Even more aggravating was Lorentz, who was ordering more guards into the room, as if she needed the entire Royal Guard to protect her in her own palace.

"You need only sit and we will protect you," Siegbjorn said, seemingly reading her mind. He stood protectively in front of her in the center of the room, a curved skinning knife nearly as long as a short sword gripped upside-down in one hand.

Makarria smiled tersely at him, but frowned again when she saw Lorentz was ushering even more guards in. She didn't doubt Lorentz's honor or prowess, but something had been odd about him since returning from Khal-Aband. He'd become overly protective, and while she appreciated his concern, when it came to troop numbers, more was not always better—she'd learned as much in her first year of ruling Valaróz.

"Lorentz, are all these guards really necessary? I'm sure we're quite safe here, and even if there were an attack on me, there would be no room to fight in here we're so crowded."

"Prince Caile commanded me to bring in reinforcements and guard both entrances, Your Highness," Lorentz said, his voice distant-sounding to Makarria's ear. It wasn't right. Something had definitely unnerved him in the darkness of Khal-Aband, and he'd lost his wits in this particular situation. The guards in the small chamber numbered nearly a dozen now, all of them shuffling around to find space along the perimeter of chairs, holding their upright pikes close to their chests.

"Captain Lorentz," Makarria said, her voice stern this time, "I think they would better guard us outside the doorways."

Lorentz turned to her, his eyes narrowed, as if such a thought never would have occurred to him. "Of course—" he started to say, but then someone pushed him aside.

"Get her!"

It was one of her own Royal Guards. He kicked aside one of the chairs and rushed forward, trying to raise his arms high enough to maneuver his pike into position to attack. The fool never had a chance. Siegbjorn gutted him from navel to chin with one effortless uppercut of his skinning knife. Other guards were surging forward, though. And yet others were trying to stop them. All of them in the same uniforms, armed with the same useless pikes. It was mayhem.

With a bear-like roar, Siegbjorn kicked an approaching guard, then turned back to Makarria with his free hand held out to her. "Come!"

She jumped to his side and he pulled her in close to his back hip as he kicked and slashed his way toward the nearest exit. Blood and curses filled the room. Makarria nearly tripped on the hem of her dress. With a curse of her own, she closed her eyes, forcing herself into a dreamtrance and envisioning a shirt of chainmail in place of the hopeless gown.

• • •

This makes no sense, Caile thought to himself. He was deep into the bowels of the warehouse and had seen no one. The loading bay had been empty except for a few dozen abandoned crates and pallets, and the inner rooms of the warehouse—administrative offices, no doubt—were completely empty. There wasn't even any smoke.

Caile peeked his head through another doorway and saw the shape of a man halt in the adjoining room.

"Thon?"

"Yes, it's me."

Caile loosened his grip on his sword. "I take it you've found nothing?"

"Not so much as a mouse turd."

"Where's the cursed smoke coming from then?"

"We only saw smoke coming from the top," Thon pointed out. "Perhaps the fire is on the roof? I found some stairs back the way I came."

"You didn't see Talitha?"

Thon shook his head.

"Off to the stairs then. Quickly. She's probably already up there."

• • •

Makarria came out of her dreamtrance with a gasp, now garbed in chainmail, her high-heeled shoes replaced with leather boots. In front of her, Siegbjorn cursed and pulled his knife free from a guard's breastbone. Makarria ducked away from him so he would have more room to maneuver only to back into a guard who shoved his way forward to get his hands around her neck.

"Die, bitch!"

Makarria's panicked scream was choked short as the man's fingers gripped tighter, and she instinctively kneed him in the groin. The man let out a scream of his own and Makarria tore herself free.

"Makarria!" Siegbjorn hollered, hammering the man on top of the head with a closed fist and sending him reeling to the floor where he was promptly trampled by the other guards.

Makarria reached out to grab Siegbjorn again, but something jabbed her in the back, piercing through her chainmail shirt with enough force that she stumbled forward into Siegbjorn's arms. The giant northman bellowed like a bear, grabbing her up and kicking her assailant square in the chest to fly backward.

"Hand her to me!" someone shouted.

Makarria glanced over to see Lorentz standing no more than five paces away, reaching for her through the doorway.

"Siegbjorn, quickly! Hand her to me."

With a grunt, Siegbjorn lowered his shoulder and plowed his way toward the door. Men ricocheted off him, but his feet became tangled in fallen men and he stumbled forward, pushing Makarria into Lorentz's arms. "Go!" he bellowed.

"No," Makarria tried saying, reaching back to help him up, but Lorentz was already pulling her away through the empty throne room.

• • •

Halfway up the stairs, a concussion rang out from above like a thunderclap, nearly toppling Caile and Thon back down the way they had come.

"What was that?" Thon asked, yanking himself back to his feet with the handrail.

"Sounds like Talitha," Caile remarked. "Hurry!"

They dashed up the remaining stairs to a small landing where a ladder attached to one wall led up through a hatch in the ceiling. Wordlessly, they hurried up the ladder to the roof, where they were enveloped in curling black smoke.

"Talitha!" Caile yelled out, repressing a cough. "Where are you?"

From the smoke rushed a figure. And then another, both of them brandishing swords. Neither were Talitha, and neither said a word as they attacked.

• • •

"Quickly, into the courtyard," Lorentz said, pulling Makarria along by the hand. "We have to get you on a horse and out of here."

"To where?" Makarria asked. He wasn't making any sense, but the pain in Makarria's back made it hard to think straight. She could feel blood running down her back beneath her chainmail and soaking into her undergarments. If she hadn't turned her dress into chainmail back in the chamber, she would be dead right now.

"No questions, Your Majesty," Lorentz said. "This way."

They were outside now, nearing the stables. Makarria glanced around. There should have been soldiers rushing to their aid, or at least the squires in the stables, but the yard was quiet. Makarria pulled her hand free of Lorentz's and stumbled after him into the stables.

Makarria stopped in horror.

They had found the squires. Three of them, dead on the ground, their throats slit.

"There she is!" someone shouted, and Makarria spun around to see four men emerging from the glaring sunlight of the practice yard into the stables. Lorentz stepped in front of Makarria, but held his sword only loosely. There was no urgency or purpose in his movements.

"Kill them both!" one of the men yelled.

"Wait," another said.

And someone was laughing. Was it Lorentz?

Makarria tried to close her eyes and dream something, but what? She didn't know who was who or what to do, and the pain from her wound was pulsating in her back, making it impossible to concentrate. All she could think to do was yell for help.

• • •

Caile ducked through the billowing smoke and dispatched his first assailant by stabbing him through the gap in his armor at his armpit. He had no time to see how Thon was faring, though, as three more men rushed out of the smoke toward them. Caile ducked and spun away to create more space, but his heel struck a curb and he nearly toppled backward. He shot a glance behind him and realized they were indeed on the roof, and he'd nearly fallen off the edge to his demise.

One of the men bull rushed him, and Caile simply sidestepped to allow the man to hurl himself to the street below. The fool's scream ended with his neck snapping on cobblestone thirty feet below. There was no time for Caile to congratulate himself, though. The two survivors were moving in more warily, and they had him backed against the ledge. Caile feinted to the left, then lunged to his right, somersaulting away, intent on making the men approach him one at a time. By the time he rolled to his feet, however, Thon was there, hacking the first man's head off, then bashing the other on the skull with the pommel of his sword.

"Captured a prisoner for you," Thon said, prodding the downed man with a toe. "Assuming he manages to wake up."

"Good thinking," Caile replied, only a bit off-put that Thon had handled their attackers so well. "Now we just need to find Talitha."

"Here," a voice came from the distance, and they both turned to see the black smoke clear away in a gust of wind. "Normal thugs, all of them," Talitha said, stepping toward them. "Not a single sorcerer in the bunch." Far behind her, at the opposite end of the roof, Caile could see the strewn bodies of a dozen more attackers and a smoldering pile of metal buckets.

"It was indeed a trap then, but one meant to get us away from the palace," he said, thinking out loud. "Makarria. Hurry!"

• • •

"Help!" Makarria screamed again.

Only one of the assailants lagged behind in the entrance to the stables; the other three engaged Lorentz like a pack of wolves, swinging and hacking with their swords. Lorentz moved effortlessly, like Makarria had never seen anyone move before, almost as if he knew what each of his attackers was going to do before he did it.

The fourth man stood watching, transfixed like Makarria for a long moment, but then he shook his head, remembering Makarria was there. He raised his sword and strode toward her. Makarria regained her own wits, but before she could even close her eyes to dream something, Fina was there. She moved like a wildcat, knocking the man senseless with a flying forearm to the head, and then dashing to Lorentz's aid. Lorentz had already cut one of the men down, all the while laughing like a madman and dodging blows like a drunken maniac. Fina dispatched the remaining two assailants in short order, using a sparring sword she'd grabbed up to break their legs and then stab out their throats.

Before Makarria could catch her breath, Fina was at her side, lifting the chainmail coat over Makarria's head to assess her wound.

"Sit," Fina told her.

Makarria did so gratefully. She watched Lorentz check the corpses of the three men around him, then stride toward the fourth man, the one Fina had knocked senseless.

"Keep him alive," Makarria said. "I want to know who's behind this."

"Of course," Lorentz said, but he walked with his sword ready to strike the fallen man.

"Lorentz!"

"Be still, Your Highness."

Makarria shot a glance up at Fina, who understood her look without question. "Stand down, Captain," Fina said, stepping after Lorentz.

It was too late, though. The prone man raised his head, pleaded something in a harsh whisper, and then Lorentz jammed his sword through his throat.

5
The Game

Natarios Rhodas groaned as Lady Hildrith continued her lengthy objection. "…furthermore," she was saying, "this gross manipulation of the schedule is obviously designed to benefit Lord Kobel. We all know he's the lapdog for you and the Kingdom of Golier both, Houndkeeper. Making the other candidates go first and allowing him to present his claim on the final day of proceedings opens the door for all sorts of theatrics. He of all people should be presenting now so that we can investigate and substantiate his ludicrous claims, whatever they might be. These whispered rumors of his distant ancestry to the Guderian line, the trumped-up numbers of his vassals and holdings, even his age are falsities, I tell you. It's all staged to make him look good at the end, right before we vote."

"Are you calling me a liar?" Lord Kobel asked, rising to his feet and leaning forward over the table to glare at Lady Hildreth.

Natarios rolled his eyes. It was true, Kobel was a buffoon. He couldn't even manage to make his menacing gesture look convincing. Natarios couldn't imagine why Ambassador Rives and the steam-engineer's guild were so keen to put him on the throne, but for now Natarios had to support him, at least until someone with more money or power to offer turned up to support another candidate.

"I'm not calling you anything, Lord Kobel," Lady Hildreth replied, unperturbed. "That's the whole point. You haven't claimed anything yet. We don't know where you stand, and will not until the other candidates are finished, making it impossible for us to validate whatever nonsense comes out of your mouth. It makes infinitely more sense to have you present your case now, and save some of the more established candidates for the latter days. Lords Derek, Loring, and Nagel all have long, well-documented records of civic duty. Why not rearrange the schedule so they go last?"

"Well, that's simply unfair," Kobel said. "I was told I would go on the last day. My presentation is not yet ready. I can't make my claim yet."

"We've been at this for a year!" Lady Hildreth yelled at him. "If you're not ready to present a convincing claim now, you never will be."

Kobel's face reddened, and he clenched one fist on the table in front of him. "Why not settle this like I suggested a year ago then? All the candidates in a public tourney. Last one still standing becomes king."

Things were getting out of hand. Kobel was a buffoon, but it didn't mean he wasn't dangerous. Natarios cleared his throat and rapped his gavel on the table three times in quick succession. "Thank you both, lord and lady. Lord Kobel, I'll remind you we're looking for a king, not a warlord. We all know of your prowess on the battlefield. Lady Hildreth, you give us much to consider. Unfortunately, the allotted time is over for new business. We will proceed to Lord Bertram's claim."

"But I haven't gotten a chance to motion for a vote," Lady Hildreth objected.

"I'm sorry, but you'll have to wait until tomorrow, when perhaps you'll be more concise with your objections. I won't allow any of the candidates to be robbed of their allotted time for presenting their claims."

Lady Hildreth glared at Natarios, but he made a show of ignoring her ire and turned to Lord Bertram, the candidate scheduled to present his claim today. "My good sir, if you will," he said, motioning for Lord Bertram to begin.

• • •

Makarria started at hearing approaching footsteps and pushed herself to her feet. *Please be Caile,* she whispered inwardly, but no, it was Senator Emil and Ambassador Mahalath, along with their four legionnaires. *So all of this was their doing after all. They've come to finish the job.*

Fina stepped forward to bar their path, and Makarria's eyes fluttered as she began to gather her strength and dream them all to stone or dust or fire. She wasn't sure, but yet again, before she could decide, she was taken by surprise.

"Are you harmed, Your Majesty?" Mahalath asked. "We heard fighting and came at once."

"Stand guard at the entrances," Senator Emil commanded the legionnaires. "Let no one pass but at the Queen's command. Protect her life with your own."

Makarria let her dreamstate dissipate and eyed them warily. They looked to be genuinely concerned for her safety. If it was an act, it was a convincing one.

"Are you all right?" Mahalath asked again.

"Wounded, but not gravely," Fina answered for Makarria.

"Who was it?" Senator Emil asked, kneeling down to examine one of the dead attackers.

"These men we don't know," Lorentz replied. "But it started with our own guards inside."

Makarria swore inwardly. She should have silenced Lorentz at once. The last thing she needed was the officials from the Old World to believe she had insurrection on her hands and doubt her competence even more.

"It is as we feared then," Senator Emil replied. "We've heard rumors that Don Bricio still had sympathizers and that they were planning an uprising. We should have warned you, but you were angry with us already."

"It was no uprising," Makarria told him. "It was an assassination attempt."

"They are one and the same, Your Highness. It was Don Bricio's sympathizers who killed your grandfather, if I am not mistaken. It stands to reason they would try to kill you."

"There are many reasons one might want to kill me, Senator. I'll not be jumping to any conclusions yet. And you can rest assured I will get to the bottom of this."

Senator Emil bowed. "Of course, Your Highness. Know that we are at your disposal, both my men and the entirety of the Old World Republic military should you accept our aid."

Horses approached, sparing Makarria from having to respond. The four Old World legionnaires, Fina, and Lorentz all rushed to the main entrance of the stables to confront any would-be attackers, but it was only Caile, returning from the fishery borough with Talitha and Thon.

"What happened?" Caile demanded as he dismounted and ran to Makarria, eyeing the slain squires and attackers lying on the ground around her. "Are you all right?"

"An assassination attempt is what happened, and yes, I'm fine," Makarria said. "What about the fire?"

"A diversion to get us away from you, it seems," Talitha said. "It wasn't even sorcery. Just a sulfur fire. Arson."

"Damn it all," Caile said, kneeling down next to Makarria to eye the wound Fina was still tending to. "Why didn't you stay where we left you?"

"Because that's where the first attack was," Makarria snapped back. "And Siegbjorn is still in there. Gather what men you can—trusted ones—and detain every guard in there. I want to question all of them."

"What?" Caile asked, confused.

"It was men wearing Royal Guard uniforms who first attacked," Makarria explained, reticent to divulge too much information in front of the men from the Old World but seeing no way around it. "I barely got out of there alive."

"Our own men hurt you?"

"I'm fine. Just go and figure out what happened."

Fina grabbed Makarria around the shoulders. "I will tend her, Prince. She will be fine. Go."

"Yes, go," Talitha concurred. "We will protect the queen. Capture the men who did this, and for the love of Tel Mathir, bring back Siegbjorn alive."

• • •

It was painstaking business sorting through the bodies and questioning the survivors in the meeting chambers, among them Siegbjorn, whose only notable injuries were bloodied knuckles from fighting off those who attacked him when he fell to the floor. Upon examination, no one could recognize or identify the slain attackers, not even Captain Haviero who knew every man in the Royal Guard. Even worse, none of the attackers seemed to have survived. Caile interviewed every single living person in that room and could identify them all as loyal Valarion guards. Furthermore, no one saw any of the attackers escape the room. It appeared they had all died in the attack, leaving no one to interrogate.

"How is this possible?" Caile demanded.

"It was mayhem, my lord," one of the guards replied. "Too many people were in the room and all of them wearing the same uniform. If I didn't recognize someone's face, I stabbed him in the throat with my boot knife. My men did the same. The traitors didn't surrender and we didn't think to take prisoners. It was kill or be killed."

Caile couldn't believe he'd left Makarria in such a situation. It was a miracle she had gotten out of there alive. "Damn it all, Lorentz! I left you in charge. How did you allow these men to enter in the first place?"

Lorentz shrugged. "I don't know. I summoned more men when you left, and guards kept coming. I simply thought them part of the same unit. By the time I realized anything was amiss, it was too late."

"It happened very quickly," Siegbjorn corroborated. "Be not angry at your man. My hands were full. If Lorentz were not standing by to drag Makarria away to safety, she would not be breathing and alive, I am to think."

Caile rubbed his forehead. Siegbjorn was right. It was his own fault, he knew, not Lorentz's. He was mad at Lorentz merely because he was mad at himself. "All right, here's what we're going to do. Siegbjorn, go to Makarria and Talitha. Make sure Makarria's safe and stay with her—we don't know who we can trust right now. Captain Haviero, have your slain men removed and their families notified. Once our casualties are cleared, I want all the attackers' bodies searched for anything that might give us clues. After they've been searched, take their bodies to the sparring yard. Lorentz, take a few men and gather the slain men from the stables and do the same. The city watch is bringing me the bodies from the fire in the fishery borough, and hopefully one attacker who is still alive, who I'll deal with. Once we have all the dead bodies in the sparring yard, have the commander of the city watch look them over and see if he can identify any of them. None of us recognize the attackers, but they look to be Valarion—maybe they're ruffians or cutthroats who have a history of criminal activity in the city. Also, let's gather up any men we have who served in Sol Cavarel, Sevol, Talvera, Valeza, anywhere besides Sol Valaróz, to see if they recognize the assailants. We need to know who these attackers are and where they came from if we're to determine who sent them. In the meantime, I'll find out where these stolen uniforms came from and then go get Fina to examine the bodies—if they're part of Don Bricio's old regime, maybe she'll recognize them." Caile pursed his lips, running the plan over in his mind one more time to see if he was missing anything. "That's all for now. Notify me immediately if you find anything. If no one else can identify our attackers, I guess I will…"

"Will what?" Siegbjorn prodded.

Caile let out a low, long breath. This would have to be handled delicately. "I'll have to ask the most probable suspects, our guests from the Old World, to see if they can identify the bodies."

• • •

Makarria was resting in her personal chambers, the wound on her back cleaned and dressed, when Caile came to her three hours later, disappointment written on his face. Lorentz stood at his side, his eyes wandering over the room from face to face: Makarria, Talitha, Fina, Siegbjorn, and Makarria's mother, Prisca.

"Well?" Makarria asked Caile, not bothering to get up from where she sat in her chair by the reading table.

"Nothing," he replied. "No survivors. The one man who was still alive died in a fit of seizures before he ever woke up to talk. No one recognizes any of the bodies. No one knows where they came from. Including the ambassadors from the Old World."

"And you believe them?"

"No, but I'll leave it to you to call them liars when the time comes. Are you all right?"

His expression was pained. It was clear he was worried about her, but Makarria wasn't letting him off the hook so easily. "I'm fine. Everyone, leave us. I will talk with Caile in private."

The women and Siegbjorn left wordlessly. They had all heard Makarria's telling of the attack in the council chamber, and even Siegbjorn had been swayed by Makarria's concerns. Only Lorentz lingered. *Of course.*

"'Everyone' means you too, Lorentz."

Lorentz glanced at Makarria, then nodded and walked out without complaint or any apparent self-consciousness. *Maybe he doesn't even realize I can't trust him anymore,* Makarria thought. *Does he not see how he's changed?*

When everyone was clear of the room and Lorentz closed the door behind him, Caile knelt down beside Makarria. "Your wound, does it hurt?"

"It's fine," she said, standing up from her chair and walking away from him. This was hard enough as it was without him being overly worried about her. "I dreamed myself a chainmail shirt when the attack started, so the knife point didn't go deep. The bruises where the chain links bit into my skin hurt more than the cut itself. Fina stitched it up for me… She told me who she is."

"Yes," Caile replied, standing up awkwardly from his kneeling posture. "I was going to tell you, but then…today happened."

"I've reassigned her. She will be my personal attendant from now on. My royal bodyguard. I'll have a scribe draw up the official appointment and a pardon for whatever supposed crime she committed during Don Bricio's reign."

Caile nodded. "Of course. It's a wise choice."

Makarria stared at him for a long moment, steeling herself for what she was about to say. "I want Lorentz sent away, Caile." There. She had said it. *Now the argument will begin.*

Caile's lips tightened. His brow knotted above his nose. "What?"

"Our trip to Khal-Aband rattled him, Caile. That's all I can figure. He is not the same man he was. He nearly got me killed today. I don't trust him anymore. I *can't* trust him anymore. Send him back to Pyrthinia and your sister so he can clear his head, figure out who he is and what his job is again."

"How could you even ask me that? Lorentz is like a father to me, and has been since the day I was sent away from my *real* father to be a ward of Don Bricio's. To say what happened today is his fault is unbelievable. If it's anyone's fault, it's mine. I shouldn't have run off chasing smoke and left you there trapped."

He was pacing furiously in front of her. Makarria held her ground, standing still and keeping her demeanor calm, though her heart was fluttering inside her. She hated confrontation as it was, but particularly with Caile.

"Look Caile, I'm not saying Lorentz was responsible for the attack, but he *was* the one who kept ordering more guards into the sitting room when it was already too crowded. I told him to send the men away, Caile, but he ignored me. And twice now he's disregarded my commands and killed men who we could have easily taken prisoner—once in Khal-Aband and again today in the stables. He's become overly protective of me—distanced and overbearing as if I'm his helpless child or charge to protect. I don't question his loyalty, Caile, but his judgment. He's trying too hard, not thinking clearly, and we can't afford any mistakes. Not now. I'm on the cusp of losing my people's trust entirely."

"You're imagining it," Caile said, shaking his head. "Lorentz has been nothing but dependable all day, assisting me with the investigation. And Siegbjorn himself said it was Lorentz who dragged you out of that room. How could you turn your back on him like this? After all he's done for you? After all he's done for me?"

Makarria sighed. He was right. Lorentz had been a protector, a mentor, a father figure, and so much to the both of them, particularly Caile. But something wasn't right about him anymore. Makarria couldn't explain it, but she felt it in her guts.

"I'm sorry, Caile, but I'm queen. These are the sort of decisions I have to make. Lorentz has to go."

Caile turned away. "You're making a mistake. If you send him away, you send me away too. You send away the two men you can trust more than anyone."

Makarria closed her eyes. She had known it might come to an ultimatum like this. She'd tried not to think about it, but here it was. The wise decision would be to send both of them away if that's what it took, but when she looked at Caile, even with his face furrowed with anger and insolence, she couldn't send him away. She just couldn't. He was the one person she had relied upon all this time, even more so than her mother. And there were other feelings for him, too, but she pushed those thoughts away.

"You trust Lorentz with your life?" she asked.

"Always."

"Do you trust him with my life?"

He paused only for a moment before answering. "Yes."

"So be it then. He can stay, but talk to him and keep him at your side from now on. Keep him away from me. I have Fina now to watch over me. I don't want him anywhere near me."

"Thank you," he said. Already the anger was draining from his face.

Makarria turned away from him and sat in her chair again, not trusting herself to look into his eyes. "Go then. Find yourself some dinner, then see if you can't find us some clue as to who's behind this attack. We meet with the Old World ambassadors tomorrow—the last thing we can do is approach them unprepared, and right now this all looks very bad. Senator Emil has all the bargaining power in his hands."

"I know. I'll figure this out. I promise."

Makarria watched him leave and then let out a long, tired breath. She wanted nothing more than to lie down and go to sleep, but there was no time for rest, not when the fate of the Five Kingdoms depended on her response to the Old World's demands. If the rulers of the Five Kingdoms—two of them newly appointed young women, and another still undecided—were going to prove their strength, they needed to respond in unison, and that meant they needed to communicate. They had only fourteen days left until the Sargothian council elected a new monarch, and the Old World ambassadors had made their impatience abundantly clear: if there was no clear direction for the Kingdom of Sargoth, then they would use military force. The only way the Five Kingdoms could survive was if they could coordinate actions, and that meant communicating in real-time. Couriers would not suffice. Not even messenger ravens. And there was only one Siegbjorn and his airship. They needed relics like the Old World ambassadors had, a way of sending messages great distances with sorcery. The moment Makarria had returned to her chambers and gotten stitched up by Fina, she had sent word to her tutor, the scholar Natale, to search through his tomes for a way in which she could do just that.

It was well past dusk and she had not eaten supper, but with the Lorentz situation taken care of for the time being, she stepped outside her room to where the others awaited her.

"Mother, Siegbjorn, it's late, why don't you return to your rooms and get some sleep. I'll be fine." She hugged them both goodnight, then asked Talitha and Fina to follow her. The three of them strode quietly through the marble halls of the palace to the library in the lower levels of the keep where Natale dwelled. He looked up from his pile of scrolls and books when he saw them approaching, his cherubic cheeks extended in a forced smile, but clearly not bearing good news.

"Natale, please tell us you've discovered something," Makarria said. "I can do much with my powers, but only if I can imagine it first, and I can't for the life of me imagine how to talk to someone a thousand miles away."

Natale averted his eyes downward. "Yes, Your Majesty, I've found a way. It will be a trifling matter for you to work your magic, and then you can communicate with whatever liaison you have in Col Sargoth easily. But you ask much of Queen Taera in Kal Pyrthin if you would speak with her."

Makarria clenched her teeth. It was Taera who had first given Makarria confidence in using her powers. It was Taera, more than anyone, who she needed to counsel with to address the Old World ambassadors.

"Why should it be any different for Taera?" Talitha asked.

"You need magical conduits to communicate," Natale replied. "Makarria could use her powers to create new ones, but that would require her to deliver the relics to Kal Pyrthin and anywhere else she needed to communicate with."

"We don't have time for that," Makarria said. "If I had anticipated the need earlier, I would have done something months ago, but not now."

Natale nodded. "Your only option, then, is to use an existing magical conduit, and unfortunately, the only feasible conduits we have access to are the scent-hounds Emperor Guderian created. We have one here in Sol Valaróz, and the hound in Col Sargoth still lives, but—"

"But my grandfather killed the scent-hound in Kal Pyrthin during the war," Makarria finished for him. "That means we can't communicate with Taera in Kal Pyrthin?"

"I'm not saying that, exactly. As long as there is a part of the scent-hound apparatus still intact it could still work, but with the living portion dead—the sorcerer, bloodhound hybrid part—the person on the receiving end would have to be a sorcerer herself to establish the connection."

Makarria shrugged. "That's not a problem. Taera is a seer of no modest means."

"It's not a matter of her power," Natale said.

"What is it then?"

"It's a matter of how much pain you're willing to put her through."

"No, Makarria," Talitha said, shaking her head. "It's not worth it. You can't put Taera in such a position. Besides, we don't even have access to the scent-hound in Col Sargoth. Only Natarios Rhodas does. Let Siegbjorn and me go to Kal Pyrthin. I will help you use your powers to create a new speaking relic and take it to Taera. With our airship, we can be there in two days. From there, we can take a third speaking relic to Col Sargoth and the three of us can speak on our own terms. Without subjecting Taera to any torment."

"We can't afford two days," Makarria said. "I meet with the Old World ambassadors in the morning. The Sargothian council elects a new king in fourteen days. We have to act now. Taera will understand. She would be more angry if I did not ask her to do it."

Talitha sighed and glanced away. "So be it then. Tell us what we need to do, Natale."

6
Dangerous Visions

Taera awoke with a gasp, expecting to find Makarria looming over her, expecting to find herself shackled and screaming in pain, but there was no one there. She was safe beneath the covers of her own bed in Castle Pyrthin. It had all only been a vision, albeit a peculiar and unusually strong one.

Since being coronated as Queen of Pyrthinia a year past, Taera's premonitory visions had diminished only to be replaced by formless dreams fueled by her new civic responsibilities. Faceless graves. Shriveled fields of grain. Lifeless cattle mewing at her pleadingly. An endless maze in the throne room. An ever-expanding staff of attendants who swarmed around her asking, "What now? What now? What now?"

These were the images that held her in suspended animation at night, half-asleep, only to awake in the morning as weary as when she went to bed.

Pyrthinia had shouldered the brunt of the casualties in the war against Emperor Guderian and the sorcerer Wulfram. As short as the war had been historically speaking, Guderian's steam-powered war wagons had decimated Pyrthinia's ground troops, most of them enlisted militia men who would now never return to their fields, ranches, mills, workshops, and storefronts. The entire infrastructure of the kingdom was in turmoil. Taera had opened the royal treasury to hire migrant workers from Valaróz and the East Islands, but even so the planting season got off to a late start, meaning the autumn harvest wouldn't yield enough to get them through the impending winter. To compound matters, the cattle grazing in the highlands east of the River Kylep had been stricken by pestilence, killing more than half their numbers. Nearly all the farms and ranches east of the Forrest Weorcan were experiencing the same phenomena. Their water supply was tainted, her agricultural advisors told her, rancid and sulfuric thanks to Guderian's smelting factories in Col Sargoth, which were shut down now, but for years had been belching poisonous smoke into the clouds that drifted eastward and rained over the vast grasslands between Weordan and the Barrier Mountains.

These were the very real nightmares haunting Taera's dreams at night. She had gone half a year without having a vision or premonition. Until a month ago. In that vision she had seen Captain Lorentz fall, deep in a lightless tunnel, wearing another's body. She cried that night, for she had no way of getting word to her brother Caile and warning the two of them. Even if she sent her fastest ship, her message wouldn't arrive in Sol Valaróz for days, and wherever Lorentz was in her vision, it certainly wasn't Sol Valaróz—she discerned that much from the dream if nothing else. And even if she did send a message, even if it wasn't too late, what would she say? The visions were too vague for her to discern any clear warning, or to be of any help to Lorentz.

When Taera had been young, still just becoming a woman, she had loved Lorentz in her own adolescent crush sort of way. But then he had gone to Valaróz with Caile, and it was years before she saw him again. When she next met him, on the outskirts of Kal Pyrthin, she was older and there were more pressing matters on her mind—namely a firewielder who was about to attack them—but still Taera held a place in her heart for Lorentz, even at times entertaining the daydream of taking him as her husband. It would never work, of course, with him being a career soldier from a poor family with no pedigree, but she was comforted by the thought of it. It made her feel safe. And now he was gone. She had dreamt it, and so it was, or would be soon enough. She wasn't sure how, but the man who had looked after her as an adolescent, the man who had practically raised her brother, was dead.

A sense of guilt and foreboding filled Taera now. Perhaps she should have sent warning. In the new vision that had awoken her this night, Makarria was calling to her. Telling her to wake up and go to the dungeon cellars and do something unspeakable. The Taera of two years prior would have ignored the vision, dismissing it as a childish nightmare, a warrantless fear. The Queen Taera she was now, though, knew better. Fear reverberated through her guts, but she ignored it, discarding her sleeping gown and dressing herself in simple riding clothes, not bothering to summon her women in waiting. The fewer people who knew about this midnight excursion the better.

In the corridor outside her chamber, two guards jumped to attention when she opened the door.

"With me, gentlemen."

They fell in behind her wordlessly as she strode down the corridor, down a marble staircase to the first floor, and then to the front of the keep to the antechamber above a stairway leading to the dungeons. "Not a word of this to anyone, gentlemen," she commanded as she opened the gate. "If anyone finds out, I'll have both of your tongues."

"Of course, Your Majesty."

Taera led the way down, letting the vision of her dream fill her mind. It was the scent-hound she was seeking, but the scent-hound in the tower of Kal Pyrthin was long dead. Makarria's grandfather, Parmenios Pallma, had killed it in an act of mercy, chopping its hound head from its woman's body to end its suffering. The rest of the scent-hound contraption, however—the six-foot brass compass portion—had been stowed away in the dungeon beneath Castle Pyrthin with the rest of the relics of Emperor Guderian's reign.

"Who's there?" the dungeon-keeper demanded as they reached the bottom of the stairwell. His aggravated expression disappeared when he realized it was Queen Taera standing before him. "Oh. Your Majesty, my apologies. How can I be of service?"

"Grab two sets of manacles, a length of chain, and take me to where the houndkeeper's belongings are stored."

The dungeon-keeper raised one eyebrow, but did not voice any objections he might have had. He gathered his things, and then with the manacles and chain in hand, along with his key ring and a sputtering torch, he led the way deeper into the dungeon, past a series of umbral cells, all of them unoccupied but a few. The stone ceiling was low and the air was stagnant. It wasn't as bad as it had once been—Taera had made certain the dungeon-keepers kept the place as sanitary as possible, even if the few occupants were murderers—but it was still a subterranean dungeon, saturated with the damp mustiness that infiltrated all such places built near the sea.

In the far back reaches of the dungeon, the ceiling became higher and the corridor opened into a room: the torture chamber. It was no longer used for anything of that sort, and instead Taera had turned it into a storage area to keep all the effects from the scent-hound tower that once belonged to the houndkeeper, Natarios Rhodas, or Wulfram. She had considered simply destroying all of it the year before when she took control of the tower and the messenger ravens within, but she'd had a premonition that the items might be needed one day, and she had been right.

The scent-hound contraption rested upright against the far wall of the chamber. The scent-hound's corpse itself, Taera had ordered removed and buried, but the brass compass still bore signs of the hound's coupling to it. Taera ran her hands over the corroded sections of brass where the scent-hound—a naked woman's body, she remembered all too well—had been melded together with the contraption. The sections where the hands and feet had been melded, particularly, had left serrated scars in the outer ring of the compass, as if her skin had eaten into the metal like acid. Bits of hair still clung, embedded into the brass itself, where the hound's head had rested on one of the cross supports. The spike extending from the main compass axle that had once protruded through the scent-hound's navel had been cut away to remove the body, but the exposed nub of the axle still remained, jagged and rimmed with metal burs.

The two guards who had accompanied Taera from her chamber

were ill at ease, keeping themselves as far away from the contraption as possible.

"Is the compass secure against the wall?" Taera asked, trying not to think about what she was on the verge of doing.

The dungeon-keeper nodded. "It's chained up there tight so it won't fall over and hurt anyone who might have to work back here."

"All right then, we'll do this standing up," Taera said, slipping off her riding boots and stockings. Barefoot, she turned to face away from the contraption and backed herself into place.

"Manacle my ankles and wrists to the outer ring."

"Your Majesty…" he started to protest.

"No questions. Do as I say."

He approached her warily and opened the first of the manacles wide to slip it around both her left wrist and the ring of the compass. His hands were shaking, and he latched the manacle only loosely, terrified of harming her.

"You'll have to do it tighter than that," Taera told him. "My skin needs to couple with the metal if the magic is going to work. Go on. Tighter. I won't break."

He did as she commanded. She inhaled sharply as the scabrous metal bit into the back of her wrist. "Good. Now the other hand and my feet." Again he followed her orders, and each time Taera winced in pain as the metal bit into her flesh.

Taera let out a long breath, trying to calm herself. Already she was trembling and she hadn't even gotten to the most painful part. "All right, now the chain. Wrap it around my waist. You'll have to lift the back of my blouse so the axle touches my skin."

The poor man blanched, more terrified at the prospect of lifting her shirt than anything else he'd already done.

"Go on," Taera prompted him.

With shaking hands he lifted the back of her blouse only as much as was needed to clear the jagged nub of the axle. Taera shifted her weight and leaned back into it with a groan as it bit into the skin along her spine. "Quickly now. Wrap the chain around me to hold me in place."

The man did so deftly, even if he was terrified. Taera cried out in pain as he pulled the chains tighter, pressing the burs of the axle into her unprotected backbone. He shied away, but she yelled at him. "No! Tighter. And secure it quickly."

When it was done, Taera stood there shaking, sweat beading on her forehead and running down the front of her chest beneath her blouse. She kept her voice calm, though. "Good. Now go. All of you. Back to the other end of the dungeon and wait."

"Wait for what?" the dungeon-keeper asked.

"For me to go silent. I will be speaking, perhaps howling, screaming. When you hear me stop, return and unbind me. If I'm unconscious, take me to my chambers and summon the physician and my chambermaids."

The man's eyes went wide, but he said nothing. He merely nodded and turned tail after the two guards who were already hurrying back down the corridor the way they'd come. With them out of the way, Taera closed her eyes and opened her mind to her visions. She didn't know exactly what to expect. As a seer, her magic was different than Makarria's or Talitha's. Visions came to her unbidden. It wasn't a magic she summoned on command. Still, she knew how to clear her mind to the visions when they came, and that's what she did now, pushing through the pain in her limbs and spine.

Makarria, she called out silently. A deep, thrumming tone grew and resonated through the compass and into her body, a tone she more felt than heard. The brass biting into her flesh began to tingle, then sting, then burn. Pain, like white-hot fire, pulsated through her spine, filling her belly and forcing itself out her lungs.

Taera, the voice came. *I'm so sorry I had to ask this of you.*

It was Makarria, speaking through her. Distantly, Taera could feel her body shaking, could hear herself bawling, audibly growling out the words she heard in her head, but she paid her physical body no heed, enraptured as she was in the magic.

We are queens, you and I, Taera responded inwardly. *What sort of rulers would we be if we were unwilling to make personal sacrifices for the well being of our kingdoms?*

Indeed. Still, I would not have asked this of you if there were not imminent danger. The Old World Republic has come, Taera. The election in Sargoth is not going well. Talitha has been impeached, and the Old World knows. They offer me a treaty in name, but in reality they offer me only the choice of surrendering to their occupation of Valaróz. From there they mean to take the Five Kingdoms, I'm certain.

What will you do?

Again, Makarria's response came like a bellows blowing white-hot heat through Taera's core. *The only thing I can do: refuse them. They will leave and return with their armada, and we must be ready for them. I will go to Col Sargoth myself and ensure the council elects a strong ruler. Caile I'm sending to Veleza to prepare my western naval fleet to protect the Ocean Gloaming. We can expect no help from the Kingdom of Golier on that front. My admirals here in Sol Valaróz will continue to patrol the Sol Sea, but they are too few to protect the eastern front alone. I need your help, Taera. You must prepare the Pyrthin navy. Our two kingdoms are all that holds the Old World at bay.*

Pyrthinia cannot afford the toll of another war, Makarria.

I know. That's why we can't let it come to that. The Old World is testing us, I believe. If we let them, they will walk into the Five Kingdoms and make them their own. But if we show our strength, our unity, they will back down. I'm certain. They never attacked during Emperor Guderian's reign. We must show them the Five Kingdoms are as strong and unified as they were under his rule.

Very well then. I have a few surprises for their armadas, if it's a show of force they want. I will prepare my fleet.

Thank you. I'm sorry we had to speak like this.

The pain was infiltrating through the magic, and Taera could feel herself convulsing on the compass wheel, could hear herself moaning. She burned to be released, but then she remembered her other vision, her vision of Lorentz. She might not have another chance to speak with Makarria again, she knew.

Makarria, wait. Don't go. Lorentz—has he died?

There was a long moment of silence before Makarria's response coursed through her. *No, but he is not himself. Something happened to him in the tunnels of Khal-Aband.*

It is as I've envisioned then. Be careful, Makarria. He cannot be himself, for I saw him die in another's body.

I don't understand, Taera.

Neither do I. I'm sorry.

And with that, the magic flowed out of Taera and she collapsed with an exhausted moan.

7
Speaking to the Void

Her friends had all been briefed at first light as to their individual missions and Makarria sat now on her throne with Caile to her side, once again watching as the Old World delegation approached. She had initially intended to meet with them in private, but after all that had happened the previous day she decided a formal hearing in the throne room with an audience was better suited to her ends. She needed her people to know that she was fighting for them and had no intention of letting the Old World occupy the Five Kingdoms. If nothing else, she needed to gain her people's confidence. If she failed in that, then Valaróz was doomed. She wouldn't allow it. Couldn't allow it. She was a descendant of Vala and a long line of compassionate, just rulers. Her grandfather Parmo had died to wrestle the throne away from Don Bricio and Emperor Guderian, to make Valaróz great once again. The thought of letting him down was too much to bear.

"Gentlemen, welcome," Makarria greeted the Old World delegation.

Ambassador Mahalath and Senator Emil bowed before her at the foot of the dais.

"We are glad to see you safe and in good health this morning, Your Highness," Ambassador Mahalath said, his white teeth gleaming against the backdrop of his burgundy lips and black mustache.

"Thank you," Makarria replied. "And thank you both for meeting with me again this morning."

"Of course," Senator Emil replied. "We will have you know that we are even more determined to provide the Kingdom of Valaróz assistance considering the attempt on your life yesterday, Your Highness. Our offer of aid stands. We are confident we can come to agreeable terms, and working together the Old World Republic and Valaróz can solidify the stability of the Five Kingdoms and ensure decades of peace." He sneered, as if Makarria's agreement were a foregone conclusion. "The Senate has empowered me with full authority to negotiate with you on the Republic's behalf."

"As to that, I would first like to thank you for your offer of aid," Makarria said, projecting her voice so the entire audience could hear her. "I have spoken with Talitha of Issborg and have been appraised of the election situation in Col Sargoth. A new King of Sargoth will be elected in thirteen days, by decree of the new lord of proceedings. I am confident this development, carried out in accordance with the dictates created by Sargoth Lightbringer himself, will result in the election of a strong king who will solidify any instability in the Kingdom of Sargoth. In fact, I mean to attend the proceedings myself to ensure an appropriate candidate is lawfully chosen. Furthermore, I spoke with Queen Taera of Pyrthinia last night."

Makarria watched Senator Emil's face carefully as she said this, but if he was surprised at her newfound ability to communicate over thousands of miles, he made no indication. He was a good politician indeed. The crowd, at least, tittered in surprise at hearing the news.

"Together," Makarria continued, not daring to scrutinize the senator too blatantly, "Queen Taera and I have coordinated an elevated naval presence in the Ocean Gloaming, the Sol Sea, and the Esterian Ocean. We will protect all lawful merchant vessels and be ready to respond to any civil unrest you suggested might occur with the absence of a king in Sargoth, Senator Emil."

That was her official stance, anyway. Senator Emil was smart enough to read between the lines and see what Makarria was really saying: our navies are ready for you if you decide to invade.

"I will additionally coordinate efforts with the Kingdom of Golier when I arrive in Col Sargoth to secure the safety of vessels passing through the Gothol Sea. Taking all this into consideration,

I am confident that the Five Kingdoms are perfectly capable of solidifying themselves and securing decades of *domestic* peace. So while we thank you for your offer of aid, we must decline."

The smug smile was gone from Senator Emil's face. Behind him, the audience members whispered to one another.

"If you gentlemen would like to discuss a treaty to ensure the continued peace between our nations, I would love nothing more," Makarria offered. "We could additionally talk trade treaties and lowering tariffs if you would like."

Senator Emil was shaking his head. "The Republic will not sign into any treaties when the stability and certainty of the Five Kingdoms is still in question, Your Highness. It is all well and good for you to give us your assurances, but they are only words. As we saw very well yesterday, you are barely capable of ensuring your own personal safety."

"You forget yourself, Senator," Caile barked.

"Our apologies," Ambassador Mahalath jumped in. "We meant no disrespect. I too would love nothing more than to work with you, Your Highness, in securing new trade treaties, but Senator Emil is right—the Republic will not sign into any peace treaties with a nation in turmoil."

"It is a simple decision to make, Your Highness," Senator Emil said. "One does not refuse the aid of the Republic. Hear and accept our terms, and Valaróz will be well rewarded."

Hisses and angry whispers filled the throne room.

"My answer is no, Senator."

Senator Emil bowed his head. "So be it. Your choice is made. I leave with the tide to return to Khail Sanctu. Be forewarned, the Republic too will be escalating its naval presence, and at the first sign of further unrest in the Five Kingdoms, we will do whatever is necessary to secure the safety of our nation."

Makarria read the message in his words loud and clear. It was just as she had known it would be: forced aid or threats of invasion.

"You have my leave to go, Senator," Makarria said flatly.

He spun on his heel and strode away, ignoring the hisses and muttered insults the audience threw at him. Ambassador Mahalath, however, lingered behind. "Your Highness, with your permission I would stay here as ambassador of the Old World Republic. Through me, you can still work on perhaps…easing tensions between our two nations."

"Of course," Makarria told him. He could prove useful if war indeed grew imminent. "You have been given your quarters in the embassy wing already. They are yours until such time as you choose to leave." Not exactly inviting words, but as accommodating as Mahalath made himself out to be, Makarria still didn't trust him.

Mahalath bowed wordlessly, and turned on his heel to follow Senator Emil out of the throne room.

Makarria let out a slow breath, making sure not to change her demeanor outwardly. She still had an audience.

"People of Valaróz," she addressed them. "I apologize, but again we must postpone the day's scheduled hearings. I leave today for Col Sargoth to oversee the election of the new Sargothian King and ensure our continued stability. As before, my mother, Princess Prisca, will rule in my stead, along with the help of Captain Haviero. I will return with all possible haste. Until then, may Vala watch over us all."

It was done. The herald called for everyone to bow, and Makarria stood and exited the throne room alongside Caile to pass into the sitting room, which was still in shambles from the day before.

"That was well done," Caile said.

Makarria let him give her a sidelong hug and smiled wanly. "Thanks, but we don't have time to congratulate ourselves. You need to pack. I need to debrief my mother to rule while we're gone, and then go meet with Natale and Talitha again. We're putting together something that will make our task much easier. I'll summon you when I'm ready."

Caile's face turned serious. "I'm still not thrilled about the prospect of splitting up. You're sure you want to go to Col Sargoth alone?"

"I won't be alone, Caile. I'll have Talitha, and Siegbjorn, and

Fina with me."

"Sure, but I won't be with you, which is as good as being alone." Only a trace of a smile at the corners of his mouth hinted at his mischievousness.

"Go, pack your bags," she said pushing him into the corridor and smiling despite herself as she turned the opposite direction to go meet with her mother.

• • •

Back in his own quarters, Caile packed his rucksack absently, his mind occupied instead by the monumental task before them. They would be taking Siegbjorn's airship, first to Valeza, where Makarria would put Caile in charge of the western Valarion naval fleet, and then Makarria would continue on to Col Sargoth. Her plan was sound enough, he had to agree, but he didn't like being away from her, especially with her going headlong into a Sargothian political maelstrom. He'd been thrown into a similar situation not so long ago and had nearly lost his life. Indeed, he would have died if Talitha hadn't found him and saved him in the underworld beneath Col Sargoth.

Caile sighed. He would have to trust Talitha to look after Makarria now, although Talitha had already proven herself out of her element in the political realm.

"What are you huffing about, Prince?" Lorentz asked him.

Caile snapped out of his reverie and glanced over to where Lorentz was placing the last of their wet weather clothes into a traveling chest. "It's just that I'm worried about Makarria going off to Col Sargoth," Caile said, plopping himself back into a chair beside the dormant fireplace. "She has no easy task before her."

"Nor do you."

"No, I don't," Caile had to agree. "And I'm already weary from running around in that wild goose chase yesterday. If I'm weary, Makarria must be exhausted. She was up all night doing some sort of sorcery to communicate with Taera. And now she means to set sail on the airship as soon as she's finished with whatever new sorcery she and Talitha are cooking up."

Lorentz latched the lid closed on the chest and sat down across from Caile. "You should urge the queen to rest then," he said.

"We don't have time. Only thirteen days until the council votes, and Makarria needs to get there as soon as possible if she's going to sort through the mess and make sure a worthy candidate is elected."

"One night added to her travel time will make little difference in the execution of the queen's plans, but one night of rest can make all the difference in her frame of mind. Well rested, she will think more clearly, be better able to face her enemy. I worry for her well-being."

Caile nodded, and leaned forward to rest his elbows on his knees and look Lorentz fully in the face. This wasn't going to be easy, but he owed his mentor the truth. "Look, Lorentz, I know you're worried, but maybe you've been worrying too much. Makarria asked me to speak with you…"

"Oh?"

"She feels like you're being overprotective, disregarding her orders and over-reacting. She was not happy you killed all the attackers in the stables. That's why she's taken Fina as a bodyguard and pawned you off back into my care."

Caile smiled to soften the half-hearted jest, but Lorentz merely shrugged.

"I was only keeping the queen safe."

"I know that. You know that. But she's not like you and me. She's seen enough killing and she wants to avoid it at all costs. And you know, she's probably right. She says a lot of the things you used to tell me about the virtue of holding my tongue and keeping my sword in its scabbard. Whatever the case may be, she's aggravated with you. You'd do best to steer clear of her on our voyage. Give her space and try not to be overbearing in protecting her."

Caile couldn't bring himself to mention anything about Makarria's original request, the request to send Lorentz back to Kal Pyrthin. *It would pain him too much, and I gave him the meat of the truth, at least.*

"You *can* be a bossy ass sometimes, you know?" Caile added. "I used to get so aggravated with you when you wouldn't let me ride off into a fray, or speak up in one of Don Bricio's council meetings, or climb up the rigging on a ship. I wanted so much to be a man and do things myself. I know how Makarria feels. She's not a girl anymore. She's a woman and a queen."

Lorentz regarded him silently for a long moment. "But now you see things from my perspective, don't you? You understand what it means to care for someone and want to protect them. You feel more deeply about her than you want to admit, even to yourself."

"Well, yes. I suppose."

"It is a fine line to tread—protecting, overprotecting?—but in this case, you must protect the queen while you still can. She has been using her power much these last few days, and it will leave its toll on her. Urge her to rest and leave in the morning. You must make her stay the night if any of this is going to work. I can't do it for you now. It's up to you, Caile."

Caile frowned. Makarria wouldn't want to hear it, but he knew that Lorentz was right. Makarria needed rest, and he was the only one who could convince her.

• • •

It was many hours later. Makarria didn't know how many, but she knew she had been in a dreamstate for a long time and that she was exhausted. Despite that, she was overcome with a surge of triumph as she slid back into her chair to admire her handiwork.

"Are you all right?" Talitha asked.

"Yes, just tired."

They were in the reading room of the library, deep in the basement beneath the palace, sitting at a round oaken table. Natale had culled more texts on creating magical conduits, and after consulting them and solidifying their methodology with Talitha's knowledge, Makarria and Talitha had done it, together as a team.

They'd taken seven smooth river rocks—the most spherical ones they could find, all nearly the size of grapefruits—and turned them into speaking relics. Once they were delivered into the right hands, never again would Makarria or her friends have to use the scent-hounds to communicate long distances.

"They're beautiful," Natale said, getting up from where he sat alongside Fina in the corner of the room, safely distanced from injury or interfering with the sorcery Makarria and Talitha had performed.

The stones were indeed beautiful. Whereas before they had been a flat gray granite, mottled with small flecks of white quartz, they now had taken on an opaque hue, marbled with colored swirls that spiraled inward, the design reminding Makarria of a sea-snail's shell.

"We must test them, to verify they work," Natale said.

"They will work," Talitha replied. "Trust me."

Natale pursed his lips. "It's my way, to test and verify phenomena, whether they be natural or magical."

"Magic and nature are one in the same," Talitha told him. "Both are the children of Tel Mathir."

"Go ahead, Natale," Makarria said, sparing the man from further lecture. "Grab one and go to the darkest corner of the library you can find."

Like an excited schoolboy, Natale grabbed one of the stones in both hands and scurried off to disappear between the shelves of leather-bound tomes.

"Fina," Makarria said as she sat waiting. "Would you send a servant to go fetch Caile? I want to show him what we've done."

"Of course," Fina replied, emerging from the shadows of the corner where she had been standing in silent watch.

"And, Fina, make sure it's Caile alone."

Fina nodded, catching Makarria's meaning—*No Lorentz*—and strode off silently.

Once Fina was gone, Makarria turned to Talitha. "Well, let's show our skeptical scholar what we've created then." She grabbed the nearest of the stones, held it close to her face in both hands, and closed her eyes. Each of the stones had its own signature, a unique hue that colored your vision when you held the stone. This particular one was yellow. In her mind, Makarria imagined red, the color of the stone Natale held. "Hello, Natale," she spoke. "Where are you hiding?"

With the connection established, Makarria opened her eyes.

"Vala's teats!" came Natale's voice through the stone. It was muffled, distant sounding, as if they were speaking from opposite ends of a corridor, but she could hear him clearly. "It works," Natale said. "And you startled me near to pissing myself."

Makarria couldn't help but laugh. "Well, I'm glad you managed not to soil your garments or any of your precious books."

"Indeed! Even knowing it was coming, it's unnerving to hear your disembodied voice."

"Unnerving as it may be, it'll suit our purpose. No more waiting days or weeks to send messages through ravens." She said that as much for herself as she did for Natale. She wouldn't admit it outwardly, but she had not been as confident as Talitha that the stones would work. It was one thing for Makarria to physically change an object—to turn her gown to chainmail like she'd done in the council room, or even to remove the floor beneath someone's feet like she'd done to Emperor Guderian—but it was an entirely different matter creating a magical device. She had not so much changed the rocks as she had enhanced them, made them in-tune with one another, and sensitive to reverberations in the air. That's the way Talitha explained it, at least. Makarria still didn't fully understand it, and Talitha had been forced to give her directions throughout the entire process, using her words to describe things Makarria needed to envision in her dreamstate. It was done now, though, and Makarria was relieved the stones indeed worked.

Natale returned with the red speaking stone, more excited than when he'd left.

"Grab the storage cases and let's pack them for travel," Makarria said.

Natale dutifully set the red stone down and ran off to retrieve the wooden crate containing the seven cases he'd ordered the royal carpenter to build to their specifications earlier that afternoon. He returned a few moments later from his office and laid the crate on the floor, where he pried off the lid. Inside were six padded boxes, each of them lined with a different color of silk.

As they were placing the stones in their respective boxes, Fina returned with Caile.

"Perfect timing," Makarria said, waving Caile to her. "Look what we've created. Speaking stones. The red one is for your sister in Kal Pyrthin." She held it up for him to see, then placed it back in the red silk cloth and grabbed up another. "The silver one is for Talitha and the Snjaer Firan in the Caverns of Issborg. The blue one is for King Hanns in Norg, the green for King Lorimer in Golier, though neither of them will get theirs until I'm sure they're allied with us. The black one is for Col Sargoth—I will keep it with me until a new king is chosen. The yellow one is for here, Sol Valaróz. My mother will keep it until this is all over and we return. And the orange one is for you to take. We'll be able to communicate with each other no matter where we are, Caile."

Caile took up his stone in both hands and stared into the orange swirled orb. "This is wonderful, Makarria. It really is. You might have just saved the Five Kingdoms. This changes everything. We can coordinate our actions and compete with the Old World now. No more being two steps behind."

Makarria smiled. "Let's not get too proud of ourselves yet. We have a lot of work before us still, and an airship to get on to deliver the stones. What time is it? I still need to pack my things."

"Dusk," Caile told her.

"Already? We best hurry then."

He frowned and shook his head. "No, Makarria. You're exhausted. You need sleep. When's the last time you rested?"

"I don't know, but it's not important," she said, refusing to think about the last few days. "I can't afford sleep right now."

"We can't afford for you to not sleep," Caile told her. "This plan of yours hinges on you having your wits about you to deal with the Sargothian council. You'll do none of us any good if you're sleep deprived and addled. Look at you—you can barely keep your eyes open. Attacked yesterday, then up all night talking to my sister, and then today the Old World ambassadors and the speaking stones. You're wearing yourself thin, Makarria."

"He's right," Talitha said. "You need rest."

Makarria didn't want to admit it, but it was true. She wasn't certain she could even stand right now. But still, she was queen. People were counting on her.

"I can sleep on the airship…"

"But you won't," Talitha chided her. "I know you. Winter is nearly upon us and it will be a rough voyage. You won't be able to sleep and you'll insist on helping Siegbjorn. You can't help yourself."

"Give yourself one night, Makarria," Caile pleaded. "We'll leave at dawn, and I promise, the time resting will be well spent. You've laid our plans well. Another seven or eight hours will make no difference."

The thought of one last night of sleep in her own bed was awfully enticing, she had to admit. *And if both Caile and Talitha think I should…*

"Fine," Makarria relented, deferring to her two most trusted advisors and friends.

Caile smiled and offered his hand. "Thank you. C'mon, I'll help you upstairs and have food sent to your chambers."

8
Shadows in the Dark

Ambassador Mahalath ate his late dinner in the solitude of his new quarters in the embassy wing of the royal palace of Sol Valaróz. Only a single candle lantern at the corner of his desk illuminated the odd-tasting food on his plate. Without the sour *kishk* yogurt he was accustomed to having in Khail Sanctu, the meat tasted dry and flavorless, and the rice was spicy in a way he had never experienced before. Or maybe it was just that he had lost his appetite. He pushed the plate aside, wiped his mustache clean with a napkin, and then took up the unsigned treaties the Senate had provided him with.

Senator Emil made a mess of all of this, he thought, ruing the missed opportunity with Queen Makarria. *I should have insisted that we meet with the queen in private, rather than confront her in her own courtroom.* What was done was done now, though. Mahalath would just have to make the best of the situation. He would have some time to figure things out with the queen away, it seemed. While she was off in the Kingdom of Sargoth, perhaps he could forge a relationship with her royal mother. If nothing else, he would get a chance to meet with the other ambassadors and get a true sense as to the stability of the Five Kingdoms. Perhaps they weren't as bad off as the Senate had suggested.

A chill ocean breeze gusted through the open window and Mahalath shivered. It had been hot during the day, which he was accustomed to, but it never got cold like this at night in Khail Sanctu. Seeing nothing else to do for the moment, Mahalath closed the window, blew out the lantern, and tucked himself into his foreign-feeling bed.

• • •

Fina sat at the foot of her bed, nearly as stiff as the mattress itself, and thumbed the hilt of the plain dagger at her belt. The antechamber to Queen Makarria's personal quarters was sparsely furnished, with only two padded chairs for waiting visitors to sit at, and a narrow bed off to the side, intended for chambermaids to use when waiting on the queen during night time hours. The spartan room suited Fina fine. Since taking on the charge of being Queen Makarria's personal guard the day before, she had brought in a chest for her new clothing, and a folded dressing screen divider to provide her some privacy when changing. She needed nothing else.

The door handle to the main bedroom rattled and Caile stepped quietly out into the antechamber. "She's asleep already," Caile said.

Fina nodded. He had been in there with her no more than twenty minutes by her estimation, not enough time to eat the entire meal the kitchen had sent up.

"I got her to eat a little," Caile said, seemingly reading her mind. "And she had a glass of wine. That was enough, I suppose, and at this point, she needs sleep more than she needs food." Caile staggered a little as he stepped away from Makarria's door, but he caught himself and blinked his eyes. "It seems I'm more tired than I realized, too."

"Or perhaps you had more than one glass of wine," Fina suggested.

Caile smiled. "Don Bricio took it upon himself to teach me to drink. I can handle my spirits. I'm just weary is all. I best be off to bed, too."

"Goodnight, Prince."

"Goodnight, Fina," Caile said, opening the door leading into the corridor and glancing back at her. "I'm glad you're watching over Makarria. Don't let anyone in here but me or Talitha. Or her mother, of course."

Fina stood up from the bed and ushered him away. "I've been doing this longer than you've been alive, young prince. Off to bed with you."

Caile smiled as he walked away, and Fina closed the door behind him. She locked the door, then opened the door at the opposite side of the anteroom to step quietly into Makarria's spacious chambers. The dishes and remaining food from their meal rested on a tray in the center of a small, round dining table, just as Caile had indicated, along with a bottle of wine, half drank. One red-tinged crystal glass sat beside the bottle on the table. The other was still half-full, sitting on the nightstand next to Makarria's canopied bed. Fina padded silently over to the bed and looked Makarria over. She was deep in sleep, and Prince Caile had pulled the down-filled comforter over her so she was snugly tucked in.

Fina liked the young prince, she decided. She had protected Don Bricio's harem for nearly twenty years before Don Bricio sent her to Khal-Aband, and in that time she had encountered men of all sorts, most of them bad. Don Bricio had kept his most prized girls to himself, but a few he would offer up for a night in exchange for political favors—Fina could not protect them from that. Other men, those Don Bricio wished to taunt or punish, would be paraded through the harem only to be denied access to the women they so wantonly desired, the lust written on their faces as plainly as if they were dogs drooling over a cut of beef. More than a few tried to sneak back in during the silence of the night, and those Fina gladly killed, or gelded if she really didn't like them. Others, like Don Bricio's guards and attendants, would sometimes pass through, and though they tried to veil their desire, Fina always saw their sidelong glances and the desire in their trembling fingers. Not Prince Caile, though.

Fina remembered him well from the few times he had accompanied Don Bricio into the harem. It was clear to Fina that he hated Don Bricio, and the very existence of the harem. Don Bricio did not see it, but Fina did. Caile had still been a young teenager in those days, but he had learned already to carry himself with a wall around his true feelings. His expressions were always even, the words coming out of his mouth respectful to Don Bricio, but the glances he stole at the women told a different story if you knew what to look for. Those glances were filled not with lust, but rather with a fire of a different sort—a fire of righteous anger.

Fina had made little of it at the time. Here was simply a young man consumed with ideals the world had not yet crushed. Fina disliked the fact that her girls—and so she thought of them—were playthings for Don Bricio, but such was the world they lived in. There were worse fates for pretty young girls than to live in a palace as concubines. If young Caile had disapproved, had burned inwardly to kill Don Bricio and free them all, such were the foolish thoughts of a royal-born boy who had learned more from books than experience. So Fina had thought then.

But here she was now. Caile had indeed killed Don Bricio. Makarria had freed the harem girls. And Caile had grown, his righteousness undeterred by all he'd seen and experienced. He loved Makarria, it was plain, and would do anything to protect her.

Fina sighed contentedly. There were times during her ordeal in Khal-Aband when she had given up hope. Certainly, she had never thought to have warm feelings for anyone ever again. It was only with pure stubbornness, vengefulness, that she had held on to life. The things done to her in Khal-Aband…she would not even think of them anymore. When Caile and Makarria had rescued her and told her Don Bricio was dead, she felt she ought to be angry for being robbed of the opportunity of killing him herself. But she was not. She instead found satisfaction in having outlived the pig, Don Bricio. And she felt gratefulness for being rescued. The gratefulness was turning into something more, she had to admit now, looking upon Makarria.

Makarria was still deep in sleep, her breaths long and even. Fina smiled and turned away to walk the perimeter of the room. She checked every window and the door latch at the balcony. All was safe, all was sound. Satisfied, Fina exited back to her small anteroom and sat herself at the foot of the bed again. She was weary, but she would not sleep tonight, she decided. She could sleep come morning once they were on the airship and Makarria was surrounded by people she could trust.

Her mind made up, Fina sat there, purposefully thinking of nothing, pushing away the dark memories that constantly bobbed at the surface of her thoughts. She focused only on the sounds of the sleeping castle around her. After a time, her eyelids grew heavy, but when they dipped near to slumber, she pushed herself up and paced the room for a while, then sat in one of the waiting chairs. She did not know how much time had passed when a knock sounded at her outer door.

She cracked open the door, her dagger drawn and at the ready, but it was only Caile. "What's wrong?" she asked. "I thought you were sleeping?"

"I was, but Makarria summoned me."

"Summoned you? How? No one's been here since you left."

"She summoned me with her magic," Caile said, wiggling his fingers as if that was all it took to be a sorcerer.

The grin left his face when he saw Fina's lack of amusement.

"She must have had a nightmare," he said. "She came to me in my sleep and told me to come immediately."

Fina opened the door for him to pass through. She had not heard Makarria stir or speak, but Fina was the first to admit she knew little about Makarria's powers. "All right, I best go in there with you and check the perimeter again."

Caile stopped at the door to the inner chambers. "No, it's fine. I'll call for you if she needs anything."

Fina opened her mouth to object, but Caile had already opened the bedroom door and was slipping silently through. Seeing no good reason to cause a stir, Fina turned away and sat back at the foot of her bed, still absently clutching her dagger. Caile's coming this late at night was odd she felt, but she knew better than to be presumptuous. She had only been Makarria's guard for two days now. Makarria and Caile had been close for well over a year. Why wouldn't the young queen turn to him for counsel or comfort from a bad dream?

The minutes passed and Fina grew restless, increasingly ill at ease. Something was not right. She wanted to convince herself everything was fine, but she couldn't shake the feeling that Caile had not been himself. When he'd stopped her from going in, the look on his face…it no longer had that righteous confidence she had recognized in it before, but instead…something smug. *Well, don't just sit there then,* she chastised herself as she stood. *There's no harm in checking in on them.*

Before she took two steps toward Makarria's door, though, a knock sounded at the other door. With a frown, she opened it to see who was there and was baffled to find a half-dozen servants standing in the corridor.

"I'm here with the wine and meal the prince sent for," one of the kitchen servants said in a hushed tone, apparently as ill at ease as Fina was with this late night disturbance.

"Prince Caile sent for this?" Fina asked, looking at the platter of food the man bore. "And the rest of you?"

"We're the queen's chambermaids," one of the three women still in their nightgowns said. "We received word from the prince that we were to come at once."

"And I'm a courtier," the other man standing in the corridor replied. "I was told to come fetch a message to take to the raven keeper."

"Let me guess, Prince Caile sent for you?" Fina said, not bothering to wait for his response. She still had her dagger gripped tightly in her right hand as she strode away and turned the doorknob to Makarria's chambers. The door caught on something when she tried to open it, but she forced her way through, toppling over a chair that had been placed on the other side to wedge the door shut.

Fina stopped and inhaled sharply at what she saw. At first she thought Makarria was strewn across the bed, murdered and dead. But no, it was worse. The covers had been thrown aside, her clothes ripped off her, and she lay there, unconscious, naked, with the half-undressed Prince Caile scrambling away from her. A bottle of wine lay overturned beside him, its spilled wine soaking into the mattress.

"What, what are you doing?" he stammered, looking back at Fina.

"You—" she growled at Caile, stalking toward the bed. "I'll

kill you!"

Caile slipped off the opposite side of the bed from Makarria and fastened his trousers shut. "Save your anger, woman, and tend to your queen." His voice was distant and cold. "Touch me and I'll put you right back where I found you."

Anger welled up in Fina, but before she could reach him, the servants from the corridor burst into the room, gasping and openly gaping at the scene before them. "All of you, leave at once!" Fina yelled at them. She glanced away from Caile, just for a moment, to push them back into the anteroom, and before she knew it Caile slipped right past her and the servants both, right through the anteroom and out into the corridor. "Stop!" she yelled, but the fool servants were blocking her way.

Behind her, Makarria groaned and began to stir. Fina grimaced, wanting nothing more than to chase down Caile and cut out his venomous tongue, this smiling prince who had duped her, but she would have to deal with him later. Right now the young queen needed her. "Be gone," Fina barked at the servants who still stood there gawking as she ran to Makarria's side. "And someone go fetch the queen's mother!"

9
Familiar Enemies

Natarios Rhodas looked up with disdain from the message in his hand to the messenger standing before him. "Ambassador Rives summons me? Oh no, I don't think so. I'm lord of proceedings, not him. If he wants to speak, he can come to my tower."

"Sir?"

"You heard me. Go! Tell that fool to come here if it's so damned important to talk. And make sure he brings a message to send to Lon Golier so it looks legitimate."

The lackey scurried away, out of Natarios's living quarters and down the spiral staircase of the tower. Natarios tried to pick up where he left off before the man had arrived, enjoying his morning snack of hard Bergian cheese and nutbrown ale from Lepig, but he was too aggravated to take any pleasure in food and drink. With a snort, he pushed himself up from his cushioned couch and exited his room into the stairwell, up to the chamber above him. The caged ravens warbled when they saw him, but there were no new messenger arrivals waiting on the landing. Natarios threw a couple handfuls of nuts and seeds to the clamoring birds in the cages, then went back to the stairwell and climbed the last twenty steps to the chamber where the scent-hound lay in perpetual slumber on its brass compass.

That was where Ambassador Rives of Golier found him ten minutes later. "Who do you think you are, summoning me?" Rives demanded, barging into the chamber before fully realizing where he was. When his eyes landed on the scent-hound, he froze in his tracks.

"I'm the lord of proceedings," Natarios said, amused. "Let's not forget that. It looks unseemly for me to be beckoning at your every call. If we must communicate outside the council meetings, it makes more sense for you to come here, on some pretence of sending a message to your Capital, for if you'll remember, I'm also still the houndkeeper—master of messenger ravens and master of our lovely hound here."

Rives ripped his eyes way from the part-woman, part-dog contraption that was the scent-hound. "Of course, you're right. I was merely impatient to tell you the news: we've secured three more votes for Lord Kobel. That puts us at nine, two away from a majority."

Natarios was surprised by this turn of events, enough so that he was unable to feign indifference. "Already? That was fast, I must say. We still have twelve days left until we vote."

"When the money and incentive is there, it's best to strike. No sense in waiting."

"Perhaps," Natarios replied. "I simply worry about revealing our gambit too soon. Sure the steam-engineer's guild and the sorcerer's guild and a couple of the lesser candidates are happy to take your money now, but your King Lorimer of Golier isn't the only man with deep pockets, you know? What if someone like the Old World Senate sets their mind on getting control of Guderian's war machines?"

Natarios said this as a mere hypothetical situation, never before having thought of it as a possibility, but the way Rives suddenly grinned made Natarios realize he was far closer to the mark than he realized.

"You needn't worry," Rives assured him. "King Lorimer is a visionary. His aims and allies extend beyond the Five Kingdoms."

"Well, why didn't you tell me so before?" Natarios demanded.

"Because it was not something you needed to know."

"And it is now?"

"Yes." Rives turned away from Natarios and walked toward the scent-hound, holding one hand over the outer ring of the compass as he circled it slowly. "Our financers need assurances. When Lord Kobel is elected, we need to know we'll have control of the steam-powered war wagons. More importantly, we need to know that we'll have control of the smelters and the war-wagon factory."

A sense of danger coursed through Natarios, but he maintained his demeanor of arrogant indifference—he had mastered the skill long ago in dealing with the sorcerer Wulfram. He was admittedly a coward, but judging by his outward appearance, Natarios Rhodas was the bravest man in all the Five Kingdoms. Or the most foolish.

"I can give you no assurances," Natarios said, displeased about this sudden revelation of the Old World's potential involvement. "The dreamwielder swore the Sargothian cavalry to her allegiance until such time a new King of Sargoth is chosen, and they are the ones who guard the war machines, the smelters, the factory, all of it. If Kobel is elected, the cavalry will obey him, so it's him you must deal with. Me—I'm just in charge of rigging the election."

• • •

More than anything, Makarria wanted to sleep. Her body ached and lethargy hung over her like a leaden mantle, but she pushed away the weariness, the nausea threatening to make its way out, and listened to Fina's story.

She couldn't believe the words she was hearing. It was like being outside of herself, watching someone else's life. This could not be her life Fina was talking about. This was not something that could happen to her. And certainly not something Caile would do. He would never. All she remembered from the night before was returning to her room, nibbling on some food and sipping at a glass of wine. But Makarria's mother and Talitha were corroborating everything Fina said, telling her of how they had found her. Telling her how her mother had set guards at Caile's chamber door to keep him prisoner. Describing how the attendants had walked in to see everything, and how their gossip had spread like wildfire through the palace and into the city as the people awoke and went about their morning business. Telling her about the crowds outside the palace protesting, and of the Brotherhood of Five demanding a hearing.

"The people are saying it's an illicit affair," Talitha said. "Rumors are flying around that you have been bedding Caile from the beginning, ever since your coronation."

"It was nothing of the sort," Fina said. "There was no blood, and you're a virgin still, so I'm sure Caile did not rape you. But he meant to, and he'd undressed you already. Likely touched you. He would have done more if I hadn't walked in."

Fina's words hung in the air.

"The rumors are easily fixed," Fina continued when no one said anything. "Tell your people that Caile assaulted you and when I cut off his balls for you to show them, your name will be cleared."

"A bit barbaric perhaps," Talitha said, "but warranted if that's what you decide, Makarria. A public shaming and banishment would achieve the same effect."

Still Makarria said nothing. She merely sat there, propped up in her bed, staring at them. She couldn't believe it.

Prisca wiped away the tears on her face and stood from where she'd been sitting off to the side of the bed. "Leave us for a while if you will, ladies."

"Of course," Fina and Talitha both agreed, and they shuffled out of the room to wait in the antechamber.

Prisca sat herself on the bed beside Makarria and grabbed her daughter's hand. Her face was a mixture of sorrow and fury, her eyes red from crying, but her lips pursed into a thin line. "I'm so sorry this happened, darling. Talk to me. This wasn't your fault. Tell me what you're feeling."

Makarria still said nothing. She gripped her mother's hand, hearing Fina's words over and over again in her mind. Faster. Louder. Until it grew in a deafening roar. And finally Makarria broke. She wailed like a child and fell into her mother's arms.

"It's not fair," she sobbed over and over again, and all Prisca could do was hold her. Makarria sobbed and cried and shook until she grew dizzy and then slumped back to her pillow.

Prisca's countenance hardened as she looked upon her distraught daughter. "I'm so sorry, Makarria. This is all my fault for leaving you to bear the burden of ruling. But I'll take care of everything now. You just rest. I'll send your father to watch over you, and I'll take care of everything. I'll send Caile to the dungeon, then I'll summon Captain Haviero, Natale, and the rest of your advisors and figure everything out. This is my fault, not yours."

Her mother's words stoked something inside Makarria. "No, wait," she said, pushing herself upright again. "It's not your fault at all. None of this is."

"It is, Makarria. You're wise and strong beyond your years, but you're still barely a teenager. It's so easy to forget, but now—with what's happened to you—I can't let…I can't let my little girl get hurt like this."

Prisca was crying now, and Makarria again leaned into her arms. "It's not your fault, Mother, not any more than it's my fault. I don't know how or why, but Caile did this, not us." The words sounded foreign on her lips. *Caile did this.* She knew rationally that it had to be true, but at the same time she knew in her heart that it couldn't be. It made no sense.

"I just can't stand it," Prisca said, shaking her head. "I've come to see Caile as almost a son, and now I want to hurt him for hurting you. I want to stow you away where you'll always be safe."

"I know. I love you, Mother, and I want your help, but if I give up now—if I let my mother sweep in to protect me—you know how it will look. Valaróz will be lost. The Old World will know I'm too weak to stop them and will invade. There will be nothing you or I or anyone else can do to stop them."

"But, Makarria," Prisca started to protest.

"No, I won't give up. I need your help, but I can face this."

• • •

With Talitha and Fina at her side, Makarria steeled herself for what she was about to do and strode past the guards into Caile's chambers unannounced.

"Your Highness," Lorentz said, standing from where he had been sitting at a small table in the anteroom. "I heard what happened. My deepest apologies. Caile must have been deep into drink last night. He is still bed-ridden and sick, and remembers little."

"We'll find out exactly what he remembers," Makarria said. "Step aside."

Lorentz opened the door to the bedroom for her, and made to follow the three women inside.

"No," Makarria told him. "Stay outside. I will speak with him alone."

"Alone? You have two women with you, one of which threatened to kill him last night. Please, Your Highness, let me be here for him through this. Whatever he might have done, he has been loyal and deserves a friend at his side. I'm sure he's very sorry for whatever he's done. Let him say sorry, send the guards outside away, and all will be better again."

Makarria glared at him, anger welling up in her, but Talitha spared her from having to speak. "Caile has no better friend than Makarria. She's a more loyal friend than he deserves, in my opinion. If it were not for her compassionate hand, Caile would be dead already, at the hand of any one of us, or worse, her mother." Talitha placed two fingers firmly on Lorentz's sternum and pushed him back into the antechamber. "Now go, and wait. No harm will come to Caile, I promise you. Not yet, at least." She closed the door and nodded for Makarria to proceed.

Caile had awakened at hearing the voices and pushed himself up in his bed to lean heavily into the headboard behind him. His face was pale and dappled with beads of sweat. He could hardly bear to look Makarria in the eyes. "Is it true?"

"Is what true?" Makarria asked, striding over to his bed and standing over him. She had been given no choice in what happened to her; she was not about to let him off so easily. She would hear all of it from his own lips.

"Lorentz told me I was found on top of you. And you

were naked."

Makarria had never seen Caile afraid before. She had never seen him abashed or even humbled. He was a trembling child now, though. Broken like she'd never seen him before. Dark circles surrounded his bloodshot eyes. Pity and sorrow washed over Makarria seeing him like this, but she held onto the anger. Being pathetic didn't make right what he had done to her.

"Indeed," she said. "Three of my chambermaids, a kitchen server, and a royal courtier all walked in to find you dismounting me."

It was as if Makarria had run him through with his own sword. His face constricted in pain and he doubled over, clutching the bed covers up to cover his face. Makarria thought he would vomit, or break down into racking sobs. When he sat up a few seconds later, though, his face was constrained. Only a few tears wetted his eyes. He took a deep breath, as if he'd just been sentenced to death and had accepted the punishment. "I'm so sorry, Makarria. I would never do that to you. I don't know *how* I did that to you. I can't even remember. Did we…did I…"

Caile couldn't bring himself to say it. Did he bed her? Did he rape her?

"She was still asleep, drunk on wine," Talitha said. "How could she know what you did to her?"

Caile choked, trying to keep his sobbing at bay.

Makarria looked pointedly at Fina, who reluctantly stepped forward.

"I know matters of the flesh more than most," Fina said. "I checked over Makarria when I sent you away. She was naked, but I saw no evidence that you had raped her."

A semblance of relief washed over Caile's face, but that only made Makarria angrier.

"It matters little whether you did or not, Caile!" she yelled, slamming her fist down into the mattress beside him. "You tried to. There were five witnesses who walked in on it. They've been telling everyone we consorted, and now the entire city thinks it's the truth! Do you understand me? I'm Queen of Valaróz. You are my advisor, not my husband. Do you know what people are saying? My people? The Brotherhood of Five has already demanded a hearing to publicly chastise me. Why would you do this?"

"Wait," Caile pled. "I still don't understand why there were witnesses. Why were there people there?"

"Because you sent for them, Caile! Food. Wine. My chambermaids. What were you thinking? That you would have them dress me up for you? That we would have a feast and that I would beg you to take me? Is that it? And then, after all your planning you were too impatient to even wait for them to arrive?"

"I sent for them?" It was barely a whisper, the way Caile asked it. "I'm sorry. I don't remember. All I remember was saying goodnight to Fina and then coming back here. Lorentz was already asleep, so I poured myself another glass of wine and went to bed..."

"You said you could hold your spirits," Fina spat.

Caile merely nodded, unable to respond, but Talitha narrowed her eyes. She glanced from Caile to Makarria to Caile again. "How much wine did you have?" she asked, walking up to Caile, who flinched, but relented when he realized she only wanted to touch his forehead and check his temperature.

Caile squeezed his eyes shut and open again. "I don't know. One glass in Makarria's room. Less than that even when I got back here."

"And both of you are sick," Talitha said. "Neither of you remember a thing."

"Vala's teats," Fina swore beneath her breath. "I should have seen it. The wine was drugged."

Talitha nodded in agreement. "Is there any of the wine left from Makarria's room?"

"No," Fina answered. "The rest of the bottle was spilled on the bed."

"What about the other bottle?" Talitha asked. "Where's the bottle you drank from here in your room, Caile?"

Caile pointed toward a decanter of wine sitting atop his dresser, the stopper lying upturned a few inches away.

"It's not likely both bottles would be drugged," Fina said,

walking over to the decanter and sniffing at it. "Too complicated. Too many loose ends."

"You're probably right," Talitha agreed. "Still, it might be worth testing it."

"You think I was drugged?" Caile asked.

"So what if you were?" Makarria snapped, not seeing how this explained anything. "It still doesn't excuse you for what you did. Drunk—drugged—or whatever the case might have been, it doesn't give you the right…" Makarria couldn't even bring herself to say the rest.

"No, you're right," Caile agreed. "I don't know what I can do or say to make up for what I've done to you."

"There's nothing you can do," Makarria said. She turned away from him and sat in one of the chairs beside the hearth, once again feeling sick. She closed her eyes and forced herself to push the emotions away. *Think, Makarria. How could this happen? Who would drug the two of us? And who could make Caile do what he did if he were drugged?* The answer was so obvious she couldn't believe she hadn't realized it before. *Lorentz!* Taera had warned her about him.

"What is it you mean to do, Makarria?" Talitha asked, breaking the silence. "I don't think it wise for you to leave now. Everyone will think you are running away."

"I'm not sure yet," Makarria said, standing and walking over to Caile's bed again. "Let me talk with Caile alone for a moment, and then I will decide."

"Are you sure that's a good idea?" Fina asked, eyeing Caile.

"I'll be fine."

"Come," Talitha told Fina, leading the way out of the room. "We'll be right here in the anteroom if you need us, Makarria."

When the door closed behind them, Makarria turned to Caile. His face was forlorn, as if he feared she were about to strike him.

"Tell me everything you remember from last night," she said.

"Makarria—" he began to object, but she silenced him.

"Tell me, Caile!"

He swallowed and nodded tersely before beginning. "After

meeting you in the library, I saw you to your room. We ate a little. Drank a glass of wine, and then you were falling asleep. I pulled the covers up over you and left. Fina and I talked for a moment. She teased me about drinking too much wine, I think, but I hadn't, I swear. I felt dizzy, but I'd only had one glass. I was just tired and wanted to go to bed. Even drugged, there would be no reason for me to go back to your room. Lorentz was already asleep in his room when I passed through to my mine." Caile furrowed his brow, deep in concentration trying to remember. "I poured myself another glass of wine to drink as I undressed, I think, but it's very hazy. I don't think I even got my clothes entirely off. I just fell back onto my bed and laid there."

"You're sure Lorentz was asleep when you returned? He didn't speak to you?"

Caile furrowed his brow and shook his head. "No, I don't think I spoke to Lorentz. I just sort of remember lying there on my bed, weary, dizzy, and then"—he closed his eyes, trying to recall whatever had happened—"and then waking up, or being half awake, and seeing myself sitting on the bed beside me. It seems like it must have been a dream, but I remember it now, looking into my own face, watching myself getting up from the bed and walking away."

Caile looked up at Makarria. "I'm sorry. I know that must sound absurd. I had to have dreamt it."

Makarria pursed her lips and turned away. It did sound absurd and it was not what she was hoping to hear, but her instincts told her that Lorentz was still somehow involved in this. And at this point, it mattered little. She was on the verge of losing the confidence of her people entirely, and if she couldn't maintain rule of her own kingdom, how could she hope to save the entirety of the Five Kingdoms from the Old World? Talitha was right. Makarria needed to stay here and regain the trust of her people. And with rumors going around the city of Makarria and Caile having an affair, Caile couldn't stay, not unless she accused him of assaulting her and threw him in the dungeon, and she wasn't about to do that. That left only one question: after what he had done, did she trust Caile enough to send him to Col Sargoth to attend the election council, or did she banish him to his own kingdom of Pyrthinia?

Makarria turned to face him again. "I can't begin to understand how or why this happened, but if any part of you cares for and respects me, Caile, answer me honestly. If I tell the Brotherhood of Five what you have done in a public hearing, will you accept the punishment they demand?"

Tears welled up in Caile's eyes and ran down his cheeks, but his face remained stolid. "If that's what you think is best, then yes. Absolutely. I will face the punishment I earned."

"Thank you," Makarria said.

Caile turned away, unable to look her in the eye. "How soon will the hearing be? I'll need time to make myself presentable. I'm still a prince of Pyrthinia and will own up to my crimes with dignity and respect."

"There's no need for that. You're not going to be at the hearing."

"But you just said—"

"I know what I just said," Makarria interrupted him. "I had to know whether I could trust you at all anymore. I can't let you stay here in Sol Valaróz, but I trust you enough, I think, to send you to Col Sargoth in my place. It's up to you now to make sure the right candidate is elected to the Sargothian throne."

"But what about the western naval fleet?"

"I'll send a raven, and my admirals will have to do their job on their own. You just make sure you put a king on that throne we can trust. I have to tend to Valaróz now and keep the Old World at bay, so I'm counting on you to make things right in Sargoth. And you're going to have to do it without Lorentz. I need him here with me."

"Lorentz? But why? You said you didn't trust him."

"I know what I said, Caile. No more questions. You have to *trust* me. You'll have Talitha and Siegbjorn with you, and I'll send an official writ, pronouncing you my emissary. I want you to take Thon with you, too. He's from Col Sargoth and has shown his loyalty to you—he may prove to be helpful. Can you do this?"

Caile stared at her for a long moment, in no position to question or deny her. "Of course."

"Good. Say nothing to anyone until you're on that airship and safely away. Not to Talitha, Siegbjorn, Fina, Lorentz, not anyone. I'll tell them everything they need to know. Do you understand?"

"Yes."

Makarria looked upon him, crushed by the weight of what had happened between them. "You'll have your speaking stone, so we can speak if need be," she said, forcing her voice to remain even. "Now dress yourself and gather your things, then fetch Thon. You set sail immediately. The morning is already half gone." She turned away and made toward the door.

"Wait," Caile said, urgency in his voice.

Makarria stopped to face him. "Yes?"

"I... I..."

Whatever it was he meant to say, he couldn't get it out, and she didn't wait for him to find the words. She walked out, and in the anteroom spoke curtly to the others. "Talitha, I need you to set sail at once. Take Caile to Col Sargoth in my stead. I ask that you stay there and help him if you can, but if you must return to Issborg, I understand."

Talitha weighed Makarria's words for a long moment, then nodded. "The Snjaer Firan have managed on their own for decades without me. They can do without me for another few weeks."

"Thank you."

"And me, Your Highness?" Lorentz asked. "I assume you'll want me keeping an eye on Caile? Our things are already packed. We can be at the airship within the hour."

"No. Caile goes by himself. You're staying here with me." Makarria watched Lorentz carefully as she said this, but she could read nothing in his reaction—his facial expression was muted. "There are enemies in our court," Makarria continued, "and I'll need both you and Fina protecting me if I'm going to survive."

"Of course, Your Highness."

"Good, you're in charge of securing the throne room. My mother is making arrangements for a hearing with the Brotherhood of Five within the hour. Make sure it is safe. Work with Captain Haviero and handpick only guards you trust. We'll not have a repeat of what happened in the sitting room. Understood?"

Lorentz nodded. "Yes, Your Majesty. I understand completely."

10
The Sanctified

A gust of wind howled outside, buffeting the cabin of Siegbjorn's airship and sending Caile's stomach lurching. He choked down the bile rising in his throat and wiped the sweat from his brow. The wine he had drank the night before—or perhaps the drug in it, if indeed it had been drugged—had given him the worst hangover of his life. Compounded with the sway of the airship and the knowledge of what he'd done to Makarria, he felt little better than a corpse. He still didn't understand how he could have forced himself on Makarria. In his heart and mind, he knew he would never dream of doing such a thing. Even drunk, he could never do it. And yet somehow he had. A half-dozen witnesses, including Fina, had seen him there. He felt like he was losing his mind.

"Why didn't Makarria just turn me over to the Brotherhood of Five?" Caile asked Talitha, too ashamed to even look at her where she sat across from him in the small cabin.

Talitha lowered the sheaf of papers she was reading. "Makarria didn't deem it fit to tell me why she chose to send you to Col Sargoth. I don't know what she said to you, or what you said to her, but clearly she trusts you with this task."

"How could she? I don't even trust myself." Caile sagged his head into his hands. He felt like vomiting. Again. As soon as they had taken off in the airship toward Col Sargoth, he had puked off the side of the deck, fertilizing some poor farmer's field below with his half digested breakfast.

"If you cannot trust yourself, then trust her, at least," Talitha said. "Young as she is, she has a way of seeing the true nature of things. It is part of her power as a dreamwielder to have a connection with Tel Mathir. If she trusts you in this matter, it is good enough for me."

Caile nodded at her words, but still felt no better about himself.

Talitha regarded him for a long moment, then continued. "If you're going to prove to yourself that you're trustworthy again, Caile, then I suggest you quit wallowing in self-misery and focus on the job Makarria has tasked you with."

The words stung, and the anger it stoked in Caile made him want to retort something back.

Talitha winked when she saw him straighten his posture and clench his jaw.

Of course, he realized. *She said that on purpose, knowing that angering me would get my attention and get me refocused.*

When the two of them had first met, he had been annoyed by her tight-lipped attitude and coy remarks. She had rescued him from Emperor Guderian and was taking him to the Caverns of Issborg to free Makarria and Taera, but, like now, he had been caught up in his own misery, distraught over leaving behind Lorentz and the rest of his troops in Emperor Guderian's hands. Yet, little by little, she had prodded him in the direction of the task at hand, and by the end of their journey together, he had seen the effectiveness of her ways. She was a teacher at heart, and it saved him and Makarria both.

Talitha was staring at him now, he realized, and she motioned him up and away with her hands.

"Go on already," she said. "Get outside and speak with Thon. He probably knows more about Sargothian politics than whatever is in these reports I have. See what you can find out from him and we'll discuss tonight what exactly it is we mean to do when we arrive in Col Sargoth."

"Of course," Caile said. "Thank you."

Caile crouched his way out the door onto the main deck of the airship, where he was assaulted by the biting cold wind. Beneath his feet, the deck of the airship shimmied. While the canvas shell of the hot-air-filled hull was massive, blotting out the sun and clouds overhead, the deck of the gondola itself was tiny, no larger than that of a fisherman's skiff. The vessel was the only one of its kind, constructed by Siegbjorn himself under the direction of the sorcerer Kadar, who had been inspired by the hot air balloons that were once fashionable in the Old World. Caile had learned all this from Siegbjorn the last time he was on the airship, a year before. On that voyage, Siegbjorn had delivered Caile to the Esterian Ocean where they intercepted Don Bricio's Valarion fleet. Had it really been a year now since Caile had foolishly jumped from the airship into the frigid waters, pulled himself aboard Don Bricio's caravel, and killed the usurper in his own cabin? The time had gone by so quickly: first, the funeral for Caile's father, King Casstian, then the coronation of his sister as the new ruler of Pyrthinia, and then the voyage to Sol Valaróz for Makarria's coronation, and all the subsequent work the two of them had done to root out the corrupt factions Don Bricio had institutionalized into Valarion politics. It had all happened so fast, and yet at the same time, the war against Don Bricio, Wulfram, and Emperor Guderian felt so removed, so long ago. *Only a year ago? Already a year ago? Which is it?*

Caile pushed the memories aside. He had work to do, he reminded himself, and if Talitha found him brooding again, she wouldn't be so nice this time around.

Siegbjorn stood only a few paces in front of the cabin, manning the rudder wheel and levers that controlled their flight, and Thon stood only a few paces beyond that at the prow. Caile slipped past Siegbjorn and leaned against the rail beside Thon, taking in the crisp autumn air, letting the cold numb away the nausea in his stomach. Far off in the distance to their portside, a wall of black clouds blotted out the western horizon. Below them to their starboard side, the Barren Mountains stretched northward to where they intersected with the Forrest Weorcan and divided the kingdoms of Sargoth and Golier.

"I never thought to see the world from the perspective of a bird," Thon said. "It's amazing."

Caile nodded, feeling foolish. Here he had been feeling sorry for himself when Thon had spent the last year or more in chains, locked up in Khal-Aband.

"It is something to behold," Caile agreed. "Wait until we get to Col Sargoth. I don't know how long you've been away, but the city is full of motorized wagons and rickshaws now—the smoke and steam they sputter out is worse smelling than the horse manure littering streets of normal cities, but it is a sight to behold."

"It's been over two years," Thon said. "I never thought to see my city again. It's all been one wonder after another since you and Queen Makarria freed me. How long before we get there?"

"That's the best part about the airship—we'll be in Col Sargoth in less than two days. And when we get there, I'm going to need your help, Thon."

"I figured you didn't just bring me along for a ride. What is it I can do?"

"Help us get the right man put on the throne," Caile said. "Makarria formed an election council after she killed Guderian. She did everything in accordance with Sargothian law, but the council proceedings broke down into political brinkmanship, none of the candidates seem altogether trustworthy, and, worse, they've mandated themselves to holding the election in twelve days. Unless you know something redeeming about one of the candidates, it seems to me we have an impossible task before us."

Thon nodded. "Talitha told me who the main candidates are, and I'm afraid I don't have anything good to say about them. All of them are warmongers and profiteers, or at least they were when I was last there. I mean, not even good-intentioned people in Sargoth could openly voice their dissent against Guderian, but some people embraced Guderian's methods a little too enthusiastically. That's the ilk we're dealing with, particularly Lord Kobel, the one the houndkeeper apparently supports."

"I'm starting to get a sense of why Guderian sent you off to Khal-Aband," Caile said.

"I wish it were so simple. The truth is I don't have any idea why I was imprisoned. I never voiced my dissent, and certainly not among the ranks of the cavalry. I mean, how does a Sargothian nobody, a stableboy with dead parents who has risen only to a modest position as a sergeant in the cavalry, manage to pose a threat to the Emperor himself? I was always dutiful and honorable."

"You honestly don't know what you did to get sent away?"

"Honestly. It's never made any sense to me. One moment we're escorting an official from Norg to speak with Guderian in the throne room, and the next I'm dragged from my bunk in the barracks by my own comrades, tied up and beaten senseless. The last thing I remember my captain saying was that Guderian had caught me 'staring at him the wrong way.' But it was a lie. I knew better than to ever glance at the Emperor. The last thing I wanted was *him* questioning me."

Caile nodded, remembering all too well his own encounters with Guderian in that throne room. "I spoke with Guderian on a few occasions—not the sort of man you have a casual conversation with. I think he may have been a genius in his own perverted way, but he was mad with his ideas, and would not tolerate any sort of argument. Perhaps one of your comrades picked up on your anti-imperial sentiments and told your superiors. Or maybe some of your comrades were jealous and simply lied about you. It's not unheard of among soldiers."

"Perhaps," Thon conceded with a shrug. "I'm afraid I'll never know now that Guderian is gone, but what's done is done. I'm free now, and if I can help in some small way to make Sargoth great again, I will feel redeemed."

"All right then, you know the candidates, or of their reputations at least. Is there not one of them at least who has some sort of honor and pride in the Kingdom of Sargoth?"

"Lord Nagel is the only one of them who was in a position of power before Guderian's reign. He was one of the three wards, in fact, who jointly ruled Sargoth after the Dark Queen was killed at the end of the Dreamwielder War and before Guderian returned from hiding in the Old World. But Nagel is too old—probably ninety by now. He would make a good advisor, no doubt, but he's not fit to be a king. The rest…well they're all entitled noblemen and landowners who came to prominence during Guderian's reign. They might not have been as openly hostile to the common people of Sargoth as Guderian's generals were, but they caused just as much damage the way they exploited the strict labor and trading regulations, not to mention the favors they traded in for ratting out their own vassals who exhibited any sort of ability with sorcery. All we can expect from them is carrying on the status quo."

"Which has everything to do with this new technological revolution Guderian tried starting," Caile said, frowning. "He really thought humankind could conquer nature with coal, ether, and steam. We could look to the sorcerer's guild for help—they'll certainly be pushing for the reintegration of sorcery into commerce—but I don't trust them. They're more in league with the Old World than they are with the Five Kingdoms, and they've already betrayed me once."

"What about the labor guild and the sailor's guild? In thirty years' time, Guderian did nothing to improve the quality of living for the working people of Sargoth. They will want a king who has their interests at heart."

"Agreed, but they comprise only two of the twenty-one voting members," Caile pointed out. "And even if we had a majority backing, we still don't have a candidate. It's a shame Sargothian law prohibits a female monarch. This Lady Hildreth who is part of the council sounds like she could be what we're looking for. Talitha said she was her greatest ally on the council. Is there any way we can use the Dark Queen's reign as a precedent to amend the law and put Lady Hildreth on the throne?"

"Not likely. Even if the Dark Queen's legacy wasn't a stain on Sargothian history, she was technically only the regent, ruling until Guderian came of age. Guderian's birthright came from his father, not her. Besides, I'm not certain Lady Hildreth is the ally you might think she is."

"Oh?"

Thon raised one eyebrow. "Not if you believe the rumors

whispered in taverns. And I've heard enough of them to believe there might be some truth to it."

"Rumors of what?"

"That Lady Hildreth was Guderian's mistress. At least for a while, when they were both younger."

Caile was taken aback. Could it be true? And if so, where did Lady Hildreth's allegiance lie now?

A gale of wind abruptly slammed into the airship, nearly knocking Caile overboard and dismissing whatever thoughts he had about Lady Hildreth.

"The storm will be upon us soon," Siegbjorn hollered at them from the helm. "It will be a rough voyage. Throw more magnesite into the furnace if you would help, Prince, and then both of you best tie-in if you are to stay on deck."

"Will it get all that bad?" Thon yelled back, looking to the approaching cloudbank in the west.

"Sandwiched between the storm and the mountains we'll be," Siegbjorn replied. "If we do not reach the Weordan Pass in time, we will have to cross the mountains in the southern reaches, where the peaks are high and the air is thin."

"Right, I'll start shoveling magnesite," Caile said, glad for another task to distract him from the guilt that threatened to overwhelm him.

• • •

Makarria sat once again on her throne. More so than anything else, this one responsibility had dominated her life over the last year. Here she was, the morning after being assaulted by her best friend, trying to avert an invasion by the Old World, and she was conducting a public hearing where she was the one about to be accused of adultery.

She'd had no time to speak privately yet with Fina to question her further about the night before, but Makarria knew there was something she was missing. Lorentz had been involved in her assault somehow—Makarria just knew it. But that would have to wait until after the official hearing, and until then Lorentz and Fina both stood behind Makarria as her guards. Makarria's mother stood at the foot of the dais with several other advisors and a small detail of the Royal Guard. Next to them were several of the foreign ambassadors, including Ambassador Mahalath, Makarria saw with displeasure. Behind those in the forefront was the usual assortment of audience members, although there were many more of them this time. The throne room was filled near to capacity.

Everyone watched as representatives from the Brotherhood of Five approached and bowed before Makarria. The Brotherhood was one of the oldest organizations in the Five Kingdoms. It was different than the guilds in that it represented not any one vocation, but rather an ideology. Members of the Brotherhood were an enigma, embodying values partly from the Old World of three hundred years before, partly of the founding five sorcerers of the Five Kingdoms. They were fundamentalists who had nearly been decimated during Emperor Guderian's reign, but had reemerged in Valaróz since Makarria's coronation. Their followers were ubiquitous now, present in every facet of Valarion society and commerce. In many ways, their views were harsher than even Guderian's, but to disband the guild just because she didn't like it would undermine all the work Makarria and Caile had done to bring justice and fairness to the realm.

"Welcome, good men of the Brotherhood," Makarria greeted them, not feigning to smile.

"Thank you for meeting with us, Your Majesty," their spokesman, Master Rubino, replied, a rotund man with a sweaty, balding forehead. "Our grievance today is not one we can speak of in courteous terms, so I ask your leave to be blunt."

"You'll say what you came here to say, good sir," Makarria told him. "Out with it."

The man bowed before proceeding. "We have heard word—the whole city has—of your indiscretion with Prince Caile of Pyrthinia. We demand an explanation."

"You misspeak, sir," Makarria corrected him. "You may request an explanation, but it is not in your right to demand anything of me. I am Queen of Valaróz, and beholden to no one."

"My apologies, Your Majesty. I should say, we request an explanation, so the good people of Valaróz might understand why their queen has consorted with a man outside of wedlock."

Even though they had all undoubtedly heard the rumors themselves, the audience tittered at hearing the rumor voiced so.

"You give too much credence to rumors and hearsay," Makarria said, speaking over the murmurs. "I have consorted with no one."

"Yet five of your royal servants will testify otherwise," Rubino insisted. "We can summon them if you wish?"

Makarria sighed. It was obvious where this was going. She could deny the accusation, but then the Brotherhood would call for an official trial where they would besmirch her reputation and call for her resignation if not outright incarceration. In all of the Five Kingdoms, only Valarion and Pyrthin law allowed for female monarchs, but even with ancient laws allowing so, the Brotherhood took exception—that was the influence of their antiquated Old World views. Not even the Old World Republic itself begrudged women a role in politics anymore. Makarria's only course of action if she wanted this matter to disappear quickly would be to accuse Caile of assaulting her, as Fina had suggested earlier that morning. The Brotherhood would have no choice but to stand by her if she did so, but Makarria wasn't about to do that, even if Caile was safely away.

Still, too much was at stake to let the Brotherhood bring her down now—she would not relent without a fight. *Even men of the Brotherhood must acknowledge truth when they see it, right? All I can do is be honest with them. I owe it to my people, if nothing else.*

"I will not deny what my servants think they saw," Makarria said. "But you must trust me when I tell you—all of Valaróz—that what happened last night was a plot against me, one involving my wine being drugged. My investigation is still ongoing, so I can't say anything further. All I can tell you is that I did not consort with

Prince Caile, and never have."

"You have witnesses to attest to this?"

"You have my word," Makarria said flatly. "As your rightful queen, that should be enough."

Master Rubino shrugged without apology. "With all due respect, Your Majesty, your word means little in this case. You were seen bedding a man. Either you provide the people of Valaróz with witnesses to corroborate your story, or…you can prove your innocence by showing this court concrete evidence of your virginity."

Makarria could hardly believe what she was hearing. Even prepared, she had not expected the Brotherhood of Five to be so bold.

Before Makarria could respond, her mother emerged from the crowd of advisors and approached the spokesman. "How dare you," Prisca said, slapping him across the face. "If Makarria were a man, no one would ever question her word." She raised her hand to strike Rubino again, but he caught her wrist.

"If she were a man, she would be a King and could bed whoever he chose, but he is a *she*, and the laws of Sargoth Lightbringer are clearly written!" The man raised his free hand to strike Prisca back.

"Stay your hand!" Makarria snapped, jumping to her feet. "If you hit her, I will have your head."

The crowd gasped. Master Rubino released Prisca and turned to regard Makarria, his eyes bulging with self-righteous anger. "And yet you will let this woman strike an innocent, law abiding man without punishment?"

Makarria forced herself to take a long breath. She had never threatened someone's life like that before—she was horrified by her own actions, but at the same time, she loved her mother for striking the pompous fool Rubino. Indeed, she ached to turn this petty man into a roach and stomp on him. It would be easy to close her eyes and do so… *No,* she told herself. *I'm not like Guderian. I can never do that. I must apply the laws fairly to everyone.*

"Guards," Makarria said, summoning the most official tone of voice she could muster, "Take the Princess Prisca away and place her in a holding cell."

Prisca said nothing, nor did she look at Makarria as two guards ushered her away. Makarria was thankful for that. Her mother was as unaccustomed to court life as Makarria was, but she knew better than to undermine Makarria's authority in front of retainers.

Master Rubino bowed in thanks as Prisca was escorted away. "As I was saying, Your Majesty, if you ask for our trust, you must prove your maidenhood. The Brotherhood has an impartial physician who would be glad to examine you."

"No one will examine me, physician or otherwise," Makarria said, unable to take the man's insolence any further. There was a fine line between tolerance and weakness. "You have my word: I consorted with no one. This hearing is over. Be gone and be glad I have tolerated your false accusations."

The man nodded and turned away with the rest of his ilk from the Brotherhood, but Makarria knew this was not the end of the matter. Far from it. At best, Makarria had bought herself some time. At worst, she had added fuel to the rumors already gone rampant.

She motioned for the herald to announce the end of the hearing, then stood and quickly exited back into the adjoining sitting room with Lorentz and Fina.

"Lorentz, please go fetch Captain Haviero and meet us in the holding cells of the dungeon to release my mother," she said. "Fina, come with me."

It was a short walk from the sitting room to the side passage and stairs that led to the subterranean dungeons below. In the last year, Makarria had sentenced more than a few of Don Bricio's crime lords to make the very same walk to where they wasted away in the deepest, darkest of cells. Prisca was being held in the uppermost level of the dungeon, though, where the spacious cells were dry and well lit by lanterns.

Makarria rushed to embrace her mother through the bars, when they reached her cell. "I'm so sorry, Mother."

Prisca smiled and ran one hand through Makarria's hair. "Don't be sorry. You did what was required of you as a queen. I did what was required of me as a mother."

Makarria smiled back. She wanted nothing more than to go with her mother and lie down for a nap, to sleep in her arms like she had when she was still just a little girl and they lived on their farm. For a while, at least, she wanted to forget about everything. But Makarria had to figure out what was going on and, more importantly, what she was going to do about it.

Footsteps approached, and Makarria looked toward the stairs to see Lorentz with Captain Haviero.

"Please release her, Captain Haviero, and escort her to her quarters."

"Of course."

The door opened with a squeal and Makarria hugged her mother again. "You best go with Captain Haviero now. I'll come talk to you once I've taken care of some matters."

Prisca nodded and kissed her, then followed Captain Haviero back out the way they had come. Makarria lingered behind in the main corridor of the dungeon. Now she just needed to get Lorentz out of the way so she could talk to Fina in private.

"This is as good a place to talk as any," Makarria said. "Lorentz, did Caile make any more progress in the investigation of my assassination attempt?"

"Not that I know of, Your Highness."

"I want you to check in the with the commander of the city watch again, then, and see if he's turned up anything or identified any of the attackers' bodies. I'm losing the faith of my people fast and need a victory here, even a small one. I need to put a face to our enemy. My guess is it's the Old World that was behind the assassination, but we need some sort of proof before I can make an accusation publicly."

Lorentz nodded. "Distracting your people from one accusation with another is shrewd, Your Highness."

That was not something Lorentz would have ever said before, but Makarria kept her expression neutral. "I don't care so much about being shrewd as getting to the bottom of what happened. Hurry now and see what you can find out. We've already wasted too much time today with that pointless hearing. Report back to me in my personal chambers if you find anything."

Lorentz bowed and trotted up the stairs and out of the dungeon. Makarria waited for the sound of his footsteps to dissipate before turning to Fina. "Come, let's make sure all the cells on this level are empty and that we're alone."

Together, they walked to the far end of the corridor to where another stairwell led down to the next level of the dungeon, checking to see that each cell was empty along the way. Satisfied they were alone, Makarria let out a relieved breath.

"Finally," she said. "I need you to tell me again every detail of what you saw last night, Fina. There's something else going on that we're not seeing, and I'm fairly certain Lorentz is involved. And now that I have a moment to really think about it, perhaps the Old World, too. The timing of Caile's assault on me—coming right after the attempt on my life, and my refusal of Senator Emil's offer—all seems a little too convenient. There has to be something more to it than a simple drug in my wine. Caile wouldn't have done what he did of his own accord, even drugged. And why summon my attendants unless they were there to witness what happened and spread the word?"

Fina narrowed her eyes. "Yes, you're right. How did I not see it before? Last night, everything happened so quickly, so precisely, it had to be coordinated. When Prince Caile left your room the first time, he was fine, I'm sure of it. Perhaps tired, but fine. I was thinking to myself how obvious it was he cared for you. Then, maybe an hour later, he returned and his demeanor was different. He did not seem drunk, and he was in your room for no more than a minute or two before the servants arrived. It *had* to have been carefully timed. But by whom? What did Caile tell you in private? Anything?"

Makarria shrugged. "He couldn't remember much, but when I pressed him, he said he remembered lying down on the bed and looking up at himself."

Fina's face blanched.

"What?" Makarria asked.

"What did Caile say exactly?"

Makarria furrowed her brow, trying to recall the exact words of the conversation. "He said he was lying down and saw his body sitting next to him. And then the body stood up and looked at him."

Fina closed her eyes and shook her head. "Sweet Vala, I'm such a fool."

"What is it, Fina? What are you talking about?"

"I've seen something like what the prince speaks of once," Fina said, but then went silent. Her eyes became unfocused and she strode to one of the nearby cells and peered inside.

Makarria's pulse quickened with apprehension. "You saw what, exactly?"

Fina turned to Makarria, her eyes wide. She spoke in barely a whisper. "It was in Khal-Aband. One of the guards was in my cell, having his way with me. Thon had tried to chase him off, but the guard beat him senseless and I knew better than to struggle. This guard was on me, saying horrible things, trying to make me angry, but I went to the far away place in my mind… and then all of a sudden, I wasn't in my mind in anymore. I was on top, looking down on myself, while my hips—my male loins—thrust back and forth into the real me. My own face looked up at me and smiled. I tried to scream, but then I was looking up at the guard again from my own body, and I bit my tongue. I always thought it was madness, my mind struggling to cope…"

The hair at the nape of Makarria's neck was standing on end. She grabbed Fina's arm. "This guard—do you remember what he looked like?"

Fina shook her head. "No, it was dark, and I made a point of not taking notice of his face. I only remember the change, when I was looking at my own face."

Makarria turned away, the pieces falling into place: the sunken skiff on the western shore of the Spine, the strange incident with Lorentz and the prison guard in Khal-Aband, Lorentz's subsequent odd behavior, and Taera's visions of warning that Lorentz had died. Lorentz hadn't been acting himself, because he wasn't himself. He was… she didn't know what, but if anyone did, it would be her tutor Natale.

"Come, quickly," Makarria said, grabbing Fina by the arm. "We have to hurry to the library before Lorentz returns."

11
Machines of War

Natarios Rhodas listened intently while the sorcerer's guildmaster and steam-engineer's guildmaster took turns questioning Lord Nagel. In the year past, the two of them had always been at odds, yet now they seemed to be in agreement, almost as if they were working in rehearsed tandem. *Rives has both of them in his pocket,* Natarios noted. *And poor old Nagel is taking a flogging because he's not part of the plan.*

"Furthermore," the sorcerer's guildmaster was saying, "what assurance can you give us that you are capable of re-integrating sorcerers into a viable arm of the Sargothian workforce? If I'm not mistaken, when you were last in charge of anything of importance, the mighty Trumball and the entirety of the sorcerer's guild were murdered."

The look of utter contempt Lord Nagel gave the man almost made Natarios laugh out loud. The old statesman wasn't cut out for this modern sort of deceitful politics, and he made no effort at hiding it.

"Sargoth's hairy arse," Nagel growled. "Were you kicked in the head by a mule? That was Emperor Guderian himself who killed Trumball and all the others. It was beyond my control. Beyond anyone's control. Suggesting I had any responsibility for what happened is moronic."

"I must agree with Lord Nagel," Lady Hildreth said. "What is the point of this constant misdirection in your line of questioning, guildmasters? Lord Nagel is the only candidate here who ever actually served this kingdom before sorcery was outlawed. Reintegrating sorcery into Sargothian life is an unknown for all of us."

"And why must *you* attack every one of our questions directed at the candidates?" Ambassador Rives asked Lady Hildreth. "We simply want to know what Lord Nagel's plan is."

Lady Hildreth put her hands on the table. Natarios could tell she was on the verge of standing up in protest, so he rapped his gavel on the table to put an end to the bickering before it went further. "Enough. Enough. We're almost out of time for the day as it is. Lord Nagel, if you would, please elaborate on your plan to integrate sorcery into Sargothian commerce."

Nagel cleared his throat and began his lengthy answer, which was much the same as what he had said during his initial presentation earlier that day. To be honest, though, Natarios was beyond caring at this point and hardly paid attention. Based on what he'd seen, Nagel had no chance of threatening Lord Kobel's candidacy for the throne. Ambassador Rives had too many voting members in his pockets and he'd put them into action, largely cutting Natarios out of the loop altogether.

The conversation he'd had with Rives the day before had begun to worry Natarios, even before the day's proceedings. If the Old World was the financial force behind this election as Rives had alluded to, why hadn't Natarios been contacted directly? He was the one in charge of the voting process, not Rives, not King Lorimer of Golier. The answer to that question was obvious enough to Natarios, and that's why he was worried: if the Old World wasn't making him part of their plans now, they had no plans for him in the future either. That simply wouldn't do. It was time for Natarios to ensure the vacant throne would only be won with his assistance, and, more importantly, with his guaranteed position of privilege when the new king was elected.

His mind made up, Natarios banged his gavel, thanked Lord Nagel for the presentation of his claim to the throne, and adjourned the meeting. As the council members and candidates began filing out, he strode over to the sole female in the room, the one who up to this point had been the biggest thorn in his side since Talitha's impeachment.

"Lady Hildreth," he said with an ingratiating smile, "I was wondering if you would have a word in private with me?"

She looked up at him in surprise from where she still sat at the table. Even better, Natarios could see out of the corner of his eye that Ambassador Rives was gawking at him. Just as he had hoped.

"It's in regard to Guderian's war machine factories and the continued welfare of the city," Natarios continued, speaking loud enough for everyone in the room to hear.

"Yes, of course," Lady Hildreth said, gathering her things. "Just give me a moment."

Natarios bowed and stepped aside to give her space to stand, smiling inwardly. *Excellent. Let everyone else worry about me now and what I'm up to for a change.*

• • •

Even having heard the foreman's bi-daily reports, Taera was surprised by the progress the shipbuilders had made. In only two days' time they had turned the royal shipbuilding hangar into an *airship*-building hangar. Already, the rigid framework of one airship was complete—looking more like a giant whale's ribcage than the frame of a ship—and workers were overlaying the tar-sealed canvas shell that would trap in the buoyant ether being generated in another facility at the opposite end of Kal Pyrthin.

"It's amazing," said Master Elias, the elderly man accompanying Taera who was responsible for the airship design in the first place.

"I'll save my praise until I actually see them flying, but I agree, the first one looks tremendous so far," Taera said, smiling for him. The truth was, the airships were only one of many concerns she had at the moment, but she needn't burden Elias with her worries. The man deserved his moment of joy after all he had been through.

He was a Pyrthinian-born metallurgist, the best Kal Pyrthin had ever seen, but Emperor Guderian had stolen him away three years prior and forced him into servitude to consult on the construction of Guderian's steam-powered war wagons. Guderian had never trusted him, and eventually—once the war wagon factory and smelters were operational—he was imprisoned. It was Makarria who had freed him, along with dozens of other prisoners Guderian had locked away in Lightbringer's Keep, including Lorentz. In Elias's case, Guderian had been right not to trust him. Quite by accident, Elias had discovered a valuable byproduct of the ether used to fuel the streetlamps of Col Sargoth and Guderian's smelting factories. After the flammable part of the ether was burned away, a portion of the exhaust was lighter than air itself. All one needed to do was filter out the noxious fumes and this alpha-ether, as Master Elias called it, could be used to levitate an airship far better than heated air could—which was how Siegbjorn's airship floated.

Elias had kept all this secret from Guderian, but happily divulged the details to Taera after returning to Kal Pyrthin. Taera saw the potential in Elias's discovery immediately. Unlike Makarria, Taera felt there was no going back to the golden age of the Five Kingdoms, where nature, sorcery, and manual labor worked in balanced harmony. For better or worse, the technology Guderian had brought about was here to stay, and Taera wasn't about to let Pyrthinia get left behind.

Nine months before, Master Elias had helped her engineers find pockets of subterranean ether in the southern reaches of the Barrier Mountains. It had taken two months to construct the mining apparatus to extract and transport the ether, and then it was a two-week long voyage for each massive storage cylinder by barge down the Highland River to the River Kylep and then to Kal Pyrthin where Taera's new smelting factory was being built. Initially, her plan had been to use the ether to power the smelting factory and start producing a new iron alloy Elias had designed. The ether would be far cleaner than the coal and ether mixture Guderian had used in his smelting factories, and the new industry would provide jobs for the struggling working class in Col Sargoth, not to mention a whole slew of superior iron products to export. The exhaust byproduct of the process, the alpha-ether, would simply be stored for a year or two until Taera was ready to start building the airships, a new industry in itself, she envisioned—a way to strengthen her navy and transport goods and people across the Five Kingdoms far faster than any mode of transportation the world had ever seen before.

But her plans had all changed the moment she spoke with Makarria through the scent-hound. The Old World Republic was on the verge of invading, and this time Taera vowed to hold the technological advantage. She had seen firsthand how Guderian's war wagons devastated her Pyrthinian cavalry and ground troops—she would not allow that to happen again. So she had ordered Elias to finalize his airship design for combat, and the incomplete smelting factory was put into service to burn off ether. It was a horrible waste of the flammable portion, as the factory forges were not yet operational, but Taera needed the alpha-ether for those airships. Her goal was to have seven of them completed within the week to set sail with her naval fleet and create a blockade from Spearpoint Rock out three hundred miles into the Esterian Ocean. Or six of the ships, at least, would head out with the navy. The other ship was designated for another, equally important, task.

"Is the shell going to give you problems where it's split around the outriggers?" Elias asked the shipbuilding foreman.

"Not at all. The shell has been reinforced with multiple layers of canvas, which we'll tack and seal with tar individually to the framework. It'll be plenty strong and leak proof, I'm certain."

Taera watched silently as the foreman pointed to where outriggers for the horizontally opposed sails protruded in a v-shape from both sides of the airship frame. *Unless Elias curbs his curious tongue, this is when I get in trouble,* she realized.

"And what of the ether rotor engines?" Elias asked. "The specs are finalized. You'll be able fit the apparatus in the aft portions of all the airships?"

Yep, now I'm in trouble.

The foreman shot Taera a sidelong glance. "Well, for this airship, yes, but it was my understanding that there was only one...."

"By my orders, only this first airship will have the ether-engine," Taera stated, saving the foreman from the awkward position he was in. "The other six ships will be powered only by their sails and the wind the stormbringers on their crew can provide." This was where Master Elias was uncomfortable. He had been agreeable to adding sails to his design when Taera initially told him her plan of manning the ships with stormbringers who could provide their own motive force, but that was only if there were sails *in addition to the ether engines*. Taera had purposely kept him out of the loop with her final design changes.

"But why?" Elias demanded. "Without the engines, the airships have no means of propulsion. They're nothing more than giant dandelions in the wind, at the mercy of nature or whatever squalls these feral sorcerers you've dug up can summon. Why wasn't I consulted on the design changes?"

"I apologize for keeping this from you, Master Elias, but time is of the essence and I didn't have time to assuage the concerns I knew you'd have. The fact of the matter is, the ether engines have proved to be rather time consuming. There's no way the builders can complete six of them in the allotment of time I've given them. I have full confidence in my stormbringers, though, and they are ready right now. They've been honing their skills with my navy, and already three of them are skilled enough to propel four ships at a time. And beyond that, the engines and ether tanks are simply too heavy. We've done the calculations—with the armament and crew I want these ships to carry, they can't carry the extra weight of the engine too."

"So that's it then. It's a matter of warfare."

Taera sighed. Elias reminded her much of her father, King Casstian. How many times had he chastised her for allowing herself to get caught up in her prescient visions before he had finally relented and declared war on Emperor Guderian? The thought of her father filled her with sorrow. She had not been with him in the Forrest Weorcan when he died at Wulfram's hands, but she had seen what was left of his body afterward; he deserved better. They all did, and that's why her decision now was so important.

"I understand how you feel about weapons, Elias," Taera said. "Willingly or not, you helped create Guderian's war wagons, and now I've made you an accessory in building my own warships. I promise you, though, I am not Guderian. I'm doing this to protect our people."

"So thought Guderian," Elias said, although not unkindly. "But it is your belief to hold, and as your vassal, I defer to you in this matter, Your Majesty. Please, just remember: in war, aggressors and defenders are not so clearly defined as historians would have us believe. The way of war is a dangerous path, no matter how good your intentions."

"Thank you," Taera said. "I will remember your words, and believe me when I say your counsel has been invaluable to me this last year."

Elias nodded and turned back to look over the airship. "So why this one then? Why will it have the ether engine?"

"Because this has another mission," Taera said, leaving it at that. Elias deserved an explanation about the airship design changes, but he didn't need to know about Taera's plans for each individual ship. This ship was not going to sea with the navy, but to Sol Valaróz to deliver a message. Taera didn't have the same ability Makarria had—the power to create a connection through the scent-hound—and that meant she had to use somewhat more conventional means for delivering messages. And this particular message was far more important than patrolling the Esterian Ocean, far too important to trust with a raven. Taera had had a vision the night before, and in it Taera had foreseen Makarria getting murdered by her own guard. A female guard Taera did not recognize. That was this first airship's mission: to go to Sol Valaróz and warn Makarria before it actually happened.

• • •

Natale looked away from the yellowed parchment for a moment and blinked the sleepiness from his eyes. How long had he been at it now? Hours? Days? His worktable, in a lamp-lit nook at the rear of the library, was littered with books and scrolls he had been poring over since Makarria had come to him. He'd been unable to answer her question, but promised he would discover the answer, if there was indeed an answer to be found, and he'd been in his books ever since. He'd missed at least one meal, and a night of sleep, he was fairly certain. He should have gone to rest hours ago; it was nigh impossible to be an attentive reader when exhausted, yet he had pushed on, and just now something had caught his eye.

He squinted his eyes one more time and then read again the name scrawled out in fading ink in the middle of the page he was holding.

Phthisicis-corporis.

It took him only a moment to translate in his head. *I've found it!* All thoughts of going to sleep were swept gone now, and he found himself half-standing up in his chair, reading over the rest of the passage. It was not much, he knew, but it was enough to get started—to *really* get started with his research. He had a phrase to work with now, a name to look up in his indexes. There would be other texts that mentioned *Phthisicis-corporis.* Particularly texts from the Old World. Makarria had been correct in suggesting he start his search there.

She needed to know at once, he decided, jumping up with a little hoot, but then he caught himself. She had given him strict orders when she had come to him. They could only speak in private, and only when she came to him. She had not said as much, but Natale surmised there was someone she was avoiding, likely the creature he was now researching. *Unfortunate that I can't tell the queen immediately, but perhaps it's for the best,* he decided, striding toward the bookshelf where all the ancient indexes were stored. *This way I can learn all there is to know about this creature before the queen returns. Pthisicis-corporis.* He let the name echo through his mind. He said it out loud to feel it on his tongue and lips.

"Pthisicis-corporis."

The literal translation was *body consumptive* but in the common tongue it translated better to *body thief.*

12
Through Fog and Fear

"I don't need eight hours of sleep," Fina said, pacing back and forth in front of the fireplace hearth in Makarria's bedroom.

Lorentz stared at Makarria from where he stood closer to the balcony door, but Makarria feigned not to notice, instead keeping her own gaze focused on Fina. Sitting beside Makarria, in the other cushioned chair facing the fireplace, was her father, Galen, who sat forward, leaning on his knees and listening intently.

"I insist, you need at least eight hours of rest if you're going to stay sharp," Makarria told Fina. "And you're the only female of the bunch, so it's settled—you sleep here in my chambers with me when I sleep at night. Lorentz, you'll take the night watch in the antechamber to guard us while we sleep, you'll attend war council meetings with me in the mornings, and then sleep in the afternoons. Same as Fina—at least eight hours of rest every afternoon." She looked lastly upon her father.

It had been tough on him this last year, living in the palace. The first several months he had simply recuperated from the wounds he'd suffered in Guderian's captivity, but once he regained his strength, he hardly knew what to do with himself. He couldn't read, knew nothing of politics or warfare, and so was of little use to Makarria in that capacity. But he was still her father and a workingman in the prime of his life. He was accustomed to toiling every day, as he'd done on their farm near Spearpoint Rock. The only thing that had made sense to Makarria was to put him in charge of the exterior doings on the palace grounds—everything from up-keeping the royal gardens to overseeing the care of the stable horses and the maintenance of the exterior buildings themselves. Galen had embraced these duties gladly, and excelled at them, but Makarria had also insisted that he take lessons in swordcraft and statecraft. He had objected at first, but Makarria pointed out that he *was* her royal father and there were certain expectations of royal males, just as there were of females. Men of noble families, even if by marriage, were expected to take on some pretence of being capable warriors and politicians, and so Galen obliged, eventually coming to enjoy it—the sparring more so than the studying. He was by no means a skilled fighter, but he was proficient, and he would do anything to protect Makarria, which was all she could ask for in her current predicament.

"Father," she told him, "you'll be my second bodyguard in the afternoons when Lorentz is resting. I'll be fine at night with only Lorentz on guard since I'll be here in my room with Fina, but in the afternoons, I may need to meet with retainers or my generals, so I'll want both you and Fina with me." Makarria paused and looked at the three of them, being certain to make eye contact with each, particularly Lorentz. "Do you all understand? With Caile gone, you are the only three I can trust with my safety. Captain Haviero is occupied protecting my mother, and after what happened in the council room, I can't trust even the Royal Guardsmen. The Old World is out to undermine my rulership, if not outright kill me. I don't completely understand what's happening, and until I do, you're all I have."

Fina and Galen nodded wordlessly, as did Lorentz. The man was unbreakable. If he found this misplaced trust in him odd—if he suspected that Makarria, in fact, did not trust him at all—he showed no sign. He was either oblivious to Makarria's suspicion, or he was playing along. It was a tricky game Makarria was playing, but she didn't see any way around it. Until she knew what she was dealing with, she felt safer keeping Lorentz close-by. If he'd really wanted her dead, he would have already done it. He'd certainly had ample opportunity. *He wouldn't have saved me from those attackers three days ago if he simply wanted me dead. So what then? What exactly is he after?*

"Well?" Makarria said. "Unless any of you have questions, we best get to it. Father, you're free to see to your own duties until this afternoon. Fina, Lorentz, we have two shorelines we need to figure out how to protect. My admirals are waiting in the council chambers."

• • •

It was a long, tedious council meeting, with much talk of troop numbers, ship numbers, travel time, and naval strategy. Makarria's generals and admirals knew their business, though, and as the hours passed, they moved toward consensus.

"So, are we all in agreement then?" Makarria asked, recapping their plans as much for herself as for them. "We send only a small detachment of cavalry to help defend Sol Cavarel, Sevol, and Lightbringer's Wall, keeping our entire eastern fleet here to blockade the Sol Sea? That leaves much of our southern border undefended, and leaves our Pyrthin allies alone to protect the Esterian Ocean."

"I don't see that we have any other choice," Admiral Biton, her topmost naval commander, said. "We have no idea what we'll be facing, but we *can* be certain any attack from the Old World will come at us by sea rather than by land. If we spread our eastern fleet too thin and the Old World comes at us en force, they could sail straight through us. It's been almost three hundred years since the Old World tried to invade the Five Kingdoms in earnest. They are not known as a warring nation with a large standing army or strong navy, but they have a massive trading fleet they can conscript, and they undoubtedly will have more sorcerers than us."

"And you agree, Lorentz?" Makarria asked. Throughout the meeting, he had been attentive and forthcoming when called upon, almost to the point that Makarria again began doubting her suspicion about him. But she forced herself to remember the man she had known for the last year—the fatherly figure who was quick to rebuke her for foolishness and quicker to lighten the mood with a well-timed joke or smile. Whatever he was, the Lorentz sitting here with her in this meeting was no longer that man. She hadn't seen him smile, let alone jest, since they'd returned from Khal-Aband.

"I do agree, Your Highness," Lorentz said. "The Old World Republic sees itself as an enlightened nation. It would reflect poorly upon their leadership to openly invade. It is more probable they will send smaller forces under the guise of peacekeeping envoys to aid our troubled nations. If you show a unified, strong defense to turn them away, I do not think they will risk outright warfare."

"It's done then," Makarria said. "Admiral Biton, you're in charge of readying our eastern fleet. Notify trading vessels of the impending blockade, and prepare our fleet. I want tactics and contingencies for facing adversaries wielding sorcery: stormbringers, firewielders, you name it."

"Yes, Your Majesty."

"And that leaves us at an impasse with the western fleet," Makarria said. "With no clear strategy or knowledge of where the Kingdoms of Norg and Golier stand in this matter, I have no choice but to keep our fleet on standby in Veleza. Once Caile arrives in Col Sargoth and speaks with the ambassadors there, we can decide whether to secure the Gothol Sea with their assistance. If they refuse...well we'll worry about that if and when it happens. Clearly, the Old World sees Sargoth, Valaróz, and Pyrthinia as the weak points: one kingdom still without a ruler and the other two with young women as rulers. We must prove to them there is no weakness here. That is all, gentlemen. Thank you. We'll meet again tomorrow."

Fina came to Makarria's side as the admirals and advisors gathered their things and filed out of the council room. She had sat at the perimeter of the room during the meeting, but she was never more than three paces away from Makarria at the meeting table and her eyes were ever vigilant. Apart from Makarria's mother and father, Fina was the only person who knew of Makarria's suspicions about Lorentz. Although wary, Fina had seen the wisdom in Makarria's decision to keep Lorentz nearby; she played along in pretending to trust him, but she was more on guard than ever, never letting Makarria out of her sight.

Outside the council chamber, Galen was waiting, right

on schedule.

"Good afternoon, Father," Makarria said, hugging him before turning to the counterfeit in their midst. "Lorentz, thank you for your help in there. I'm much relieved now that we've finally made plans for action. Go rest, now. I'll see you tonight when you're back on duty."

"Yes, Your Highness," Lorentz said with a slight bow of his head, and then he strode away without further ado.

Makarria couldn't help but feel a sense of relief watching him go. She felt tight as a bowstring having him around, constantly worrying what he might do, although she had not realized it until he was gone now and she could actually relax. It left her weary, but less scared, at least.

"Your Majesty," a courtier spoke, stepping forward from where he'd been waiting in the hall near the entrance to the council room.

Makarria hadn't even noticed him, but Fina had. She stood barring his way, a dagger in hand. The poor man shied away, but Makarria smiled to try and ease his discomfort.

"Yes, go ahead," Makarria told him. "Speak freely. No sudden moves and I promise Fina won't cut you."

"Uhm, yes, Your Majesty. It's Master Natale. He's requested your presence in the library."

Makarria thanked the man, a surge of excitement sweeping through her and pushing aside the weariness she'd felt just a moment before. She didn't even care that Natale had disobeyed her orders in summoning her. If he'd deemed it necessary to send a courtier, it meant he had found something important, and she wanted to know. Now.

"Please, lead the way," Makarria told the courtier, and she fell in line behind him with her father and Fina to make their way through the palace and down into the basement library.

"Well?" Makarria asked Natale when they got there. "Please tell me you've learned something."

Natale glanced up in a daze, nearly dwarfed among the stacks of books piled on his worktable. "Your Majesty! Yes. Yes, I have."

He made room at the worktable and motioned for her to sit.

"What we're dealing with here is a *pthisicis-corporis*, or in our tongue, a body thief." He slid a book in front of her and pointed to the words on the page.

"A body thief?" she asked, more interested in his explanation than the book.

"That's right, an ancient form of a sorcerer long thought to be extinct. The last full account I can find of them is from the 12th Century P.I., *post illuminatio* as the Old World reckons time, which is about five hundred years ago. These sorcerers were used in a great civil war, much the way dreamwielders were used here in the Five Kingdoms during the Dreamwielder War. From what I can gather, a *pthisicis-corporis* literally switches bodies with his victim. His consciousness inhabits your body, and your consciousness transfers to his old body."

Makarria turned around to look at Fina. "Does that sound right?"

"Yes, that's exactly what happened to me."

Makarria nodded and faced Natale again. "So the body thief can switch back and forth if it so chooses?"

"I imagine so, but that is not their normal mode of operation," Natale said. "When the switch happens, there's a moment of disorientation on the part of the victim, during which time the *pthisicis-corporis* typically kills the victim. So in a sense, the sorcerer wears your body as a mask, taking over your identity and killing you in your new body before you realize what's happening. You can imagine what sort of turmoil this could cause in a civil war with the bodies of public figures and generals being taken over by sorcerers with their own ulterior motives."

Makarria in truth was having a hard time imagining a war five hundred years ago; all she could think about was poor Lorentz.

"It's just as Taera dreamed it," she said. "Lorentz really is dead, not just ensorcelled or possessed as I had hoped. The body thief switched places with him in Khal-Aband and killed him right in front of me. Lorentz is dead."

The memory of the scene in Khal-Aband replayed over in her

mind. The shackled guard suddenly lunging toward her. Lorentz jumping between them to grab the guard's wrists. A brief struggle and then the guard's sudden confusion, causing him to fall back. *No, Lorentz's sudden confusion when he found himself in the guard's body, looking up at his own face.* And then the body thief had stabbed him. Makarria had yelled out for him to stop, but the body thief had murdered Lorentz right before her eyes. Lorentz had watched his own body stab him in the heart.

Natale put a sympathetic hand on Makarria's shoulder. "Yes, I'm afraid your friend is dead. I am sorry for that, but thankful he is all we have lost. It could be much worse. The turmoil the body thieves created in the Old World nearly destroyed the nation. They went rogue, it seems, intending to rule the realm themselves, breeding among themselves to bolster their numbers and placing their kind in key positions of power. Unlike other forms of sorcery, their power appears to breed true: a *pthisicis-corporis* begets another *pthisicis-corporis*. If two of the body thieves have a child together, their offspring is especially gifted, sometimes with additional powers, like precognition. Some ancient scholars conjectured the *pthisicis-corporis* was not human at all, but a different species altogether.

"In any case, the warring factions in the Old World had to put aside their differences and join together to defeat the body thieves. It was a horrible time. Hundreds of body thieves, including their children, were put to the torch, and a law was ratified to outlaw body thieves in the realm forever. The Old World's goal was to eradicate their race forever. Complete genocide. That was the idea, at least, and my understanding is that after that first extermination, while the Old World did not actively continue to seek out and destroy body thieves as Emperor Guderian did sorcerers here, there was still a policy—a promise—that the government and military would never use *pthisicis-corporis* for political purposes again.

"I *have* discovered a few allusions to them since then, though. A hundred years ago, the then king of the East Islands accused the Old World of using a body thief to infiltrate his court to remove trading tariffs. In a separate occasion, the sorcerer's guild here in the Five

Kingdoms prior to the Dreamwielder War had some sort of internal uprising, and a few accounts suggest there was a body-changing spy from the Old World that caused the turmoil. I've found enough to suspect that the Old World Senate, or certain factions of it at least, have not lived up to that law they enacted five hundred years ago, and have, in fact, been using body thieves as spies to influence foreign affairs to their benefit. What you have here in your court, Your Majesty, is a spy sent by the Old World to sow discord and undermine your authority."

"But not kill me?"

"No, I don't think so. If he, it, whatever we want to call the body thief, wanted you dead, I think he could have done so easily before now."

"It makes sense, I suppose," Makarria agreed. "The Old World doesn't want to appear like a warlike nation, so they strike with subterfuge. Weaken my kingdom and my authority in hope that I accept their aid, then become indebted to them, ultimately becoming their puppet."

Natale smiled. "So you have been paying attention to your history lessons after all?"

"Yes, not that it helps us a bit right now. We know what we have—a *pthisicis-corporis*—but how do we subdue him?"

"Are we even sure we have the right him?" Fina asked. "He must have switched bodies with Caile to accost you. Do we know he switched back?"

Makarria's eyes widened in sudden horror. She hadn't even considered the ramifications of the body thief in the incident with Caile. Caile had been innocent all along, she realized, and she had accused him of violating her trust and then sent him away. Or had she sent the body thief away?

Makarria's father cleared his throat. "I could be wrong, but if both Caile's and Lorentz's bodies are still alive, then the body thief must have switched back that night, right? The body thief couldn't risk letting Caile wake up in someone else's body and figuring out what was going on. If he had wanted to inhabit Prince Caile's body permanently, he would have killed Caile in Lorentz's body to keep his secret safe."

"You are exactly right, sir," Natale said. "Unless we find a dead body, we can safely assume the body thief is still wearing the same body."

"Yes, it has to be Lorentz," Makarria agreed, reassuring herself. She had spoken to Caile before sending him away, and despite her anger, she knew it was still him she was talking to. The same couldn't be said for Lorentz.

"If we're certain it's Lorentz, then, we have to kill it," Fina said. "You've played with fire long enough keeping him nearby, Makarria. Kill him. I've felt this creature's touch. It is nothing but pure evil. Kill it. Kill your friend's body if that's what it takes. He's sleeping as we speak. Send your soldiers in and kill him right now."

"That's not exactly lawful," Makarria said. "I can't expect my vassals to honor laws if I hold myself above them. And even if I wanted to, who's to say he wouldn't swap bodies with one of my guards? We'd end up killing an innocent man and the spy would still be in our midst, and now unknown to us."

"Let me go then. I'm quiet, and he can't use his magic if he's still asleep."

"No, we can't risk it. We have to be more cautious than that." Makarria pursed her lips and turned back to Natale. She knew what she was up against now, but that didn't make her task any easier. "In any of this stuff you read, did you find details about how the *pthisicis-corporis* switches bodies?"

"Not much, but enough to know that the body thief must touch its victim to make the change. *Tangere* is the expression in the Old World. *To touch*."

"A crossbow bolt to the heart then," Fina said. "If we go now, we can turn him into a porcupine where he lies on his bed."

"No," Makarria said. "I want him alive."

"Makarria," Makarria's father said. "You know me—I'm never one to suggest violence or murder, but I'm scared for you. I think Fina has the right of it. We can't risk having this creature near us anymore. Who knows what he has planned? Remove the danger so you can focus on repairing the damage he has done."

"That's exactly what I'm thinking about," Makarria said. "If I can capture this body thief alive, I then have evidence of the Old World's treachery. I can prove Caile's innocence, and my own. I will have fuel to unify the Five Kingdoms against the Old World's treachery. If we're smart about this, we can capture the spy and defeat the enemy in one fell stroke."

"We don't have time for long, drawn out plans," Fina said. "Lorentz sleeps only for a few hours before he's on duty again. You must act now."

Makarria sighed and took in all their advice. They had the right of it, she knew. Time was already against them, and who knew if she would ever have this chance to capture, or kill, the body thief again. Lorentz—the real Lorentz—had often warned her against making rash plans, of rushing into battle, whether it was on the field with swords and pikes or in the political sphere with pens and words. There was no way about it now, though. She had to act fast.

"All right, here's what we do then," Makarria said at last. "Fina, round up my best crossbowmen and a few stout guards from the dungeon. Also, summon the kennel master."

"The kennel master?"

"That's right. He'll have pole lanyards for capturing feral dogs. We're going to need his tools and his expertise if we're going to take our *pthisicis-corporis* without him touching any of us."

"Of course," Fina agreed. "I'll never say you're not bold, young queen."

"That's only half of my boldness. Father, you're coming with me. We're summoning the Brotherhood of Five, and we're going to confront Ambassador Mahalath. It's time the Old World knows we're on to their scheming."

13
Cornered Prey

Makarria had intended to summon all the ambassadors to the throne room, but when she learned they were already eating dinner together in the embassy wing of the palace, she decided to confront Ambassador Mahalath there instead. It would be less formal that way, which was good considering she had not yet captured the *pthisicis-corporis* and was not prepared to make official accusations against the Old World Republic.

There were six ambassadors in all sitting in the private dining hall, one each from the other Five Kingdoms—Pyrthinia, Sargoth, Golier, and Norg—and also the ambassador from the East Islands, in addition to Ambassador Mahalath from the Old World. They were sitting at the long dining table in the hall, along with a dozen or so of their personal servants when Makarria walked in, flanked by her father and a contingent of four soldiers she knew and trusted from their trip to Khal-Aband.

"Your Majesty," greeted the ambassador from Pyrthinia, a middle-aged man with a curly mane of brown hair and a giant hook nose. "If we had known you would be joining us, we would have waited to begin eating."

"It's quite all right," Makarria assured him, coming to a stop at the head of the table so they all could see her. "I'm not here to eat. In fact, I apologize for disturbing your meal, but my business could not wait. There is a spy in my court, gentlemen, and I wanted you to be the first to hear of it."

"A spy?"

She had everyone's undivided attention now, including Ambassador Mahalath's.

"That's right, and not just any spy. A *pthisicis-corporis*. A sorcerer who can steal bodies. He's killed one of my men already and inhabited his body, and he temporarily stole Prince Caile Delios's body to accost me the other night. You no doubt heard of the ordeal. It seems this spy is out to soil my honor and undermine my authority as queen."

Ambassador Mahalath had turned away to whisper something to his assistant sitting beside him, but he cleared his throat now and stood, bowing his head slightly to Makarria. "Queen Makarria, might I speak? The other ambassadors here have not likely heard of a *pthisicis-corporis* before, but I have, so I understand your implications. The *pthisicis-corporis* is a scourge from the Old World Republic's past. A race of beings—meddlesome tricksters—that steal a man's body and identity for nefarious purposes. At one time they were used as instruments of subterfuge and war, but they have long been outlawed in the Old World Republic, and I assure you, if indeed you have a *pthisicis-corporis* here, it is not here at the bidding of my nation."

"So I thought you might say, and yet the timing of his disruptive actions coincides with your arrival and Senator Emil's treaty proposal. The Old World stands to gain more than any other nation by creating chaos and instability that would force me to agree to your concessions. And Valaróz wouldn't be the first nation to accuse the Old World of using body thieves as spies."

Makarria glanced over at the ambassador of the East Islands, hoping the stout, dark skinned man knew his own nation's history better than she knew hers. Thankfully, his shrewd eyes picked up on her cue immediately.

"Indeed," he said. "King Aola made grievance to the Old World thirty-seven years ago. The Old World Senate denied the accusations, but there was ample evidence to prove the spy's guilt and he was executed. And though few know of it, one other such spy was captured and executed in the last decade, under the reign of

King Kana. The people of the East Islands have long been wary of the political manipulations of the Old World."

Ambassador Mahalath inclined his head again before speaking. "I understand your concerns. I promise you, though, I was sent here to work with the Five Kingdoms, and yes, the East Islands, in good faith to procure trade agreements that benefit all of our nations. I'm not out to manipulate the internal politics of your kingdoms. I myself have participated in senatorial inquiries to investigate claims of the unlawful usage of subterfuge and sorcerers, and I have discovered no evidence my nation has done anything wrong. As I said before, if indeed there is a body thief in your court, it acts of its own accord, as is their wont."

"We shall find out soon enough," Makarria said, not willing to risk pushing Mahalath further. "When we have the spy in custody, he will be questioned and I will get answers."

"I'm certain you will find the Old World acquitted of any responsibility," Ambassador Mahalath said. "Do proceed with caution, however, Your Highness. A *pthisicis-corporis* is formidable prey and not easily captured."

"Thank you for your concern. I'll return the sentiment. All of you, be careful. I ask that you stay here in the embassy wing of the palace tonight. Don't admit any unexpected guests. We are taking precautions, but it is possible the spy could escape."

"Or has already escaped," Ambassador Mahalath suggested. "Some body thieves of old were said to have the same powers as seers. It could be that your spy already knows you're coming."

Makarria stared at him, trying to read his intentions. Was he trying to scare her into making a mistake or was he honestly warning her for her own safety? The man seemed earnest enough, but she was unused to his accent and demeanor—he was impossible to read.

"As I said, we shall know soon enough," Makarria said, anxious to be away. She'd put her plan into action now, and there was no turning back. "I will hold a hearing in the morning, regardless of what happens," she told the ambassadors. "I request that you all be there."

They all nodded in agreement, and she turned away without another word, with her father and guards in tow. She had hoped to get something of use from Ambassador Mahalath and had gotten nothing, but it was of little consequence. She had accomplished her primary goal in making the existence of the spy known. Subterfuge held sway over her only when it was secret. The spy had already done its damage in tarnishing her reputation, and capturing him would only be half the battle. The other half was redeeming herself in the eyes of her vassals, and that began with making the truth public.

A dozen doubts popped to the surface of Makarria's mind, but she pushed them away. Her mind was made. She was committed. She thought briefly of the speaking stones she and Talitha had created. She could speak with Caile at any time. Or Talitha. Or both of them. But she was afraid of doing so. She was afraid their advice would weaken her resolve. *Trust your feelings,* Talitha had told her once. *You have a way of seeing the true nature of things.* And that's exactly what Makarria was doing now—trusting her instincts.

She made her way to the armory with her father and her guards. Waiting for her and standing at the ready were Fina, four crossbowmen, two dungeon guards, and the kennel-master and his apprentice, both of them equipped with long pole-lanyards. They waited still, however, for the last member of their party, the one person out of all of them that it had pained Makarria to summon. No one said a word as they waited. They knew their tasks. All they could do was wait.

When Master Rubino, the spokesman from the Brotherhood of Five, finally arrived in the armory a half hour later, Makarria sighed in relief. In a few hours more, it would have been time for Lorentz to resume his shift as Makarria's night bodyguard, and she absolutely did not want to confront him out in the open. The plan was to corner and subdue him in his own quarters—the anteroom of Caile's bedroom—but the plan also hinged on the presence of a representative from the Brotherhood. *Capturing the pthisicis-corporis is only half of it…*

"You summoned me, Your Majesty?" Rubino demanded, beads

of sweat running down his bald head and jowls despite the cool evening air.

Makarria swallowed her disdain for the man and spoke evenly. "Yes. Thank you for coming on such quick notice. You wanted proof of my innocence? Well, you're about to get it. I did not consort with Prince Caile. I was drugged and accosted by a spy who used sorcery to steal Prince Caile's body."

"What?" Rubino sputtered. "That's outrageous."

"Have you ever heard of a *pthisicis-corporis*, Master Rubino? It's what we call a body thief. They originate from the Old World, and we have one who has been hiding here in our court. The entire incident with Prince Caile was planned by this spy to sew discord in our kingdom, and now we're about to capture him and find out who sent him. I want you there as witness. You and I are both Valarion, Master Rubino. We must help one another for the good of our kingdom, because I promise you, this threat does not come from within."

Makarria's flattery had its intended effect. Rubino puffed up his chest and nodded solemnly. "Well, of course, Your Majesty. If there is indeed a spy in our court, I will make sure the people of Valaróz know about it. By the Five, we will clear your name."

"Thank you," Makarria said. It was exactly what she needed to hear: her most outspoken detractor would now spread the truth of Makarria's innocence to the people of Valaróz. "Come with me then, Master Rubino. And use caution. Stay well behind the guards."

She led the way out of the armory, down a long corridor to the central hall of the keep, and then up the stairwell to the second floor where she navigated a long series of intersecting corridors to bring them to Caile's private chambers. Unless he somehow knew of their coming, Lorentz would be in the anteroom, asleep on his slender bed.

Makarria wordlessly stepped aside from the door and nodded for the soldiers to take their positions. One of the jailors took hold of the door handle. Two crossbowmen took their places at his side, ready to rush in. The other crossbowmen were split to either side of the doorway as backup. The kennelmaster and his assistant stood at the ready behind them. Galen and Fina guarded Makarria, and behind them all, Rubino watched.

The jailor at the door looked to Makarria for her order. She closed her eyes and took a deep breath to calm herself. She had planned this the best she could, but she knew it might come to her having to use her power to capture the body thief. If so, she had to be calm and ready to slip into a dreamstate. She breathed out the anxiety inside her. Relaxed her shoulders and neck. Let the warmth of her meditative state wash over her. Only then did she open her eyes again and give the order.

"Now."

What happened next was a blur of moving bodies. The jailor threw the door open. The two crossbowmen rushed in, each taking aim toward opposite sides of the antechamber, only to find it empty. "Clear!" one of them barked, and the jailor ran through the anteroom to the interior door, opened it and stepped aside to let the crossbowmen pass through into the main bedroom. "Stay down!" one of them yelled. "Don't move!" said the other. The two other crossbowmen rushed in behind them. The four of them spread out along the perimeter of the room, their weapons trained on Lorentz, who laid propped up on his elbows in Caile's bed, watching them with an indifferent air.

Makarria watched it all from the corridor, detached, still halfway in her trance-like state.

The kennelmaster and his apprentice rushed in next, their pole lanyards held out before them, the rope loops at the ends ready to grab Lorentz around the neck and arms.

"Nice and easy now," the kennelmaster said. "Do this our way and you don't get hurt. Get down onto the floor. Kneel and put your hands behind your back."

"Today is not the day I kneel before any man," Lorentz said, sliding his feet from the bed to stand.

Makarria pushed her way past the jailor in front of her and stepped through the anteroom into the main bedroom. "Do it. We know what you are, *pthisicis-corporis*."

Lorentz stood there at the side of the bed, eying her for a long moment before responding. "And what, Your Highness? Now you're afraid of my touch?"

Adrenaline coursed through Makarria, stealing away her dreamstate. "I would show you mercy and hear what you have to say for yourself, body thief, but only if you do as I say. Disobey me and I will have you shot."

Lorentz narrowed his eyes and smiled. He began to kneel, and just when Makarria dared to hope it might all work, he leapt to the far side of the bed, and rolled away out of sight. One of the crossbowmen fired, but his bolt flew wide to stick into the far wall with a twang.

"Hold your positions," one of the others yelled. "There's no place for him to go."

That's when the bed was upended and Lorentz charged them from behind the protective shield of the mattress. Like fools, the other three crossbowmen fired their weapons into the down-filled mattress. Lorentz plowed ahead, unharmed. He knocked over the kennelmaster with the mattress and dumped it on top of him, its bulk pinning him to the ground. Then the first crossbowman was down, Lorentz's sword cutting through the flesh of his belly before he could reload his weapon.

Makarria closed her eyes, imagining Lorentz's limbs chained to his sides with his own skin, just like she had done with Warden Aymil in Khal-Aband. She did it fast, before Lorentz could get to the next guard, to kill him, or worse—touch him. She breathed out and exerted her will to push through the resistance to make it so…

…and something went horribly wrong.

She gasped as pain exploded through her body. She had felt pain like this only once before. *Is it Emperor Guderian? Back from the grave to staunch my magic?* She could barely open her eyes enough to see her hands before her, let alone take in her surroundings. Instead, she felt herself falling. She tried to hold her hands out to catch herself, but they would not respond. She watched the marble floor flying toward her face. And then nothing.

• • •

When consciousness came to her, it was only to be welcomed by more pain. She could not move her arms or legs. Her head throbbed. Her skull ached all around, like a crown of white-hot fire. *I cracked my skull open,* Makarria thought, remembering her fall and then all that happened leading up to it, like a bad dream. A sense of dread filled her. *Lorentz? Did we capture him? Did my magic work?* She willed herself to open her eyes and her vision slowly came into focus.

"He's coming to," someone said.

Makarria had to blink her eyes several times to believe what she was seeing. It was herself she was looking at, her own body that was staring back at her and speaking.

"He lives, it appears," the *pthisicis-corporis* said, wearing Makarria's body. "And we're all safe now thanks to this wondrous device."

The body thief reached out toward Makarria's head, or rather toward some sort of contraption that was attached to the top of her head. Makarria could just see the perimeter of it above her brow, a brass ring of some sort, connected to a larger framework out of her line of sight. Blinding pain shot through her head when the *pthisicis-corporis* touched it. It was like a thousand of Guderian's war machines, their cacophonous engines roaring in her head.

"The mind cage is screwed into his skull, blocking him from performing any sort of magic," the *pthisicis-corporis* said, turning away from Makarria. "He won't be able to switch bodies anymore, nor use whatever other powers he might have."

The body thief was talking to others in the room, Makarria realized, focusing through the reverberating thrum in her mind. Yes, there was her father. Fina. Master Rubino from the Brotherhood of Five. All of them listening to the body thief, thinking he was her. All of them staring at the real her, thinking what? Makarria knew the answer before she could even focus her eyes downward at her legs below her. She was wearing Lorentz's clothes. No. She was in Lorentz's body, and she was chained to the wall in the dungeon. In one of the dank cells, deep in the dungeon.

She tried to speak, but her tongue was foreign in her mouth, tripping over the gaps where Lorentz had missing teeth. *It's me, Makarria,* she tried saying, but the words came out as garbled nonsense.

The body thief turned back to face her and leaned in close. "Hush now, Your Highness," it whispered in her ear. "I'm you now, and if you start to fuss, I'll have your head."

Makarria began to tremble. She tried closing her eyes and going into a dreamstate, but white pain shot through her head again, from the backs of her eyes to the top of her spine. Whatever it was attached to her head made it impossible to concentrate.

"You look so surprised," the *pthisicis-corporis* whispered when Makarria's eyes opened again. "You really should have known better. I can make the switch whenever I make contact with another, and the touch needn't be physical. No, the mental touch is much more effective, in fact, so thank you for that, Dreamwielder. You just made my job all the more easy. And perhaps a little more fun as well."

14
Flames and Shadows

The four-mast galleon flying the blue and red pennon of the Old World Republic was given leave by the Pyrthin navy blockade and laid anchor in Pyrthin Bay at midday. Queen Taera was notified immediately and was waiting at the docks with a regiment of spearmen before the ship was even secured to the berths at the main pier. She had no intention of letting the Old World emissaries set foot on Pyrthin soil.

"Ahoy," the ship captain hollered, eyeing Taera and the soldiers warily as his men bustled about deck, battening down the sails. "We come on a diplomatic voyage. I bear representatives of the Old World Republic. They wish to meet with the Queen Taera."

"Then send them topdeck forthwith," Taera barked. "I am Queen Taera. I will speak with your representatives now and send you on your way, so don't let your crew get comfortable, captain."

"Aye," the captain muttered, and turned to speak to a crewman who ran off to disappear belowdeck.

"Permission to come aboard, captain?" Taera asked.

The captain looked from her to her soldiers crowding the docks, then back to her before nodding wordlessly and motioning for his men to lower the gangplank.

Once the plank was secure on the pier, Taera walked aboard with six of her guards and stopped to wait there at the portside of the ship, effectively blocking anyone else from embarking or disembarking. Custom, as well as common wisdom, would suggest that Taera should greet the emissaries in the palace, where she would welcome them from her throne. She was queen, after all, and they were coming to treat with her. On the ship, she was meeting them on their territory. Plus, she was exposed. Even with her regiment of spearmen, she was vulnerable onboard a foreign ship with a crew of seasoned sailors who were well accustomed to working and fighting on-deck. Her father, if he were still alive, would have called her a fool for even considering such a risk. Taera was many things, but she was no fool. She had already foreseen this day in a vision, so she knew she was safe. From physical harm at least. The Old World wasn't here to attack her. They were here to seduce her.

She was here to scare them away.

When the two emissaries—clearly not sailors, judging by the opulently fringed togas they wore—emerged from the stairwell beneath the poopdeck, they at least had the good taste to not look surprised to see Taera standing there. The taller of the two men had graying blond hair, and the corner of one side of his mouth was lifted in a perpetual sneer. The other man was dark skinned and wore a cylindrical cap upon his head.

"Your Highness," the man with the graying hair said, inclining his head. "You honor us with your presence. This is Ambassador Membai, and I am Senator Emil of the Old World Republic, endowed by the Republic Senate with the honor of sending our greetings and support to the new ruler of Pyrthinia."

"Save your flattery for someone else," Taera said. "I don't know how things work in the Old World, but here in the Five Kingdoms news travels faster than ships. I know you've visited Queen Makarria, and I know what it is you're out to get from me."

"Your Highness, we are not here to 'get' anything. We are here merely to speak with you. There was a time when Pyrthinia and the Republic were the closest of trade partners. Now that Emperor Guderian has passed, we would rekindle that relationship. We ask nothing of your kingdom that would be unrequited."

"Fine then. What is it you have onboard that you would like to trade?"

Senator Emil smirked, as if he had expected such a response

from Taera. "You mistake my words, Your Highness. We have nothing onboard at the moment. We are merely ambassadors, here to forge trade agreements."

"Then, by all means, state your terms. What commodities do you wish to trade? What tariffs do you wish to negotiate? I would hear them now and expedite matters."

"Well, Your Highness, the Old World needs assurances that Pyrthinia and its surrounding kingdoms are stable first. We are concerned about the instability in Sargoth. We are concerned about your friend Queen Makarria who was nearly assassinated before my eyes a few days ago. I will be forthright with you, as you clearly are not here for pleasantries. The Republic is offering financial and military aid. That is the commodity we offer you. Once the Five Kingdoms are secure, we will move on to negotiating other commodities."

Taera smiled at him. "Then I'm afraid I will have to pass, Senator Emil. Tell your senate they need to return to their scrolls and brush up on basic economic principles. Why would I want to trade for a commodity that I already have in surplus? Return home and tell your senate about the ether caverns that Pyrthinia has tapped in the Barrier Mountains. Tell them of the forges. And of our fleet of airships."

Taera turned her head to the left, and there they were, right on schedule: two flying warships closing in from the north faster than any sea-faring vessel ever could hope to attain. The Old World emissaries followed her gaze and gasped in surprise. Even having seen hot air balloons and perhaps even having heard of Siegbjorn's airship before, they were unprepared to see the spectacle of these ships—thin, sleek, and menacing in their silent approach.

The ships passed by overhead, and even though they were two hundred feet above the docks, the gale of wind summoned by the stormwielder pilots onboard the airships slammed into all of them standing there at sea level. Ambassador Membai had to hold both hands on his head to keep his cap from blowing away, and both his and Senator Emil's clothes whipped up around their legs.

It was a good show of force, just the way Taera had planned. In reality, these were the only two warships completed, but Emil had no way of knowing that.

"As you can see, Senator, military aid is the last thing we need, and our trading outlook is looking up, I must say, even without your aid. So I will bid you a good voyage. Return home and tell your senate there is no need to worry. I am in contact with Queen Makarria. We are monitoring the election in Sargoth. All is well. Return if you will when you have something worthwhile to trade."

Taera turned to walk away, but Senator Emil called after her.

"But, Your Highness. This treatment is uncalled for. We have just arrived. Our state status demands your hospitality. Send me away if you will, but at least accept Ambassador Membai as our official emissary. You will find him most accommodating and helpful."

Taera turned on her heel to level her steely gaze upon Senator Emil. "You demand nothing of me. Be gone, and return only when you have the authority to negotiate in good faith a trade agreement that doesn't involve your military presence and Pyrthinian concessions. And know this, Senator: any ships from the Old World discovered sailing in Pyrthin seas before then will be treated as vessels of war."

With that, Taera turned her back on the emissaries for good. She walked down the gangplank, back onto the pier, and toward Castle Pyrthin. "Captain," she barked out to the leader of her guards when they were out of earshot of the Old World vessel. "Send word to the shipyards. Our airship fly-by was a success. *Casstian's Breath* is to set sail for Sol Valaróz immediately with my message."

• • •

It had been a harrowing flight. With the storm bearing down on them, Siegbjorn had been forced to cross the Barren Mountains east of Talvera, taking a winding path between craggy peaks. Then the storm collided with the mountain range and the valleys turned into wind tunnels that sent the little airship careening recklessly close to the copper-toned rockfaces. As if that were not enough, next came the torrential hail, pummeling the air-filled hull above them and sounding like a thousand-horse stampede. Night descended then, and they were still in the thick of mountain maze, the wind and hail unrelenting. Caile could do nothing but retreat with Thon to the cabin with Talitha and silently hope the ship would withstand the beating. Siegbjorn was unperturbed, though, and when they finally poked through the eastern edge of the mountain range, all was calm, the airship no worse for the wear.

From there, it had been a smooth night's sailing over the Forrest Weorcan, and now only a few low afternoon clouds hung over the Gothol Sea as Siegbjorn piloted his airship to land in the open meadowland south of Col Sargoth.

"Thanks for getting us here alive, my friend," Caile told him.

The big man smiled in return, then turned to Talitha for his orders.

"Get some sleep if you can," she told him. "I'll return before nightfall."

And with that, Caile, Talitha, and Thon strode across the meadow to the south gate of the dark city: Col Sargoth.

It was the same gate Caile had used on his first trip to the dark city, but on that occasion he had been on horseback along with Lorentz and a small contingent of troops to consign themselves as hostages to Emperor Guderian. On that trip, the dark city was crowned in a halo of black smoke that rose up from the two smelting factories, one each at the north and south ends of the city. On that trip, Caile had barely escaped alive. This time Guderian was gone, the factories dormant, and Caile was wiser perhaps, but far less certain of himself. *Or maybe that's what wisdom is, realizing you have little control of anything in this world.*

The city was much the way he remembered it. The buildings were dreary, squat looking things, tarnished black with age and soot. Ether-fueled streetlamps burned even in the midday light, and the rutted tar-paved streets were crowded with a mixture of traditional beast-drawn carts and noisy steam-powered wagons and rickshaws. It took the three of them the better part of an hour to reach Lightbringer's Keep at the center of the city. The keep was a monstrous structure, far more imposing than the royal palaces in either Sol Valaróz or Kal Pyrthin. Its five black towers were twice again as tall as the watchtower in Lon Golier, the second highest structure in the Five Kingdoms.

Guards at the main entrance challenged their approach, but they recognized Talitha when she identified herself. She had been a regular fixture at Lightbringer's Keep for the last year, so nearly all the staff and guards knew her on sight. As they had discussed on the airship, Caile let Talitha do all the talking, first with the guards, and then with a porter who led them into the keep and showed Caile and Thon to their guest quarters in the dignitary wing. Talitha took no room.

"I'm merely here to introduce Prince Caile Delios to the council, and then I'll be on my way back to Issborg," she told the porter, who smiled at her warmly and entreated her to at least stay for the night.

It was encouraging to Caile to see that the porter liked Talitha. The houndkeeper and the other politicians had schemed to kick her out of the election council, but the working people of the keep genuinely admired her, Caile could tell. That gave him hope that they weren't on a fool's errand. More importantly, it gave him a sense of purpose, something to keep his mind off why he'd been sent away from Makarria, maybe even a way for him to redeem himself in some small way. *I'm here to keep the Old World at bay, but also to make sure the people of Sargoth get a king who is worthy of them.*

"I wish I could stay," Talitha told the porter, "But I've been away from my own people for too long now."

It was a lie, of course. Talitha would make a show of leaving the city and flying away with Siegbjorn, but Siegbjorn would drop her off as soon as night fell, and she would sneak back into the city. That was their plan, at least. Just like a year and a half before, she would take to the streets as a turnip vendor and learn what she could from the shadows and whispers in the streets of the city, while Caile would throw himself publicly into the lion's den that was the election council.

Thon, for his part, was simply introduced to the porter as Caile's attendant and so would share Caile's room. As they had discussed on the airship the night before, they made no effort to clean up or change into more formal attire. They simply dropped off their belongings in the room and met back out in the corridor, whereupon Talitha bid goodbye to the porter and then led the way to the other side of the keep and to the election committee hearings. The two guards standing at attention to either side of the closed doors stepped forward when they saw the three of them approaching, but took pause when they recognized Talitha.

Talitha gave them no opportunity to object or question her presence. "I'm escorting a royal observer. Make way and announce Prince Caile Delios of Pyrthinia to the assembly. Immediately."

The two guards exchanged unsure glances, then scurried to do as she bade them. They opened the double doors, and twenty-odd council members all turned their way at the sudden disruption.

"What is the meaning of this?" Natarios Rhodas demanded from his seat at the head of the table.

"A royal observer," one of the guards announced. "Prince Caile Delios of Pyrthinia."

"He is here at the bidding of Queen Makarria and Queen Taera," Talitha interceded, again, just as they had planned. She strode in halfway around the table, nearly brushing her hand upon the houndkeeper's shoulder as she passed, so that everyone there could see and recognize her. "Upon my dismissal as lord of proceedings, I traveled to Sol Valaróz and spoke with Queen Makarria. I urged her to return here and dissolve the election council, and to anoint a king of her own choosing if she would not rule Sargoth herself, but she instead gave the council her blessing. She applauds this council's decision to put a time limit on the proceedings. She asked only that Prince Caile be allowed to observe and provide his counsel along with the ambassadors of Valaróz and Pyrthinia."

"Well, this is quite irregular," Natarios Rhodas huffed.

"I care not," Talitha said, her face stolid, purveying a sense of insolence. "Accept him or don't. I have done my duty and mean to return to Issborg. Sargoth is your problem now."

With that said, she turned away and walked out the way she'd come. Caile smiled inwardly. She had played her part perfectly, distancing herself from him so that the houndkeeper and the council would be more willing to accept him. He had a reputation, he knew, as a young man who was hotheaded and petulant, but also strong enough to defeat Don Bricio and Wulfram. It was best to temper that reputation with some calming reason. Hence Talitha's act. And now it was his turn. He stepped forward from Thon, who stood nervously holding his hands behind his back.

"Council members, my deepest apologies for the interruption," Caile said, inclining his head slightly. "I know my intrusion is unorthodox, but so again is this council. I come here only to observe and to help as I may. It is not only the Five Kingdoms who watch these proceedings carefully, but also the Old World." Caile swept his gaze across the room, taking in the faces of all the council members, whom he had at his complete attention now. He knew a few of the ambassadors, but that was all. The houndkeeper, Natarios, was easy to identify by his position at the head of the table, as was Lady Hildreth, being the only female in the room. The two of them particularly glared at him, although maybe it was just his imagination.

"The Old World has called upon Queen Makarria," he continued, "offering military support to bring Sargoth under her dominion. She sent the Old World away, just as she did the sorceress Talitha. She has placed her trust in this council to choose a capable and strong king. I am merely here to make sure you have the opportunity to do so."

"Then by all means," Natarios Rhodas said, "sit down so we can proceed with our hearings."

Caile nodded and led Thon to the empty seats behind the ambassadors from Valaróz and Pyrthinia. He had stretched the truth a good deal, but better to have the council think he was on their side than openly opposed to them. And better to get the Old World's motives out in the open. He was certain there were Old

World sympathizers on the council. He had set the bait. Now it was just time to wait. Whoever came after him would be more in league with the Old World than the Five Kingdoms. *I just hope I'm ready for them.*

15
Faithful Servants

With Lorentz, the body thief, safely locked away in the dungeon, Fina slept like a baby for the first time in years. Dreamless and heavy. It was as if her body was making up for lost time now that she'd finally given it license to relax, now that she wasn't on constant alert for some thief or murderer in the night. *How many years has it been? Ten years, at least, protecting my girls from Don Bricio's cronies. Then it was Khal-Aband, fretting every echo, every footstep in the dark corridor, waiting for the guards to come punish me. And the creature—the body thief—who stole my own skin and then gave it back, just to torture me. But he's gone now, thanks to Makarria.*

Fina would have slept right on into the afternoon if Queen Makarria hadn't awoken her. She was abashed to be awoken so, and apologized profusely, but Makarria was not angry with her. In fact, the queen, too, seemed to be more at ease. The two of them lounged about in Makarria's room, eating the breakfast the servants brought to them, content to eat in silence and enjoy the view from the balcony overlooking the city and harbor below. *It should be her mother spending this time with Makarria,* Fina thought as she nibbled at a pastry stuffed with spices and lamb. *But a good ruler must make sacrifices, I see now, and I'm glad to share this moment of peace with the girl. She's been through so much these past few days…*

The morning hours ebbed away, and finally Fina felt compelled to remind Makarria of her day's responsibilities. "Your Majesty, you should begin preparing. The ambassadors will be expecting you in the throne room within the hour."

"Right, of course," Makarria remarked absently. "Send my handmaidens in to dress me."

Fina did as she was commanded and waited obediently in the anteroom until the queen was ready, and then she escorted her down to the sitting room adjoining the throne room. Just four days earlier, the young queen had almost been murdered there, but it was tidy now, the blood scoured from the floor and the room furnished with new carpets and chairs. Scented candles flickered warmly in the sconces along the wall.

"Are they ready for me in the throne room?" Queen Makarria asked, adjusting her gown. The poor girl never seemed to be comfortable in her royal garb.

"Let me check, Your Majesty," Fina replied, and she slipped the door open a crack to peer into the throne room. It was as packed to full capacity with retainers, aristocrats, and representatives from all walks of life in Sol Valaróz. Fina could make out among the ranks Makarria's parents, Prisca and Galen, guarded closely by Captain Haviero. She also spied in the forefront the ambassador from the Old World, and, of course, that pig, Master Rubino. Fina understood why Makarria had summoned him to witness Lorentz's capture, but it still sat wrong with her. Fina knew men of his ilk well. Men who outwardly scorned women and proselytized the sanctity of female chastity always did so to compensate for their own perversions. *What is your perversion, Master Piggy?* Fina mused. *Little boys? Animals? Or maybe you simply can't perform, and that's why you hate women.*

"Well?" Makarria asked.

Fina let the door close and turned back to the queen. "It looks like all is ready, Your Majesty. Are you ready? Shall I have the crier announce you?"

"Yes. Let's get this nonsense over with."

Fina opened the door fully this time and nodded at the herald who stood waiting on the other side.

"Her majesty, Queen Makarria Parmenios!"

Makarria pushed her way past Fina and the herald, and took a seat at her throne with little grace, looking as if she were some common wench taking a seat in the mess hall. Something seemed awry to Fina, but she dismissed the thought. *She's just nervous,* Fina told herself, following in Makarria's wake and taking up her place behind the throne.

"People of Valaróz," Makarria spoke, wasting no time. Her voice, at least, was clear and strong. "You come here today because you have heard stories. Stories of a queen and a prince. Stories that titillate your senses and send you off tittering to your neighbors. Did she really do it, you have asked yourselves. Did our queen lie down to rut with the prince from Pyrthinia?"

Whispers and surprised murmurs filled the courtroom.

What in Vala's name is she doing?

"Well, I come here today," the queen continued, "to tell you that I did not. It was all a ploy. A carefully orchestrated scheme. We have had a spy in our court, a clever trickster of the most devious sort. A brilliant creature who staged a good number of misdeeds in order to undermine my authority in your eyes. You will be happy to know that, as of last night, that meddlesome trickster has been captured and, as I speak, rots in the dungeon beneath our feet. So leave here well-assured, my people, all is right once again. You can trust me. My maidenhood remains faithfully intact. Return to your women. Your wine. Whatever diversions you hold dear, and leave the ruling to me."

Makarria stood from the throne and bowed extravagantly. The crowd began murmuring again, unsure of what they had just heard, uncertain of whether they were meant to stay or go.

Fina's hair stood on end at the base of her neck, and she edged forward instinctively. *This is not right.* In the front ranks of the crowd, Master Rubino was scowling and gesturing frantically at the queen.

"Your Majesty," Fina hissed. "You're supposed to let Master Rubino speak. As witness."

The queen shot a sidelong glance at Fina and nodded with a grin. "But wait, my people! Do not leave yet. I have a witness. Our esteemed Master Rubino stands as a witness. He would corroborate my story."

Master Rubino had the presence of mind—or pomposity—to ignore the crowd's tittering and stepped halfway up the dais to pump up his chest and face the assembled court. "Good people of Sol Valaróz, it is I, Master Rubino, speaking on behalf of the Brotherhood of Five. I was summoned last night by the queen to witness the capture of a spy. While I cannot attest firsthand to his powers, I saw well enough that he was an enemy intent on killing the Queen. Indeed he killed one soldier and injured another trying to get at her. After having bore witness to this, and hearing the evidence Queen Makarria provided, I have no doubt as to the perversions of this spy. Your Queen is innocent, a victim of this perversion, as so many are, which is why the Brotherhood of Five will be bringing forth to the queen in the days and weeks to come a series of proposed morality laws. It is our goal to wipe clean the stain of perversion on this great city."

"Thank you, that is quite enough," Queen Makarria interrupted, stepping down from her throne to clap Rubino on the shoulder. "I've just told my people they are free to celebrate. Let's not dampen their spirits. Be gone, my people! You are dismissed. Go out, drink, and know one another!"

There was no quieting the crowd this time. The throne room filled with their animated voices, mixed with laughs and a few indignant shouts in Makarria's direction. Fina stared at the queen, stunned. Was this really Makarria? Had something happened in that room with the body thief? *But he never touched her, never even got close.* Fina didn't know what to think, but she knew the hearing was turning into a spectacle and she needed to get the queen out of there before she did more damage.

"What is the meaning of these theatrics?" Master Rubino was sputtering, stepping self-consciously away from the queen's grasp. "You undermined me in front of the entire court!"

"Just as you did to me a few days past," the queen remarked, tapping him on the tip of the nose with her pointer finger. "Remember yourself, fat man. I'm the queen, and if you continue to be bothersome, I'll be happy to relieve you of that jowly monstrosity you call a head. Now get out of my sight."

Fina could hardly believe what she was witnessing. "Your Majesty, we best exit the throne room. Now!" The queen obliged and retreated back behind the throne to the adjoining sitting room.

"Are you feeling well, Your Majesty?" Fina asked when the doors were safely closed behind them.

"Fantastic. Couldn't be better. Why do you ask?"

Again, the hair on Fina's neck stood on end. She picked her words carefully. "Well, Your Majesty, because of the scene you just caused. I don't mean to be presumptuous, but I thought the whole purpose of today's hearing was to not only clear your name, but also put the blame on the Old World as the likely perpetrators."

"Bah," the queen replied waving one hand at her dismissively. "The *pthisicis-corporis* is captured now. That's all that's important."

"And the threats from the Old World? The election in Col Sargoth?"

"That's quite enough," the queen snapped. "You're my bodyguard. Nothing more. You think I don't worry enough about these matters without you harping on me?"

Fina lowered her eyes. "My apologies, Your Majesty."

"No need to apologize. Today is all about regaining good spirits. We've addressed the court, now let's go visit our injured compatriots. The kennel master and another guard were injured last night, if I'm not mistaken. Where will we find them?"

"In the infirmary, Your Majesty."

"Excellent," the queen said, starting for the rear exit of the room, but just then the main doors opened behind them to admit Prisca, Galen, and Captain Haviero.

"Makarria," Prisca said, concern plainly written on her face. "What's going on? Are you all right?"

The queen pushed her mother away. "I'm quite fine, Mother, and I know exactly what I'm doing, so don't be bothersome. You know the rules. It's too dangerous for us to be together like this, so off with you to your room. Captain Haviero, if you would?"

The captain nodded and motioned for Prisca and Galen

to leave.

"Makarria," Galen objected, but the queen waved him away.

"Go! Both of you! I have people to see. Important things to do!"

Fina bit her tongue, her mind scrambling for what she should do. She needed to get to the dungeon to question Lorentz, the prisoner, she knew, but at the same time she didn't dare leave the queen alone. Something horrible had happened, and until she could verify her suspicions, she had to make sure the queen—whoever she was—did not ruin everything.

• • •

In his dream, something was dripping. A leaky roof. Or a loose bung on a cask of wine. *Drip. Drip. Drip.* Each one a loud plunk on the stone floor. Each drip louder than the previous. He tried to make out his surroundings, but all was gray and formless, except the floor, which was liquid stone, rippling with each drip, rising ever closer to his prone form. He tried to get up, but was paralyzed. All he could do was crane his neck to see the black lake rising around him. *Drip. Drip. Drip.* Was it water? Wine? Or something else? *Drip. Drip. Drip.*

Yes, something else. Blood, he realized with sudden panic, and he awoke with a gasp.

The approaching footsteps stopped and Natarios Rhodas looked up from his bed to see two dark figures standing over him.

"Stay back!" Natarios yelped, scurrying beneath the covers to cower against the wall on the far side of the bed. "Who's there?"

Without warning, one of the figures lunged forward and grasped Natarios by the ankle. Natarios screamed and kicked, but the man was strong. He yanked Natarios toward him and punched him in the side, right below the ribs. Natarios gasped in pain and curled up into a ball, still clinging to the edge of the bed.

"We're friends of a friend," the other man said. "Here with a friendly reminder about the election. You were put in place to perform a certain task, and that's to make sure Kobel wins the throne. This other business—whatever you spoke to Lady Hildreth about, and the sudden arrival of Prince Caile—will not be tolerated."

Natarios didn't recognize the man's voice, but it was obvious enough these two were hired muscle. Even reeling in pain, Natarios knew exactly who had sent them. "Tell Rives the meeting with Lady Hildreth was nothing. She has some influence with the cavalry. I was just feeling her out to find her thoughts on the war wagon factories. I wanted to make sure she wouldn't interfere once Kobel is elected. And the prince—I had nothing to do with that. I had no idea he was even coming. Tell Rives. Please, you don't need to hurt me."

"No more games," the man said.

"No more games," Natarios agreed with a glimmer of hope that the ordeal was over. But no. The silent ruffian grabbed him again and twisted Natarios onto his stomach, only to punch him again, this time in the opposite kidney. The pain was blinding, stabbing deep into his abdomen and stealing away his breath. Natarios sobbed, and tears ran down his face to wet the crumpled bed sheets beneath him. When he finally caught his breath, the men were gone.

Bastards! he swore silently after them, too afraid to actually yell. He pushed himself up and lit a candle. Even the dim light it emitted was comforting, and within a few moments he poured himself a glass of wine, drank deeply, and felt his wits return to him. He should have expected something like this, he knew. It was foolish to have not taken precautions, particularly after his talk with Lady Hildreth. *At least I know the others view me as a threat now,* he consoled himself. He would post guards at the tower entrance below, and perhaps a personal bodyguard was in order, too. *Rives is a fool to think he can intimidate me into being his lapdog. If he wants to play rough, it will only be worse for him. I may not have as much gold at my disposal to hire muscle, but there are other ways to make a man suffer.*

16
Clockwork Evil

It took every ounce of willpower for Makarria to raise her head. The contraption attached to her skull—or Lorentz's skull, as it was—had slowly weighed her down to a limp heap hanging from the shackles against the dungeon wall. It wasn't so much the physical weight of the device as it was its unrelenting ticking. At the edge of her vision, near the center of her forehead, a turnkey protruded from the contraption. As it slowly spun, the unwinding of springs and clicking of gears reverberated through her head. At first, she had felt acutely the four screws embedded into her skull that secured the contraption to the crown of her head, but now all she sensed was one pulsating mass of pain where her mind should be.

She had lost count of how many times she tried to slip into a dreamstate. The clicking, the whirring, made it nearly impossible to do so. One time, maybe twice—she couldn't recall anymore—she had almost touched her power, and it had been the same as that first time after the switch when the body thief had awoken her: a cacophony of metallic clanging and screeching in her mind, like she were inside the inner workings of a bell tower pealing out a song of chaos. Her mind would go blank, and when she awoke from the stupor it was only to be welcomed again by the clicking and whirring. She couldn't sleep. She couldn't dream. All she could do was remind herself to breathe in and out. Guards that she didn't recognize came occasionally and poured tepid broth down her gullet with a funnel. In between the gagging and swallowing, she would cry out to them.

"Help me. I'm your queen! Makarria." The words came out

barely intelligible, garbled by her pain and the foreign feel of her tongue rubbing against the gaps of missing teeth in her new mouth.

The guards would only laugh at her. "Nice try. You think us fools?" they'd ask, and if she persisted, if she pleaded them to summon Fina or her mother, they'd punch her in the stomach, sending her undigested broth back up the way it came. The last time they'd come, she'd said nothing. She just focused on her breathing, and spoke to herself, trying to drown out the machinery by repeating over and over the names of her friends: Mother, Father, Caile, Taera, Talitha, Siegbjorn, Natale, Fina… Someone, please come save me. Mother, Father, Caile…

• • •

Lord Derek droned on for what must have been the third straight hour about the noble lineage of House Derek. Caile groaned inwardly. *Who cares if his great, great grandmother was the second cousin to some lord descended from Sargoth Lightbringer? He could be a direct heir to the Lightbringer himself, and Lord Derek would still be an arrogant moron, unfit to lord over a pigsty, let alone a kingdom.*

The past three days had been exactly the same. The hearings were nothing more than a well-orchestrated show, posed to stage Lord Kobel as the only viable candidate as the hearings came to a close in the coming days. Now that Caile saw what a farce all of it was, he was angered, exasperated, and, more than anything, overcome with a sense of helplessness. After his arrival and little speech about the Old World, he had been certain that someone would come to him, whether it be to gain his support or gauge his threat as an adversary. But nothing. On top of that, his private entreaties to the ambassadors from Golier and Norg to secure the Gothol Sea with a heightened naval presence had been for naught. Ambassador Rives had scoffed at the notion the Old World might invade, scoffed a little too readily in Caile's estimation. The ambassador from Norg didn't scoff at the prospect of invasion through the Gothol Sea, but rather was forthright in saying his nation didn't care. The Kingdom of Norg's primary concern was with maintaining naval dominance of the Norg Sea.

What made Caile feel more helpless than anything else, though, was that he had heard nothing from his friends. Siegbjorn's airship was gone three days now, yet Caile still had not heard from Talitha. Had the northman dropped her off as planned? Was she able to sneak back into Col Sargoth during the first night? The second? Had something gone wrong? *And why haven't I heard word from Makarria?* Caile had foregone dinner in the mess hall and waited in his room each night since arriving, holding his orange marbled speaking stone in his lap, waiting, hoping that Makarria would contact him. If nothing else, he told himself, she would want to check in to learn how the election was progressing. But again, nothing. Had something happened to her? Or was she still too disgusted with him? Twice Caile had held his orange speaking stone to his face. Twice he had closed his eyes and concentrated on the image of Makarria's yellow speaking stone, and both times he had changed his mind. He couldn't bring himself to call out her name. *What would I even say to her? That I've accomplished nothing?*

He'd contemplated calling out to Talitha's stone that morning before the hearings began, but the sorceress had made him swear to do no such thing before she had left. "Who knows where I might be hiding," she had told him. "The last thing I need is your voice coming out of my rucksack and giving me away. Just wait. I will contact you if need be."

That left him on his own, with only Thon to help. *And I'm tired of waiting around,* he decided as Lord Derek droned on. *It's time to poke the hornet's nest and see who comes flying out.* The houndkeeper couldn't be working alone, he knew, and everything that had transpired so far pointed to the Old World. They had to have an agent in Col Sargoth bribing or intimidating people into voting for Kobel, and if Caile could figure out who—if he could eliminate that agent—then just maybe he could turn this election into a fair contest.

When the houndkeeper finally banged his gavel and adjourned the day's hearing, Caile waved for Thon to follow him, and made straight away out of Lightbringer's Keep to the northern courtyard.

"Where are we off to?" Thon asked, half-jogging to keep up.

"The northern smelting factory to inspect Guderian's war wagons," Caile told him, not bothering to keep his voice down as they exited past the guards at the gates into the streets of Col Sargoth. *If someone is watching us and hears, all the better.*

"I thought the factory was locked down and guarded by the cavalry," Thon said. "Will they let us in?"

"I'm an official emissary from Queen Makarria. They'll have to."

Thon shrugged, seemingly content to trust Caile and enjoy the walk through his home city. Caile led the way north, sticking to the main thoroughfare, dodging between carts and steam-powered rickshaws. Despite not having a king in place, the city actually seemed to be thriving more than when Caile had last been in Col Sargoth. At least it was more lively. Under Emperor Guderian's dominion, the city dwellers had lived and worked in muted fear. By night, the taverns were full enough of gests and laughter as people lost themselves in spiced grain spirits, but in the daylight hours people had gone about their business with little joy. It was different now. There were more people in the streets, and there was an excited energy about them, even among the poor beggars, which they saw in increasing numbers as they walked farther from Lightbringer's Keep into the industrial borough alongside the Sargothian River. The buildings became smaller and more ragged, the people poorer, even those who weren't beggars. The residue of the dormant smelting factory became worse, too. The wood paneling walls of the ramshackle homes were covered in black soot. The side streets weren't paved like the main thoroughfare, but rather consisted of hard-packed dirt, wet and dark with oil stains. The air reeked of rotten eggs.

"Sargoth's hairy arse," Thon said. "I remember the river borough being a bit rundown, but it was never this bad."

"It was probably worse when the smelting factories were still running," Caile replied. "When I was here last year, you couldn't even see the sky because of the smoke and soot, and that was from

Lightbringer's Keep. I can't imagine how bad it was here."

The smoke stacks of the smelting factory loomed ever larger as they drew closer to the river and the rundown houses gave way to warehouses. The whistles and shouts of sailors and dockworkers filled the air, carried on the chill breeze coming off the Sargothian River. The cold air did nothing to staunch the smell of tar and rotten eggs, though.

Caile and Thon came to a halt as they passed a warehouse and the smelting factory itself came into view. It was not so different from the surrounding warehouses in size or shape, but it was made of brick rather than wood, and it had smoke stacks: three of them, protruding from the crestline of the steep-pitched roof and towering a hundred feet into the air. *This is where they were made,* Caile told himself. *The war wagons that cut down my countrymen outside Lepig.* Caile had killed Wulfram on the rain-soaked battlefield that day, but along with the fallen sorcerer, thousands of Pyrthin cavalrymen also died, mowed down by the war wagons like wheat beneath the scythe. The sounds of men and horses screaming still haunted Caile's dreams.

With a deep sigh, Caile pushed aside the memories. "The place is ass-ugly from the outside," he remarked. "Let's see if it's any nicer on the inside, shall we?"

"I'm doubtful," Thon replied, but the two them strode forward nonetheless.

The giant bay doors were closed and chained shut, but two armed guards stood at attention in front of the nearby walk-in doors. Their horses were nowhere to be seen, but it was clear by their armament that they were Sargothian cavalrymen, the elite fighting force of the Sargothian army. They carried round shields and flails with spiked balls, and wore black surcoats emblazoned with the symbol of Sargoth—a white sun radiating five shafts of light—over the top of their light armor.

Caile made straightway toward them and handed over a letter from inside his doublet.

"I am Prince Caile Delios, emissary of both the Kingdom of Pyrthinia and the Kingdom of Valaróz. I have been charged by

Queen Makarria Pallma, Dreamwielder, Merciful Conqueror of the Kingdom of Sargoth, to inspect the war wagon factory and ensure the Sargothian cavalry has kept it secure."

The guard with the letter gave no more than a cursory glance at Makarria's note.

Good thing, Caile thought. *All Makarria had time to write was a vague letter proclaiming me her official emissary. It says nothing specifically about the factory.*

"You'll have to speak with the commander," the guard said, handing the letter back to Caile.

"I don't have time to wait for the commander to stroll on over from the keep, soldier," Caile said. "Summon whoever is in charge here on the premise. I know Queen Makarria left more than two cavalrymen and a couple of chains around the door to secure the factory."

"She left an entire squadron and the commander himself."

"The commander is stationed here?" Caile asked, surprised. That was a good thing as far as the security of the facility went, but not such a good thing for Caile's prospects of talking his way inside. "Well, why didn't you say so? Send for him immediately."

The soldier frowned at Caile's flippant remark, but did as he was told, slipping through the doors into the factory and leaving his comrade alone to guard the exterior. Within moments, the soldier returned with a similarly adorned man, tall and lithe, with narrow shoulders, but long, lanky arms beneath his black surcoat. He carried in the crook of one arm an open-faced helm with ram horns, and the dark hair atop his head was trimmed short, little more than a week's stubble after having shaved it clean.

"Prince Caile of Pyrthinia, this is Commander Buell of the Sargothian cavalry," the soldier introduced them.

Commander Buell lowered his head in a poor semblance of a bow. "Your Majesty. I'm told you brought a letter from Queen Makarria authorizing an inspection of the facility?"

Caile handed over the letter. "Commander, you'll find the writ pronounces me as Queen Makarria's emissary, with full authority to act on her behalf."

"It says nothing about inspecting this facility," the commander said, glancing over the letter.

"Queen Makarria couldn't possibly be expected to anticipate every task I need to undertake while overseeing the election. Perhaps you haven't heard, Commander, but a new king of Sargoth will be elected in eight days, and the Old World is watching the proceedings very carefully. If anything goes wrong with the election, if they sense any sort of civil unrest—if anything happens to this factory—then they *will* attack the Five Kingdoms."

Commander Buell snorted. "What does the Old World care about a kingdom two thousand some odd miles away?"

Caile took pause. It was foolish of him to speak so cavalierly of the Old World to this man. It was one thing throwing names around at a bunch of politicians, but what if the Old World had already gotten to the commander, too—perhaps bribed him or threatened him? Commander Buell was a man who could do something about Caile's meddling. *Too late now,* Caile decided, almost hoping for violence so he would have a clear-cut enemy to fight.

"Well Commander, you can ask the Old World yourself when they invade in a week, or you can let me inspect this facility," Caile said. "They've already made demands of Queen Makarria. She's turned them away, but only her promise that Sargoth is secure keeps them from attacking. It's our belief they're after the war machines, or at least the steam technology to make them. That's why I was sent here with such haste. I need to see the factory, Commander. I need to confirm Queen Makarria's faith in you that the machines are secure."

Commander Buell pursed his lips and glanced from Caile back down to the letter, and then up to Thon, just noticing him for the first time. His eyes narrowed. "And who's this with you?"

"Thon Hilliard," Thon answered. "One of your countrymen."

"More than a mere countryman," Commander Buell said. "I know you."

Caile shifted his weight so the hilt of his sword moved clear from the edges of his doublet. *It's looking more like a fight with each passing moment. What did you do to get sent off to Khal-Aband, Thon?*

"Yes, I was a sergeant in the cavalry once," Thon told the Commander, righting himself to stand stiffly at attention.

"And you were taken prisoner by order of Emperor Guderian himself. I remember well. Your captain was commanded to restrain you and hand you over to Guderian's private guards. We were not told why, and we never saw you again. We thought you dead."

"Queen Makarria and I freed him from Khal-Aband," Caile said, still unable to read Commander Buell's demeanor toward Thon, still ready to fight if need be. "He and another prisoner were the only survivors."

"Khal-Aband actually exists? I suppose I shouldn't be surprised, not when it comes to Guderian's paranoia." The Commander stepped forward and Caile tensed, but the tall man merely smiled and clapped Thon on the shoulder. "I'm glad to see you survived, soldier. I would be happy to discuss reinstating you back into the cavalry if you so desire."

"Thank you," Thon said, "but I owe Prince Caile and Queen Makarria a debt for saving me. I am in their service now."

Caile smiled, relief washing over him. *He was a good soldier after all, just like he said.* "Commander, if all goes well over the next week and we avert war with the Old World, then Thon is free to do as he pleases and rejoin you if he likes."

"All right, but make sure to keep him in one piece for me," Commander Buell said. "Let's give you the grand tour, shall we?"

The two guards threw the doors open and Caile and Thon walked into the smelting factory behind Commander Buell. The interior of the building was expansive, but there was little wasted space. A massive forge dominated the area nearest the entryway, a potbellied furnace larger than some castles Caile had seen. It was fed by an array of black iron pipes thick as tree trunks and an iron-track conveyor belt as wide as the city streets outside. Caile spied two more identical ones farther back in the factory.

"The raw ore from the mines is purified into iron ingots in

the southern factory," Commander Buell said. "This is where the second stage of smelting occurs and, of course, where the actual construction of the wagons takes place. The pipes you see are for the ether, which fuels the smelters. The belts feed the coal and ingots into the furnaces. From there the liquid alloy that forms flows downstairs. Up here, everything has been secured since Guderian's death—shut down and locked up. The only dangerous component topside would be the ether storage tanks, which are in the stockyard out back. They too are sealed, secured, and guarded day and night. If anyone managed to get past the sentries outside the wall surrounding the stockyard, they'd still have to scale the wall and face the sentries inside the stockyard before they could get anywhere near the tanks. By then, the sentries would have raised the alarm and the attackers would have an entire regiment of cavalrymen to contend with."

Caile recalled his own tank he had constructed on the outskirts of Lepig. That tank had been made of wood and stored five thousand gallons of naphtha. It was meant to fuel the hydraulic cannon Caile used to combat Emperor Guderian's war wagons. In the end, it had been successful, but Caile had been terrified the entire time that Sargothian archers would set it aflame before the hydraulic cannon could ever be put into action.

"What are the ether tanks made of, Commander?" Caile asked. "Are they flammable?"

"They're made out of the same iron alloy as the war wagons. They're not flammable. Sustained heat could cause the ether to expand and the tanks to explode, but the stockyard is equipped with an equal number of water tanks, ready to extinguish any flames. My cavalrymen are trained to do exactly that."

Caile nodded and followed after Buell, who led the way toward the center of the factory. In the open area between the first two forges, an encampment of sorts had been constructed. Nearly a hundred cavalrymen mulled about, playing dice at square tables, sparring with wooden practice flails, nibbling food at the cook stations, or napping in their cots.

"My best regiment is stationed right here in the factory," Buell said. "The men are on rotation and get two days leave every week. Otherwise, they are here on call, even when not on patrol. I myself have made it my interim headquarters. We have a fully stocked larder and armory. We've built a stable and a riding arena in the loading yard near the river docks to conduct our practice drills."

Thon brightened at the mention of the armory. "Commander, I know I'm not part of the cavalry—not anymore, at least—but do you suppose you could spare a flail? Prince Caile was kind enough to lend me a sword, but it's not anywhere near the same as a proper flail."

Buell smiled. "Of course, it pains me as much as you to see you carrying a pedestrian weapon." He barked a quick command to one of his men, and within moments Thon had himself a new flail. Thon grinned as he grasped the long ash handle and felt the weight of the spiked head swinging on its chain.

"We can tour the rest of the topside," Buell said, all business, "but you'll find it's more of the same. The areas of interest are all in the subterranean levels."

"By all means, lead the way below," Caile told him. "And perhaps you can tell me, has anyone else come asking to see the facility? Anyone from the election council, perhaps? One of the candidates?" *Or a turnip lady?* Caile wanted to add, but he dared not give up Talitha's cover.

Beyond the makeshift encampment was a broad stairway leading to the lower levels of the facility. Commander Buell glanced back as he led the way down. "One or two of the guildmasters have come by asking to inspect the facility," he said, "but none recently, and none but you have been admitted."

Caile nodded congenially, but he wasn't sure he believed the commander. Just because Buell seemed fond of Thon and had agreed to let them inspect the facility didn't mean he was trustworthy. *He has no reason to tell me anything, but if he's in league with the houndkeeper, Lord Kobel, or the Old World, he has all the reasons and more to tell them about me.*

They came to a stop at the first subterranean level, where they found more pipes and more manufacturing machines.

"Here, the liquid alloy is poured into casting molds," Buell explained. "Smelter number one feeds the molds for the wagon chassis components. Smelter two feeds the armor molds. Smelter three feeds the steam engine molds. The rest of the machines are for grinding, honing, and polishing the cast pieces so they fit together properly. Like topside, everything is locked down. The casts themselves are harmless. The grinding machines are inoperable without ether."

Caile stood mesmerized, looking upon the expanse of machinery. He had never seen anything like it before. Metal chutes hung down from the ceiling, a spiderwork of channels that fed the ceramic molds, some of them larger than a horse-drawn cart. The molds weren't as foreign looking as the grinding machines, though. Each machine had a central steam engine fed by smaller water pipes, with a boiler and piston box that powered a crankshaft attached to a cluster of giant gears and flywheels, which were in turn attached to the operational grinding wheel.

I've seen smithies before, where swords, axes, and arrow points are made alongside horseshoes and wagon yokes, but nothing like this. This is a death factory.

"Would you like to inspect any of the molds or machines, Your Majesty?" Buell asked. "Or would you prefer to go straightaway to the lower level and inspect the wagons themselves?"

"The wagons," Caile said.

Buell led the way back to the stairwell and down to the next level. Caile caught his breath halfway down the stairs and stopped in stunned silence. Topside, the smelting factory was no larger than any of the other warehouses, but down here the factory sprawled outward in every direction for leagues, seemingly. Pillars and buttresses supported the ceiling above them, and in the spaces between were the war wagons. End to end. Side by side. Thousands of them, stretching into the distance as far as Caile could see.

"This is where the wagons are assembled and stored," Buell said, looking up at Caile from the bottom of the stairway. "As you can see, it's already filled to capacity. The factory was operating double time in anticipation of the war with Pyrthinia, right up to Guderian's death. In the end he had more war wagons than soldiers to man them."

Sweet Pyrthin, Caile swore inwardly. *Makarria should have come and seen this herself before she left to claim the throne in Valaróz. She should have destroyed it. Now it's too late. The wagons will belong to the next King of Sargoth and no one will be able to stop him. No one.*

17
From the Clouds

"Your Majesty, I think I've spotted them."

Taera strode across the deck to the forecastle, her feet still unsure beneath her. She was no stranger to sailing, but this airship, *Casstian's Breath*, was nothing like the seafaring ships she had been on before. Even Siegbjorn's airship had been more stable than this. Unlike Siegbjorn's vessel, *Casstian's Breath* was sleek and long, which made it fast, but also prone to cross winds. Any sudden cross breeze would rock the gondola from side to side, and if the gust was strong enough, the ether-filled hull above them would shudder, sending its reverberations through the entire framework of the airship. Admiral Giorgi, the captain of the ship, had already nearly lost one sailor overboard, and that had been over land, before they had reached the turbulent winds of the Esterian Ocean.

"It's definitely a fleet of ships," Admiral Giorgi said, lowering the spyglass from his face.

"You sure it's not just some fishing boats?" Taera asked.

Giorgi handed her his spyglass. "Look for yourself. Sails on the horizon to the south. I can only make out two for certain, but I'm sure there are more."

Taera closed one eye and peered through the spyglass, finding her bearings with the Pyrthin shoreline to their starboard. From there, she scanned slowly to her left along the curving blue horizon of the sea. Sure enough, there they were, two white sails due south. Nervous energy filled her belly. She'd had no premonitory visions, but ever since rebuking the Old World emissaries, she'd had a growing sense that the Old World was on its way to attack. *Maybe they're just fishing boats,* she tried convincing herself.

She rotated the eyepiece to better focus the spyglass and scanned farther to her left, toward the morning sun in the east. *Nothing, not for a hundred leagues to the east. Maybe it really is just a couple of fishing boats.* She swung the scope back to her right, finding the sails more easily this time and seeing it wasn't two boats at all, but rather a galleon with two main sails. Already it was larger in the spyglass. She knew enough to know that a vessel that big was no fishing boat. She scanned farther to her right and glimpsed something new. A glimmer of white that was gone a moment later. She held the scope steady and waited.

There it was again, and then another sparkle of white. And another. Within moments, there were dozens of them—little white glimmers that sprouted into sails on the horizon.

"It's them," Taera said, handing the spyglass back to Admiral Giorgi. "The Old World is here."

Giorgio stole one more quick glance through the spyglass himself and nodded grimly. "You best head belowdeck, Your Majesty," he said, and then turned on his heel and began hollering at his crew as he made his way to the helm. "All hands on deck! Prepare to come about!"

Taera frowned at Giorgi's presumptuousness. She was happy to move out of the way as the half-dozen crewmembers came bustling out from the small cabin beneath the sterncastle, but she had no intention of hiding belowdeck. This campaign was her doing, and while most of the crew members were veterans from the Pyrthin navy, the airship had been her doing, and Dekle, the wild-eyed stormbringer who propelled the ship, was her recruit. On top of all that, she was queen, not Giorgi.

Relax, she reminded herself. *They all know what they are doing. There's no reason to step on their toes.*

As she watched, the men indeed moved with well-practiced precision, which put her more at ease. In a matter of seconds they were all in position and "raised" the portside sail. With outriggers instead of a traditional mast, it wasn't so much raising the sail as it was extending it, but the effect was the same.

"Wind!" Giorgi barked, and Dekle the stormbringer closed his eyes and summoned a tail wind. With only the portside sail raised, the ship came about to its starboard with dizzying dexterity. Taera had to close her eyes as the Pyrthin mainland swept by in front of them a full one hundred and eighty degrees.

"Starboard sails!" Giorgi yelled.

Dekle killed the wind as the crew extended the starboard sail, and then Giorgi shouted "Wind!" again, and both sails filled with a snap as Dekle summoned a new gale. *Casstian's Breath* lurched forward, and within seconds they were racing forward, due north now, away from the advancing armada and toward Taera's own fleet anchored off of Spearpoint Rock.

They moved twice as fast as any seafaring ship could hope to, and at the helm Giorgi manned the steering levers that controlled the rudders on the air-filled hull above them, two horizontal rudders to either side of the hull and a vertical one at the crest of the hull. Steadily north and downward he steered them, with Dekle providing a steady source of wind. Before long, Spearpoint Rock and the Pyrthin navy came into view.

"Prepare the flags," Giorgi shouted, and when they drew within a hundred yards he yelled for Dekle to stop the wind. The airship lurched to a halt, then buffeted sideways as the natural westerly wind caught the sails.

"Drop sails and send the signal: all ships, full sail, south."

A sailor holding a bundle of colored flags ran to the bow and communicated the signal. First, two red flags, one straight up in the air and one extended horizontally. *All ships.* Then the two yellow flags, both straight up in the air. *Full sail.* And last, two green flags held out to either side. *South.*

Taera had been briefed about the mode of communication, but it was one thing to hear about it in a war meeting, and quite another to see it in action. Within moments of the last flag signal, the entire fleet came to life: fifty seafaring vessels, and two additional airships, which cut loose their tie-lines and rose into the air from where they'd been tethered to the two largest sea ships.

With all the vessels ready, Giorgi gave the next command. "Half sail now so we don't outrun them, and bring the wind!" Dekle closed his eyes and the wind was upon them. The stormbringers on the other two airships did the same, along with the three stormbringers crewing the sea ships below.

The sails of fifty-three vessels filled with a boom and lurched forward, due south.

Taera couldn't help but smile. They had done it. They had put together a fleet of traditional ships integrated with airships and sorcerers, all in a matter of days. Master Elias had tried talking her out of using sorcerers, as had Admiral Giorgi and most of her other advisors, and yet here they were—seven stormbringers—propelling an entire fleet of ships. Now it was just a matter of whether it was enough of a spectacle to avert battle, and failing that, enough to win the battle.

Admiral Giorgi kept *Casstian's Breath* low to the water so that Dekle's wind combined with that of the other stormbringers, and at the speed they were traveling, the Old World armada came into view within minutes. It was still bearing straight for them. Taera took a deep breath, remembering what Makarria had told her and hoping she had been right.

If we show our strength, show our unity, they will back down, Makarria had said.

So far, though, the Old World armada was not backing down.

"Arm the ballistas!" Giorgi commanded from the helm. "Ready the naphtha charges!"

The crew sprang into action around Taera, taking up their battle stations and readying their weapons. Below and all around *Casstian's Breath*, the other ship crews were doing the same, just as they had practiced. The plan Giorgi and Taera had devised was to split the fleet into three wedges, one in the air and two in the sea. The airships would fly up high enough to stay out of striking distance of any weapons and firewielders the Old World ships had onboard. *Casstian's Breath* and her two sister vessels would pass over first, dropping their naphtha charges and firing their ballistas into the enemy vessels below. With the aid of gravity, their striking range was nearly limitless. Or at least as limitless as the crews' aim. With any luck, they'd connect with half their targets, blowing holes in the decks of the enemy ships with the iron ballista bolts, soaking them in naphtha, and sending the enemy crews into disarray.

Meanwhile, the Pyrthin sea ships would split into two groups, one breaking off to beat windward and the other charging full sail ahead with the aid of their stormbringers. The first wave of seafaring ships would cut through the Old World fleet, striking with their own unique weapons: twin ballistas with chain-linked bolts to sweep across the enemy decks and cause mass casualties, and then the Pyrthin firewielders to ignite the naphtha the airships had dropped. By the time that first wave of sea ships passed through, the second wave would be charging with the natural wind at their back, twenty ships with reinforced prows to plow broadside through the crippled Old World fleet and send them to the bottom of the Esterian Ocean. And then, with the sea ships clear, *Casstian's Breath* and the other airships would pass by again to pick off any surviving vessels from the safety of the air.

That was the attack plan, at least. Taera hoped it wouldn't come to that, and even if it did, Giorgi had been forthright in admitting that naval battles never went to plan. That was doubly true with the Old World—they were bound to have their own tricks. Explosive weapons. Firewielders. Beastcharmers with whales or giant squids at their command. Stormbringers who could very well negate the Pyrthin stormbringers' efforts and snuff out the wind altogether, leaving both fleets still in the water. If that happened, it would turn to hand-to-hand combat. The grappling hooks would come out and then the cutlasses. Any way it happened, both sides were sure to suffer heavy casualties if it came to a battle.

I hope you were right, Makarria, Taera thought as the enemy fleet loomed closer. The Old World armada was massive, easily outnumbering the Pyrthin fleet two vessels to one. And they weren't backing down.

"Full sails!" Giorgi commanded the crew, and he pulled the control lever back to start gaining elevation. To either flank, the two sister airships did the same.

Taera held her breath. Within moments, it would be too late to turn back. They would be fully engaged and thousands would die. "Please," Taera whispered, imploring the spirit of her father and Pyrthin himself for something to avert this battle, and as if in response, the Old World fleet veered away sharply, turning due east into the wind.

"Yes!" she hooted, but at the helm above her, Admiral Giorgi's voice drowned hers out.

"Come about to the portside!" he shouted.

"What? No. Stand down," Taera yelled, but her voice was lost on the wind as the ship careened to its portside.

"More wind!" Giorgi commanded Dekle.

Taera cursed and grabbed onto the rungs of the ladder leading to the top of the aftcastle to haul herself up to the helm. Halfway up, she nearly lost her footing, but she held tight with her hands and heaved herself onto the aftcastle.

"Admiral!" she screamed as she pushed herself to her feet. "Stop."

"Get belowdeck, Your Majesty," he yelled, waving her aside. "This is no place for a woman."

Cold fury filled Taera, and she came within half a breath of striking the admiral, but she stayed herself at the last moment and turned to her stormbringer instead. "Dekle," she yelled, "make the wind stop."

Dekle did exactly as she told him and *Casstian's Breath* stalled in the sky, nearly knocking her and everyone else over.

"What do you think you're doing?" Giorgi demanded, regaining his balance and shooting her a look of utter contempt. "How dare you contradict me in front of my men."

Taera heard every word coming out of his mouth, but her attention was focused on the Old World armada before them. Even with Dekle pushing *Casstian's Breath* at top speed, the Old World armada had outdistanced them after turning to the east. Taera couldn't begin to imagine how many stormwielders they must have had at their disposal. She glanced back toward the stern and saw that in Giorgi's haste, he had also managed to separate *Casstian's Breath* from their own fleet, just as Taera had feared.

"Damn it all," Giorgi cursed, following her gaze. "They've strung us out."

"No, you've strung us out," Taera replied. "And now the Old World is about to attack."

She spun around to look over the bow as the entire Old World armada came about to the north and looped back toward them.

If they charge now with their sorcerers and the natural wind to their backs, we're done for.

But nothing happened. It looked as if the enemy ships were furling their sails, in fact.

Giorgi raised his spyglass to look closer and lowered it a moment later with a perplexed expression on his face. "They're dropping sails and dropping anchor. But why?"

"Because the dreamwielder was right," Taera said. "They were only testing our resolve. We've shown ourselves to be more than eager, thanks to you, and now they're content to wait."

"Wait for what?"

Taera had heard enough from the fool.

"That's no longer your concern, Admiral. You are hereby dismissed from command."

Admiral Giorgi scoffed, as if he were regarding a child. "What? You can't do that."

"Don't make me repeat myself again, Admiral. You are dismissed from command for disobeying my direct order. Keep talking and I will have you thrown into the dungeons."

"You ungrateful little bitch," Giorgi said, shaking his head in anger. "I was captaining ships for your father before you were even born. You know nothing."

Taera laughed, short and humorlessly. She didn't even feel

sorry for the fool. "Dekle," she said, "show our former admiral how to fly."

"What?" Admiral Giorgi asked, turning to Dekle. "No, I'm in charge here. Don't listen to her."

Dekle didn't even hesitate to obey Taera's orders. He closed his eyes and a second later his blast of wind hurled Giorgi over the stern rail to plummet to his watery death below.

• • •

Fina watched silently from the perimeter of the sitting room as the queen signed Ambassador Mahalath's treaty, helpless to stop her. *No,* she told herself, *the queen is not Makarria, but something else.*

The last three days had been one trial after another for Fina. First it had been the public hearing in the courtroom, then the visit to the infirmary where the queen had suggested the injured kennel master and crossbowmen visit her private quarters when they were "feeling up for a romp." Fina quashed that notion on the spot, under threat of dismemberment to the injured men, and urged the queen to retire to her quarters. Instead, the queen had ordered a feast prepared, and that night she got so deep into the wine in front of the Valarion aristocracy that Fina had to carry her up the stairs to bed. That very night, Fina had attempted to visit the prisoner in the dungeon, but she was turned away by the guards, which only strengthened her suspicion as to who was really trapped in that cell wearing Lorentz's body and the mind cage.

The guards must have spoken with the fake queen, because after that the queen would not let Fina leave her side. The following day the queen was more debaucherous than the previous one, first visiting a wharfside tavern, and then a bawdy theatre show with performers that coupled naked on stage. Everywhere the queen went she drew a crowd of astonished onlookers. It was all Fina and the other guards could do to keep her from getting mobbed.

And then this morning had happened. The queen agreed to everything Ambassador Mahalath proposed: the military aid, financial aid, the opening of the naval blockade in the Sol Sea. Everything suddenly fell right into the Old World's hands. Makarria's reputation was ruined, and now the Old World controlled Valaróz.

"You have made a wonderful decision," Ambassador Mahalath said, smiling as he signed beneath the queen's signature on the treatise. "I will send word to Senator Emil and the Senate in Khail Sanctu immediately. We can expect reinforcements by tomorrow afternoon, which leaves us with six days still before the Sargothian election. We'll have to act quickly, but with our combined resources, we'll ensure a new age of prosperity."

Fina couldn't believe what she was hearing. *The Old World ships will be here by tomorrow?* That meant they had ships laying in wait somewhere in the Sol Sea, and that Ambassador Mahalath had a means of contacting them.

"Prosperity is all I want," the queen said.

Mahalath's mustache quivered as he smiled again. "Excellent. And you'll be sure to send a raven to Valeza with word to your admirals to relinquish command to the Republic's armada in the Ocean Gloaming?"

"I'm on my way right now," the queen said, rising to her feet and shaking Mahalath's hand.

Mahalath bowed and departed, and the queen followed after him, motioning for Fina to come along. Fina couldn't understand why the fake queen bothered to keep her around, except perhaps to keep the appearance of normalcy. The body thief had to know Fina suspected something was awry.

In the corridor outside the sitting room, a courtier was waiting for the queen along with a sailor who wore a tunic bearing the red and gold stripes of Pyrthinia.

"Your Majesty," the courtier said with a bow. "An airship has arrived from Kal Pyrthin. The captain here carries a message from Queen Taera."

The queen looked the sailor over for a moment before holding out her hand. "An airship, hmm? Well let's have it then. Give me the letter."

"Queen Taera did not dare put the message to paper, Your Majesty," the sailor replied. "She entrusted me to tell it to you in person, and then to return at once with your response to Kal Pyrthin."

The queen snorted, and then strode away and motioned for them to follow her. "This way then, good sirs. I have urgent business in the scent-hound tower, but we can speak as we walk."

"But Your Majesty," the Pyrthin sailor objected as he followed after her. "The message I bear is urgent, and secret. No one else can hear. Not even your most trusted advisors or friends."

Fina's skin prickled. This was perhaps her one chance to gain someone's help, she realized. Makarria—the real Makarria—trusted Queen Taera. Fina needed to find out what Taera's message was, or if nothing else, at least send a message back to her with word of what had happened to Makarria. What little influence Fina had over the fake queen was tenuous, though, so she would have to play up her role as a worried bodyguard.

Fina steeled herself and pushed her way past the courtier as the four of them continued their way down a marble staircase to the central hall of the palace. "What is your name, sailor?" she demanded of the Pyrthinian messenger. "How do we know Queen Taera sent you?"

"I am Captain Hierome. I sailed a newly built Pyrthin airship to deliver Queen Taera's message. Her message is known to me only, but you can see the official warrant she prepared for me, if you like. It pronounces me her royal messenger."

"Let's see it," Fina commanded him.

The sailor produced the folded piece of parchment from his tunic and handed it over. Fina read it over quickly as they continued walking toward the rear of the palace. There wasn't much to the warrant, simply a short sentence proclaiming Captain Hierome an official messenger to treat with Queen Makarria, followed by Queen Taera's signature and her wax seal.

"It looks official," Fina admitted, handing the parchment back to the sailor.

"Good enough for me," the queen said, coming to a stop at the spiral staircase that led to the scent-hound tower. "Come along then, Captain Hierome. You can tell me your secret message as we climb the stairs. Fina, you have my leave to go. Find yourself a meal or whatever you please. Meet me in my quarters in an hour, and we'll go speak to my generals."

"But, Your Majesty, it's not safe," Fina protested.

"Go on," the queen said with a flippant wave, and then she disappeared into the tower stairwell with the courtier and Captain Hierome right on her heels.

Fina stood there for a moment, uncertain what she should do. She considered trying to sneak up the stairwell to eavesdrop on the messenger, but she knew getting caught would be the end of her. It would be wiser, she decided, to utilize this moment of freedom to finally do what she'd been hoping to do for the last day and a half and go speak with the one person who could perhaps help her.

Her mind made up, she hurried back to the main hall and down the stairway into the library. There she found Natale at his usual reading table.

"Madame Fina," he greeted, surprised to see her but pleased nonetheless. "Where is our young queen?"

"Sending a raven to Valeza with orders to surrender the western fleet to the Old World."

"What? How can this be?"

"She signed the treaty with the Old World ambassador just now."

"What? Why?"

The rotund scholar seemed to be filled with more questions than answers.

"Where have you been the last three days?" Fina asked. "Have you not heard the gossip of the Queen's doings?"

"No, I've been here with my books."

"I hope you've been reading more about body thieves then."

"Yes, as matter of fact I have, but why? What's happened?"

Fina told him everything, about all of the queen's uncharacteristic behaviors and actions over the last three days, sparing no detail.

"I noticed the change as soon as the body thief was captured," Fina added when she was done. "The way she paraded us through the dungeon to gloat over his body, even, was so unlike her. The body thief must have switched with her, even though she never touched him."

"I don't see how that's possible. You're sure he did not make physical contact with her in some way?"

"Makarria stood in the doorway beside me. When Lorentz—the body thief—started attacking the soldiers, Makarria used her power to fell him. She never got within ten feet of actually touching him."

Natale's face paled. "Wait. She used her magic to do what to him exactly?"

"I have no idea. She closed her eyes, and Lorentz's body went limp."

Natale turned to his desk and rummaged through his stack of books frantically until he found the one he was looking for. He thumbed through the pages, stopping at one that was dog-eared to scan over it with one finger. "Here it is. *Tangere.* To touch. 'In order to switch bodies the *pthisicis-corporis* must touch the victim…' Sweet Vala." He looked up from the book to face Fina, his face ashen. "You're right. I took the passage to mean the literal translation of *tangere*, to physically touch someone, but there are other usages of the word in the old tongue. It can also mean to use your magic upon another to manipulate or change them, something only dreamwielders can do. Makarria *touched* the *pthisicis-corporis* when she used her power. That means he could have switched with her. What have I done?"

Fina felt bile rise up in her throat. There was no satisfaction in confirming her suspicion. "Don't blame yourself. We have both failed Makarria. We led her right into the body thief's trap, and now he rules the kingdom in her guise and the real Makarria is chained up in the dungeon wearing the mind cage."

"Mind cage?"

Fina closed her eyes and shook her head, overcome with shame. "I had assumed it was your finding, that you had given it to her while

I was off fetching the kennel master. But of course not. It was the body thief, the fake queen, who knew where the contraption was stored when we went to the dungeons. She had the jailors screw it into Lorentz's skull to keep him from using his power, but it wasn't the body thief in Lorentz's body. It was Makarria, and now she's helpless to use her magic."

"We have to rescue her at once," Natale said, pushing himself to his feet and knocking over a stack of books onto the table in the process.

Fina grabbed his arm. "I've already tried. The dungeon is well guarded. Neither one of us will be able to gain access without the fake queen's permission. If we just barge into the dungeon, we'll be taken captive and then the body thief will know we know. Is there any other way to subdue this thing? Haven't you found anything in your scrolls?"

"Such as what?"

"We need to make it give Makarria's body back."

Natale shook his head. "I'm sorry. The *pthisicis-corporis* is a creature that acts of its own free will. It will only switch bodies back with Makarria if it so chooses."

Fina let out a long breath. She was at her whit's end. "We need help then."

"Help from whom? We can speak to her parents, but they have no real power."

"No," Fina agreed. "Captain Haviero might help, but I'm not sure we could convince him. We need someone with real power who we can trust: Queen Taera. She sent an airship. It arrived this morning with a message to Makarria, with orders to return immediately with Makarria's response. We need to sneak a message back on that ship to tell Taera what's really happened."

Natale's face brightened. "Or better yet, we can send her a speaking stone. I have it here. Queen Taera's stone is still in my possession!"

"Of course," Fina said, stunned she hadn't thought of it herself.

"Makarria sent Talitha and Prince Caile away with all the other stones, though," Natale said. "That leaves us with only Makarria's yellow stone. Do you know where it is?"

"It's in her room, still untouched," Fina said. "The body thief wasn't here when you made them. It probably doesn't even know the stones exist."

"We must be quick then," Natale said, scrambling away from the reading table in the direction of his office. "I'll go to the airship at once and deliver Queen Taera's stone and a letter. You go fetch Makarria's stone before the *pthisicis-corporis* returns from the scent-hound's tower."

Fina didn't need to be told twice. She sprinted away, past the shelves of books and back up the stairs into the main hall. *How long have I been away?* she wondered. The fake queen had told her to return to the royal quarters in an hour, and she couldn't have been with Natale for more than a quarter hour, she was certain. *Just act normal,* she told herself, slowing to a brisk walk as she went through the hall and up the grand stairway leading to the royal chambers.

A Royal Guardsman stood on guard in the corridor outside Makarria's private quarters, but he recognized Fina and let her pass by without a second thought. Fina didn't even have to say a word. Still, she was on edge and had to pause to catch her breath once she closed the door behind her in the anteroom. After giving herself a moment to calm herself, she went to the opposite door and listened for any signs of life in the main bedroom.

It was dead silent.

She knocked before entering, just in case, then entered Makarria's opulent bedroom to find it unoccupied. With a relieved sigh, she went to the fireplace mantle where the yellow speaking stone sat alongside a half dozen decorative baubles. She grabbed the speaking stone and turned back for the door, but realized she couldn't just walk through the halls with a yellow stone in her hands. She needed to hide it somehow. She glanced about, looking for a loose handkerchief or something she could wrap around the stone, but of course the room was immaculately kept by the household staff.

A rucksack then. I have one in my room.

Fina darted back out the way she had come only to find the outer chamber door open and someone standing there.

"Hello, Fina," the fake queen said. "What have you got?"

Fina glanced down at the speaking stone, her mind racing. "I beg your pardon, Your Majesty. I returned early from the kitchens and thought to grab this decoration."

"Oh?"

"I mentioned to you that I liked it last week, if you recall," Fina lied. "You said I could keep it in my room, since I have little in the way of decoration. I thought to grab it while I waited."

"I see," said the fake queen. "Well, I've changed my mind, so go put it back where you found it."

Fina nodded, not trusting herself to speak further. She turned back into the main room and placed the stone onto the mantle, her heart thrumming in her chest.

The fake queen closed the door behind her, trapping Fina in the main bedroom alone with her.

"Our little messenger from Pyrthinia bore strange news," the fake queen said.

Again, Fina only nodded, wary of leaving her place beside the hearth lest she get too close to the body thief.

"It seems Queen Taera has had a vision," the fake queen went on. "She's foreseen my murder."

"Murder? She's certain?"

The fake queen narrowed her eyes at Fina. "That's right, and the perpetrator in her vision is someone who looks an awful lot like you."

18
Behind Enemy Lines

A warm, rank gust of wind filled the tunnel, sending the torch sputtering and making Natarios Rhodas gag. "Gah!" he spat. "It smells like a privy."

"Right you are," Old Kram replied, bringing the torch in closer to his chest to shield it from blowing out. "These ancient tunnels must overlap the sewer canals below West-End by my reckoning." He stared down at his map, squinting his eyes and leaning in close to see it in the flickering torchlight. "We're past the king's tower now, getting close to the dignitary wing, but we're veering too far to the west. If the tunnel doesn't swing east soon, we'll have to backtrack and try a different branch. Could be there ain't no tunnels under the dignitary wing."

"There has to be," Natarios insisted. "Why would anyone build tunnels in the first place if they weren't made to spy on foreign ambassadors?"

Old Kram shrugged and shuffled his way forward, holding his torch out in front of him. Natarios was beginning to have doubts about the old architect he'd bribed out of retirement, but he had no choice but to follow. Without Kram, he was as good as lost. Kram was the only one who could make sense of the architectural drawings of Lightbringer's Keep, and the chalk symbols Kram had drawn on the passage walls to mark their route were completely indecipherable to Natarios.

As far as Natarios knew, he and Prince Caile were the only ones in Col Sargoth who knew about the tunnels beneath Lightbringer's

Keep. Natarios had learned about them from Wulfram when Prince Caile had escaped Emperor Guderian the year past, and that's exactly where Natarios had started—in the room from which Prince Caile escaped. He'd briefly entertained the idea of exploring the secret tunnels alone, but after prying away the floor stone and lowering himself into the tunnel, he realized venturing on alone would be as good as suicide. True, he had a knack for escaping trouble, but the tunnels beneath Lightbringer's Keep were a complex maze of intersecting passages, many of them collapsed or filled-in thanks to remodeling efforts over the decades, and all of them choked in centuries of dust and cobwebs. He didn't dare explore them alone. And so he'd sought out an expert.

All it took was some discreet questioning of the household staff to find "Old Kram," the architect who had overseen the building modifications Emperor Guderian ordered at the beginning of his reign. Old Kram had never heard of the tunnels, but he was more than willing to go explore them when Natarios offered him a small purse of gold and the chance to get away from his shrew of a wife.

They had been at it for three nights now, mapping out the tunnels as the people in the keep above them slept, and tonight they were finally on the verge of finding the passage Natarios sought. *If we hurry, we'll arrive just in time to find our guests returning from dinner.*

"The passage is curving in the proper direction," Kram said. He'd tucked the map into a pocket in his breeches and was eying an old compass. "Indeed, almost due east now. Maybe thirty yards and we'll be beneath the dignitary wing."

"Keep your voice down then," Natarios hissed. "Just because you're half deaf doesn't mean the people sleeping in the rooms above us are."

Kram grunted, but said nothing in reply. The passage became more narrow, and the ceiling lower, forcing them both to crouch. Twenty yards farther they began hearing voices. They were little more than disembodied echoes, but definitely voices. Forty yards in, the passage came to an abrupt end and the voices were clearer and louder now but indecipherable—a half dozen disparate conversations, all garbled nonsense in the still air around them. Kram held his torch up to examine their surroundings and discovered two side tunnels, one each to their right and left, teeing off from the main passageway. They were a good five feet off the ground and narrower than the main tunnel. Kram held a cupped hand to one ear and leaned in closer to the tunnel on the left to verify the voices were coming from within, then turned to Natarios and put a finger over his lips to keep him quiet.

Obviously, I'm going to be quiet, you old fool, Natarios thought. *Do you think I'm a moron?*

Old Kram, oblivious, lowered the torch and scanned the wall beneath the side tunnel, expecting to find something, but all Natarios saw was more rough-carved, black rock. Kram knew his business, though. He brushed his hand across the wall and found a foothold obscured beneath a veil of dusty cobwebs. And then he found another, and another. Within moments, he had cleared out five footholds carved into the wall—a ladder of sorts, leading up to the side tunnel. Kram motioned for Natarios to climb up, and Natarios felt his throat tighten in fear.

You go, he wanted to tell Old Kram, but no, of course, it had to be Natarios. *Kram wouldn't understand what he was eavesdropping on even if he didn't break his hip climbing up there.*

Seeing nothing else for it, Natarios took a deep breath and hiked up his black robes to get his right foot into the first foothold. From there he reached his hands up to grip on the ledge of the tunnel above him and pushed himself up. The ledge was smooth, with nothing to properly hold on to, and Natarios felt himself slipping backward as he blindly tried to find the next foothold with his left foot, but then Kram's hand was on his arse, shoving him upward. Natarios felt old webs clinging to his face as he scrambled up, and then he cracked his head into the ceiling of the side tunnel.

Natarios choked back a curse as he fell heavily into the narrow tunnel, kicking up a cloud of dust Natarios couldn't see but could smell and taste well—bone dry, and enough to send a man into a fit of sneezing. Natarios closed his eyes, grabbed his nose, and willed himself to do nothing of the sort. Around him, the echoes of conversations continued unheeded. When the tickling in his nose was finally gone and he opened his eyes, he found it to be just as dark as with his eyes closed. A twinge of panic ran through him, but he pushed that away too. The passage was too narrow to turn around and get the torch from Kram. He would just have to worm his way forward in the darkness, then back out the same way he came.

Seeing nothing else for it, Natarios crawled deeper into the blackness, flailing one arm out in front of him to knock away the bulk of the cobwebs. *At least I know with all these cobwebs still intact, there can't be anything too big living back here,* he told himself, but the thought did little to calm his nerves.

Eventually, one of the conversations became clearer as he wormed forward, coming suddenly into sharp focus in his right ear. Taking a page from Old Kram, he brushed a hand over the wall and discovered a hole, no larger than his fist. He cleared away the cobwebs and wiped them off on his robe as he slid in closer. *A sound hole.* The conversation from the room above was as clear as if he were in the room itself.

"…the same for me, so do not be discouraged," someone was saying. "The other voting members humor me and hear me out, but with Queen Makarria two thousand miles away, they see me as little threat."

Ambassador Elvio.

"How is that not discouraging? I'm supposed to take solace in the fact that no one takes either one of us seriously? The election is a week away, Ambassador."

It was Prince Caile's voice, this second one.

"I was certain snooping around the war-wagon factory would stir up something, but no one seems to care," the prince continued.

This was all information Natarios already knew. His own informants had told him of the prince's tour of the war wagon factory, and Natarios had passed the information on to Ambassador Rives. Rives had certainly already known about it, too, but Natarios needed to maintain the guise of being a dutiful servant for the time being.

The prince was still whining about his futile attempts to influence the council, so Natarios resumed crawling deeper into the tunnel, seeking his real quarry. The voices of Prince Caile and Ambassador Elvio garbled behind him, only to intermix with new voices. After several yards, those new voices came into focus, and Natarios stopped, cleaned out the sound hole, and listened.

"...you hungry for more than just supper tonight, m'lord?"

It was a woman's voice.

"Aye," a deep, gravelly voice replied. "Come here, you filthy wench."

Ambassador Lanhorne. Natarios rolled his eyes and crawled deeper into the tunnel. *A Norgman through and through, that Lanhorne.* The wench's giggles garbled behind him, and then there was only the confusion of mixed voices for a long time. *One of the rooms must be empty up above.* He trudged forward, though, and eventually a new conversation came into focus. He cleared the sound hole.

"...you ask me, we should kill him."

It was the steam-engineer's guildmaster. Natarios would recognize his nasally voice anywhere.

"Let's not be hasty. The prince is of little threat to us for the time being."

Rives!

"The votes for Kobel are still there," the Ambassador Rives continued. "We stick to our plan unless we hear otherwise."

"Well, let's speak with them already."

The third voice was the sorcerer's guildmaster. Natarios's skin prickled at hearing him. The man was by all accounts a powerful sorcerer himself. *Might he sense my presence down here?*

"Well?" the sorcerer demanded.

"Yes, it is time," a fourth voice responded, a voice Natarios did not recognize at all. "Close your eyes as I establish the link."

A low buzzing noise filtered through the sound hole from the room above, and then all was silent for a long moment. The hair at the nape of Natarios's neck stood on end. *Sorcerery. Lightbringer's arse,*

I hate sorcery.

"You may open your eyes."

"Good evening, Senator Emil," Ambassador Rives said. "All goes according to our plans here in Col Sargoth, with the exception of one new wrinkle."

"And the wrinkle?"

Another new voice, this one more distant sounding than the others. *They're speaking with the Old World,* Natarios realized. His neck was beginning to cramp from holding it up alongside the sound hole, but he dared not shift his position and risk giving himself away. Especially now, knowing there were two sorcerers in the room above him.

"Prince Caile Delios continues to snoop around," Rives was saying. "He was granted access to the war wagon factory. I see little harm in his actions, but the others feel he is a danger."

"Abduct him," the distanced voice said. "Be discreet about it, and don't harm him seriously. As a hostage, he might be useful in persuading his sister to acquiesce. She is our last hurdle."

"The last? What of the dreamwielder?"

"She bowed to the Republic and signed the treaty this morning. All is going as planned."

Natarios could hardly believe what he was hearing. *The dreamwielder is in league with the Old World, too? I wonder what our spoiled prince would think if he were to find out she's abandoned him.*

"Our western fleet is en route," the Old World senator continued. "They should arrive on the day of the election. Once Lord Kobel is elected, you know what to do. Make sure the entire council has signed the decree and then kill them all."

"That's probably not necessary," Rives said. "Once Kobel is elected, no one will have any recourse to undermine his authority."

"Kill them all," the senator repeated. "The houndkeeper and Lady Hildreth have proved themselves meddlesome, and the others vote for us only because we have bribed them. We'll have no loose ends. The death of twenty some odd individuals will avert outright war, so you'll actually be saving thousands of lives, gentlemen."

Righteous anger welled up in Natarios. *Ungrateful bastards. After all the work I've done, you mean to kill me like a common cutpurse?*

"It will be done," the sorcerer's guildmaster said. "I will have two firewielders with me. I will see to it myself that no one besides those of us in this room walk out alive."

"Excellent."

"And what of Queen Taera?" Rives asked.

"You let me worry about her. Just capture the prince, and get Kobel to those war machines as soon as he's elected. Once Queen Taera sees she's caught between the Republic armada on one side and Kobel's war wagons on the other, she'll have no choice but to surrender Pyrthinia."

"And Norg?"

"With the other four kingdoms in the fold, King Hanns will bend the knee quicker than King Lorimer himself."

"You forget yourself," Rives growled. Natarios knew that tone of voice all too well. Rives was quick to anger and wore his emotions on his sleeve. "King Lorimer did not bend the knee. He was the one who proposed this pact with the Old World Republic. Without him—without me—none of this would have been possible."

"My apologies, Ambassador Rives. You are correct. The Kingdom of Golier has been instrumental in this expansion, and you and King Lorimer will be rewarded greatly for your services. Now I must go. I will contact you tomorrow night after I arrive in Sol Valaróz."

The buzzing noise filled the room above him again, and then all Natarios heard was the shuffling of feet and a few murmurs as the conspirators left. Natarios took that as his cue to leave as well, and began the long scramble backwards through the tunnel, his mind racing. *Bastards,* he kept repeating to himself. *If you think I was meddlesome before, just you wait.*

• • •

Makarria willed herself to raise her head when she heard the keys rattling in the lock of the iron door. She had expected to see the jailers returning to feed her, but no, it was the *pthisicis-corporis*, still wearing Makarria's body. It was like a horrible dream seeing her own body approach her. The fake queen carried a rucksack in one hand, but tossed it to the ground once the guards lit the wall torches and left, locking the door behind them.

"How's my little pet enjoying the mind cage, hmm?"

Makarria's head slumped, but the fake queen clapped her on the cheek three times, as if Makarria was a disobedient child in need of reprimanding.

"No, no, stay with me. You should be used to the clicking and clacking by now, I would think."

Why? Makarria tried saying the word out loud, but all that came out was a groan, followed by a mouthful of drool that ran down her chin. *Not my chin,* she remembered. *Lorentz's.* She had discovered the stubble of a newly sprouted mustache and beard earlier, when she'd tried wetting her lips before the guards shoved the feeding funnel down her gullet.

"How uncouth," the fake queen said, wiping the drool away for Makarria. "I have exciting news for you, but you'll need to concentrate. Ignore the clicking and whirring in your head and focus on my words. Come now. You can do it." The *pthisicis-corporis* wore the royal gown in a negligent, wanton manner, with the neckline unlaced and hanging open. Makarria's body, too, looked mistreated. The fake queen had dark circles beneath her eyes and the skin on her face had an unhealthy pallor.

What have you done to my body? Makarria raised her head and blinked her eyes clear again, her anger giving life to her weary mind and limbs.

"Excellent," the *pthisicis-corporis* said, stepping away from Makarria to pace back and forth in the small cell. "Now all this must be quite a shock for you, I'm sure. One moment, you're the queen, on the verge of capturing your nemesis, and the next, you're trapped in his body and chained to a wall. Even worse, you can't dream up your little magical tricks any more. Do you still remember what you did wrong, my dear?"

Makarria's thoughts since being locked up had been fragmented and torn, but she had over time pieced things together, as if in a nightmare. She knew who she was still—it took effort to remind herself with each breath, but she knew who she really was—and she knew what had happened to her. And even over the whirring and clicking of the mind cage, she understood the body thief's words. Makarria ran her tongue over the roof of her mouth to wet it and focused on the fake queen's face. She formed the words carefully, but even so it came out in a horrible lisp, unaccustomed as she was to Lorentz's tongue and missing teeth. "I touched you with my power."

The fake queen gave her a melodramatic grin. "Well, well, very good. You are still sane, after all. I should have never doubted you. You've proved to be an enjoyable adversary, particularly considering you're barely more than a child. You sniffed me out quickly, and even though I knew you were coming for me, bringing the kennel masters with their pole nooses, well, that caught me by surprise. A couple of years training and seasoning in the Old World, and you would almost be a worthy opponent for me. Even so, it's been an entertaining diversion."

The pthisicis-corporis is toying with me, Makarria realized. *But for what purpose? I'm already chained. Beaten.* She knew the answer to the question before she finished asking it. The *pthisicis-corporis* was here for the same reason Emperor Guderian needed to pontificate in front of his court about mankind's dominion over magic and nature. Without someone to share his crazy ideas with, they were simply that: crazy ideas. Emperor Guderian had needed the validation of those around him to convince himself he was righteous in his tyranny. The *pthisicis-corporis,* in turn, lived a life of secrecy, subterfuge, and solitude. The creature needed someone to speak to in order to validate its genius, and what better person to talk with than Makarria, the victim who no one would ever believe even if she did try to tell the guards?

"It was your skiff on the western shore of The Spine," Makarria said, the words coming to her more easily now.

The fake queen beamed. "Of course. I had a vision of the dark caves of Khal-Aband, and you coming in like a white knight to rescue some pauper that was already dead, so I made haste to get there before you. You took a bit longer arriving than I anticipated, but I found enough diversions to keep me entertained. A few of the prisoners might have gone mad after feeling my touch—and a handful of the guards as well—but it was of no consequence. You swept in as I knew you would, and I took your very own bodyguard to take my place at your side."

"But why?" Makarria asked. If the *pthisicis-corporis* was in the mood to talk, she would have answers out of him. "Who sent you? Senator Emil?"

The fake queen shrugged. "Emil or another senator of the Republic. What does it matter? I was held captive, in a cell not so different than this, wearing the very same mind trap you wear now, when some man in a white robe came to me. He gave me his proposition, and when I agreed to his terms, my release."

"His terms? You mean to kill me?"

"To kill you? Good dear no. The Old World Republic thinks much too highly of itself to resort to simple assassination. My task was to merely create havoc and undermine your authority until you had no choice but to sign the Republic's treaty, which I signed on your behalf this morning, by the way."

It was just as Makarria had suspected then, a plot by the Old World to weaken her authority as queen. The confirmation of her suspicion did little to lift her spirits, though. Nor the news of the signed treaty. Even helpless and chained to the wall, it stoked a cold anger inside Makarria. This body thief was too confident, too smug by far. *I goaded Guderian into making a fatal mistake by showing him the truth. Why not the body thief?*

"Your over-confidence will be your undoing," Makarria said. "Already, you almost lost me once."

"Oh?"

"The assassination attempt in the council chamber and then the stables. If I had died, your plan would have been foiled. You're not half as clever as you think you are."

"Oh please," the fake queen scoffed. "You think something like that happened by happenstance? I was the one who paid those men, uniformed them, and got them inside the palace. That's why I had to kill them all, lest they ratted me out."

"You'd be a fool to risk to do such a thing."

"A gambler perhaps, but not a fool. What better way to regain the trust of the Queen and Prince than by foiling an assassination? And even more important, what fun!"

The *pthisicis-corporis* spoke with mock enthusiasm. There was no glimmer of mirth in its face. It leaned in close to Makarria, so close Makarria could smell the sour wine on its breath. Makarria had to turn away, not because of the stank breath, but because looking into her own distorted face was unbearable.

"You mistake me, dreamwielder," the body thief said in barely a whisper. "Just because I was captive, just because the Senate gave me orders, does not mean I am a slave. I am a *pthisicis-corporis*, and like the rest of my fallen race, I serve my own whims and purposes. You and the Republic senators are one and the same. You seek control over others. You use words like 'peace' and 'order,' but you really mean control—bending others to your will so the world makes sense in your eyes. Well, I don't see the world as you do. I am an agent of anarchy. I do as I please, when I please. My only pleasure in life is to destroy peace and order so others are forced to *really* make their own decisions for the first time in their lives."

Makarria raised her head and met the fake queen's stare unblinkingly. "You're wrong about me, body thief. I'm not the same as the Old World senators. Everything I've strived to do as queen has been to give people the liberty to live as they please, but every time I change a law to give people more freedom, someone takes that as license to exploit those around them. Sometimes it's greedy merchants. Sometimes it's self-righteous groups like the Brotherhood of Five. And sometimes it's an entire nation like the Old World Republic."

Makarria wet her cracking lips, ignoring the foreign sensation of the fleshy gumline where her teeth were missing. "I know what they did to your race," she continued. "The Old World Senate exterminated the *pthisicis-corporis*. All but a few, who were kept alive in captivity to do the Senate's bidding. You grew up as such, in chains, and I'm sorry for that. I really am. I may have grown up on a farm, but I lived with the same fear, the fear of extermination. Emperor Guderian hunted down anyone with the ability to perform sorcery. And as a dreamwielder, you can be sure he wanted me dead. I ran at first, but like you, I realized I needed to face those who would control me. I faced Guderian, and he placed me in a dungeon before I killed him and set his people free. Has it all gone as I hoped? No. But it's not too late. Why perpetuate the injustice that was done to us, when we can end the cycle of hate and violence? The treaty you signed can be undone. Let me go, give me my own body again, and we can work together. Together, we can turn the Old World away and make the Five Kingdoms truly free. You must have a real name. Tell me and I will accept you for who you are, make you one of my most trusted advisors. Clearly, you have wisdom beyond my understanding."

The fake queen stepped back and smiled again, this one seemingly genuine. "Oh you are amazing, young queen, to tempt me so. You actually believe what you're saying, which is endearing. But you'd be a fool to trust me, and besides, even if I bought into the notion a kingdom could be free, it's much too late for that now. I've put into action a series of events that can't be stopped. Even your feeble seer friend has foreseen it."

"Taera?"

"Indeed, she's been a busy little bee. She built an airship and had a message delivered to me. She's foreseen my murder in her visions. Or your murder rather. Fina, your bodyguard has figured me out, and with no way of saving the real you down here in the dungeon and with no one to believe her except your fat scribe in the library, she will try to kill me in your body rather than let me cause further damage to the kingdom."

Makarria couldn't believe it. She'd only known Fina for a short time, but she'd come to trust the woman, and she couldn't imagine Fina killing Makarria's body and condemning her to live the rest of her life in Lorentz's broken body. The very thought frightened her more than death itself.

"You don't think she's capable of it," the fake queen said, guessing Makarria's thoughts. "Likely she wouldn't have done it of her own accord, but that's the beauty of prophecy—more often than not it is self-fulfilling. Your seer friend has a vision and tries to warn you, but warns me instead. I pass on this foretelling to Fina, who pretends like she doesn't know what I really am and swears she would never harm me. 'I trust you completely,' I tell her in turn, but I know, like you know now, that I've planted the seed in her mind. Her other options will suddenly seem hopeless and futile. The foretelling will grow in her mind until it seems like it is her destiny, that there is no escaping it. On the morrow, or the next, she *will* give in to her destiny, and render this body I've taken from you lifeless. But I'll be ready, of course. Into her body or another's I'll jump, and then all will be chaos. I'll escape in the confusion, and when the Old World finally regains order—as they most certainly will—I will be long gone, and Senator Emil, or someone like him, will find you down here wearing the mind cage and think you are me. Off you'll go to Khail Sanctu to be locked away in a prison just as I was."

"Why are you telling me all this?" Makarria demanded, seething with anger, wanting nothing more than to use her power, but not daring to do so. "Did you come here just to gloat about how clever you are?"

"I'm not above gloating, it's true, but this is much more important than simple gloating." The *pthisicis-corporis* leaned in close again and tapped two fingers on the framework of the mind cage. Blinding pain shot through Makarria's head, and she reeled backward only to clank the cage into the wall behind her and send another shock of pain through her skull and down her spine.

"Do I have your attention again?" the *pthisicis-corporis* asked after a moment. "This is important, so listen carefully. I am doing you a favor, dreamwielder. I am setting you free. How can you live your potential when you're bound to the duties of a queen, beholden to the laws of some self-righteous sorcerers who crossed the Spine three hundred years ago? I've been living your life for only four days, and I'm already fed up with it. The responsibilities. The expectations. The propriety. You'll finally be free of all of it. You'll be sent off to a secret prison in Khail Sanctu as a *pthisicis-corporis*, where you'll have plenty of time to ruminate on the purpose of your existence, maybe for a year or two, maybe for a decade. Who can say? But eventually you will be released. The Senate might have a task for you, or if not, they will bring you a new body when the one you wear now is old and close to dying. Either way they will remove your mind cage, thinking you a *pthisicis-corporis*. But you are much more than that, and in that moment you will be truly free for the first time in your life. It's no secret, I hope you will show the Old World Republic what you think of their idea of liberty and freedom. The Old World has not seen a dreamwielder of your likes in thousands of years, and they are long overdue to be humbled. But you can do as you please. Perhaps you'll seek me out, wiser and more prepared to face me the second time."

Words were beyond Makarria. Emperor Guderian had been belligerent in his beliefs and easily angered, but the *pthisicis-corporis* was unflappable. All Makarria could do was return the fake queen's glare.

"You stare back at me in defiance, still not believing what I say," the fake queen said. "You think—what?—that one of your friends will save you still? Perhaps this will convince you." The *pthisicis-corporis* turned away and grabbed the satchel lying on the floor. Makarria had completely forgotten about it. The *pthisicis-corporis* hefted it up with one hand, and Makarria could see something dark and wet dripping from the bottom of it. A sense of dread filled her, but what the *pthisicis-corporis* pulled out of the sack was the yellow speaking stone.

"Another clever trick, this," the *pthisicis-corporis* said. "A magical stone for speaking to your friends. I had not foreseen it. In fact, I would have been oblivious to it if Talitha of Issborg had not called out to you the other night. Alas, Fina was not there to witness my discovery. When Queen Taera's airship arrived this morning she sent your fat scribe to deliver a red stone, and Fina tried to sneak into my room and steal this one. I was not fast enough to catch the fat man in time, but I did catch this one."

Makarria felt a surge of triumph at hearing the news of Natale's success. *I might be locked up, but now Caile and Taera and Talitha can help one another, at least.*

"Don't look so pleased," the *pthisicis-corporis* said, and with a grunt hurled the speaking stone against the wall, where it shattered into a thousand pieces of yellow gravel that skittered across the stone floor. "Your friends can talk now, but none of them know about you. The only ones who know about you are Fina and…" The pthisicis-corporis paused to reach back into the rucksack.

"No!" Makarria shouted, realizing what it was too late.

"…the fat man," said the *pthisicis-corporis*, hefting up Natale's severed head. Jagged chunks of the scholar's vertebrae hung from the bottom of the sundered neck, and his wide, glassed-over eyes reflected the flickering torchlight dully.

"I couldn't very well have loose ends lying around, could I?" the *pthisicis-corporis* said. "And besides, it will give Fina one final nudge to fulfill her destiny and murder me when she finds Natale's dismembered body in the library."

Makarria sobbed, slow, tearless heaves that wracked through her body. "No," she moaned. "Why?"

"In fact, I dismissed Fina from duty for the rest of the evening," the *pthisicis-corporis* said, ignoring Makarria's weeping. "She is very likely making her grisly discovery as we speak. It was much messier than I intended. I had to do the dirty business myself, and your waifish arms aren't well suited to hefting a short sword. But it is done and done, and you are all alone, dreamwielder."

Makarria screamed, a wordless, feral cry of anger and anguish.

The *pthisicis-corporis* grinned and reached up and wound the turnkey on Makarria's mind cage, five quick turns, and on the fifth turn Makarria screamed herself into oblivion.

19
Corporis Amiserunt

Caile sat by himself in the room he shared with Thon, holding the orange speaking stone in both hands. Thon was gone, off fetching food for the both of them from the mess hall, and now that Caile was alone with his thoughts, he felt more helpless than ever. He had tried everything he could think of since arriving in Col Sargoth and had gotten nowhere. The election council was moving inexorably forward to elect Lord Kobel, and Caile was completely out of the loop. No one on the election council would even meet with him anymore.

He let out a long breath and spoke into his orange speaking stone, too lost and too worried to care about his pride anymore. "Makarria, can you hear me? Makarria? Makarria?"

Nothing. He closed his eyes and concentrated on the image of her yellow speaking stone in his mind, and tried again.

"Makarria? Are you there?"

He kept at it for a good ten minutes to no end before finally flinging the stone onto his bed in frustration. *Only six days until the election, and I've made no progress. I'm worthless here. I should have stayed in Sol Valaróz with Makarria. Something's happened, or she would have contacted me by now.*

"Damn it all!" he yelled, punching the pillow on his bed and then flinging it across the room. He snatched up the speaking stone again and looked into its orange swirls, this time imagining the color silver. "Talitha! Talitha! It's Caile. Can you hear me?"

Nothing.

Caile closed his eyes and concentrated harder. "Talitha!"

He waited, and still nothing.

This time he pictured Talitha's face and squeezed his speaking stone so hard the color drained from his fingers. "Talitha! Talitha, please…Talitha?"

• • •

Fina twirled the stem of the wine glass between her fingers, then set it back down on the nightstand and picked up her letter to read it over one last time. The ink was dry and the words were as good as she would ever get them, so she folded the parchment and grabbed her candle to dribble out a dollop of wax to seal it closed. She had no official seal, so she used her thumb instead. When the wax was dry, she flipped the letter over, dabbed her quill into the inkpot, and addressed the front: *Princess Prisca.*

With the letter done, she examined the short sword at her side and the dagger in her belt one last time to make sure they were loose in their scabbards. Satisfied that all was ready, she grabbed the wine glass and lifted it to her lips. *We knew each other only briefly, Natale, but you were a good man and deserving of better,* she toasted silently, sipping and savoring the sharp tang of the red wine on her tongue for a moment before tipping the glass back to drain the rest of it in one giant gulp.

I must hurry now, and do my duty, she told herself. Already, the fake queen was downstairs, readying to enter the throne room for the *official proclamation*, the body thief called it, but *surrendering to the Old World* was more accurate. Makarria's royal parents would be down there already too, along with the ambassadors and the newly arrived delegation from the Old World. Fina needed to move fast if she wanted to deliver the letter to Prisca's room and make it to the throne room in time.

• • •

Caile tossed the speaking stone onto the bed again, disgusted. Makarria had sent him away thinking he had betrayed her, and now something had happened to her, he was certain. Otherwise she would have contacted him to discuss the election if nothing else. It had been five days since he'd arrived in Col Sargoth, seven days since he'd left Sol Valaróz, and nothing? And what of Talitha? Where could she be? Caile was utterly alone, and even Thon was gone now.

For too long now, Caile realized. *Where is Thon?*

He walked to the door, opened it, and peered out into the corridor. He saw three cavalrymen at the far end of the hallway, but no sign of Thon. With a dissatisfied grunt, he slammed the door closed again. It shouldn't have taken Thon so long to go fetch a few trenchers of stew from the mess hall. *Maybe someone struck up a conversation with him. But who?* Thon had elicited less attention than Caile himself had here in Lightbringer's Keep, and Caile was a prince.

Someone knocked at the door.

Caile frowned and opened it.

"Prince Caile Delios," one of the cavalrymen said in a hushed tone. "Come with us. Quietly."

Caile looked down and saw the man held a dagger two inches from his stomach.

• • •

Even though they recognized her as the queen's personal bodyguard, the guards at Prisca and Galen's door refused to let Fina in. One of them, at least, agreed to step inside himself and set Fina's letter on Prisca's desk for her to find when she returned. "Won't you see her in the throne room?" the other guard asked. "Why not just give it to her there?"

"Because a throne room is no place for reading letters," Fina said simply, and hurried away toward the stairs.

• • •

It was madness to try and push past three Sargothian cavalrymen, but that's exactly what Caile did. He slapped the dagger out of the hand of the first solider, then lowered his shoulder into his chest to drive him back into the other two men. Before they could regain their balance, Caile spun aside into the corridor and dashed away.

The cavalrymen cursed and their heavy footfalls echoed through the corridor as they chased after him. Caile reached down to grab his sword as he sprinted toward the end of the hallway and realized his sword wasn't there. He'd taken his belt and scabbard off as soon as he'd returned to his room from the council meeting, he remembered. *Fool!* he cursed himself, but it was of no matter. He was a fast runner and he was nearly to the end of the corridor where it opened up into the grand hallway of the keep. The hexagonal hallway of Lightbringer's Keep was always bustling with people and there were dozens of side corridors he could slip into to lose his assailants.

Caile chanced a glance backward and grinned when he saw he was already outdistancing his followers. *Finally, something is happening!* he rejoiced, but when he turned forward again he saw three new cavalrymen rush to block the exit.

• • •

Fina stepped quietly into the sitting room adjoining the throne room and closed the door behind her. Inside, the fake queen was joined by Ambassador Mahalath, as well as Senator Emil and two legionnaires, both armed with shields and stout short swords. Senator Emil had arrived by sea not three hours earlier with an escort of twenty ships from the Old World. At the fake queen's command, the Valarion generals welcomed a thousand Old World legionnaires into the city, into the royal palace itself, and now the fake queen was about to officially turn over power of the city, and the kingdom, to Senator Emil. The satisfied look he wore on his face made Fina want to take his head off, but she remained focused on the task before her.

The fake queen glanced up from her chair to see Fina standing there and winked. *The body thief taunts me. It knows what I'm about to do. It wants me to. Perhaps it already knows my inner thoughts, but it's too late to turn back now.* Fina ignored the fake queen and went to stand at the ready by the double doors leading to the throne room. Her stomach cramped, and she could feel sweat beginning to bead on her forehead. *You only have one shot at this, Alafina Infierno,* she told herself, blinking away the blurriness in her eyes. *May your dagger be true and your grip strong.*

"Is all ready out there?" the fake queen demanded.

Fina wiped the sweat from her brow and pushed one of the doors open a crack to peer inside the throne room. As before, it was packed with tittering aristocrats, guildmasters, generals, and more. The herald stood at the ready to announce the queen, and a dozen Royal Guards stood at the foot of the dais, six to each side so as not to block the view of the throne.

"All is ready, Your Majesty," Fina said, turning back to the fake queen. "You're certain this is what you want to do?"

Senator Emil shot her a black look. "The treaty is already signed, and this hearing is nothing but a formality. Who are you to question a queen?"

"Never mind her, Senator," the fake queen said, rising to her feet. "She means well. A loyalist to the end, she is. Go on then, Fina. Open the doors and let's face the Kingdom of Valaróz."

• • •

Caile's second attempt at plowing through his assailants proved less successful than the first. He managed to knock the first cavalryman down, but the man was ready for him. He grabbed Caile around the waist as he fell and they both tumbled to the hard basalt floor. Caile elbowed him in the stomach and managed to slip free of his grip for a moment, but before he could regain his feet beneath him, one of the other cavalrymen punched him square in the nose. His head flailed back and stars filled his vision, and it was all he could to do maintain consciousness. Not that it helped him. One of the soldiers wrenched both of his arms behind his back to clap them in irons, and another shoved a black hood over his head.

Caile yelled for help once, but that only earned another punch, this one to the soft spot beneath his ribs that knocked the air out of him. When he finally regained his breath and his senses, he was being dragged away and knew better than to struggle.

• • •

The fake queen was announced first, and Fina stepped out onto the dais behind her to take her place to the left of the throne while the men of the Old World waited in the sitting room. Fina's hands were trembling now. The blurriness in her eyes was worse, and she could feel sweat from her armpits soaking the short sleeved gambeson beneath her chainmail, could feel sweat trickling down between her breasts.

"My people," the fake queen spoke, sitting up straight in the throne. "You have heard the rumors of the Old World Republic and, today, have seen the ships in the harbor. You have also heard the rumors of my missteps, the accusations from the Brotherhood of Five. I will deny them no longer. I am young. A woman, and prone to foolishness."

Fina bristled at the words. *Makarria would never say such a thing. I should kill the creature now, before it speaks further ill or announces the senator.* But the senator's words were true. The treaty was already signed and this was nothing more than a theatrical farce for the benefit of the court. The only way to undo a treaty signed by the queen was to kill the queen. From there, rule would fall to Makarria's mother, the Princess Prisca. *And if I'm going to kill the body thief along with Makarria's body, I have to time it perfectly,* she reminded herself. Her stomach cramped again, but she gritted her teeth against the pain.

"I have made mistakes, I admit," the fake queen went on. "But always I have loved you, my people, and I love our kingdom more than anything. Emperor Guderian and Don Bricio left our fair kingdom in tatters, though. Even with the aid of the finest advisors and generals Sol Valaróz has to offer, I have been unable to restore the peace and harmony we deserve. That is why I have enlisted the aid of the Old World Republic."

The fake queen stood and held up one hand welcomingly to the doors at the back of the dais. "My people, I present to you Senator Emil and Ambassador Mahalath of the Old World."

Soon now, Fina told herself, blinking the sweat and blurriness from her eyes. *Very soon.*

• • •

Blinded as he was with the black hood, Caile had no idea where he was, but it was far from Lightbringer's Keep, that was for certain. His captors had dragged him away through some hushed corridor and outside into a courtyard. He was able to discern that much by the noises and smells around him, but then he'd been heaved into the back of a horse drawn wagon and carted off. The city noises all sounded the same to him. Someone better acquainted with Col Sargoth might be able figure out where they were by the unique calls of vendors or roaring of steam-powered rickshaws, but not Caile. All he knew was that he'd been in the cart for a quarter hour before it came to a stop and he was dragged out again.

It had to be Commander Buell who had ordered him captured, Caile knew. It was cavalrymen who had taken him, and they wouldn't act except under Buell's orders. The real question was, who was Buell in league with? Caile had a brief glimmer of hope at the thought it might be Talitha, but that made no sense. If Talitha needed him, she had simpler ways of summoning him.

Well, you're about to find out soon enough. You did ask for it.

The cavalrymen dragged him through the dirt of another courtyard and then into a corridor. Caile could hear the footsteps of his captors' boots clacking on stone. And then it was down a stairwell, through another corridor, and into a chamber that echoed with the cavalrymen's footsteps, where Caile was dumped onto the stone floor.

"Up onto your knees!" one of the soldiers barked.

That proved to be easier said than done with his hands secured behind his back, but after a few moments he managed it. Someone yanked the hood off of his head then, and he was assaulted by the light of a dozen torches in sconces at the far wall of the tiny chamber. Caile had to squint to focus his eyes. He was in what looked like a cell, he realized. *Not good.* To either side of him were his armed escorts—four cavalrymen—and standing in front of him were two figures cloaked in black. With the torchlight behind them, he could see them only as silhouettes.

Well, I am a prince, Caile thought. *I best play the part.*

"What's the meaning of this?" he demanded. "I'm here under the authority of Queen Makarria of Valaróz, Conqueror of Sargoth, Dreamwielder."

"Queen Makarria cannot help you," one of the figures said.

Caile recognized the voice immediately. *Lady Hildreth?*

She stepped closer into the light so that he could see her face beneath the dark waves of her hair. Beside her, the other figure lowered the hood of his cowl and Caile saw it was Commander Buell.

"As we speak, the dreamwielder is surrendering Valaróz to the Old World," Lady Hildreth said. "And you, young prince, are utterly alone. And a fool."

Caile didn't believe it—Makarria would never surrender—but Lady Hildreth was right about the second part. Caile was utterly alone and a fool both.

• • •

Senator Emil was addressing the court, but the words meant nothing to Fina. They were merely background noise to the high-pitched buzzing in her ears. Her stomach was in knots, and her hands trembling. *It's time.*

She blinked the blurriness from her eyes and glanced from the fake queen sitting at the throne to the crowd of people below her. Prisca was out there, near the forefront, watching the creature she thought was her daughter, shaking her head in confusion alongside Galen and Captain Haviero. *I'm sorry, Prisca. Read my letter and you will understand.*

Fina wiped the palms of her hands on her breeches and reached for her dagger, knowing the sword would end things too quickly. The Royal Guards were a dozen steps away. The Old World legionnaires were intent on their own masters, paying Fina no heed. None of them would be able to reach her in time. *Only the body thief knows what I'm about to do.* Fina pushed aside the pain of the knots in her belly, and pulled the dagger from its sheath.

The fake queen looked up and smiled just as Fina lunged forward.

Someone in the crowd screamed, but Fina was focused on gripping her dagger tight. She jabbed it once into the fake queen's belly, right below the ribs. *Hold tight!* she screamed in her mind. On the second jab, the fake queen grabbed her around the wrist and everything was chaos: a cacophony of sounds, a blur of smells and colors, and a prickling sensation like a million needles in her skin. *Hold tight, Alafina!*

When she opened her eyes with a gasp, she was sitting on the throne, looking up at herself. A knife was buried in her belly, the pain blinding and hot, but she pushed through it and held tight to the wrist in her grip. Guards were rushing up the dais, she realized. *To save the queen.*

"Halt!" she croaked. "Stay back!"

The guards stopped, uncertainly, pikes lowered and ready.

"It's all right. Stay back."

Blood was spilling out to soak the royal gown and trickle down the throne, but Fina was calm. She still held tightly to the hand that wielded the dagger. The body thief, wearing Fina's body, stared down at her, amused. "Fool," it whispered. "You're bleeding out, and as soon as you die the guards will abduct me, and I'll be gone, out of this body and into another."

But then Fina saw a cramp convulse through the body thief's

body. Slow realization dawned on the creature's face. It blinked its eyes. Once. Twice.

"What have you done?"

The body thief tried to pull away, panicked, but lost its footing in the blood spattered on the floor and fell to the ground with Fina still holding tightly. Fina willed herself off the seat of the throne to kneel beside the body thief and hold the trembling body down.

"It's all right, everyone," Fina said, her voice trembling, motioning the guards to stay back. The pain in her belly was excruciating. Only the blue sashes of the royal gown held her guts from spilling out.

"What have you done?" the body thief asked again. The skin it wore—Fina's skin—was soaked in sweat now, and pale as a corpse. Trembling.

"Wolfsbane," Fina whispered. "Poison. I was ready for you this time."

The body thief's breaths were shallow now. The guards on the dais were stepping slowly toward her.

"Stay back," Fina said, coughing up a gout of blood.

Someone screamed, "Help her!"

Prisca, Fina realized. The guards were rushing forward. The body thief's breaths had stopped, but she had to be sure. With the last of her willpower and strength, she yanked the dagger from her belly and slit the body thief's throat. Only then did Fina finally let herself go.

20
Lost

The woman stabs Makarria in the stomach, once, twice, but it's not Makarria—only Makarria's shell. Both of the women fall from the throne to melt away into a pool of blood that becomes a turbulent sea. A woman's scream becomes a crack of thunder, and lightning peels down from the veil of clouds stretching from one end of the horizon to the other. A ship glimmers in the distance, rising to the crest of a wave for a moment, then disappearing in a trough the next. Waves crash down upon the deck, splintering the main mast, but the ship somehow stays afloat. A flame grows from where the mast is sundered, yellow and strong, a beacon of light in the darkness of the storm. In the center of the light is Makarria, but the waves build up and crash down upon her, dragging her beneath the sea.

And then all is black.

Caile is alone, in a tomb of rock. He cries out someone's name. Makarria, he calls out, but hears nothing in response. Talitha, he calls out. Taera, he calls out.

But Taera is watching her factory as airships fly out of the hangar, one after another. Guderian's war machines approach from the west. To the east, the surf in Kal Pyrthin Bay grows as the Old World ships draw nearer. The waves lick at her ankles, then her calves and thighs. And her hands are covered in blood, viscous and dark like naphtha…

Taera awoke with a strangled gasp, the bed sheets of her tiny bunk wrapped around her face and neck, her body soaked in sweat. It took her a moment to remember she was still onboard *Casstian's Breath*, not in her own room. She threw the bed sheets aside and stepped out of the tiny cabin onto deck, expecting it to be deep into the night, but the crescent moon was still low in the sky to the east. She had been asleep for not even an hour, she realized. Far below, she could see the silent forms of the Old World ships at anchor. Beyond them, to the south, was a sprawling darkness that blotted out the stars along the horizon, just as in her vision.

A storm is coming, she told herself and then slipped belowdeck back to the warmth of her cabin and bed.

• • •

"What do you know of this? Why did the dreamwielder send you here?"

Caile shook his head, still not believing what Lady Hildreth had told him. *Makarria surrender to the Old World? Never.* But at the same time, Caile hadn't heard from her since leaving, and he'd left her in a dire situation with the Old World and the Brotherhood of Five both pressuring her. After what Caile had done to her, perhaps it was all too much and she had bowed the Old World's will. Caile took a deep breath. All he could do now was take care of himself and do what he was tasked to do.

"I was sent here to make sure the Old World had no possible excuse for invading," Caile said at last, shifting the weight on his knees, which were already aching from kneeling on the stone floor. He didn't know who Lady Hildreth and Commander Buell were in league with, but he would throw the truth in their face to find out, he decided. "The Old World sent emissaries to Queen Makarria, insisting the Sargothian election would fail and that chaos would break out. They offered her aid, but their offer was little more than a demand to join them and solidify the Five Kingdoms under their rule. She told them no, and I was sent here to make sure the Sargothian election was carried out lawfully and fairly."

Lady Hildreth narrowed her eyes. Beside her, Commander Buell stood, his expression implacable.

"The Old World would come offering more than threats," Lady Hildreth said. "Daggers mixed with honey has always been their way."

Caile narrowed his eyes. "Yes. They urged Makarria to disband the election committee and claim dominion of Sargoth herself, as was her right when she killed Guderian. They suggested the Five Kingdoms would be stronger and more unified under her rule."

"And you mean to tell me she was not seduced by the prospect?"

"I could ask you the same, Lady Hildreth."

Lady Hildreth shot up one eyebrow in surprise. "The Old World Republic has nothing to gain from me, but it makes sense they would see an opportunity in a young queen, just as they have seen an opportunity here in Sargoth where there is no king at all."

Caile nodded, wanting to believe Lady Hildreth, but not daring yet to believe she might be an ally. "If Makarria wanted to rule Sargoth," he said, "she would have claimed it when she killed Guderian."

"That was before she was even coronated Queen of Valaróz. Before *you* became her advisor; the young prince who served as ward to Don Bricio in Valaróz, and then to Guderian himself here in Col Sargoth; the prince who killed Wulfram and stood by as his father's throne was given to his older sister instead of him. It seems to me, you might have motives for ambitions beyond simply advising Queen Makarria."

Caile was shocked by the insinuation. She trusted him less than he trusted her, it seemed. "Pyrthin law dictates the throne to fall to the eldest child, regardless of gender," he told her. "It has always been such. And Taera and I had a brother—Cargan—older than both of us before Guderian killed him. The throne was never meant to be mine. I knew that. I never wanted it. And I'd never council Queen Makarria to lust for more power. Trust me, we've had our hands full as it is trying to remove the stain of Don Bricio and that madman Guderian from Valaróz."

Lady Hildreth's face hardened at Caile's mention of Guderian, but only for a moment before returning to her placid expression. "Why then would the dreamwielder submit to the Old World?"

Caile stared at her for a long moment, debating how much to

tell her. *What does it matter?* he decided. *She seems to be just as concerned about the Old World as I am, and I know little and less. Let her be as flummoxed as me.*

"I have to admit, I don't know. Makarria's initial plan was to come here to Col Sargoth herself to oversee the election, but then something happened…"

"What something happened?"

"Our wine was drugged and I did something horrible to the queen, though I can't for the life of me remember doing it…"

"Perhaps it was more than drugged wine," Lady Hildreth suggested. "Sorcery, perhaps? As I said, the Old World mixes honey with daggers."

Caile's eyes widened. The thought of ensorcelment had not even occurred to him, but it made sense with the timing of it all. His inexplicable assault on Makarria had followed right on the heels of the Old World arriving and the assassination attempt on Makarria. A sorcerer, a spy of some sort, would explain much.

"I don't know," Caile admitted. "You may be right. Whatever happened, Makarria sent me here in her stead, and I've not heard from her since. She was under vast pressure, both from the Old World and the Brotherhood of Five. If, as you say, the Old World had something to do with drugging—or ensorceling me—perhaps they did the same to Makarria. That's the only thing I can imagine that would explain it. There's no way Makarria would surrender to the Old World of her own accord."

Lady Hildreth regarded him silently for a moment, then turned to Buell, standing beside her. "What think you, brother?"

Brother? No wonder Buell went to her. Caile had gone to inspect the war wagon factory fully expecting Buell to rat him out to the houndkeeper or one of the guildmasters who might be in league with the Old World. He'd never suspected it would be to Lady Hildreth, though, or that the two of them were siblings. Apparently, it wasn't well known, otherwise Thon would have mentioned it to Caile.

"He's either a fine actor, or he's telling the truth," Buell said.

Lady Hildreth huffed. "All princes are fine actors, but you're right. I see no reason for him to be in league with the Old World."

"You're satisfied then?" a voice said from behind Caile.

Caile craned his head to the side to see who it was speaking, expecting it to be one of the cavalryman, but it was someone new who had snuck into the cell silently behind him: the houndkeeper.

Natarios Rhodas gave him a lopsided grin, then turned to Lady Hildreth again. "I told you he was nothing more than a pawn in all this."

"Why is this worm here?" Caile demanded. He'd had no interaction with the houndkeeper outside the election council meetings, but Caile's father had told him enough about Natarios Rhodas to know what sort of man he was. "If anyone is in league with the Old World, it's him."

"Sweet prince, I'd be offended by your cruel words if there weren't some truth to them," Natarios said. "But I promise, we are bonded by a mutual foe now."

"The schemer has turned to us for aid," Lady Hildreth told Caile, "if only because those whom he schemed with have turned their schemes against him."

The houndkeeper smiled wanly. "Yes, well, maybe we could discuss all this someplace more comfortable now that we're all friends. Someplace beside a warm fire, perhaps?"

"Soldiers, unchain Prince Caile," Lady Hildreth said, but she grabbed onto his shoulder before they unbound him and gave him an apologetic frown. "I'm not holding you as a prisoner, Prince Caile, but you're not exactly free either. You must stay down here and out of sight. Ambassador Rives wants you taken captive to use as leverage against your sister, and I trust not even my own household staff to keep our secret. Idle gossip could easily reach his spies' ears and implicate me. We can't afford that yet, and it's best if you're not seen here either, houndkeeper."

Caile said nothing as the cavalrymen unlocked the irons binding his wrists and helped him to his feet. It was best to stay silent and learn what he could, he decided. He was in Lady Hildreth's own estate he knew now, and in no imminent danger.

"There's no fireplace, I'm afraid, but we can retire to the guardroom and speak there," Lady Hildreth said, leading the way out of the cell.

"And perhaps some wine?" the houndkeeper suggested.

"No wine."

Caile followed in the wake of Lady Hildreth, Commander Buell, and the houndkeeper, who cowed away from Caile's presence but dared not push his way past Buell in the cramped corridor of the dungeon. Behind Caile, two cavalrymen stayed on his heels. *They trust me some, but not wholly.*

Lady Hildreth led them to a larger room, more brightly lit, and replete with a square table and chairs, but otherwise no more comforting than the jail cell. "Sit," she told them.

Caile took the seat across from her, leaving the houndkeeper to sit to his right, who looked none too pleased by the prospect judging by the way he scooched his chair as far away from Caile as possible.

"Comfortable enough for you?" Lady Hildreth asked Natarios, not waiting for his answer. "Go on, tell the prince what you heard, and we'll see if he can be of any help."

The houndkeeper cleared his throat and turned to Caile. "Yes well, it was actually your escape from Emperor Guderian, Prince, that gave me the idea. I overheard him speaking with Wulfram about how you escaped through tunnels beneath the keep. The two of them had no knowledge of it before your escape, and to the best of my reckoning, the four of us here now are the only ones still alive who know about it."

"The details of your sneaking aren't important," Lady Hildreth snapped. "Get to what you heard."

"Right. I knew Ambassador Rives was up to something, so I used the tunnels and found one beneath Ambassador Rives' room. I overheard him having a secret meeting with the guildmasters from the steam-engineer's and sorcerer's guilds. And also with someone else, a sorcerer from the Old World, I think. They somehow were able to speak with a senator from the Old World Republic."

"Yes," Caile interrupted. "Makarria and I suspected the Old

World of using some sort of speaking relic that allows them to communicate over great distances. They knew about Talitha's impeachment before we did in Sol Valaróz. Was it Senator Emil they spoke with?"

The houndkeeper's eyes lit up. "Yes! And he was definitely the one giving orders. All this time I had thought it was King Lorimer orchestrating things through his ambassador out of simple greed. I was glad to help when it was just a king and a few guildmasters and I was promised a big slice of the pie. I mean, what harm was there in putting Kobel on the throne and firing up Guderian's factories again if everyone was out to make a little money, particularly me? But it's not as simple as that. King Lorimer has put everything into place to turn the Five Kingdoms over to the Old World. In return, he'll be the overlord."

"The Kingdom of Golier has a long history of treachery, but I never suspected King Lorimer would commit outright treason," Caile said. "I'll take his head myself if I ever get my hands on the bastard."

"We can deal with King Lorimer and his treachery later," Lady Hildreth said. "We have more pressing matters first. The senator told Ambassador Rives that Queen Makarria was surrendering Valaróz and that a fleet from the Old World would arrive here in Col Sargoth on the day of the election. The votes are secured to put Kobel on the throne and he'll open the city to them, then unlock the factory gates to march out the war machines. Once that happens, there will be no one who can stop them, not your sister, and certainly not King Hanns in Norg."

"And to prevent any objections," the houndkeeper interrupted, "the senator ordered Rives to murder the entire election council once the vote is secured. Even me. The sorcerer's guildmaster intends to burn us all alive with firewielders."

"Everyone except you, prince," Lady Hildreth added. "You, he ordered captured immediately. You've garnered a reputation as being rash in your actions. He didn't want you to give them any unexpected surprises. That's why we had to abduct you so hastily. In order to save you from them."

"A surprise of its own," Caile said. "But thank you. Whatever hasty actions I've made were to stir up my enemies, and now that I know them, I mean to act. If Kobel is the key to their plan, then we'll get rid of him. I'll accuse him of treason in the council hearing tomorrow, and challenge him to a trial by combat. He's more of a hothead than me. He'd never refuse."

"That's noble of you, but Rives would never allow it," Lady Hildreth said, shaking her head.

"She's right," the houndkeeper agreed. "I may be lord of proceedings in name, but Rives has wrestled control of that council from me with Old World money. He'll refuse your demands, and vote you out of the council chambers. And then his men will know exactly where to find you, and they won't be content to simply capture you anymore."

"Then I'll denounce Rives and demand a trial by combat with him too," Caile insisted.

"Did you not hear the part about the firewielders?" Lady Hildreth asked. "Try anything rash in that council room and the sorcerer's guild will cook you before you can draw your sword."

"What then?" Caile demanded, annoyed by their casual refusal of all his ideas. "Commander, you have control of the war-wagon factory. You can fortify it and refuse to turn it over to Kobel, right? Whoever controls those wagons holds the might of Sargoth."

"Even if I wanted to, the factory is too big to defend indefinitely," Buell said. "It has a half dozen entry points and easy access from the river. I wouldn't be able to defend it for more than a day against the Royal Guard, let alone the Old World legionnaires who will be on those ships. My cavalrymen are trained to fight on horseback outside, not to defend a fortification."

"We appreciate your enthusiasm, Prince," Lady Hildreth said, "but the only answer is to offer up a superior candidate to the council, one that they would have no choice but to elect."

The houndkeeper laughed. "Like who?"

"How about you, Commander Buell," Caile suggested.

"My brother would make a fine king," Lady Hildreth said. "The council would not find him to their liking, though. No, there is someone better suited." She turned to Buell, who nodded for her to proceed. Lady Hildreth took a deep breath. "I have a child, grown now," she said. "And he is the son of Thedric Guderian."

The houndkeeper gasped, but Caile managed to keep his surprise contained. Thon had told him of the rumors that Lady Hildreth had been Guderian's mistress. It only made sense that she would have a child with him.

"If you have a direct descendant of Guderian, then we can bypass the council vote altogether," the houndkeeper said, grinning like a stupid animal. "Who is he?"

"Yes," Caile agreed. "Who is he, and why hasn't he come forward? Where is he?"

"I was hoping you could answer that question," Lady Hildreth said. "When we abducted you, we had hoped to steal him away too, but he was not in your room."

21
Code of War

Taera lowered the spyglass and handed it back to Admiral Laud, newly promoted to the position following the demise of Admiral Giorgi. The storm had drawn closer, but the Old World armada seemed oblivious. Whereas Taera had ordered the rest of the Pyrthin fleet to retreat for the safety of Kal Pyrthin Bay at first light, the Old World armada had done nothing; their ships still laid at anchor some sixty miles offshore, and the storm was nearly upon them. The massive bank of clouds coming from the south was dark as night, and even though it was still miles away, they were feeling its effects. The air was thick and heavy with moisture, and the buffeting winds were strong and unpredictable. Already, Dekle and the airship crew were having difficulty keeping the *Casstian's Breath* steady in the air.

"They're done for," Admiral Laud said, peering through the spyglass one last time. "That's a hundred year storm bearing down on them. They'll be lucky if a quarter of their ships survive."

"You really think it will be that bad?" Taera asked.

"It's nearly winter, Your Majesty. Most storms this time of year come from the north, riding the cold air out of the Norg Sea and the Barrier Mountains. This one is coming from the south, riding the warm waters out of the Sol Sea. It'll be wet and powerful, mark my words. The Badlands and Mount Pyr will be seeing their first downpour in twenty years. The best chance the Old World fleet has is to ride the headwind and hope to outrun the storm north and west. If they can make it past Tyrna, they could salvage their losses, but they don't seem intent on moving. They'll try to ride the storm out and when they realize their folly, they'll make for the Bay and try to cut through the strait, which will be the end of them. What few ships manage to get past the reefs in the high waters will be easy pickings for us when the storm finally blows over."

Taera wished Laud were right. She didn't doubt his assessment of the storm; Laud, after all, had more experience than any sailor in the Pyrthin fleet, and was not prone to making bombastic declarations in the way Admiral Giorgi had. Still, Taera remembered her vision from the night before well. Parts of it had been shrouded in the symbols endemic to dreams, perhaps, but the storm had been very literal, along with the threat of the Old World armada. Those ships would still be there when the storm passed, she knew.

Beneath their feet, the deck rumbled as the wind pummeled the airship's ether-filled hull.

"We've seen enough," Taera said. "You best get us back to the safety of Kal Pyrthin, Admiral."

Laud bowed sharply to her, then strode to the helm of the ship. "Full sails!" he barked at the crew. "Dekle, feast on the power of this storm and make a zephyr to take us home."

• • •

The people of Sol Valaróz reacted to their queen's death with violence. The riots had lasted throughout the night and well into the morning before the Republic legionnaires and Sol Valaróz's city watch were able to restore order, and even then it was a tenuous order at best. Fires still burned in the poorer boroughs, and the marketplaces were abandoned. The casualties were mostly rioters, but numerous innocent bystanders had been trampled to death in the mayhem, and a handful of skirmishes had broken out between the legionnaires and the city watch themselves thanks to Senator Emil's orders to kill all rioters on the spot. The legionnaires obeyed, but of course the city watch was reticent to stand by and watch their own people get killed by foreign soldiers. Ambassador Mahalath had warned Emil as much, but Emil had been adamant, and Mahalath had to admit in hindsight, however reluctantly, the tactics worked.

Apart from the fires, all was quiet now. The citizens had retreated to their homes, and the looting and killing was stopped. Mahalath just hoped the peace would hold until more legionnaires arrived. As it was, the Republic armada ships entering the harbor from the Sol Sea were arriving in only a sporadic stream.

The royal palace, at least, was safe. *It had been mayhem for a while when Queen Makarria was first murdered,* Mahalath reflected. The throne room had been utter chaos, with people screaming, shouting, and trampling over one another—some of them to get to the dais and aid the queen, others to flee. *I was as aghast and panicked as any of them,* Mahalath recalled. Senator Emil, ever in control of his emotions, was quick to take charge, though. Within minutes, Emil had orchestrated everything: the clearing of the throne room, the transport of the queen's body to her bedchambers to be attended to and mourned over by her parents, the immediate burning of the assassin's body, and the deployment of legionnaires to all the key points throughout the palace and the city to secure Republic control.

The Valarions, for their part, were completely inept without their queen. Queen Makarria's mother was hysterical and distraught, the captain of the Royal Guard preoccupied with attending to the mother, and no one else was even present to step forward and take command. Prince Delios was in Col Sargoth, they were told, and Queen Makarria's other advisors all conspicuously absent. The pompous fool representing the Brotherhood of Five, Master Rubino, was the only one to stick around and make his voice heard. He demanded a hearing, citing some ancient law, but Emil had him thrown out of the throne room, and just like that the Republic was in control of Sol Valaróz—the queen dead and Emil with the signed treaty to back up his claims of authority.

It's what we wanted, but it didn't have to be this way, Mahalath thought. *Queen Makarria already signed the treaty. It was done. There was no reason for her to die needlessly.* Mahalath had liked the young queen. She reminded him of himself when he was a youth: headstrong and idealistic. She had been caught in an impossible position, between a crumbling empire and the Republic eager to expand, but she had acted with honor and decisiveness. Mahalath had nothing but respect for her, but her own servant apparently didn't see it that way. Now Makarria was gone and Mahalath was left to reassemble a functioning Valarion government along with Emil, who had all the tact of a drunken bull.

"It is not up for debate," Emil was telling Admiral Biton, the man in charge of the Valarion navy. They were seated in Queen Makarria's council chamber—Mahalath, with Emil and the commander of the legionnaires, as well as the highest-ranking military officials in Sol Valaróz—and Emil was having his way with all of them. "Your ship captains will be demoted to first mates, and be replaced by Republic captains," Emil continued. "The Pyrthin navy is threatening to disrupt the peace we've worked so hard to gain. Do more need to die? I've shown you the treaty your queen signed, Admiral. If you or your ship captains refuse me, it's treason. I am well within my right to have you all executed."

"Save your threats," Admiral Biton said. "I'll see to it. The captains will step down and allow your men aboard."

"Good. Each of your forty naval ships will get a new captain and a protector—a sorcerer, to be clear. I'm quite aware of the kinship between Valaróz and Pyrthinia. The sorcerers will be there to ensure we have no mutiny. And if that's not enough, let your crews be reminded that it is Republic legionnaires who 'guard' what's left of the royal family. If there is any sort of mutiny, they will be less inclined to keep the royal family safe. Am I understood?"

"Aye."

Emil nodded, self-satisfied and unafraid to show it. His smirk stretched nearly ear to ear. Mahalath could barely stomach his arrogance, but the Senate knew what they were doing in sending him. Emil got results.

"Good," Emil said. "The tide goes out three hours after sunset, if I'm not mistaken. Your ships will leave with the tide and make straight away for Kal Pyrthin Bay to aid the Republic armada."

"It would be wise to wait a few days," Admiral Biton said. "A heavy storm is bearing out of the southern waters. It's veering away from the Sol Sea and is headed into the cold waters of the Esterian. It will be a ship-breaker."

"He speaks the truth of the matter," Mahalath spoke up. "Our reinforcements from Khail Sanctu have reported high seas and heavy cloud cover."

Emil shot Mahalath a dark look and then turned his gaze back upon Admiral Biton. "Your ships and sailors are renowned for their seaworthiness. I refuse to believe a little storm will get in their way. They will leave with the tide, or I will have your head."

"Aye," the admiral said, though his tone made it clear he didn't like it.

"Be away then," Emil said, shooing him away with a flippant wave of his hand. "All of you: admirals, generals, whatever you might be. Go."

The Valarions all filed out of the council room, leaving Mahalath alone with Emil and the captain of the legionnaires.

"Good then," Emil said. "Now all we need to do is put a Valarion face to our rule here. We'll follow standard protocol and appoint a council of Valarion governors. Mahalath, you will sit on the council as well, and as the only Republic senator here, the council will answer to me, at least until the Senate appoints chancellors for the Five Kingdoms. So then, what Valarions do we appoint as governors? Obviously, we have to appoint the Queen's mother, so as to acknowledge their archaic system of monarchy by birthright. But the woman is nothing more than a farm wench. She will be easily cowed. In addition to her, I was thinking of the man from the Brotherhood of Five, Master…"

"Master Rubino," Mahalath supplied. "Are you sure about him? He is outspoken, and his views are hardly progressive."

"Bah," Emil scoffed. "He pines to make Valaróz in the image of the Republic."

"Yes, but the Republic of three hundred years ago, when we still had slaves, and women were considered inferiors under the law."

"Women still are our inferiors," Emil said. "And the masses of imbeciles who drive the Republic economy are slaves in all but name.

Having someone on the Valarion council to voice such conservative views will do no harm. And besides, Rubino has more influence in the city than anyone else from what I can discern. We'll need him to keep the people in line. We'll also need a military figurehead. None of these generals or admirals we met with today will do. They're too stubborn and loyal." Senator Emil turned to the commander of the Legionnaires. "Commander, you're in charge of finding a good candidate among the officers in the Royal Guard and city watch. Pick someone who is young and ambitious, a man who is willing to sell out his own people for power."

"As you say, Senator," the commander replied.

Emil looked back upon Mahalath. "Who else then? That's only four, including yourself. We need to find two more, at least, in order to represent a wider selection of the Valarion people. A working man, I think. One of the guildmasters, perhaps?"

"Yes," Mahalath agreed. "I'd recommend the scholar Natale, too, as he provided council to Queen Makarria, but my men discovered him dead this morning. He was slain where he worked in the library. Beheaded."

"Unfortunate," Emil remarked. "Most likely killed by the same mad woman who killed the Queen. Exactly the reason women shouldn't be given swords or seats in government. They're beholden to their emotions."

Mahalath faked a thin smile and bit his tongue. *My wife is five times the senator you are. You're nothing but a blunt instrument.*

"Well?" Emil demanded. "Who else? A dead scholar can't sit on the council. You've been here over a week. Surely you've made contact with someone suitable."

Before Mahalath could respond, there was a commotion at the door, and two Valarion guardsmen pushed their way into the council room along with the queen's parents, who were clearly distraught. The two legionnaires who had been guarding the door were grabbing at the Valarion soldiers, trying to pull them back outside, their hands reaching for their short swords.

Mahalath jumped to his feet. "Legionnaires! Stand down. Let

them pass."

Everyone went suddenly still at his command. The legionnaires shot a glance at their commander who sat to Mahalath's side. At his nod, they composed themselves and exited, leaving only the royal parents and their two guards. One of them Mahalath recognized: Captain Haviero. Mahalath had been about to recommend him for the council, even knowing Emil wouldn't like it.

"Senator," the queen's mother said. "Ambassador. Your soldiers have barred our entry to the dungeons."

"What need have you to visit the dungeons?" Emil demanded, showing little courtesy to the woman who had just lost her child, and was a queen by right.

Before she even responded, Mahalath tensed, knowing what she was about to say. *The pthisicis-corporis.* Everything had happened so quickly since Emil's arrival that he'd had no opportunity to broach the subject yet, but it had been nagging at the back of his mind, like a midge that kept buzzing in his ear. Mahalath couldn't imagine why the queen's parents would want to see the prisoner, though, even if he was a *pthisicis-corporis*, which Mahalath highly doubted.

"There's a prisoner down there," the queen's mother said. "My daughter, the queen."

Senator Emil laughed, but Mahalath was stunned. *Why would she think the prisoner is Makarria?* he asked himself, but in the back of his mind, he feared he knew the answer.

"Please do explain," Emil said. "If I'm not mistaken, you were there in the throne room, along with me and hundreds of others, when your daughter was murdered by her own bodyguard."

"That wasn't my daughter up there. That was the body thief."

Mahalath's skin prickled to hear her say it.

"A body thief?" Emil asked incredulously. "No such thing exists. You are simply distraught. Denial is a natural part of grief."

"No, I have a letter explaining everything. Fina left it for me. The body thief was wearing Makarria's skin." The queen's mother held up a folded slip of parchment for them to see.

"Fina, you say?" Emil asked. "The same woman who killed

your daughter on the public stage of the throne? You must excuse me for not believing anything a mad woman would write."

"I'm skeptical myself," the queen's father spoke up. "But there's no harm in letting us see the prisoner and making sure. Tell your guards to let us pass."

Mahalath shot a glance at Emil, and wet his lips. "Perhaps we should all—"

"Absolutely not," Emil interrupted. "I'll read this letter you speak of and investigate matters, but we can't risk the queen's royal parents getting injured visiting the dungeon, not after what's happened already."

"You have no right to bar Queen Prisca from anything," Captain Haviero said suddenly. "With Makarria gone now, Prisca is Queen of Valaróz."

"The queen is dead," Emil replied. "The treaty she signed was a royal proclamation, declaring the Republic as steward of the realm, and we take that responsibility very seriously. Before you barged in we were discussing the formation of a council of governors to rule the kingdom, a council which Lady Prisca would sit at the head of." Emil smiled ingratiatingly and stood up to walk toward the queen's parents. "Here now, let me have the letter to look over, and all of you retire back to your rooms. This is a mournful time for you, I know. Let me look into matters with this prisoner."

Senator Emil slipped the letter from Prisca's hand and called for the legionnaires outside. "Soldiers, please escort the queen's parents back to their rooms." And then he spoke quickly to the legionnaires in the Old Tongue. Mahalath did not speak the Old Tongue fluently, but he knew it well enough to make sense of what Emil said. His jaw clenched and he took half a step forward to protest, but Emil made a terse hand motion in his direction.

Say something, you coward! Mahalath told himself, but he couldn't bring himself to speak, and then it was too late. The queen's parents were escorted out, along with Captain Haviero.

Emil returned to his seat, and finally Mahalath found his tongue. "That was unnecessary, Senator."

"Don't be naive," Emil said. "You know as well as I do that the woman won't relent, and as long as she has soldiers loyal to her at her side, she has the ability to cause trouble. Especially that captain. The Royal Guard will be loyal to him and he looks fool enough to try a coup. If anything I've just saved lives by ordering the captain killed."

Mahalath knew he would get nowhere with this argument. It was done. Captain Haviero was as good as dead.

"As you say," Mahalath said, sitting himself back down. "But as to this matter of what they call a body thief, there is more you don't know. While you were gone—"

"The queen captured what she thought was a *pthisicis-corporis*," Emil interrupted. "Yes, I know. I have my own eyes and ears in the city. Trust me when I tell you that the *pthisicis-corporis* are long extinct. This prisoner might be a sorcerer, and a traitor by all accounts, but he is no *pthisicis-corporis*."

"But Queen Makarria was not herself after confronting and capturing this man," Mahalath said, surprising even himself with the admission. *She never would have signed my treaty so readily. I knew better.* Mahalath wetted his lips. Beneath his turban, his shorn scalp was soaked in sweat. "The queen came to us ambassadors and claimed there was a *pthisicis-corporis* in her court and that she meant to capture him, and then…"

"And then what, you damn fool? She came to you, complaining of her inadequacies as queen, and tried to lay the blame for her troubles on the Republic. She all but accused us of plotting to destroy her. And like the spineless lickspittle you are, you sat there and took it. Have you no pride?"

He's lying. Trying to humiliate me to hide the fact he knew all along.

"I want to see the letter," Mahalath said.

Emil stared at him for a long moment, then ripped the letter in half, and then in half again. "Absolutely not. Get out of my sight, and I'll not hear another word of this."

22
Into the Eye of the Storm

Her tears had dried, crusting the mustache whiskers on her face with salt. *It's Lorentz's face that I wear,* she reminded herself, but she was not certain of that anymore. She didn't even know whether her eyes were open or closed half the time, not since she'd been visited by the creature wearing her body. *It can't be true what the body thief told me,* she'd tried convincing herself, and yet she had seen it with her own eyes. She had watched as Fina drove the dagger into her body, once, twice. And then the confusion. She watched as Fina's body fell to the floor. As her own body stood and straddled Fina's. She watched the blood soaking through the gown and spreading across the white marble dais. The color seeping from flesh. The final breath of two bodies. And then the panic of the people in the throne room. The screaming. Her mother. Father. Rushing to her body. The guards pulling them away. And then everything again from the beginning—the jabs of the dagger, once, twice. The blood. The fading flesh. Over and over again.

It's just a vision, she tried telling herself. She had experienced a vision once before, when she was locked in Emperor Guderian's dungeon. She had seen his past in that vision, his very real past. But this vision was not the past. The body thief had just been with her the day before. Or was it two days before? Or a week before? She couldn't be certain. *Just a vision,* she repeated to herself. *Just a premonition. It doesn't have to be true. Talitha told me prophecy is only a potential future. Even the pthisicis-corporis said visions are unreliable.*

But still, Makarria kept seeing it over and over, whether her eyes were open or closed. The dark, dank walls of her cell had become the repeating nightmare vision of Fina killing her body. The guards had come thrice to feed her, she thought, but she couldn't know for sure. Maybe the guards and the feeding funnel were just a memory. Or a vision, like the throne room. *Maybe it's all a vision. A dream. A nightmare that won't stop… Do you even know who you are?*

Yes. Makarria. Your name is Makarria. Wake up. Wake up. Wake up…

"Wake up!"

The voice was not hers. Harsh, yellow light assaulted her eyes. Torchlight, she realized. She was in her cell, and a man wearing a turban was standing before her, barking at her to wake up. *Ambassador Mahalath?*

"That's right, open your eyes," he said. "Look at me."

Makarria blinked the blurriness from her eyes and willed herself to raise her head, though her neck muscles were a knot of pain from supporting the weight of the mind cage. Mahalath was no more than a foot away, holding up a torch in one hand to see her. Behind him stood two servants, both of them holding torches of their own. The cell door was closed and Makarria saw no sign of the usual guards.

"Who are you?" Mahalath asked. "Tell me your name. Please."

It was the please that did it. Makarria knew she had no reason to trust Mahalath. He was from the Old World, and it was the Old World that had plotted to steal control of Valaróz from her, that had released the *pthisicis-corporis* upon her. But Mahalath's voice was tender rather than demanding, and he said please. Makarria needed some form of kindness more than anything, and please was enough.

"My name is Makarria." The words passed through her lips in a raspy whisper. "The *pthisicis-corporis*… I touched it with my power and…"

"It switched bodies with you," Mahalath finished for her.

"Please, believe me," Makarria whispered. "I came to you and the other ambassadors, remember? Wearing my real body, not this one. You warned me to be cautious with the body thief. I thought I was being cautious, but I used my power. I didn't know."

"Enough," Mahalath said. "Save your strength. I believe you. I didn't want to believe it, not when you came to me that night to accuse the Old World, nor when I thought it was you signing my treaty. I saw what I wished to see, and I let Senator Emil deceive us both. I am sorry." Mahalath glanced back to his men and motioned them forward. "Help me unchain her from the wall."

Makarria didn't believe what she was hearing. *Is this some sort of trick?* But the servants did as Mahalath commanded. They had the jailor's keys, and together they unlocked first her feet and then the manacles at her wrists that had been supporting her weight for days now. The servants were gentle in lowering her down, but even so, when her arms were released from their restraints to flop to her sides, the flesh came alive with pain—a million pinpricks of fire from shoulders to fingertips.

The guards sat her down on the floor and leaned her back against the wall, and then Mahalath knelt in front of her. "I'm sorry, but this is going to hurt very badly. Men, hold her still."

Makarria didn't think she could possibly be in more pain than she already was, but she was wrong. When Mahalath grabbed the first of the thumbscrews that attached the mind cage to her skull and then twisted, it hit her like a bolt of lightning, shooting down her spine and blinding her with white and blue flashes. Vaguely, she could hear herself screaming and feel herself struggling against the strong hands holding her down, but her body felt far away and foreign. The pain was all-consuming. By the time Mahalath got to the second thumbscrew, Makarria blacked out.

When she came to, Mahalath was wrapping a long linen bandage around her head. "You're free of the cage now, but do not try to use your power. The screw holes in your head have become infected. I'm wrapping the bandage loosely so they may bleed and purge the contagion. Let them heal, and your body rest, before trying anything. I cannot conjecture as to what might happen if you try to use your power in your condition. You very well might die."

"Thank you," Makarria told him. Her body was weak and ached everywhere, but with the weight of the mind cage gone, without the clicking and whirring of gears in her head, she felt alive again. She held up her new hands, calloused and wide-knuckled, the hands of a career solider. It didn't seem they could possibly be hers now, but when she willed them to move, they did so.

"What are you going to do with me?" she asked Mahalath, lowering her hands, not wanting to see them. "Will you take me to my mother, please?"

"I am sorry, but I cannot. That would be as good as killing you myself. Emil likely suspects who you are now. He's content to have you locked up down here for the time being, but no doubt he means to kill you eventually, and if I free you into the palace, he'll have you killed immediately. No, I am sorry, but you cannot stay here. If you were in your own body, it would be one thing, but no one will believe you are the queen in this man's body. Valaróz is lost to you. Emil controls everything, and there's nothing either one of us can do to stop him. I've risked much already in coming here, but I owe you your life, at least, for the deception and treachery I unwittingly allowed to happen."

Mahalath stood and motioned for the servants to help Makarria up. Makarria groaned, but managed to support most of her own weight as the guards lifted her and placed a cloak over her head and shoulders. Lorentz's body was stout and accustomed to physical punishment, it seemed.

"Where are you taking me, then?" Makarria asked.

"I'm putting you on a ship to Kal Pyrthin. Quiet now. Your Valarion guards outside will obey my commands, but they will not understand who you are, so don't try to speak to them. Be our silent prisoner."

Makarria allowed herself to be led forward, leaning heavily upon the servants to either side of her as Mahalath opened the cell door. He spoke curtly to the two Valarion jailors standing in the corridor, and then led the way past them toward the rear stairwell, which led up to the service wing of the palace. At the top of the stairs, Mahalath and his attendants guided Makarria into the servants' courtyard, walking so fast Makarria couldn't keep up and was left dragging her feet below her. Pained as she was, the cool night air in the courtyard was the most refreshing thing Makarria had ever smelled. Even thick with dust and the odor of horse dung, it was better than the moldering stank of the dungeon.

A horse-drawn coach was already prepared for them, and Mahalath stepped up first to help Makarria in, whereupon she collapsed onto the hard wooden bench at the rear of the cabin. Mahalath closed the door, sat down on the bench across from her, and then rapped his knuckles on the front wall to signal the driver to go. The driver whipped the reins and the coach lurched forward, out of the courtyard and into the streets of Sol Valaróz.

Makarria could still hardly believe what was happening. To be alive and free of the mind cage was wondrous, but her thoughts couldn't escape the memory of her visions, of the scene the *pthisicis-corporis* had foretold. Ambassador Mahalath had said Emil was in control now, but had said nothing about the *pthisicis-corporis*. She looked up at Mahalath, who sat looking back at her.

"My guard Fina," Makarria said. "Did she…"

"Yes. Your body is dead, I am afraid. And your servant Fina, as well."

Makarria slumped in defeat. Her body had been murdered just as the *pthisicis-corporis* told her, and now Makarria was trapped in Lorentz's battered body forever. Her parents would never see her again. Nor Caile. She was utterly alone, and the weight of it all was crushing. She couldn't cry, couldn't think beyond the surface facts.

"The body thief knew what Fina was going to do," she said, as if outside of herself. "It told me it was going to switch with her, and then switch with one of the guards when they came after her. It happened just like it said, and now the *pthisicis-corporis* is free again, in someone else's body."

"No, I think not," Mahalath said. "I did not understand what was happening when I witnessed it, but now knowing what your friend Fina was facing, I understand. She poisoned herself first. My men and I just examined her room and found the wolfsbane. Both the *pthisicis-corporis* and your friend were dead within moments. No one else touched them, your friend made sure of it. She was a loyal servant to the end, though she will be known forever as the one who murdered the Dreamwielder."

This time Makarria couldn't hold back the tears, but she cried for Fina and the sacrifice she had made, not for herself. The reality of her own plight was still too much to comprehend, and so she cried quietly for Fina as the coach moved through the streets of Sol Valaróz toward the harbor. When they drew close, Mahalath roused her from her misery.

"I am putting you on a Valarion ship. It is captained by a man of the Republic and making way for the Esterian Ocean to aid the Republic armada in defeating Pyrthinia, but the crew are all your countrymen. Go with them, pretend to be a sailor, and the old gods willing, you will survive the storm and battle before you. If so, go and make a new life for yourself. There is nothing for you here any longer. Your mother and father still live and are safe, but you can do nothing for them. Emil needs them, if for nothing more than to maintain the cooperation of your people. I am sorry. I wish there was more I could do..."

Makarria could only bring herself to nod.

The wagon came to a stop a moment later, and she allowed herself to be escorted from the coach and then up the gangplank to a ship. Mahalath spoke briefly to the captain, who summoned sailors to escort her below deck to the sick bay where she collapsed into one of the hammocks. Her last thought before falling into the oblivion of sleep was, *I'm dead and I've failed everyone...*

• • •

She awoke to find her hammock rocking. The cabin was dark, lit only by a sputtering tallow candle on the table at the center of the room. She was alone, and the walls and ceiling around her were pitching from side to side. It took her several seconds to remember where she was, and who she was. *Not Makarria any longer,* she reminded herself as she ran her fingers over her face, the face that once belonged to Lorentz. *I'm on a ship to Kal Pyrthin. I'm a sailor now, like my grandfather.* The thought of Parmo and how he had been assassinated moments before being crowned King of Valaróz grieved her. *Grampy is gone, and now Lorentz, Natale, Fina, and even me. What am I without my body? Just a stupid girl trapped in the body of a broken soldier.*

She sat up in the hammock and nearly fainted as a wave of nausea washed through her. Her head throbbed like someone was beating on it with a sledgehammer. She probed the blood-caked bandage wrapped around her head and gasped. The four spots where the mind cage had been screwed into her skull were inflamed and wet with discharge. Makarria could tell by the rotten smell that the dampness was puss, not blood. *I need to clean it with hot water and a poultice of wormroot and bee balm before it's too late,* she thought, pushing herself to her feet. She went to the table in the center of the cabin, intent on grabbing the candle lantern and exploring the room—it was the sick bay, after all, and bound to have some sort of medicinal herbs—but she found the lantern was fastened to the table. *Of course, this is a ship. Everything is nailed down to keep from flying around in rough seas.*

A bowl of food had been prepared for her, she saw. It sat in a recess in the table carved especially for keeping the bowl from sliding around, and next to it, in a similar recess, was a tin cup filled with water. Just seeing the simple plate of hard bread, cheese, and pickled anchovies made Makarria realize how hungry she was. Cleaning her wounds could wait, she decided.

She sat in the chair, also secured fastly in place to the floor, and began devouring the food, oblivious to the floor beneath her swaying with the ocean swells. She didn't normally care for anchovies, but she found she couldn't get enough of them now. It was Lorentz's body that craved the fish, she realized, and gave it no more thought. When the food was all gone, she gulped down the entire mug of water.

Feeling more alive, she pushed herself to her feet and found the floor beneath her was rocking more violently than before.

Ambassador Mahalath mentioned she would be sailing into a storm, she recalled, taking stock of the sick bay. The cabin was sparsely furnished, with only the small round table and two chairs, four hammocks—two along the back wall, and two along the side wall—and a large chest and wooden bench along the other side wall. Makarria went to the chest and opened the lid. It was dim in the room, but she could make out inside the chest a collection of operating knives and bone saws, a pile of clean bandages and ties, and a corked bottle. She grabbed the bottle and a wad of clean bandages and sat herself onto the bench. The cabin was rocking more wildly now, and through the walls she could hear the shouts of sailors, whistling wind, and the prow crashing through waves.

She uncorked the bottle and gave it a sniff, instantly regretting sticking her nose in too close. It was no herbal elixir, but distilled alcohol, pungent and vaporous. With a grimace, she recorked the bottle and began unwinding the bandage from her head. The alcohol would burn like fire in her wounds, but she had little choice if she wanted to stay the infection. The last several windings of her bandage were stuck to her scalp, and broke free of the scabbing wounds begrudgingly. Makarria felt the first twinges of nausea returning, but forced herself to breathe deeply and relax.

Again, she uncorked the bottle, this time keeping it well away from her face while she soaked one of the clean bandages. She took a deep breath again and then wiped the mess away from the first wound on her head. The pain was excruciating, but she refused to let herself waver. By the time she scraped away all the gunk from the first of the wounds, her body was shaking and covered in rivulets of sweat. Undeterred, she grabbed a new rag, soaked it in the alcohol and went to work on the second hole. Meanwhile, she could feel fresh blood trickling down her scalp from the first wound. *Good,* she consoled herself. *The bleeding will flush out the infection.*

When she finished cleaning the second wound, she moved onto the third, her hands shaking so much now she no longer noticed the ship careening beneath her. The fourth wound was the worst of them all, the one at the back of her head above her right ear.

When she touched it with the alcohol-soaked cloth, she could feel something squish out and was assaulted by a rotten odor that made her gag. *I have to get the infection out,* she thought, and willed herself to press harder on the wound, yet when she did so she blacked out and collapsed onto the bench.

She came to a few moments later, lying on the floor in a puddle of her own vomit and the residue of the broken alcohol bottle she had inadvertently knocked over. *I knew I shouldn't have eaten all those anchovies,* she reflected, but found little humor in the thought. Her head was throbbing even worse than before and she was overcome with the sudden realization she was going to die. The bone saws and knives might work well enough for an arm or leg with gangrene, but there was no salvation in amputating her head. Oddly, the thought of dying didn't disturb her as much as she thought it might. *I died the moment the body thief took my body away. I just didn't want to believe it.*

Resigned to this thought, she pushed herself to her feet and exited the sick bay into a narrow passage, her legs weak and wobbling beneath her. The entire ship was creaking now under the strain of the ocean swells, and Makarria had to keep her hands on the passage walls to keep herself upright. It was dark, but she felt her way to the wooden stepladder that led up out of the hold. The hatch at the top was closed, but seawater was trickling down the ladder nonetheless. *If I'm going to die, at least it will be in the ocean air,* she told herself. *That's the way my grampy wanted to go.* She climbed the steps and turned the lever lock on the hatch above her, only to have the lever ripped out of her hands as the howling wind wrenched the hatch open to slam on the deck above her. A gout of water rained down through the opening and the roar of the wind and waves outside was nearly deafening.

The violence of the wind sent a rush of energy through her, and Makarria scrambled the rest of the way out of the hold only to be thrown to the deck as the ship careened suddenly to the portside.

"Batten down that hatch!" a sailor yelled, and Makarria realized the man was yelling at her.

Makarria snapped to order, and grabbed the edge of the hatch.

She lifted it easily enough, but a sudden gust of wind slammed it back into her legs and sent her sprawling again. What little energy she'd had a moment before drained out of her, and she was overcome by the pain in her head.

"Hurry," the sailor yelled at her again. "You'll sink us, you damn fool."

Makarria willed herself to her feet, got her legs firmly beneath her this time, and used what little strength she had left to pick up the hatch and drive it through the face of the wind into its resting place. She collapsed on top of it and turned the lever tight not a second too soon, for another wave washed over the deck. Only her handhold on the lever kept her from getting washed overboard.

"Here!" a sailor near her shouted, and a length of rope hit her on the face.

She grabbed the rope and lurched to her feet to see the sailor had given her a lifeline that was tied off to the mainmast. Makarria wrapped it three times around her waist, then knotted it, just the way Siegbjorn had shown her on his airship. Now secure, she clamored up the steeply sloped deck to the starboard rail and grabbed hold as best she could alongside the sailor who had thrown her the rope.

"You're no sailor, are you?" the man asked. He was staring at the open wounds on her head, probably at her missing teeth too, but he was polite enough to say nothing.

"Not exactly," she said, taking a moment to finally take in her surroundings. She was on a massive carrack, she saw. The main sail had been furled, but the square sail of the foremast still billowed in the wind, as well as the lateen sail of the mizzenmast. They were tacking, she saw, which was why they were heeling so much to the portside. All around the ship, sailors were clinging onto rails or ropes to keep from getting blown or washed overboard. The sea was turbulent, with waves nearing twenty feet high, and above them the sky was near black. Makarria's first thought was it was night still, but in the far distance to their stern—to the west—she could see a lighter patch of gray clouds indicating the sun. It was evening, she realized, which meant she'd slept the entire day through. Or two days, which would explain why she'd been so ravenous and how her wounds had become so infected. Even more disconcerting than the time she had lost was the storm before them, a shroud of clouds dark as night, with the very real darkness of night looming no more than an hour away.

Makarria caught a glimpse to their portside of what she thought was a whitecap at first, but when she looked again she realized it was a ship sail in the distance. And the more she looked, the more ships she saw, bobbing up and down on the waves, coming in and out of view, looking to be little more than toys among the massive waves.

"How many ships are out there?" Makarria hollered at the sailor beside her.

The man shrugged. "We started with forty, but I saw *Windrunner* lose her mainmast as soon as the storm hit. If we lost her, we've no doubt lost more."

Anger welled up in Makarria. These sailors had no business being trapped in this storm. Had Senator Emil sent them off to aid the Old World armada or to die in this storm? *Either way, he wins,* she realized, and that made her even angrier.

"We have to turn around," Makarria yelled. "This is suicide."

The man laughed, a short, humorless snort. "Too late for that, land lubber. Even if we didn't have Old World sorcerers in command, we couldn't turn back now. We're in the thick of the storm. We come about and we'll be going against the current and the wind. All we can do is call upon the Five to save us. We get past Pyr Point and could be we ride it out." The sailor shrugged. "If not, we drown."

Makarria glanced from the man back out over the stormy sea. *The Five are all dead and gone, and they were nothing more than sorcerers. Not even Vala herself, mightiest stormbringer the world has ever seen, could help us in this storm. This is the work of their goddess, Tel Mathir. The earth is showing us how insignificant we are against her might.*

It had been a long time since Makarria had thought about Tel Mathir. The Five had been followers. Talitha was also a follower, and she had taught Makarria a little about the link between magic and nature, and how the both of them were an outgrowth of Tel Mathir. But that had been more than a year ago, and their time together had been brief. *Talitha told me I had a unique gift to see the true nature of things as a dreamwielder, that my magic was a gift from Tel Mathir meant to give life and create, not destroy. If only I had my own body back, maybe I could save these men from the storm.* She imagined a giant wave around the ships, shielding them from the wind like a massive wall. With such a wave, she could push the ships back to the safety of the harbor in Sol Valaróz. She remembered watching dolphins ride the waves into the shallows around Spearpoint Rock when she was younger, and how much fun it looked. *If only I was myself, I could make a big slow wave for us to ride all the way into Sol Valaróz.*

The sudden shouts and cursing of the crew around her snapped Makarria out of her daydream. Her eyes had been closed, she realized. She blinked them open and followed the terrified stares of the ship crew off to their starboard side. In the far distance, a giant wave had begun to form, towering up into the sky higher even than the storm swells, but as Makarria watched, it began to dissolve now into the smaller waves around it. *That was my wave!* she realized. A surge of triumph coursed through her. She still had her power, even trapped in another's body, and it was as strong as ever. It was no wonder the body thief had put the mind cage on her. She had just been too caught up in her own misery to give it any thought.

My body or not, I'm still a dreamwielder. How could I have ever doubted it? My grandfather was dying once and I made him young and whole again. I remade his flesh in the image of his ideal self. That's how Talitha had explained it, at least. However it had worked, Makarria was confident she could make her wave now, but she wasn't foolish enough to forget the cost of her magic. When she had made her grandfather young again on the shore near her farm, she had inadvertently killed thousands of sea creatures swimming in the nearby surf. The wave Makarria needed now would have to be massive, and even with the enormous power of the storm raging around her, if she tried to create the wave from where she stood on the deck of the ship, she'd draw the life right out of the sailors.

She knew what she had to do.

"Here," she said, untying the lifeline from around her waist and handing it to the sailor beside her.

"What are you doing?" the man started to ask, but before he could finish his question, Makarria sprinted down the sloping deck and dove over the portside rail into the sea.

23
The Heir Apparent

Natarios Rhodas yawned and shook his head, trying to shake off his weariness. Around him, the candidates and council members were trickling into the room to take their seats at the table. It was Lord Kobel's day to present his claim—the last day of presentations—and Natarios needed to be sharp, but instead he was bleary eyed and addled thanks to the infernal scent-hound. When he'd returned to his tower after the previous day's council session, the hound had been howling like mad. Natarios couldn't begin to imagine how it had awoken from its magical slumber, but the fact remained, it was awake and it smelled something.

He had never seen this particular hound in action before, but he knew well enough what its crying and baying meant: the dreamwielder was up to something. Only a dreamwielder's magic prompted it to cry so. *Perhaps Queen Makarria has changed her mind and decided to resist the Old World Republic after all,* he thought initially, but then he checked the coordinates of where the scent-hound was pointing on its compass wheel. Once he marked them out on his map, he discovered the dreamwielder was not in Sol Valaróz at all, but somewhere farther to the east. Without coordinates from the other scent-hounds he couldn't triangulate the exact location, though. The dreamwielder could have been as close as the Forrest Weorcan or as far away as the southern reaches of the Esterian Ocean well beyond the Old World. He had no way of knowing, and with problems of his own to worry about, he had retired to bed.

And yet the scent-hound had continued baying and whining

throughout the entire night. Even two floors below, he could hear it. He tried piling pillows over his head, stuffing the ends of old socks in his ears, but nothing would block the piercing cry of the scent-hound. Twice, Natarios had strode upstairs with a dagger in hand, intent on killing the hound, and twice he chickened out and returned to his room to toss and turn in his bed. Come morning, the hound was still fussing, although not as loudly, and when Natarios glanced at its coordinates, he saw they had shifted. Wherever she was, the dreamwielder was moving westward.

But none of that helped Natarios. Here he was, a day off from the election—a day away from getting burned alive by the sorcerer's guild—and he and Lady Hildreth were no closer to finding the true heir to the throne. Lady Hildreth's illegitimate son, Thon, had returned to Col Sargoth from a secret prison only to up and disappear before she had gotten a chance to tell him who he was. The poor fool didn't even know she was his mother, and now he had either run away or was dead, probably the latter. Ambassador Rives had no idea who this Thon lad was, but that didn't mean he would hesitate to kill him.

And that damn Prince Caile, Natarios swore inwardly. *I convinced Lady Hildreth to set him free so he could search for the heir, and now he's disappeared too. Likely, he's run away. That's what I would do if I were him. That's what I'll be doing come morning if this illegitimate prince doesn't turn up.*

The last of the council members had entered, and all of them were sitting, waiting for Natarios to begin, including Lady Hildreth. Natarios glanced her way, but if she had any pressing news for him, she made no indication. Seeing nothing else for it, Natarios squinted his eyes one last time and called the meeting to order.

"I see that we still have no Prince Caile Delios present," he remarked. "I don't suppose anyone has heard word from him?"

He received only blank stares in return. It was a dangerous game he was playing. He couldn't let on that he had eavesdropped on Ambassador Rives, but at the same time he couldn't play at being too accommodating toward Rives's cause or else Rives would know something was awry.

"Very well," Natarios said at last. "We shall proceed, and if Queen Makarria ever inquires, at least it can't be said we didn't ask about him. Unless there is any new business, we shall give the floor to Lord Kobel."

"We have no business but to hear Kobel today," Rives said. "Let's be on with it."

"Indeed. Lord Kobel, the floor is yours."

Lord Kobel stood and bowed. "Lords, gentlemen, and lady, I mean to show you why I am the one and only true choice to become the next King of Sargoth."

Natarios rolled his eyes. *You could show us the black forest of hair between your arse cheeks and you'd still get elected. It's Old World money that buys your throne, not your qualifications.* But, of course, Natarios said nothing and merely smiled as Lord Kobel continued on.

• • •

If only Thon and I had known who he really was, none of this would be happening, Caile thought miserably. *I would have disbanded the council, Thon would be sitting on the throne, and the war-machine factories would be sealed up forever.* But it hadn't happened that way, of course. Lady Hildreth, paralyzed by pride, had waited too long to tell Caile she had birthed a son with Guderian, and now Thon was missing, oblivious to who he really was. Lady Hildreth had her servants asking about Thon among the household staff in the keep; Commander Buell had his cavalrymen keeping an eye out in the city; and Caile, with the unlikely support of the houndkeeper, had convinced Lady Hildreth to release him so he could search as well, but all of it was too late, he feared. *Only one day left.* And what if Ambassador Rives's men had found Thon and killed him? They didn't know who he was, but simply being Caile's companion might have been enough to warrant his death in their eyes. Or what if Thon had seen the cavalrymen coming after Caile in the keep and simply ran away? Even if he was alive and safe, Thon had no way of knowing he was the true king. And without Thon, all was lost. Caile would fail Makarria utterly and completely.

With a dissatisfied grunt, Caile pushed his black-dyed hair from his face, and squinted at the assault of the sun in the crisp, clear sky. It was mid-morning, and the streets of Col Sargoth were bustling with activity: people running errands, vendors hawking their wares, wagons carrying loads to the harbor, and rickshaw drivers hustling up customers. Caile, dressed as a commoner in a gray tunic and armed only with a simple dagger at his belt, fell into line with the flow of pedestrians making their way south, trying not to draw attention to himself, but keeping his eyes on everyone who passed by. *Come on, give me a turnip lady or a lost-looking heir to the Sargothian throne.* But, of course, he saw neither Talitha nor Thon. He stopped several minutes later when he got to the street where he'd first encountered Talitha more than a year before, when she'd been posing as a vendor and had offered him her produce. She was nowhere to be seen now, though, and Caile wasn't even sure why he bothered to keep looking. He had been at it for three days, combing the city in places where he hoped to find Talitha by day, and then lurking through the tunnels beneath Lightbringer's Keep by night to spy on Ambassador Rives. Not that his eavesdropping had done him any good in finding Thon. Rives had met each night with a few of the guildmasters to discuss bribes and votes, but they made no mention of Caile or Thon, and the Old World sorcerer with the speaking relic that the houndkeeper spoke of failed to ever appear. Caile had serious doubts about the houndkeeper's story, but it mattered not. Whether Rives had intended to capture Caile or not—whether the sorcerer's guild meant to burn the council assembly alive after the vote tomorrow or not—the fact remained that Lord Kobel was on the cusp of becoming king, and once he did he would unleash the war-wagons and all would be lost. The only way Caile could stop him was to find Thon, and he only had one day left to do it.

Caile gazed over the busy intersection one last time, and then turned in the direction of another familiar place, The Thirsty Whale. He had no choice now but to sneak into Lightbringer's Keep itself, he decided. Slinking about in the tunnels below was getting him nowhere. Lady Hildreth had warned him to not show his face anywhere near

Lightbringer's Keep, but he needed to see people's faces, to ask questions, and he needed to find his belongings; his sword and speaking stone had both been left behind in his haste to get away from the cavalrymen who captured him. His black-dyed hair and disguise of common Sargothian garb would have to suffice, and if anyone recognized him, well, he'd deal with that when the time came.

With the decision made, he felt a brief glimmer of optimism and moved with new vigor in his step. He pushed his way through the crowds in the street, and then slipped down an alley alongside The Thirsty Whale. He stopped when he came to the back entrance of an abandoned warehouse and glanced about quickly to make sure no one was around to see him. Finding the coast clear, he pushed his way through the boarded-up doorway into the warehouse. It was the same warehouse where he had met with the sorcerer's guild and offered to help them overthrow Emperor Guderian a year before. And it was in the cellar below where he had met with the sorceress Roanna who tried to kill him. Talitha had saved him on that occasion and sent him back through the tunnels to return to Lightbringer's Keep where he was being held as a ward. Caile retraced the very same path now. He trotted to the stairwell in the corner of the warehouse and made his way down three flights of dilapidated stone steps to the cellar, which was in shambles thanks to the brief skirmish the two sorcerers had had there. The doorway and parts of the ceiling were collapsed, piles of smashed bricks littered the floor, and the place reeked of old fire.

Caile grabbed a new torch from the pile he had stashed near the trapdoor leading down into the sewer tunnels. It took him a few moments to light it with the cheap dagger and piece of flint Lady Hildreth had given him, but once the torch came to life, he lowered himself down through the trapdoor, and made his way through the sewer tunnels to where they intersected with the tunnels beneath Lightbringer's Keep. From there, he made his way through the winding passages. He'd made the trip enough times over the last several days that he didn't even need the maps the hound-keeper had given him, and even when his path veered from where he had been exploring recently, the memory of his flight the year before was good enough to navigate by. Before long, he found himself standing beneath another trapdoor of sorts, this one beneath the very room he had stayed in when he was held as ward to Emperor Guderian. *This is where I killed Lindy,* he recalled, still not proud of what he had done. The man had just been doing his duty in keeping an eye on Caile, and Caile had killed him to make his escape. *There's no changing the past now,* he reminded himself. *Your job is to find Thon, not mourn over what's already been done.*

He reached his hands up to find the stone that covered the secret passage into the room above. *I hope no one's up there.* The stone made a low grating noise as he pushed it up out of its slot and off to the side on the floor above him. He grabbed the dagger from his belt and poked his head up through the hole, ready to duck away if need be, but the room was empty. With a relieved sigh, he sheathed his dagger, and pulled himself up. He replaced the floor stone, then brushed the dust and cobwebs from his hair and clothes. If this was going to work, he needed to look like a common servant, not someone who had been mucking about in the sewer and climbing through abandoned tunnels.

Satisfied he looked as presentable as he was going to, he opened the bedroom door and stepped out of the corridor to walk toward the mess hall. *Walk with purpose,* he reminded himself. *Act like you know what you're doing and no one will question you.* It had worked for him before, and it worked for him now as he passed a chambermaid with a basketful of dirty linens in the corridor who barely gave notice to him. Caile couldn't help but grin.

The corridor intersected with the main hexagonal wing of Lightbringer's Keep and Caile found himself suddenly intermingling with heavier foot traffic, but everyone was about their own business and paid him little heed. He did the same and made straightaway for the mess hall. The hall was expansive, with two dozen bench tables, meant to accommodate the entire dignitary wing of the palace. It was largely empty now, however. It was well past breakfast and only a handful of staff members sat at the tables eating an early lunch.

Caile strode across the long hall toward the serving bar, where a lone cook stood, stirring the various kettles of whatever slop was being served for lunch. *This is madness,* Caile thought, but he forced himself to walk casually.

"Lamb shank stew or lamb shank stew?" the cook asked Caile humorlessly.

"Two bowls of the lamb shank stew," Caile said. "One for me and my new employer. He's one of the ambassadors electing a king. I'm to deliver his lunch to him."

"That so?" The man's tone made it clear he didn't care.

"Yes indeed. Apparently his other servant just upped and disappeared a couple of days ago, so he hired me to take his place. It's a bit of a mystery, actually, where the fellow went. I don't suppose you've seen him?" Caile blanched inwardly at the awkward disingenuiness of his story. "His name was Thon? Average height. Dark hair. Wore a flail at his side?"

"Sounds like half the men I serve," the cook said, plopping down two overflowing bowls in front of Caile and sloshing half their contents onto the bar top in the process.

"Right you are," Caile said, grabbing the wooden bowls and turning away. "Thank you," he said over his shoulder, and walked back out the way he came, trying not to look suspicious. *The man is either too indolent to think anything of me and my questions, or he's one of those nosy sorts, pretending not to care and selling gossip to whoever is willing to pay the most for it it.* He hoped it was the former.

He made his way back into the main corridor and tossed the two bowls of slop aside into the garbage bucket one of the passing servants carried. The room he had been occupying with Thon was close, and as foolish as it was to go there, Caile had to risk it. He needed his sword and the speaking stone. With the stone, he could at least try contacting Talitha again. Perhaps she had discovered something, assuming she responded.

At the junction of the main hallway and the side corridor leading to the dignitary rooms, Caile stopped and pretended to tighten the laces of his boots as he shot a glance in the direction of his room. Seeing the corridor empty, he wasted no time and strode down the corridor. He found the door handle to his room unlocked, just as he'd left it, but when he stepped inside his brief glimmer of hope snuffed out. The room had been cleaned out. Not only were his sword and speaking stone gone from the bed, but also his trunk full of clothes and Thon's few belongings. Even the linens from the bed had been stripped away. The room was barren and clean, awaiting whomever the next occupant might be.

Caile knew he shouldn't be surprised, but he was disappointed nonetheless. With a grimace, he turned to make a quick retreat, only to find the doorway barred. A man he'd never seen before was blocking the way. He was tall and broad shouldered, but not exactly imposing. His limbs hung flaccidly at his sides, and his oily brown hair was combed up from the back of his head in a poor attempt to cover his bald pate.

"Excuse me," Caile said. "I seem to have stepped into the wrong room."

"Is that so?"

The man's voice had a distinct accent. He was from the Old World, Caile was certain. "That's right," Caile said, smiling politely to distract the man's attention away from what he was really doing.

"Leave that dagger in its sheath," the man said.

"What dagger?" Caile asked, his skin prickling with danger. "If you wouldn't mind standing aside, I should be on my way." He lunged forward, intending to bull rush the man, but before he got within two steps he was flung backwards, his feet flying over his head, his body somersaulting backward to skip off the surface of the bed and land on the cold, hard floor.

The breath was gone from him, and his vision was filled with spots, but Caile willed himself to his feet, dagger in hand, intent on hurling it at the man. Again he was too slow. The Old World sorcerer puckered his lips as if he were blowing a kiss, and a gale burst forth from his mouth to hurl Caile into the wall behind him. When his head slammed into the unforgiving basalt a moment later, everything went black.

24
The Bloodless War

Standing at the helm of the airship *Casstian's Breath* alongside Admiral Laud, Taera could see for miles in every direction. Behind them to the west, Kal Pyrthin Bay still churned with the after-effects of the behemoth storm that had passed through. The Pyrthin sailing fleet stretched back for miles behind *Casstian's Breath* as the ships made their way through the choppy waters toward the Esterian Ocean. Far to the north, the storm itself raged on, spanning across the horizon from the mainland far out into the Esterian Ocean. And to the east was the Old World armada, waiting just as Taera had known it would be—hundreds of ships just sitting there, their masts prickling the eastern horizon against the backdrop of the morning sun. The storm had seemingly barely even touched them. Taera glanced toward Admiral Laud and saw the stunned expression on his face. He had been so certain the storm would destroy the Old World fleet. *It's not his fault,* she reminded herself. *He has done well, all things considered. Airships, Old World sorcerers: they are completely foreign to him. To all of us.*

"Orders, Your Majesty?" he asked, shaking off his surprise.

"Drop sails, and signal the other airships to do the same. We wait here until the rest of the fleet catches up."

The admiral barked the orders to his first mate, and the crew scrambled to furl the sails. When they were finally stationary in the air, Laud returned to Taera's side to stare at the Old World Armada before them. "What are they waiting for? The storm has passed. They easily outnumber us."

"They're waiting for their own signal," Taera said, thinking of the red stone belowdeck in her cabin. Taera had returned to Kal Pyrthin during the storm to find Captain Hierome awaiting her. He had returned from Sol Valaróz the day before on Taera's ether-powered airship bearing the stone and Makarria's odd message. *Save yourself the trouble and surrender*, the note had said, which was so unlike Makarria because it was, indeed, not from her at all. Unlike the letter, the stone had been delivered to the airship's crew in secrecy by a scholar, one of Makarria's advisors, Captain Hierome had reported, and the scholar had told him of the *pthisicis-corporis*.

As soon as she had seen the red stone, Taera knew what it was—a means to communicate—and when she picked it up out of the box, a flood of visions had washed over her: seven ordinary granite stones sitting on a table, suddenly brought to life by the touch of Makarria and Talitha; Caile calling desperately into his orange stone, but receiving no response; Talitha tucking her silver stone deep beneath the folds of a bed mattress, trying to stifle Caile's voice; and the yellow stone shattering on the floor, destroyed by the very hands that had created the stones but, at the same time, not Makarria's hands at all.

Whatever had happened to Makarria, her stone was gone now and Taera had no means of speaking with her. That was clear enough to Taera. Everything else was a mystery. A half dozen times the previous day, she had nearly spoken into her stone to call out to Caile, but each time the vision of Talitha had come to her—the sorcereress frantically trying to hide the stone while Caile's voice called out over and over again. Taera had felt Talitha's fear in that vision, and she could only assume it was fear at getting caught. What if Taera endangered Caile in the same way? What if she called out to Caile at the wrong moment and gave him away to his enemies? She still remembered distinctly her previous vision, of Caile buried and alone beneath Lightbringer's Keep. And so Taera had waited for the storm to pass, hoping Caile or Talitha would contact her through the stone with some sort of news. But there had been nothing, and now she was out of time. Today, a new King of Sargoth would be elected, and then the Old World armada would attack.

Taera tore her eyes away from the Old World armada. In Col Sargoth, it would still be a few hours before dawn. With any luck Caile would be sleeping someplace safe. And alone. She had no choice now but to risk using her stone.

"Admiral," she said. "I'll be belowdeck in my cabin. If the Old World ships raise their sails, fetch me immediately. Otherwise I need absolute privacy."

• • •

"Caile… Caile, wake up… Caile, can you hear me? Caile?"

The voice dragged him from unconsciousness—his sister's voice. Caile blinked his eyes, but it was dark and the pain in his head throbbed against the back of his eyes. *Where am I?* He tried to sit up, but discovered his hands were bound together in front of him, as were his feet.

"Caile?" Taera's voice came again, and suddenly lamplight illuminated the room.

Caile squinted his eyes to see a man standing over him. Seeing the face brought everything back. *The Old World sorcerer.*

The man was holding open the shutter of his lamp and redirected the light from Caile to a nearby table where the orange speaking stone sat. "Caile?" came Taera's voice, thin and distant sounding.

"Well, it seems your little toy works after all," the sorcerer said, his voice phlegmy from sleep. "I'm glad I decided to hold onto the thing."

Another lamp suddenly came alive, and then another, illuminating the spacious room. Two other men approached the table, lamps held out before them. "Who is it?" one of them asked, a brutish looking lout.

"It must be his sister, Queen Taera," the sorcerer replied. "Who else could it be with the dreamwielder dead now?"

The hair at the nape of Caile's neck stood on end at hearing the words. *With the dreamwielder dead? Impossible,* he told himself, but fear and anguish filled him. Could Makarria really be dead? Is that why she had never reached out to him through the stones?

"Do you want me to drag him up?" one of the brutes asked, motioning in the direction of Caile. "I can make him talk to her."

"No, not yet," the sorcerer said. "Not until I speak to Senator Emil. He'll be pleased. Capturing the prince was a better asset than we'd dared to hope. Now that we know he can talk to her directly, we'll let him convince Queen Taera to surrender."

"What makes you think I'd do that?" Caile asked, immediately regretting his decision to speak up.

One of the brutes strode toward him and kicked him in the stomach, leaving him writhing on the floor to regain his breath.

"Because if you don't do what we tell you, I'll kick you to pieces," the brute said.

"Yes, and be that as it may," the sorcerer added, "you'll have other motives. Once Ķobel is elected and the Republic fleet arrives, Sargoth will be ours. With Valaróz already secured, and another fleet of Republic ships waiting at the ready in the Esterian Ocean, your sister is trapped. You can standby and let her fight as thousands of your kinsmen are crushed between Guderian's war wagons and our fleet, or you can convince her to surrender peacefully and be accepted into the fold of the Republic."

Caile breathed uneasily and kept his thoughts to himself this time. Had it really come to this? Had he failed Makarria and his sister both?

"Fetch my conch," the sorcerer commanded one of the ruffians, already indifferent toward Caile.

"Are you sure? It's still nighttime. Won't the senator be angry if you disturb him?"

The sorcerer went to a window and threw open the curtains, revealing the purple sky of the predawn and illuminating the room more fully. "It's nearly morning here. The sun will be up in Sol Valaróz already and Emil will want to know immediately about the speaking stone."

As the ruffian scurried off, Caile took the opportunity to take in his surroundings. He was in an opulent room furnished with velvet couches and chairs, and adjoining the room was another, a bedroom it appeared, even more ornately decorated than the den. Caile recognized it all immediately. He was still in Lightbringer's Keep—not in one of the dignitary rooms, but in one of the suites for royal visitors. It had to be King Lorimer's suite, Caile realized, but before he could give it further thought, the ruffian returned with a golden conch shell.

The sorcerer took the conch and placed his lips to the opening. A buzzing filled the air as the sorcerer blew, and Caile could feel a fluttering sensation against his forehead, like a steady pulse of wind. The buzzing grew in intensity, like a swarm of bees growing closer, and then Senator Emil's voice filled the room.

"Good morning," the senator said through the conch. "It promises to be a glorious day. You call bearing good news, I presume?"

• • •

Ambassador Mahalath adjusted his turban, focusing on the reflection of the linen folds rather than making eye contact with himself in the gilded looking glass. He had never felt so ashamed and emasculated in his life. He was neither naïve nor idealistic—he had been in politics for over thirty years and knew the game well—but that didn't mean he had come to Sol Valaróz without a sense of purpose and nationalistic pride. He had come here believing he had something of value to offer the Five Kingdoms. He had arrived with absolute faith in the democratic principles of the Republic, but now…

He had been used like a pawn in a game. Emil and his collaborators in the security council of the Senate, whoever they were, had sent him here to merely present the guise of diplomacy. Meanwhile, the real strategy had been to unleash the *pthisicis-corporis* on Valaróz and take control of the Five Kingdoms by subterfuge. *And fool that I am,*

I played my part to perfection, Mahalath thought. *I stood there and smiled when a fake queen signed my treaty, knowing full well that it made no sense for her to do so. And when I had the opportunity to save the real Makarria, I sent her away on a ship, likely to her death. A pitiful attempt at redemption it was.*

He had asked Senator Emil to be relieved of his position, but Emil was not about to let go so easily. Emil had taken away the conch Mahalath had been given to communicate with, and he told Mahalath in no uncertain terms that he was staying. "I'll not have you running back to Khail Sanctu to decry me before the Senate," Emil had told him the day before. "You've had as much of a hand in this as I have. Your signature is on the treaties. You will stay here, and you will continue to co-chair the Valarion high council until the Five Kingdoms are completely under Republic control. Only then will I allow you to return to your home and wife. Continue to question me and you will never see her again."

Mahalath didn't know whether to take that as a threat toward his own life, his wife's, or both. His wife was a junior senator. She was highly respected, and had strong allies in the Senate, but she had nowhere near the influence Emil had. Mahalath knew Emil was right—he had Mahalath right where he wanted him. If Mahalath called for an investigation, if he told his wife what had happened here, if he did anything to arouse the Senate's attention, they would be ruined, he and his wife both. Mahalath half hoped that Emil would discover that the prisoner in the dungeon was gone. It wouldn't be hard for Emil to discern who had freed the prisoner, and it just might anger him enough to kill Mahalath on the spot. Then again, Mahalath wasn't certain that Emil knew who the prisoner really was. Even if Emil had been the one to unleash the *pthisicis-corporis* in the first place, it didn't mean that Emil believed Lady Prisca's story that the *pthisicis-corporis* had swapped bodies with Makarria. Either way, the prisoner Mahalath had freed was in a broken body and likely of little interest to the Senator now that he had control of the kingdom. *No, my death would be too easy an escape,* Mahalath rued.

A rapping came at the bedroom door, and Mahalath turned sullenly to watch his servant answer the call. It was one of Emil's lackeys at the door.

"Senator Emil demands your presence immediately, Ambassador Mahalath," the courtier said. Mahalath didn't dignify the man's insolence with a response. Instead, he merely rose to his feet and motioned for the courtier to lead the way.

After a short, wordless walk through the palace, they found Senator Emil lounging on the veranda, overlooking the city and harbor below. Emil smirked up at Mahalath from where he sat in a cushioned reclining chair.

"Don't be so glum," Emil said. "Today is a great day for the Republic. Everything is in place. Lord Kobel will be elected this afternoon as King of Sargoth, our ships will arrive in Gathol Harbor to secure the city, and then we can turn our attention to Norg."

"And what of Pyrthinia?" Mahalath asked. "Queen Taera has shown no indication she means to surrender."

"That's why I summoned you. More good news. We have Prince Caile in custody and he has a speaking relic of some sort. Once Col Sargoth is secured, we will have him negotiate his sister's surrender. If she balks, we simply threaten to kill him. She will fall into line like all the others, and then with four of the Five Kingdoms already in the fold, King Hanns of Norg will do the same. We'll have conquered an entire nation in a bloodless war."

"Bloodless?" Mahalath demanded. "You forget Queen Makarria. Her bodyguard. That innocent scholar. The captain of the Royal Guard. And what of those ships you sent off into the storm?"

Emil rolled his eyes. "Sometimes I think you must be a woman, the way you prattle on and fret about a few casualties. Would you rather that we had invaded? Would you rather see tens of thousands of soldiers die? Is that it? You want to see a long, drawn out war?"

"I'd rather that we simply offered aid like we promised! Since when did the Republic get into the business of conquering nations? We came here to provide assistance to the Five Kingdoms. To encourage freedom and democracy. That is all!"

Emil stood, his eyes flashing with anger and contempt. "Listen to yourself. You know as well as I do what is in those warehouses beneath Col Sargoth. Do you really think the next King of Sargoth would be content to leave them there, the tools to conquer the entire world? This is a matter of national security. We had to act preemptively and secure those war wagons."

Mahalath turned away to gaze over the harbor. There was no use in arguing. Emil was a hawk through and through. To him "diplomacy" was just another word for manipulation, a means for gaining control. Guderian's war wagons—regardless of whether they posed a legitimate threat or not—were excuse enough for Emil to justify his actions. Nothing Mahalath could say or do would change that.

• • •

Caile sat helplessly on the floor as the morning waxed on and daylight brightened the royal suite. One of the ruffians had left and returned with breakfast hours before, and by Caile's estimation it was nearing the hour when the election council would convene to elect Lord Kobel as King of Sargoth, and then die a fiery death at the hands of the sorcerer's guild. Caile didn't even care that the guard had neglected to fetch him any food; the pangs of hunger he felt were nothing compared to the shame and guilt he felt at having failed Makarria and his sister.

He tried in vain to pull his hands free from their bindings, but all he accomplished was tearing the skin away from his wrists. As much as he hated to admit it, he was defeated. There was nothing he could do. His orange speaking stone and sword were on the table no more than five feet away, but they might as well have been five hundred miles away for all the good they did him. Seeing nothing else to do, he slumped forward in submission and waited.

His captors, too, sat silently in anticipation, waiting for word to reach them of the official vote. None of them spoke. The brute who had kicked Caile earlier took to pacing the den occasionally, but beyond the shuffling of his feet on the floor, there was only silence. That's why the knock at the door, when it came, seemed so obtrusive.

"That was fast," the brute said, getting to his feet from where he sat at one of the cushioned chairs. "I thought they weren't meeting for another hour or two."

Caile exhaled slowly. *It's done, then. Kobel is King and the Old World has won.*

"Hold on a moment," the sorcerer said, his brows pinched above his nose in confusion as he approached from the adjoining bedroom. "It's too early..."

But it was too late. The brute had already unlatched the door, and he flailed backward in a spray of blood as the door burst open.

• • •

Senator Emil took Mahalath's silence for assent to his demands. "I will be presenting my report to the Senate this afternoon," he said. "Just as soon as I receive confirmation from our agents in Col Sargoth that Kobel has been elected. I want you to be present to corroborate my assessment and recommendations."

"Recommendations?"

"To proceed toward full annexation of the Five Kingdoms, starting by sending governors and more legionnaires to ensure the transfer of power goes smoothly. Galleys and troops stand at the ready to sail. The Senate Security Council has contingency plans prepared to guide the transition of the Five Kingdoms from sovereign nations to Republic territories, and then to full-fledged provinces within twenty years. All is prepared."

Mahalath sighed and turned away from Emil to stare out over the harbor.

"Think whatever you like about me and my techniques," Senator Emil said, "but you must see this is the best of possible outcomes. We avert war and bring the Five Kingdoms into the fold of the Republic. Could you ask for a more perfect scenario?"

Mahalath didn't respond to the senator, not because he was angry this time, but rather because of what he saw in the harbor below: approaching ships, and lots of them.

"Are those Valarion ships returning?" Mahalath asked, as much to himself as to Senator Emil.

The senator followed his gaze. "They're certainly not ours. They must be the ships I ordered to Kal Pyrthin." His face twisted in annoyance.

"Perhaps the storm turned them back?" Mahalath suggested.

"They have stormwielders with them to deal with inclement weather, and I gave specific orders to—"

A horn sounded from the harbor below, a warning call from the legionnaires who patrolled the docks. Mahalath's skin prickled. *It's Queen Makarria returned,* he thought, but immediately dismissed the idea. *No. She's broken and beaten, trapped forever in another's body.* Still, Mahalath narrowed his eyes and leaned farther over the veranda railing to discern what was happening in the distance below.

Some two-dozen ships were sailing into the harbor. One, at least, had already docked, and a handful of others were furling their sails to do the same. A squadron of legionnaires—clearly visible even at this distance thanks to their distinctive maroon uniforms—approached the first ship, and suddenly they were gone. Vanished. Mahalath blinked his eyes, not believing what he was seeing, but when he looked again, there was no doubt: the legionnaires were gone. The only movement on the pier was sailors rushing off the ship and a flock of birds streaming out over the harbor. More legionnaires rushed forward to meet the sailors, and another horn sounded the alarm. This time, Mahalath and Emil both saw clearly as the legionnaires disappeared… or rather were transformed into a flock of birds.

"What in damnation is going on down there?" Senator Emil growled.

Mahalath was too stunned to reply, mesmerized as he was by the majestic arcing path of the birds—first over the harbor and then curving back toward the city, close enough that Mahalath could make out their green feathers and hear their piercing cries.

"Parrots," Mahalath muttered.

"Guards!" Senator Emil yelled, ignoring him.

Two legionnaires rushed out onto the veranda. "Sir?" one of them, the captain, asked.

"Order the palace sealed. I want the gates closed, the walls manned, and a regiment at the ready in the main courtyard."

"Yes sir!"

"And, Captain, I want the Valarion Royal Guardsmen with you. Mix them into your ranks."

The captain again barked his assent and rushed off into the palace with the second guard at his heels.

"Is that wise, bringing in the Royal Guard?" Mahalath asked.

"Whoever just annihilated our legion down there"—Emil paused and waved negligently in the direction of the harbor—"maybe they will think twice about doing the same if there are Valarion troops in harm's way. In fact, let's go fetch ourselves even better insurance, shall we?"

Senator Emil didn't wait for Mahalath's reply, but rather stormed off into the palace. Mahalath followed reluctantly, wishing he had guards of his own with him. *Not that they would be of much help, not against whoever is powerful enough to turn an entire regiment into a flock of parrots.*

Mahalath was no stranger to sorcerers. Unlike in the Five Kingdoms, sorcerers were commonplace in the Republic, integrated into all walks of life, from the working class beastcharmers who transported goods with their elephants to the highly paid stormwielders employed by the agricultural industry. And while there were also a variety of sorcerers involved in politics and the military branches of the Republic, sorcery was, by and large, removed from warfare. Having experienced how sorcery brought to the battlefield could devastate a nation, the Senate had put strict regulations on the use of sorcery in the military. The Five Kingdoms had been slower to learn that particular lesson, as evidenced by their Dreamwielder War, which was so violent that it opened the door for Thedric Guderian to eradicate sorcery altogether with near unilateral support from his vassals.

It was that very eradication of sorcery in the Five Kingdoms that was nettling Mahalath now. There were very few sorcerers in the realm at all, let alone one who could wield the power of transformation. *It's Makarria,* a little voice kept saying in his head, but he refused to believe it. *No, it must be Talitha of Issborg, returned to avenge her friends. Who else could it be?*

"Do you have any idea what we are up against?" he asked Senator Emil, thinking Emil might know something he didn't.

Senator Emil, leading the way up the main staircase, shot a glance back at Mahalath. "A sorcerer of no small skill, obviously."

"Yes, obviously. But any idea who it might be?"

"Who can say? Talitha of Issborg? Some backwoods sorcerer Queen Taera Delios dug up? Or maybe even one of our own countrymen who has defected? He wouldn't be the first."

Or it's the Dreamwielder returned, Mahalath thought, but he said nothing, instead mulling over Emil's cavalier attitude. The senator either had unwarranted confidence in the legionnaires, or he knew something Mahalath did not.

Senator Emil led the way onward to the third level of the palace and down a long corridor. *We're fetching Makarria's parents as hostages,* Mahalath realized.

Four Republic legionnaires stood guarding the entrance to their room. Since Captain Haviero's demise—or murder, more accurately—Senator Emil had tasked the legionnaires with "protecting" the Princess Prisca and her husband, Lord Galen.

"Fetch them both," Emil commanded. "Immediately."

The guards hurried inside and returned a few moments later, pushing Makarria's parents before them. Neither spoke a word of protest at their rough handling. As inexperienced as they were at statesmanship, they were by no means fools. Nominally, they were the rulers of Valaróz, but in reality they were little more than prisoners, and they knew it. Mahalath turned away from their gaze, not able to face the shame.

Emil had no such qualms. With the royal parents now in tow, he led the way back down the way they came: through the corridor and down three flights of stairs. From there, they made their way outside into the main courtyard of the palace, by which point Mahalath was panting and already perspiring in the late morning heat.

The legionnaires were already in place; interspersed within their ranks were the Valarion guardsmen, just as Senator Emil had commanded. Emil motioned for Mahalath and the royal family to follow him across the courtyard to the outer palace walls, where he led the way up a steep stairwell, twenty feet to the battlements above. Crossbow-wielding legionnaires stepped aside to let them pass to the section of the battlements directly above the main gates.

Mahalath, still trying to catch his breath, peered through one of the crenels to the city beyond. The streets were bustling with people. Normally, petitioners would be lining up outside the palace gates, and the main avenue would be lined with vendors selling food and wares, as well as buskers and street performers, not to mention delivery wagons enroute to the palace itself. Now though, people were rushing every which way. The vendors were rolling their carts away into the adjacent side streets, while curious children and ne'er-do-wells darted back and forth across the boulevard, their faces turned to the south, looking toward the harbor, not the palace. Clearly, they knew something—or someone—was approaching. But who?

They were not left waiting long.

The chanting reached them first. Mahalath had never heard the song before, but it was obviously enough an old Valarion war chant.

"Across the Spine, whoa-a! She came in a storm! With ice in her veins—and the sun in her heart. Vala! Vala! Rose of the sun. Valaróz!"

Then the crowd came into view: a conflagration of sailors, city watchmen, and common city dwellers, chanting and hollering. At their forefront strode a woman. She was tall and lithe, with walnut brown hair that blew back off her shoulders in the morning sea breeze. She wore a simple blue dress, sleeveless and short-hemmed just below the knee. A yellow sunflower was tucked behind one ear, contrasting against her dark complexion. The crowd had formed up around her, hundreds of people, jockeying among each other to get close to the woman, some of them brave enough to reach out and touch her on the shoulder or arm. Mahalath had never seen the woman before, and at the same time he had. She was Queen Makarria, Liberator of the Five Kingdoms, Dreamwielder. She looked different than the young woman whom he had first met—taller, stronger, wiser, older yet still youthful, and very much a woman—but there was no doubting who she was. The husk Mahalath and so many others had watched die in the throne room at Fina's hands paled in comparison to the woman striding toward the palace. She emanated power and life.

Senator Emil hissed beside Mahalath. "How is this possible? We saw the bitch die."

• • •

Caile recoiled as blood spattered over his face and torso. When he opened his eyes, he saw the other ruffian rush forward to collide with a hulking figure striding through the smoldering doorway. *Siegbjorn!* Caile was flooded with sudden hope, and was not disappointed to see the burly northman nearly take off the ruffian's head with one swipe of his curved hunting knife.

There was still the Old World sorcerer to contend with, though. Caile jerked his head back, motioning toward the bedroom. "Sorcerer!" he yelled.

The Old World stormbringer's eyes were rolled back deep in their sockets and lightening was forming at the tips of his fingers.

"Watch out!" Caile yelled, but before the words even left his lips, he saw the sorcerer's forehead cave in as if it had been struck with a ballista. His eyes fluttered open briefly as the lightning died on his fingertips, and then he toppled backward onto the floor, dead.

Caile contorted himself to face back toward the door and saw Talitha standing at Siegbjorn's side. Caile had no idea what sort of magic she'd just unleashed, but it had stopped the stormwielder dead in his tracks. Standing behind Talitha in the doorway were two more familiar faces: Thon and Lord Nagel, the elderly statesman from the election council. Caile opened his mouth, but didn't know what to say.

Siegbjorn smiled and knelt down to cut Caile's bindings and help him to his feet. "You are much welcome," the hairy beast of a man said with a grin.

Caile returned the smile, but then remembered the voting. "The election meeting," Caile asked. "Has it…"

"No, it hasn't convened yet," Talitha said.

"Then there's still time to stop them. Thon is Guderian's son, and the rightful heir. We have to hurry!" Caile rushed forward, trying to gather them all up and herd them back out the way they came. "I'll explain on the way to the council room."

"Slow down," Talitha said, grabbing him by the arm. "We know who Thon is, and we still have time yet." She motioned for Thon to prop closed what was left of the door behind him.

"But how do you know? Did Lady Hildreth tell you?"

Talitha shot a glance toward Lord Nagel. "Lady Hildreth? No. It's a long story, but let it suffice to say I infiltrated Lightbringer's Keep, pretending to be a chambermaid, and investigated the rumors of an illegitimate son of Guderian's, which led me to Lord Nagel."

The old statesman nodded. "I knew long ago of young Thon. It was I who urged Lady Hildreth to give him up and hide him when he was but a babe. Yet somehow Guderian still found out, and put it upon me to kill the ill-born prince."

Caile shot a glance back at Thon, but if Thon was offended, he showed no indication.

"Guderian was mad," Lord Nagel continued. "He was convinced he was immortal. He had no desire to marry and saw any offspring as a threat to his rule. There were two things he feared: dreamwielders and a son. I convinced him to spare Thon's life, but only by sending him to Khal-Aband. Lady Hildreth never said anything of the matter to me, but between her and her brother, Commander Buell, I'm certain she knows what I did."

"I don't know if they know it was your doing, but they know who Thon is," Caile said. "It was the two of them who apprehended me. They were trying to get you too, Thon. Lady Hildreth was ready to claim you as her son and pronounce you king. We can trust her, I think. And the houndkeeper, too, if you can believe it. It was the houndkeeper who found out about Ambassador Rives's plot. It seems the Kingdom of Golier and the Old World have been plotting this entire thing to get Lord Kobel on the throne. They mean to kill the rest of the council—the sorcerer's guild is in on it—as soon as the vote is finalized. And Old World ships will be here anytime as reinforcements. They want those war wagons."

"All the more reason to be precise with our actions then," Talitha said. "I'll take care of the sorcerer's guild. Lord Nagel will take care of anointing Thon, and if it's as you say—if the houndkeeper and Lady Hildreth can be trusted—then we have nothing to worry about."

"Except..." Caile couldn't bring himself to say it.

"Except what?"

Caile swallowed. "I overheard the sorcerer you just killed say that Old World ships are ready to attack Col Sargoth."

"We'll deal with that once Thon is king. They'll be expecting to be welcomed with open arms by Kobel, so we'll have the element of surprise."

"There's more," Caile said. "More ships are heading for Kal Pyrthin—Taera tried contacting me this morning through the speaking stone. And something else. The sorcerer said Makarria is dead." The words sounded so wrong coming out of his mouth, he wasn't sure he'd actually said them. "He said the dreamwielder is dead..."

• • •

Senator Emil glared at Mahalath. "Did you have some part in this? You did. You felt sorry and released the prisoner. Traitor."

Mahalath snorted at Senator Emil. "Me a traitor? You're the one who unleashed a *pthisicis-corporis*, a master trickster. You broke an ironclad law enacted by our forefathers, and now you're surprised to discover you too have been tricked?"

It was a foolish thing to say, Mahalath knew, but at this point he didn't care. What did it matter if Emil figured out Mahalath's treachery? Mahalath would gladly confess to having known Makarria was still alive, and to secretly freeing Makarria from the dungeon. If he had not been such a coward, he would have done more. He should have done more, and sooner. As it was, he was ready to meet his fate at the dreamwielder's hands. It was she who he needed to fear, not Senator Emil. Her bearing made that clear. The woman who came to a stop in the street below them and motioned for the crowd to silence was the nearest thing to a god Mahalath had ever seen.

The immediate silence Makarria commanded was unnerving. Mahalath heard Emil gasp beside him, but couldn't tear his eyes away from Makarria.

"F… fire," Senator Emil stuttered, and Mahalath heard the distinctive twang of crossbows loosening their deadly bolts. The projectiles shot forward from either side of Mahalath, but before they closed half the distance toward Makarria and the crowd of people around her, they turned into long-stemmed sunflowers and fell harmlessly to the ground.

Makarria had said nothing, nor made any motion. All she had done was blink her eyes and the crossbow bolts were flowers.

"Let that be your last act of aggression, Senator," Makarria said then. "Command your soldiers to put down their weapons and surrender. You are in no position to bargain. Surrender and open the gates to the people of Sol Valaróz."

"Reload, fools!" Senator Emil yelled at the soldiers around them. "Fire at will."

The reaction among the soldiers was mixed. Many of them glanced at each other uncertainly. A few, however, began to re-cock their crossbows. Before Mahalath could think to warn them, they were transformed. The crossbows clanked to the marble battlements, and in the place of soldiers, two-dozen green parrots took to the skies, squawking. At witnessing their comrades' fate, the rest of the legionnaires dropped their crossbows. The Valarion guardsmen mixed among them scurried to gather up the weapons.

"And now the legionnaires behind the gates," Makarria said. "Command them to disarm."

This time Mahalath acted. "Drop your weapons, all of you," he yelled back over the battlements to the soldiers formed up in ranks in the courtyard below.

Senator Emil didn't bother to contradict his order. Instead, he grabbed Lord Galen by the scruff and shoved him forward off the wall.

"No!" the Princess Prisca screamed, but her fear was unwarranted. Makarria's father plummeted to the street below only to land in a pool of water that suddenly formed where paving stones had been moments before.

Senator Emil laughed, and grabbed Prisca by the hair to draw her in close. "You think you're so clever, Dreamwielder, but I didn't push your father to kill him. I just wanted your attention, and I think I have it now. Submit yourself and I'll let your mother live." He withdrew a dagger from his robes and pressed the edge of the blade to Prisca's exposed throat.

Makarria blinked her eyes and the dagger turned into a serpent that turned back and bit Senator Emil on the wrist. Emil screamed in pain, and Prisca took the opportunity to tear herself free and leap from the battlements into the pool below to join her husband.

"You try my patience, Senator," Makarria said. "Open the gates and surrender yourself."

Senator Emil ripped the snake off of his wrist with a grunt and flung it at Makarria. It too turned into a sunflower before it hit the ground.

"Fine, you win," Emil said, wincing in pain. "I surrender, but I demand fair treatment as my state status dictates. I am a senior senator of the Republic."

Senator Emil turned and glared at Mahalath as he made his way toward the stairs leading to the courtyard. Mahalath followed behind him, ready to meet his judgment. Royal Valarion guardsmen formed up around them when they reached ground level, and Mahalath saw that the legionnaires were all disarmed and kneeling with their arms behind their heads. The Valarion soldiers had not wasted a moment to turn on their captors.

"Open the gates," Emil started to say, but before the gatekeepers lifted a finger, the gates opened of their own accord, the giant chain pulleys ratcheting back the doors on their hinges as if manned by ghosts.

Makarria strode into the courtyard with the crowd of people massed behind her. Emil took a knee and bowed his head, but something wasn't right. Mahalath felt a tingling sensation in the air, and looked down to see Emil rubbing his fingers behind his back. He had seen firewielders do the very same thing in the Republic…

"Makarria!" Mahalath shouted, but it was too late. Emil had already lunged forward and purple flames were spewing from his hands toward Makarria. Even three paces *behind* Emil, Mahalath was knocked back by the assault of heat. The flames billowed forward, blotting out Makarria and the screaming crowd behind her. But then the flames began to condense and spiral together. Makarria suddenly came into view behind the whirlwind of fire, unscathed.

Emil barked something in the old tongue and hurled more fire at Makarria, but his efforts only fueled the tornado of fire Makarria had formed. She blinked her eyes and the maelstrom turned on Emil. With a panicked yelp he tried to scramble away, but the flames overtook him in a heartbeat and he was caught up in the spinning flames. His screams of pain were short-lived. The fire consumed him and then snuffed out, leaving only a pile of ashes on the ground.

Mahalath stared at the pile of ashes, and then at Makarria in stunned silence. "Your Majesty," Mahalath said, bowing. "Sol Valaróz is yours. I order the surrender of the Republic, and I take full responsibility for my actions. Or rather, my inactions. Punish me as you see fit."

Makarria stared at him and then nodded. She stepped forward and Mahalath closed his eyes, expecting the worst. Welcoming it.

• • •

Siegbjorn's face flinched at hearing Caile's words, but Talitha shrugged off the news. "I would not worry about Makarria. She is more than capable of taking care of herself. But you're right about needing to help your sister, and perhaps Makarria can help in that."

"I tried contacting Makarria through the stone before I was captured," Caile said. "She didn't answer."

"No, her yellow stone is destroyed. I too tried contacting her, last night, and I could not sense the stone. Something happened to it. But there is another way. You can speak to her through the scent-hound. Take your stone and go to the houndkeeper's tower. Speak to your sister through the stone. See if you can contact Makarria through the hound. Tell them both all that has happened."

"But I'm going with you to the election council," Caile objected. "You'll need my help."

Talitha shook her head. "No, there's not enough time. Your friends trust you, Caile. You must do the same if we are to succeed."

"But, the firewielders. And you'll need me to vouch for you with Lady Hildreth and the houndkeeper."

Thon stepped forward and grasped Caile by the shoulders. "This is the last thing I ever expected, Caile, but you know what? I'm ready. I'm ready to step out from the shadows and make things right for Sargoth. I've seen what you and Makarria have sacrificed for your kingdoms. Sargoth deserves no less from me. Let me do what I have to do. You go help Makarria and your sister. Please."

Caile lowered his eyes. Thon was right. Caile was a damn fool, always trying to do everything himself. "All right," he agreed, looking up to see all his friends staring back. "I'll go to the scent-hound, but be careful and send word as soon as Thon is anointed."

"I have my speaking stone with me," Talitha said. "I will contact you as soon as it is done. You are the hub between Makarria, Taera, and myself. Go. Grab your stone and hurry."

• • •

You're a damn fool for waiting this long, Natarios Rhodas told himself as he scurried about his room and stuffed his valuables into a rucksack. *Since when did you start trusting people?*

He had held up as long as he could for Lady Hildreth and the feckless prince to find this lost heir of theirs, and now here he was, still in Lightbringer's Keep, less than an hour away from the election and his certain death. Natarios had enjoyed his moment of power as lord of proceedings, but he wasn't so loyal to the position that he was willing to die for it. Particularly not when the mode of death was by sorcerous fire.

I'm no swine to be turned on a spit, he mused, checking over his room one last time to make sure he had everything important. Satisfied, he made his way out the door into the spiral stairway, only to stop short.

Someone was calling his name.

"Do you hear me, houndkeeper? Natarios Rhodas?"

The voice was full of menace. Natarios backstepped into his room silently, assuming the worst. *Ambassador Rives and the Sorcerer's Guild can't be bothered to even wait for the meeting to kill me.*

"Houndkeeper," the voice growled again. "If you can hear my voice, come to the scent-hound and say something."

The scent-hound? Natarios furrowed his brow. Why would Rives send his ruffians up there? And for that matter, why bother calling his name at all if they were simply out to kill him? Natarios's instincts told him to stick to his plan and run while he still had the chance, but his curiosity got the better of him.

He tossed his rucksack to the floor of his room and scampered up the stairs to the scent-hound chamber, expecting to find someone there. The room was empty, though, except for the scent-hound. The idiot creature's body was taut on the compass wheel like he had never seen it before, the usually flaccid arm and leg muscles flexing as if the hound were trying to tear itself free. The eyes, which had always been closed before, were gaping now, revealing milky white orbs, pupil-less and marbled with red arterioles.

"Houndkeeper, are you there?"

Natarios shuddered. The voice had come from the hound itself, though it seemed disembodied and unnatural. It was as if Natarios was hearing a ghost.

"Who's there?" Natarios croaked, his mouth dry.

"I am Makarria Pallma, Queen of Valaróz," the voice replied. "Am I speaking with the houndkeeper?"

"You are, indeed, although I don't understand how. Where are you? How is this possible? If it's magic, the hound should be baying."

"I'm in Sol Valaróz, speaking to you through the other scent-hound. Now tell me, please, what's happening there? Has the election council voted yet?"

"No, but they will within the hour, and then the Old World will have their man on the throne. Is it true you have surrendered to them?"

"No. They imprisoned me, but I am free now and the Old World threat is eliminated here."

Eliminated. The way the dreamwielder spoke, even filtered through the scent-hound's gravelly vocal chords, left no doubt about the validity of her claim. Natarios was taken aback by how nonchalant she made it sound. Then again, he was speaking to the sorcerer who had killed Emperor Guderian. He shouldn't be surprised just because she was little more than a child.

"I don't know where your allegiance lies," the dreamwielder continued, "but I call upon you now to stand for the Five Kingdoms. Whatever the Old World has promised you is nothing but lies. They mean to control us, plain and simple. I ask you to denounce them. Find Prince Caile and tell him that Senator Emil is dead, and his plot with him. Together, the two of you can reason with the council."

"I believe you more than you know about the Old World," Natarios said. "Golier is in league with them and they mean to turn loose Guderian's war wagons. Unfortunately, there is little I can do. Your prince is nowhere to be found and Ambassador Rives has bought nearly every voting member on the council. They're all far too committed to turn back now."

"Where has Prince Caile gone?"

"Off searching for a legitimate heir to the throne—Guderian's bastard born child who was locked up in Khal-Aband."

"Thon?"

"Yes, that's him. He was here with the prince, but disappeared before anyone realized who he was. It would have all been so simple if we had only known, but now it's too late."

"No, it's not," said a new voice.

Natarios gasped in surprise and spun around to discover Prince Caile had snuck up on him. Natarios let out a relieved breath. For a moment, he had assumed the worst and expected to see firewielders behind him.

"Is that you, Caile?" the dreamwielder asked through the hound.

"Yes, I'm here. Is it really you, Makarria? I'd heard…the worst."

"The worst and more, but I survived. Is it true about Thon?"

"Yes, he's the true heir, and Talitha found him."

Natarios grimaced at the mention of Talitha. "That hag sorceress is here? Why?"

"Because she's going to save you from the sorcerer's guild," Caile said.

"Well, that's something pleasant for a change."

"You best get down there," Prince Caile told him. "If you can get a moment alone with her, tell Lady Hildreth we've found her son, and then bring the meeting to order. Lord Nagel and Talitha will take care of the rest."

The thought of purposefully striding into the council chambers unnerved Natarios, even if they had found the lost true heir. "And what about the Old World?"

The scent-hound growled. "Let us deal with them," the dreamwielder's voice emanated from its throat. "Leave Caile with the hound and tend to the meeting as he says. I mean to come to Col Sargoth myself as soon as we have chased the Old World off. Do well today and you will be rewarded. Fail this task I have put upon you and…"

"No need to tell me what," Natarios interrupted. "I catch your drift. I'll do what you say."

"Thank you, houndkeeper," the dreamwielder replied. "Caile, you must contact Taera…" she continued on, but Natarios was already out the door and walking down the stairs. *You have one more chance to run, fool. Do it now or there's no turning back. Once you walk into the council room, you have to see this thing out, and it probably won't turn out well, no matter what the dreamwielder thinks.*

Natarios scrunched up his face in frustration as he reached his chamber entrance. His knapsack was there on the floor where he left it. All he had to do was grab it and run.

• • •

Taera held the speaking stone tightly in the crook of her arm as she stepped out from the cabin onto the deck of *Casstian's Breath.* Admiral Laud lowered his looking glass and glanced back at her from where he stood at the prow of the airship. "Their armada is mobilizing," he said. "They haven't raised sails yet, but all hands are on deck. They might attack at any moment."

"They're expecting their signal soon," Taera replied. "Signal the rest of our fleet to ready themselves."

"Yes, Your Majesty."

Anxiety welled up inside Taera's chest as she watched the admiral rush off to command his crew. For all her preparations with the factories and airships, and despite her stolid demeanor among her advisors, she'd never wanted it to come to actual war. She'd witnessed too many deaths already in the revolt against Guderian. The last thing she wanted was to sacrifice more of her people, and she was no fool—she knew the odds of winning this sea battle were not good.

"All is ready," Laud said. "We wait on your command."

"We wait until the Old World ships raise their sails and are bearing down on us," Taera said. "Once that happens, hang—"

Taera stopped midsentence and yelped as the speaking stone vibrated in the crook of her arm.

"Taera?" came a distant voice. "Taera, can you hear me?"

"Caile?"

• • •

Natarios took a deep breath and then stepped into the council chamber, half-expecting to be met by flames and his excruciating death immediately. Instead, he was met only by steely glares.

"We were just about to start without you, houndkeeper," Rives remarked.

Natarios forced a smile and took in his surroundings as he made his way to the head of the table. Rives sat at his normal place at one side of the table, flanked by the sorcerer's guildmaster on one side, and Lord Kobel on the other. Seated behind them, as "observers," were two sorcerers—the firewielders who were there to kill them all, Natarios surmised. At the opposite side of the table sat Lady Hildreth and Lord Nagel, but there was no sign of the sorceress Talitha, nor the bastard prince Thon. *Did Prince Caile lie to me?* Natarios wondered, but brushed the thought aside. It was too late now.

Natarios took up his gavel and called the meeting to order. "The day has arrived at last," he began. "The day we have all been waiting for. When we leave this room, the council will be disbanded and Sargoth will have a new king."

"Yes, yes, we all know why we're here," Ambassador Rives said. "Let's get on with the vote."

Natarios rapped his gavel on the table sharply. "We'll get on with the vote when I call for it!"

Rives eyes widened in surprise momentarily, but he quickly regained his composure, nodded in assent, and made sure everyone in the room saw his self-satisfied smirk.

You can burn me when the time comes, gutter trash, Natarios fumed inwardly, *but I'll be damned if I let you steal this moment from me. I've already had to truncate my speech—the one I would be saying if you hadn't double-crossed me and leagued yourself with the Old World.*

Natarios cleared his throat. "As I was saying, we've all heard now from each of the candidates, and it is upon us to choose wisely. The storied history and future of Sargoth is in our hands..." *And here's where I have to change the script.* "On this historic occasion, I find it appropriate to give the floor to our most venerable member to say a few words on the gravity of the vote before us."

A few of the council members murmured their surprise, but Natarios paid them no heed. "Lord Nagel, if you would."

Lord Nagel was already standing, and he smiled at Natarios's unexpected introduction. "Thank you, loyal houndkeeper, and thank you, fellow council members and candidates. It is with great pride that I have served this kingdom for the last sixty odd years as an advisor, and I have but one last bit of council to offer this committee."

"To what?" Lord Kobel barked. "To vote for you, so that you can henceforth command us instead of counsel us?" Kobel turned to Natarios, his brow furrowed in anger. "What is the meaning of this? Nagel had his chance to say his piece. You defy protocol by allowing him to address the council again."

"It's fine, let him say his piece," Ambassador Rives said, reaching up to grab Kobel by the wrist, but Kobel slapped his hand away.

"We've heard enough," Kobel barked. "Proceed to the vote."

Natarios rapped his gavel again. "Silence! You can give orders to me and this council if, and when, you're elected king. Until then, sit down and close your pastry hole or I'll have you thrown out."

The room tittered with nervous whispers as Kobel stared back at Natarios for a frozen moment.

That was foolish, Natarios mused. *Even if Rives's sorcerers don't cook me, Kobel will be sure to have my head now.*

Kobel clenched his right hand and reached slowly for his sword.

"Lord Kobel, I plead of you," Lord Nagel interrupted. "Give me but a moment more. I rescind my claim to the throne."

Kobel narrowed his eyes and turned his glare to the aged statesman. "You rescind?"

"Yes. I have but one piece of counsel for everyone before we proceed."

Satisfied, Kobel took his seat and nodded for Nagel to speak, as if he were already king. Natarios bit his tongue, and eased himself back into his own seat. *Where are you going with this, old man? Hopefully whatever you say will infuriate everyone enough so I can scurry under the table and sneak out of here while they're taking their wrath out on you.*

"Please proceed," Natarios said, speaking his last words as lord of proceedings.

Lord Nagel nodded and swept his gaze across everyone at the table before speaking. "My counsel to all of you is to bow before your rightful king."

Confusion swept across the faces of everyone in the room, but before anyone could say anything, the doors opened and the sorceress Talitha stepped inside with the bastard prince at her side, flanked by the giant northman, Siegbjorn, and a dozen cavalrymen.

"You?" Ambassador Rives hissed, but before he could push himself out of his chair, the cavalrymen had their crossbows leveled toward him.

"Relax, I'm not here to take over the proceedings," Talitha said. "I'm merely here to escort the crown prince of Sargoth." She stopped and leveled her gaze on the sorcerers. "Men of the sorcerer's guild, contain yourselves. If I sense so much as a hiccup in your thauma, I will signal for the cavalry to fire."

One of the soldiers stepped forward, and Natarios recognized him as Commander Buell, Lady Hildreth's brother.

"You are all in the presence of royalty," Buell said, his voice thick with menace. "Any sudden moves will be seen as a sign of aggression and result in your immediate death."

Talitha turned her gaze from the sorcerer's guild to Natarios, winked, and nodded for him to proceed.

Natarios grinned despite himself. *Well, I guess I have a few more words to say as lord of proceedings, after all. All it takes is three Sargothian lords to attest to a person's noble lineage. With Nagel, Lady Hildreth, and her brother as witnesses, the bastard can be anointed king without a single vote.* Natarios stood.

"Thank you, Talitha of Issborg. Ladies and Lords of the council, I present to you the son of Thedric Guderian, Prince Thon…"

"Thon Hildreth," the bastard prince interrupted. "I have chosen to take my mother's name as a symbol and promise that I will not perpetuate the tyranny of my father who bore the Guderian name."

"Impossible!" Lord Kobel growled, practically foaming at the mouth. He flung his chair back and reached for his sword, but before he could take a single step toward Thon, three crossbow bolts punctured his chest.

Ambassador Rives gaped at Kobel as he collapsed back onto the floor dead. "Kill them!" he squealed, turning to the sorcerer's guildmaster. "Burn them!"

When the guildmaster ignored him to only stare blankly ahead, Rives swiveled around to make his plea to the other sorcerers. "Burn them! Burn them all! What are you waiting for?"

That was as far as his hysterics got. Commander Buell, having heard enough, stepped around the table and knocked him out cold with a backhanded slap.

Natarios laughed out loud, a rich, wonderful release of tension. "Thank you, Commander," he said ignoring the incredulous stares of the rest of the council. "Now let's proceed. Lord Nagel, Lady Hildreth, Commander Buell, I will have you swear to the legitimacy of Prince Thon Hildreth's claim, and then we shall anoint him King of Sargoth."

• • •

Mahalath sat against the wall of the round tower chamber, his head in his hands, watching as Queen Makarria loomed over the piteous creature called a scent-hound. At the doorway, two Valarion soldiers stood guard silently. Mahalath had been sitting there for an hour or more now, seemingly forgotten by the dreamwielder, but he knew better than that. She had told him to follow her to the chamber and to wait, and he was going to do exactly as she said. He owed her that much. And whatever punishment she had in store for him, he intended to accept his fate when the time came. There were simply more pressing matters she had to attend to right now. Senator Emil's machinations had been complex and widespread. As Mahalath had sat there, he was privy to the relayed messages from Prince Caile of Pyrthinia: an armada was poised to attack Kal Pyrthin, another was bearing down upon Col Sargoth, and within Lightbringer's Keep itself, the Sargothian election council was about to elect a king who was beholden to the Republic. All of it brokered by Senator Emil. Prince Caile and his comrades had found a potential heir to Guderian, but Mahalath was all too aware how election councils proceeded—it was a numbers game, and Senator Emil had been too cunning to not make sure he owned every vote in the council. *He has put the pieces into action, and even with him dead now, there may be no stopping him.*

"It's done!" came Prince Caile's voice, a growl through the scent-hound's maw.

"Thon has been anointed?" Makarria asked, leaning over the creature, her hands resting on the outer compass ring.

"Yes. And Ambassador Rives and the sorcerers have been taken into custody by the cavalry."

"Excellent," Makarria said. "Tell Talitha to have Thon secure the harbor. Those ships from the Old World are close. And tell your sister to hold tight. I will take care of the rest now."

Queen Makarria raised herself away from the scent-hound and turned to regard Mahalath. Mahalath pushed himself to his feet and inclined his head. *She's done it, against all odds. And now the time has come for her to deal with me.*

"Follow me, Ambassador," Makarria said. "It's time to put this conflict to rest."

"Of course, Your Highness."

The guards opened the door and parted to allow Makarria and Mahalath to exit. Mahalath followed the queen silently, down the winding staircase to the main keep below and then through the corridors to the dignitary wing, past Mahalath's own room and to Senator Emil's guest quarters.

"Senator Emil was communicating with your Senate," Makarria said, pushing the door open effortlessly even though she did not have the key. "We're looking for a relic of some sort. A magical device."

"Yes," Mahalath agreed as they stepped inside the spacious anteroom. "He told me this morning he meant to give a report to the Senate and wanted me to corroborate. You'll be looking for his conch. That's how we communicate."

Makarria nodded as her eyes scanned across the room. Not seeing what she was looking for, she stepped into the main bedroom. "We shall stick to his plan then," she said. "The only difference is that you'll be giving the report and you'll be telling the truth, not whatever version of the story Emil concocted." Her gaze stopped at an iron-belted chest alongside the wardrobe, held fast with a heavy padlock. The padlock clicked and fell open before she even took two steps toward it.

"The truth?" Mahalath asked.

Makarria was silent for a moment as she opened the chest and rummaged through it. When she stood she was holding Emil's speaking conch.

"That's right," she said. "The truth, Ambassador. First the gravity of the situation. Emil is dead and I control Valaróz. King Thon Hildreth sits on the Sargothian throne, not some Old World puppet. And two Old World fleets sit poised to attack the Five Kingdoms, ready to plunge our two realms into a war that will destroy us both. Those fleets must retreat immediately. Once the Senate has complied, we will then talk about the rest."

"The rest?"

"That's right. The more painful truth part. What you were told you were here to do, when you found out about the *pthisicis-corporis*. All that you learned about Senator Emil's plot. Everything."

Mahalath swallowed. *This will be the end of my career and my wife's too, but Queen Makarria is right. The truth must be known if we are to avert enmity between our nations.*

"Of course, Your Majesty."

"Excellent," Makarria said, stepping toward him and holding up the conch. "Now I need your help to make the connection. Put your hands on both sides of the conch and imagine the Senate—wherever it is they meet."

Mahalath placed his hands on the shell. "The Citadel."

"Yes, picture it in your mind while I blow into the shell."

Mahalath closed his eyes and pictured the marble steps of the amphitheater in the Citadel, at the heart of Khail Sanctu. The Senate would be seated and waiting, each of the members in their official white robes, leafed coronets around their heads to signify their civic station.

A deep, mournful trumpeting emanated from the shell as Makarria blew into it. The sound and the air washed over Mahalath's face, but he held the image tight in his mind. When the noise abated, it was as if Mahalath was actually there, standing on the floor of the amphitheater looking at the hundred Senators surrounding him. In the distance, in the uppermost row, he even saw his own wife looking down at him expectantly.

"Senator Emil?" came a distant voice, the voice of the speaker of the assembly.

"No," Mahalath spoke. "Senator Emil has died a death he earned with his treasonous actions. It is I, Imad Mahalath, Republic Ambassador to the Kingdom of Valaróz."

25
Epilogue

The water is not as cold as she expects, but the violence of the waves nearly overwhelms her. Choking and gasping, pummeled with swell after swell, she is unable to slip into a dreamtrance. The sense of confidence she'd had just a moment earlier, before jumping off the ship, is gone.

How can she go into a dreamstate if she's drowning? How can she stay above the surging waves in the broken body she's trapped within? Dizziness washes over her as her weakened limbs give out. Quit fighting it, quit raging against Tel Mathir, a little voice says in her head, and she lets herself go. She lets the air out of her lungs and sinks beneath the surface, to the tranquility of the ocean beneath the storm. She closes her eyes and feels the storm above her, feels the ships and sailors getting pummeled by it. She imagines her sea wall around the fleet of ships, and draws upon the ferocity of the storm to turn her dream into reality. The power is intoxicating. She no longer feels her broken and battered body, but euphoria. She imagines herself free of Lorentz's empty shell, she imagines herself rising up to behold the fleet and sailors she has just saved.

When she opens her eyes, she is riding acrest a column of water that lifts her out of the ocean and toward the nearest ship. She steps foot onto the deck, barefoot, naked, in her own body remade. The dumbfounded Valarion sailors bow before her. The Old World sorcerer tasked to watch over the ship panics and jumps into the sea, terrified of her. Around them, the storm has gone silent, its energy sapped away by Makarria's actions. She feels invincible and tells the sailors to rise. They begin shouting her name, and the men on the other ships take up the call.

Makarria! Makarria! Makarria…

"Makarria," Taera said, shaking her shoulder gently and

arousing her from her sleep.

Makarria's eyes fluttered open and she instinctively put her hands to her face, making sure it was her own, that the ocean transformation had not been a dream, but rather a memory. It was indeed her own face, and she remembered where she was now: on Taera's airship, *Casstian's Breath*.

"We've arrived," Taera informed her. "The others are here to welcome us."

Makarria pushed herself up from the small bunk and straightened her simple, blue dress. "The others?"

"Yes. Talitha, Siegbjorn, the new King of Sargoth, and my brother."

Caile. She hadn't spoken to him since they had used the scent-hounds to communicate. Taera had offered up her red speaking stone for Makarria to use during their voyage from Sol Valaróz, but Makarria had declined, choosing instead to wait until she could speak to Caile in person. She had no idea what she meant to say to him—so much had happened since she had sent him away she hardly knew what to think anymore—but she knew they needed to talk face to face.

"Would it be all right if I spoke with Caile privately before we enter the city?" Makarria asked. "Just for a minute. I won't keep everyone waiting long."

Taera smiled. "Of course. You stay here. I'll fetch him for you."

Taera stepped out of the small cabin, leaving Makarria to fidget where she sat on the thin mattress of the bunk. When Caile entered a few moments later, the two of them made eye contact for only a second, and then he kneeled before her and bowed his head to avert his eyes.

"Makarria..." he started to say, but then his words abandoned him.

"Get up, sit next to me," she told him, not able to bear him prostrating himself before her.

He did as she said, but he still couldn't look at her. "Makarria, I'm so sorry for what I did. And I failed you here in Col Sargoth. It was all Talitha's doing that Thon was found and put on the throne. Even the houndkeeper did more than I…"

"Stop. You don't need to be sorry for anything," she told him. "You did nothing wrong. I'm the one who needs to apologize for sending you away so rashly, before thinking everything through and discovering what had really happened. There was a spy—a body-switching sorcerer—in our midst, Caile. It wasn't you who assaulted me, but this sorcerer wearing your body. You didn't do anything wrong. I'm sorry for even thinking you could."

Caile raised his head and stole a glance at her. "This sorcerer? Did it have something to do with Lorentz?"

"Yes. I'm sorry. He's gone, Caile. He died in Khal-Aband, right before our eyes."

A flicker of pain hardened his expression. "You tried warning me. I should have seen it. I should have believed you."

"Neither one of us knew what we were up against," Makarria told him, shaking her head. "And besides, it's all behind us now. We need to move past it. I don't know that things can ever be like they were between us before. I need time to make sense of everything still, but I know I trust you, and I can't bear to lose you to guilt and blame. Not now. No more blaming ourselves."

"Yes, you're right," he agreed, and it was as if a great weight was taken off his shoulders. He looked her in the face, finally. "You look different somehow, Makarria. Older, prettier. I'd feared the worst after hearing the rumors that you'd surrendered Valaróz, and that you had died."

"I nearly did die," she told him, the memory still as vivid as if it had just happened. "My body was ruined, and I'd been sent away on a ship, having lost Valaróz to the Old World. But amazingly, I was still able to use my power. I jumped into the ocean to save all these ships from the storm, and I got caught up in the power of it. I saved the ships with a wall of water, and I remade my body. In the ecstasy of the moment I thought I could make myself whole again, but all I could do was remake my body, what you see on the outside. The Makarria on the inside isn't nearly as strong as what people think they've seen these last few days."

Caile shook his head. "I don't believe that for a moment, but I know what you mean." He stood up and offered his hand. "Come. The others are waiting for us to attend to our unpleasant business. We can discuss everything afterward, on the voyage back to Sol Valaróz. If you'll have me again as your advisor?"

"I'd like that very much," Makarria told him, and she took his hand. Together they walked out of the cabin and down the gangplank to where everyone else stood waiting in the meadows outside the dark city of Col Sargoth.

• • •

Many hours later, Makarria watched alongside the other four monarchs and Caile as three men were executed by hanging: Ambassador Rives, the steam-engineer's guildmaster, and the sorcerer's guildmaster, all of them found guilty of treason. King Lorimer of Golier had nearly joined them on the gallows, coming within one vote of conviction in the meeting of monarchs. Thon and Taera had both voted for his execution. King Lorimer had voted against his own execution, of course, and pled for economic sanctions as his punishment. King Hanns had voted in Lorimer's favor, leaving the final decision to Makarria. The thought of levying sanctions—essentially punishing the people of Golier for King Lorimer's crimes—seemed vastly unfair, but at the same time, the last thing they needed was another one of the Five Kingdoms without a ruler. And so she had voted in favor of sparing Lorimer's life and waiving the sanctions altogether, with the agreement that King Lorimer take on a new advisor to keep watch over him—an advisor whose greed and ambition would keep Lorimer's own ambition in check: Natarios Rhodas. The others had agreed, as had Natarios Rhodas, and it was done. The conspirators who had been on the election council were sentenced to death, while King Lorimer and whatever Old World Senators he had dealt with—the true power players behind the entire coup—went unpunished. The injustice of it all burned inside of Makarria, but she quelled the fire behind a wall inside her and proceeded onward, just as she had since emerging from the turbulent Sol Sea the week prior. It was easier to endure now, at least, having Caile and the rest of her friends with her.

Hanging from his noose, Ambassador Rives abruptly twitched to a stop in a last spasm of death, and the scent of feces washed over the observing crowd, which included a host of Sargothian aristocrats, officials, and soldiers, as well as Talitha, Siegbjorn, Natarios Rhodas, Lady Hildreth, and Ambassador Mahalath.

King Thon grimaced at the grisly spectacle and stepped up onto the gallows platform to address the crowd. "Justice has been done this day, with all of you standing as witnesses. Please now, gather into the awaiting coaches and you'll be taken to observe the last order of business for the day—one thankfully less grim."

As the crowd dispersed toward the coaches, Caile hung back and offered his arm to lead Makarria to their coach. She smiled wanly and let him lead the way. With the two of them onboard, the procession of wagons made its way out of the courtyard into the streets of Col Sargoth, guarded by a full regiment of the cavalry. It was only a short ride from Lightbringer's Keep to the war wagon factory, and within minutes they were all filing out of the coaches again to stand in front of the massive, squat building. Makarria stepped out in front of the crowd to regard the structure. Talitha joined her, along with a half dozen Sargothian sorcerers under the direction of their new guildmaster.

"Gentlemen, you know what to do," Talitha said. "Join hands and open up your thauma. Let Makarria do the rest. We are just here to add to her strength and shield the bystanders."

The men nodded and joined hands. Makarria took her place in the middle, flanked by Talitha on one side and the guildmaster on the other. She let her eyelids droop so that the factory before her blurred in her vision. She had given little thought as to what exactly she was going to do in this moment, but that had become her modus operandi since emerging from the sea—*just react and follow your instincts. Thinking still hurts too much.*

Turning the factory to stone, or even a hill of loose rubble would be too heavy, she knew. She had walked through the factory with King Thon and Ambassador Mahalath before the meeting of monarchs. The majority of the factory was subterranean and would collapse beneath the weight of earth above it. And situated so near the river, the entire thing could wash out. *No, I need something with support... with roots.* A picture came to Makarria's mind, a drawing Natale had once shown her of a giant tree in the East Islands. A banyan tree he had called it, with a canopy the size of a palace and a root system even larger. *Yes, why negate destruction with more destruction, when I can create life? A tree to honor Natale and Fina and Lorentz...*

Makarria pictured the tree in her mind. Then three trees, one each to replace the three mammoth smoke stacks. She drew upon the strength of those holding her hands. She pushed her consciousness into the brick walls of the factory, into the mortar and stone foundation, and over it she placed the image of the trees, massive and deep-reaching to entomb Guderian's war wagons. The resistance was great, but she pushed through it, drawing upon the love she knew her fallen friends had for her. *Natale, Fina, Lorentz... Grandfather.*

The crowd gasped, then began to cheer, startling Makarria out of her trance. When she opened her eyes, the factory was gone, replaced by the banyan trees, each of them on their own larger than any building in the city except for Lightbringer's Keep itself. A great weariness fell over Makarria.

"Well done, Makarria," Talitha said, grabbing her in a warm embrace.

The other sorcerers, too, began clamoring and joined in to hug Makarria, caught up in the momentous occasion they had just participated in. Makarria smiled for them. "Thank you, gentlemen."

"Queen Makarria," Ambassador Mahalath said, "It is magnificent!"

Makarria separated herself from the sorcerers and went to him, waving the other monarchs and Caile over. "It is done," she said when they were all gathered around. "The war wagons and the factory that created them are buried forever. The Five Kingdoms have lived up to their promise. It's now up to the Old World Republic to do the same. We act on good faith from here on out."

"It will be done," Mahalath agreed, nodding gravely. "You have my word."

"Good," Makarria said, turning now to her fellow monarchs. "This is a different world than the one we inherited. The war wagons are buried forever, but the technology itself can never be buried. Steam power is here to stay, along with the ability to fly, and now we have the speaking stones to communicate with. All of this makes our world much smaller. If we work together, it can be to our benefit, but if we are driven by ambition and lies, it will be to our ruin, and I for one have seen enough ruin."

"We all have," Thon agreed.

"I'll have your vow then," Makarria said, and she looked into each and every one of their eyes as they swore to her their alliance to the Five Kingdoms.